THE TORRENTIAL THINGS
AGENT MOORE SERIES
BOOK 3

B.E. FIDLER

Copyright © 2023 by B.E. Fidler

All rights reserved.

No part of this book may be reproduced in any form or by any electronic or mechanical means, including information storage and retrieval systems, without written permission from the author, except for the use of brief quotations in a book review.

Cover By: B.E. Fidler

Editing By: Jenni Gauntt

Formatting By: Jenni Gauntt

AUTHOR'S NOTE

Each Chapter Subheading is a Song that is highly recommended to accompany or to be listened to after the chapter. Happy Reading!

DEDICATION

Dedicated to my wonderful husband who unfailingly deals with the songs on repeat and the hours of me hiding in my writing world. To my teenagers who love the story times, tossing ideas around as much as I do. To my besties who offer support, read my work, and always encourage my growth. Lastly to my editor Jenni, Thank you for helping me become a stronger writer and falling in love with my imaginary friends.

INSIGHT

Life used to be about the little things, all the bright, wonderful moments, but then things changed. Instead, those meant to protect and control introduced humanity to the abominable things; creatures with an insatiable hunger with no cure in sight, causing the death toll catapult. Our world is now overwhelmed by a torrential movement of abominations, and they seem never-ending and unyielding in their pursuit to devour the living.

CHAPTER ONE
RORY
"COMPLETELY" BY LEDGER

WAKING in the arms of your soulmate has to be the best feeling on earth, that moment before reality brims your mind. When you're still half asleep, and you can only hear the beat of his heart, the feel of his chest as it rises and falls, the smell of him is admittedly more wild and untamed than before. Briefly, I allow myself to think of "Before". The sound of thumping and crashing pulls me from the distant memories. I blink, not moving in the slightest as reality fizzles my euphoric state of existence.

My hand glides up Sterling's abs, tangling in the hair on his chest next to my head. *He is real*, my brain confirms. Fear has been plaguing my subconscious off and on through the night, that I will wake on the edge of the river vomiting up water. After last night and three rounds of mind-shattering sex and numerous bottles of water, you think my brain would let me rest, let me live in the here and now.

The gleam of my ring catches my attention, and I stare at it, really examining it now without being caught in the moment of surprise, relief, and lust that had been swirling within me yesterday. It's beautiful, like looking into Sterling's eyes when he is mischievous or extremely happy.

"Do you like it?" Sterling asks.

I jump, and he chuckles. "Yes, it is beautiful."

"My mother would be so thrilled," he sighs, running a hand through his shaggy hair.

I roll slightly, looking up into his face.

"That ring was my grandmother's as well, and when my dad got out of the Air Force, things were tight, so they used her mother's ring when they got married at some church. I've seen pictures. It was so huge and beautiful, and it was called Little Flower or something like that. My mother, being a florist, knew it was meant to be, and since it was at a church of my grandfather's friends, he agreed to pay for it. It was the last time she saw her family; they disowned her when I was born seven months later," he explains, his thumb caressing the emerald ever so gently before his eyes meet mine again.

"I feel very special that you gave me something that belonged to your mother," I admit, hugging him to me.

He smiles and kisses my forehead. "I am amazed that it fits, I was thinking we might have to put it on your dog tags, now that I can't get it fitted," he admits.

"You didn't have it fitted?" I ask, touching it gently.

"No, I asked, and then, well, you know the dead rose," he reminds with an exasperated sigh.

I laugh, and he grins at me. "They rose because I walked into a church," I tease, sitting up. He scowls, and I laugh harder. My watch beeps three times and lights up. I immediately go silent, staring at it.

"Files uploaded, tracking suspended," the watch announces.

"Files?" I ask, clicking it. I swipe through the new interface, pausing at the list of assassins that I know with the word "locate" next to them. Then swipe back out and to the file widget. I click on it, and a video of Sterling's lighter appears on the screen.

"Is that a new watch?" Sterling asks, propping himself up on his elbows.

"Yeah, when I dropped Quin off at the mines, I got it," I inform him with a shrug.

"You went to the mines?" he asks, his jaw dropping in shock.

"Yeah, to drop off Quin and Warner," I deter, flicking till I get to the pictures of Warner.

"Wait, what?" he asks, sitting up. "You went to the mines? Did they see you?"

"Yeah, one of them had Warner, and I had to kill a few of them to get him back," I admit, not looking up at him now.

"Why did you come here, then? Why didn't you stay there safe?" he asks. I look up at this. "And who is Warner?"

I hold up my watch, not answering his questions. He tilts his head, looking at the picture. "He is adorable, whose kid is he?" Sterling asks.

"Quin's," I reveal. "Honestly, I was hoping we could look after him."

"His parents are gone?" he asks, a frown pulling at his brow.

"We saved him from the mall in Playton, they had him up for sale," I explain, refusing to let the shiver of the memory show as I straighten my back to sit up.

"You wanted us to be his parents?" he asks, leaning in and hooking a finger under my chin.

"I thought about it, I know you want kids, eventually. You would be a wonderful father, and at least he would be safe with us," I say, then flick to the video in the car and show Warner talking to me. "An abomination attacked him a little while before this, and I had to toss him to Quin across the river. I think that's when I figured I might not be cut out to be his mother."

"Did she catch him?" he gasps, staring down at the blond boy on my watch in horror.

"Yeah, then the log broke, and I fell in the river. He probably wouldn't have survived that; I only did because of you."

"Because of me?" he asks, taking both of my hands in his.

"I was holding onto this old broken bridge leg, and all I could think of was that you were waiting for me."

He kisses hands, clutching them. "Aurora, why did you come

here? If it meant leaving your family? I would have eventually come back."

"No, you wouldn't have, you would have waited here for me, forever," I argue, raising an eyebrow. The look on his face clearly tells me I am correct in my assumption. "And you are my family," I add.

He squeezes my hand. "Your well-being is more important than coming to get me."

"No, it's not, you bring out all the goodness in me, you are my whole heart. I can't live without you. Just as you would have let yourself perish waiting here for me, we belong together, no matter where we are."

"We can go back, we can raise Warner. Be with our family," he insists, throwing his leg off the bed to get up.

"We can't," I deny, not releasing his hands.

"What, why?" he asks, settling back on the bed next to me.

"They are going on a year-long lockdown," I explain, watching concern take over his features. "Also, pretty sure they will shoot me on sight."

He frowns. "I thought they would be pleased that you can kill?"

"They won't be happy that their guinea pig for a cure ran out of the building. The only reason I wasn't shot was because of Alexander," I reveal, biting my lip as tension fills his features.

"They tried to shoot you?" he growls.

"Allen ordered them to shoot my leg because they need me alive. That's why my tracking is disabled, so they won't know how close I am," I explain, glancing at my watch.

"So we can stay here?" he asks. "Wait for them to cool down and the door to open back up," he suggests, glancing around his room, hope reclaiming a place in his eyes.

"Not an option, it's almost the end of August. Soon it will be too cold to survive. The nights are already dropping to below 50, so we need to go south," I say, shaking my head and plucking at the sheet.

"I still have a place in Texas. It was up for sale, but the market wasn't doing well."

"That might work, it would most likely be empty of people. Where in Texas?" I ask.

"Near North San Antonio," he responds.

I close my eyes, thinking. "So roughly 1400 miles, if we went straight there, no guarantees if that is a possibility."

"How long would it take to go 1400 miles?" he asks, scratching his scruffy face absently.

"On foot, maybe 450 hours nonstop. If we drove, it would depend on the roads and avoiding cities. We can't go south because Chattanooga is not an option. We could go west, cut around Lexington, then take the freeway on the outskirts of Saint Louis. Mind you, this is all based on vehicle accessibility and the roads being accessible. Along with other people, abominations, and if they set the FIMA centers up in or near these places," I summarize.

"We will need to get some maps at the very least," he says. I nod, watching him process everything I have said. "So we need to find a vehicle and take as much water and food as we can carry and go as far as we can before winter pushes in. Winter isn't still for a few months, and it's not even Fall yet, so we have some time."

"Not in the Appalachians, we don't. The rain will be more often, the nights will fall below 40 depending on weather patterns that we don't have access to, and we need something we can sleep in if necessary. I do agree with the water and food," I say, pulling my knees up and resting my chin on one..

"The box truck is still at Davin's," Sterling admits, gesturing toward my brother's house.

I make a face. "Do you know how to hot wire it?"

"Won't have to if the truck is, in fact, still there and it's not stolen or destroyed then we could drive it here and load up the water, except that this place is overrun by the sounds of it," Sterling admits, his attention moving wearily to the door before swinging back to me. "How did you get up the stairs and into the attic?"

"You're adorable, I came in through the roof," I reveal. "If we leave that way and cause a big enough commotion, we can draw them away like I had to when I got here."

"How did you distract them?" he asks, his eyebrow quirking up with curiosity.

"Alexander's Jeep full speed into the end house," I explain.

His eyes widen.

"I jumped out well before."

"Well then, first, we need self-maintenance, treat any injuries you have, hydrate, and eat what we have. We left clothes here, so there is that," he admits, stretching.

"I didn't bring any food, they took my supplies when we got within the fortress of the mines."

"I have some left, so we split that. How do you think we could draw them away?" he asks, getting out of the bed naked to grab his backpack.

I watch him move. I've missed these little moments of complete openness. My eyes linger on a mark above his incredibly sexy bare ass. "What happened to your back?" I ask, clambering to my knees and toward him.

He tenses slightly before turning, and I try to catch his eye, sensing that whatever happened would not make me thrilled. While he fidgets, I resist my primal urge to ogle his naked extremities. He sets his bag on the bed and sighs. "One man that was part of the rescue in Chattanooga was at Quin's the night they came to collect you. The one who came into town and tried to persuade you to come in, in front of the Sheriff's station," he explains.

"Pearson, the one I threw my knife at when he tried to kill you and Dad?" I ask, frowning.

"Yes, he was with the men that were with Trevor. When we got back, he grabbed Davin and me up real quick. He wanted to know how you survived and what happened to Gus. Davin was quick enough to ask if Cassie was there."

"Was she?" I ask, feeling hope build in my chest.

"She was, and they brought her in. She gave them the information you gave Chip about Gus. They figured out I was your boyfriend, and after letting Cassie take Davin to get rations, he and some old guy, who I guess was in charge, wanted to speak to me man to man."

"Corporal Allen," I say, letting the name hiss out of my mouth, my fists clenching as I sit back on my heels.

"Sounds right, anyway, they didn't want to believe that I didn't have any other information," he explains, his eyes dart between mine nervously..

"What did they do to you?" I ask.

"They held me for 24 hours, then they interrogated me with extensive measures," he responds, smoothing the hair on the back of his head.

"They beat you?" I ask, heat flaming in my face now as anger explodes inside me.

He nods, watching me with slight unease.

"That's why they let you come here, isn't it? So when and if I showed up, you wouldn't tell me?" I conclude, my body rigid and ready to avenge this atrocity.

He shrugs. "Probably."

"What hurts?" I ask, channeling my anger to concern as another yellowing bruise on his ribs catches my attention.

"I am fine, my back is a little sore from whatever Pearson hit me with. But I am almost 85%."

"They are dead if I ever lay eyes on them again," I snarl.

"Okay," he agrees with a soft smile.

"Allen will be quick, but Pearson, his will be drawn out."

He shakes his head in amusement, still watching me.

"I don't know how to get hold of anything strong enough to bust open that door," I admit, tapping my finger on my chin as I consider nearby options.

"You going to start blowing shit up?" he asks with a playful smile.

"I already blew up a gas station this week by accident, so I am sure doing it on purpose wouldn't be too hard." I shrug.

His eyes lock on mine, and I roll my eyes at him, pulling his bag to me. "You're joking, right?" he asks.

"You can think that if it makes you feel better."

"How do you accidentally blow up a building?" he gasps, his hands both running up into his hair now pulling at it slightly.

"Go to the restroom, and then I will tell you what happened." I offer, then open the bag.

"How do you know I need to go to the bathroom?" he asks, dropping his hands to his side with exasperation.

"Your penis makes a twitching movement when you need to pee, it's your tell," I inform. Amusement bubbles through my intense stare when I see the look on his face. "You shouldn't have asked," I say, snorting with laughter and then covering my face.

He shakes his head and walks into the bathroom, shutting the door.

I pull his supplies from his backpack, glancing at his locked door. Could Dean still be just one room over? Has he finished the rations I left him in my room? Or did he get better? I stare at the door, my task forgotten. I survived the virus in that very room. Maybe he has as well.

"Aurora?" Sterling says.

I blink, turning to find him clothed and standing next to the bed.

"You okay?" he asks, brushing his wet hair back off his forehead.

"Yeah, lost in thought," I admit. I get out of bed, looking around the room for my scattered clothes.

"What thought?" he asks, setting his brush down and watching me pull on my clothes.

"If Dean survived, or if he is still in there?" I admit, glancing back at the door.

Sterling looks toward the door and then back at me.

"Also, if he finished the rations, we left in there."

"Let's eat and then take the hall back so we can get to your room." Sterling offers, twirling a can opener in his hand.

I shake my head, sitting down. "We can go through the attic to my room and try to look."

He nods, passing out the food.

"I would feel better with you there, making sure I don't fall into the room," I admit between bites of cold raviolis.

"I can look if you want, then you can always pull me back up."

"You pulling me would be faster," I argue, my eyes pausing on his well-shaped arms.

He nods, and we dig into our canned food. I spend most of our meal watching him. "I was thinking about something," Sterling informs. "We need to be realistic about the fact that one of us may not survive at some point."

I stare at him, my heart thudding to a halt.

"We need to make a pact, that if we are a hundred percent sure the other is dead, we won't let them stay an abomination, and we will take care of it and continue to live the best we can," he proclaims.

I continue to stare at him, trying to keep my nostrils from flaring as icicles of fear lace my veins.

"I know that it's a lot to ask of both of us, but the strain of thinking about the other, letting themselves die because the other is gone, is equally unbearable. What do you think?"

I continue to stare at him, unable to form words for how horrific this idea is. I do not want to live in this world without him.

"Aurora?" he asks after my silence stretches on too long.

"Stipulations," I argue, setting the empty tin can down none too gently.

"Stipulations?" he asks, following my lead and abandoning the can.

"A stipulation is a condition or requirement that is specified or demanded as part of an agreement," I explain, whipping at my face to remove any stray sauce.

He rolls his eyes at me.

"Sorry, I have been with Quin consistently."

"What is your stipulation?" he asks, rubbing his thumb over my hand to ease my tight fists.

"I don't know how to survive without you," I whisper, my head dropping in defeat.

He takes my hand. "I am not saying it would be easy."

"My stipulation is I die first," I announce, sitting up straighter and jutting my chin out defiantly, then sigh as his face hardens. "Fine, we fight our damnedest to do everything to survive for each other, no matter what."

"I can do that," Sterling agrees with a sad smile.

"Davin made me promise we would look after each other. We need to communicate and fight together because we are stronger together. That way, if the unthinkable happens, you are as prepared as possible to make it alone."

"And vice versa," he reminds me, squeezing my hands.

"I will let nothing happen to you," I argue, trying to pull away.

"As I will do everything in my abilities to do the same for you."

I sigh, an invisible weight pushing me down at the mere idea of him being harmed.

"I know, baby, it's not a pleasant situation, but it makes me feel better that we have a pact. That I know you will fight for every breath until you die naturally or unavoidably," he says, releasing my hands and dragging his fingers up and down my arms until my breathing evens out.

"Pinkie promise? Spit shake? Or blood oath?" I ask with a smirk.

He beams at me. "Isn't it called a pinky swear?"

I hold up my pinky, and he brings his pinky to mine, wrapping them together with a sigh. "I, Sterling Karter, promise to do what I must do to protect both of us from danger and to eliminate your abomination if need be," he swears.

"I Ro...Aurora Karter," I begin with a grin. "Promise to do what I must do to protect our souls and physical existence from danger, both foreign and domestic, with malicious intent. To free you of an abomination if it rises within you," I promise. "We should have done an orgasm oath or something," I say, to break the tension.

His laugh fills the room, and my heart races in response. He kisses his hand, our pinkies still entwined.

I raise an eyebrow quizzically at him

"That's how you seal the deal," he insists.

I lean forward, kiss my hand, and seal the promise.

CHAPTER TWO
STERLING
"I DARE YOU" BY BEA MILLER

HER WORDS WERE MORE eloquent than mine, not surprising, but endearing. One of her many features I adore. *My wife*, I think while watching her prepare for the attic. We have agreed to just bring everything now, check her room, restock with water in the attic, and then go to her dad's looking for food before backtracking to Davin and Quin's new place.

"After we come back and load the truck with water, we need to go to Brooks first," she says.

I look over from my pack. "Is Brooks a town or a person?"

"A town, so we can get supplies: maps, food, weapons," she explains, packing my bag as tightly as she can so I can add some extra clothes.

"Is there an assassin there that you know?"

She laughs dryly. "No, personal storage."

I nod and then finish packing my bag with an extra pair of clothes. "Did I mention how proud I am that Quin survived your journey?" I ask. She laughs, and I relish the amusement on her face.

"After she questioned why I wouldn't share you with her, she almost didn't make it," Aurora admits, shaking her head in detest.

"Ew, what the hell?"

"We were attacked by abominations, or I would have skewered her and roasted her over the fire," she reveals, swiping her arm out as if to do just that.

"Why would she even, ew?"

"She was whining about how unfair it was that I had you, and she was stuck with Davin," she informs, releasing her pretend prey and searching through my bedside drawer.

"Bitch," I sigh, shaking my head.

"I let Davin know to make his own choices, and be true to himself."

"What did he think of the boy, Warner, right? Like your dad?" I ask, watching sadness flit through her eyes before she nods.

"Yeah, Warner, he had briefly met him before he asked where you were. I was still waiting for you to pop around the corner."

"I am sorry I wasn't there, baby," I sigh, caressing her lower back.

"No, I considered coming here first, and I should have followed my gut, but with the boy, I wanted to be direct, and I was so sure you would stay with Davin," she argues, shutting the drawer a little too hard and turning toward me.

"I figured you were tracking my beacon."

She looks at my ring and then smacks her forehead. "I don't know your code name."

"What's Davin's old code name? Maybe Trevor never changed it?" I ask, examining the ring Davin had given me a few years ago.

"Locate warbler," she dictates to her watch. The face swirls, then the arrow points at me. "At least one of us is intelligent," she growls, knocking the lamp off the bedside table and plopping onto the bed..

"What is a warbler?" I ask, ignoring her jab at her own intelligence.

"It's a type of bird, up here, we know them as Prothonotary warblers. They are rare. All the beacons have something to do with birds, Quin is Sparrow," she explains.

"And your dad is Eagle's Nest?" I ask, twirling a lock of her hair around my finger.

She nods and clicks cancel on her watch.

"It's a shame we can't reverse it and make my ring track you," I tease, tapping on the small engraving of a bird on the side of the ring that for the longest time I had thought was Davin's class ring.

"I wish Trevor had given you a watch."

"I hardly saw him, he was busy keeping Davin out of trouble."

"What about Alexander?" she asks, flicking at her watch looking for something.

"He is the reason I only have one remaining mark. He stopped Pearson's questioning. Did you know he was the person who showed up outside the last night we were here? He thought we had already been scooped up and went to check in, but when he made it back, they said no, and when he came back into town, the helicopter was already leaving."

"I guess I was wrong about him. He didn't bring Chip in, did he?" she asks, her body language changing to one full of anxiety.

I shake my head. "No one has heard from him, your dad asked."

"Did you tell him that Chip hit me with a whiskey bottle?"

"Davin did, your dad was not thrilled with me."

"Why?" she asks, frowning at me.

"Cause I came there without you."

"Davin came back without Quin," she argues, her hands flapping up in exasperation.

"He is used to Davin doing things he isn't pleased with, but he is not used to me disappointing him."

I watch her roll her eyes. She grabs the dresser and yanks it toward the closet.

"Can't you just spider monkey up there?" I ask as I help her.

"Yes, but you can't," she teases. We push the dresser into the closet's corner, and Aurora clammers up and into the attic, peering back down at me. "Get that sweet ass up here."

I grin, then move my nightstand to help me get up without overturning the dresser. Struggling at the top, I pull myself into the attic.

Aurora watches me, and I smile at her reassuringly. "Guess you'll need to limber me up," I grin.

She smiles back, her eyes sparkling with mischief. Then she leads me over to the panel of her room and takes a deep breath. Her hand shakes slightly as she reaches down and pulls the panel up. Squaring her shoulders, she braces her arms on the rim of the entrance and leans down. I see one of her hands move and then the other. I grab her hips, holding her steady. She puts her hand up, and I pull her back up. Her face is pale, and I know what she has seen before she speaks.

"He is still in there, I need to go down. His soul should be freed, and there is food on the dresser," she informs, patting herself down and then looking around for some kind of weapon.

"Then we need to both go."

She looks at me like she wants to argue, then nods. "Watch the shelf," Aurora warns before she wiggles down. When she's down, I move to follow and put my feet down first. I feel the shelf and bend my legs, placing my knees on it. The shelf creaks, and Aurora darts out of the way as it rips free and falls. I grab the attic ledge, holding myself up. Then I drop, stepping out of the closet. I look over at Aurora, who is standing staring at Dean's abomination.

It has a sheet tied around its middle, and the other side is torn and tied to the hinge of the bathroom door. It is straining against the sheet. Teeth snapping, arms stretching. I spot the tattoo on his right forearm that I know is the Heartclave family crest, but he looks so different. *It*, I remind myself, not him. This thing is not him anymore, just walking around in his meat suit. This isn't the man that my wife had become friends with. He is no longer her or Davin's brother. No longer an officer of mountain patrol or a boxing instructor. He is a shell, he is an, it.

I move to grab the food, placing it in my bag. Aurora steps forward, and the abomination follows her warily. I shoulder my bag, watching her.

"Grab me some underwear," Aurora directs, pointing at the top left drawer of her dresser.

I open her drawer, pausing as I look down at a baggy full of green pills, it's covered in a fine layer of dirt. I pocket a few pairs of underwear, then pick the bag up, turning to Aurora and holding it up to her. "Aurora?"

She turns, blood draining from her face.

"Molly?" I ask.

"I don't know what it is, but Dean did, so I left it with him in case he needed it for the pain or an out," she explains, biting her lip nervously.

"But where did you get it from?"

"A box of my mother's stuff," she informs, glancing back at Dean's remains again then back at me.

I twist the baggy open and examine a pill, then scrape it with my nail and taste it. I frown, wiping the rest on my pants. Then place it in a pocket of our backpack, glancing up at Aurora, looking at me horrified. "We can trade it," I shrug.

"Those are the pills that killed my mother," she whispers, her face pale, eyes orb-like as if she's waiting for me to drop.

"Then she must have taken over 120 mg because if she was a regular user, then it would be hard to mess it up unless she had a new dealer," I explain, opening another draw to see if there is anything worthwhile to grab..

"You mean she could have done it on purpose?"

I look into her shocked face and shrug. "Let's talk about it when we are safe later," I offer, closing the drawer which holds a few stacks of cash.

She nods, looking back at the abomination. She punches it in the face hard, dislodging a few teeth, and rotting blood splatters the wall and bed.

I step back, looking at her in earnest. She has her fists clenched and her back ridged, looking like she's ready to deck it again. "What is it?" I ask, stepping closer.

"Well, I can't punch Dean himself for going into my underwear drawer, and I didn't leave the pills in there, they were in the bedside drawer," she explains, pointing to the nightstand.

"Show me how to punch it so he gets the picture watching from the afterlife," I offer, watching as a smile tugs at the corner of her mouth, and I grin at her.

"First off, spread your feet a little; you already have great posture, so find your ground, make sure you have control of your weight, and know where your balance range is. Nothing should be able to rattle you unless you want it to," she instructs with a sexy smile.

I close my eyes, taking a deep breath, then I feel her hand on my chest, and she shoves me. I don't yield and open my eyes, looking into her blazing green eyes.

"Now put your hands in fists, okay, untuck your thumbs. We don't want any breaks or stains. Bend your knees slightly. I want you to think about your balance. Pivot your back foot and twist at the waist. Bring your arm on the side you're pivoting with into your blow," she explains, demonstrating.

I mimic her movements, and she nods at me. Then I step toward Dean, find my center, and reset my stance. I bring my fists up, adjusting my thumbs. I look up at the abomination rattling before me. Finally, I pull my arm back and then throw my weight into the punch. My fist connects with the side of its head.

"Did that hurt your hand?" Aurora asks.

"Nah, not really. It might have without the ring," I admit, flexing my hand to check it.

"Your form was great, but you overreached. Find a location that is obtainable without putting yourself open to losing your balance or putting yourself at risk for attack," she instructs. I nod, watching her. "Where is his knife? He always carried one, and we can use that," she asks, moving to the bedside table. She opens the drawer and then pauses.

"What is it?" I ask, moving over to her.

Her hand reaches down into the drawer and pulls out a piece of paper. She holds it out to me. I take it and look down.

> Rory and Davin,
> Thank you for coming back for me. I assume I have died or turned into one of those things. I am sorry I was not strong enough to hold out. I was not brave enough to cut the pain short, so here I am, my fever is high, and the coughing seems to light every working nerve in my body with pain. This sucks. I am going to tie myself up before I have no strength left so that when you come to get me, I won't hurt you. Thank you for coming back, no matter how long it took. Look after each other, the pills Rory gave me are in her underwear drawer. I figured that would be the last place looters would look, and I admit I was curious.
> I am so proud of the man you have become, look after Rory for me. She might be a hardass, but she's got a lot of heart. If your best friend hadn't scooped her up, I would have tried. I see now why you fought so hard to keep your new family, with support like Rory, you became unstoppable. I am sure she knows I am in love with her, but being her friend and her brother for as long as I got the chance was well worth seeing her happy with someone like Sterling. I wish I could tell you both everything and say goodbye, but this will have to do. Davin, if I am one of those things, take care of this, so Rory doesn't have to.
> Your Brother Dean

I look up at her and see her staring at Dean's knife. "I can do it," I offer.

"No, I will. Davin is not here, and I am his sister," she argues, clutching the knife expertly.

"We can do it together," I counter, turning to face the abomination.

She looks up at me, and I can see a tear roll down her cheek, her eyes sad. She nods. "You grab him, watch the teeth, and I will put an end to his suffering."

I can see in the way her jaw tightens; she will not bend on this, and we really need to get moving to Davin's house. I fold the note up and put it in the baggy of pills to keep it dry. Then I put my backpack back on and step toward the abomination. I grab its flailing arms and shove it back against the wall. Aurora moves, slamming the knife into the abomination's head, then steps back. As gently as I can, I lower it to the ground, then step over to her. Without a word, she collides against my chest, and I wrap my arms around her.

I hold her for a few more minutes, then sigh. "Okay, baby, we need to leave."

"Can you do a prayer? Maybe my dad will welcome him wherever he goes?"

"Of course," I agree. She backs up and takes my hands, squeezing her eyes shut as I bow my head. "God, hear my prayer, please accept this soul into your light and guide it to where his heart leads. Please tell my father-in-law just how much this man cared about both of his children. Make sure Dean knows we came back, that he is not forgotten, that he will be missed, and how incredibly strong he was to fight it till the very end. It's in your son's name. I pray. Amen."

"I am sorry," Aurora adds, swiping at her face as a stray tear tries to escape.

"Come on, love, what else do we need in here?"

She steps over the body and into the bathroom.

I look at the picture of us pinned on her bulletin board, then pull it free, looking at our smiles. I can't believe this was taken four months ago, and now she is mine. Now, after everything that has changed, here I stand, a new man. A man whose sole purpose is to protect undoubtedly one of the most dangerous people left in this world, as well as hands down the most beautiful and incredible. I glance over at the bathroom and then back at the picture.

My old self, the one next to Aurora in the picture, was still splintered from what had happened long ago. But now, with her by my side, I feel whole, even in this new insane reality. Her hand on my arm has my attention on her beautiful, determined face, she moves past me with the items she had found in the restroom and opens the backpack to store them. I fold the picture and tuck it in my back pocket.

"Up to the attic," Aurora directs, moving toward the attic access.

"Show me how to get up, and I will try it your way. I have to stop being afraid of not being able to do something."

"You can do anything. Trust yourself." She turns to the closet, walks over, and pulls the shelf out, tossing it on her bed. The bed I had first made love to her on, the bed where she had laid near death, and I had been at work, trying to honor her wishes and help a sick friend. I wonder for a moment if Vickers is dead, too. Had he gotten sick with the virus?

"Okay, when you run at a wall, you need to jump before you reach it. Do you know how your leg was bent during round three last night? Aim for that angle," Aurora explains, with a grin.

I have a second of wonder, how could I be aware of how my leg was angled when I had this minx writhing beneath me? Aurora shoots forward and springs up at the attic access, then pulls herself up.

I glance around her room for anything we might want to take that we may have missed. My focus returns to the attic access before running forward and jumping where she had instructed. My hands grasp the ledge, and my body slams against the wall. I grunt, then pull myself up. Muscling my way up into the attic spotting a hysterical Aurora watching me with a bottle of water in her hand.

"Bet that felt great," she giggles, covering her mouth.

"Oh yeah," I say sarcastically, rolling my shoulders to ease the pain.

She holds out a bottle of water, and I take it, rubbing my chest. I drink deeply, and she opens the case wider, pulling bottles free.

"Too bad we don't have another bag, then we could take more water with us," I admit.

"Is the hall closet closed?" she asks, looking deeper into the attic.

"I think so," I reply, shrugging.

She moves over about ten feet into the shadows of the attic. I hear a loud noise and see the beam of her flashlight. I move toward where she disappears, pausing as I see her reappear. She moves into the light from the window near me, pulling Dean's knife from her pocket. I look at the fabric in her hands. She sets them in her lap, pulling a sheet free, and she uses the knife to cut it into strips. "Hold these please," she requests, holding the cut sheets out to me.

I watch her shake a pillowcase, then two more. She takes the knife and makes small slits in two of the pillowcases leaving the third unmarred by the knife. She puts one cut pillowcase into the other and then puts the last one in them both. "Hold those ends tight," she directs as she takes the other end of the four strips. I grasp them tightly, looking at her hands expectantly. When she doesn't move, I look at her face. Her eyes are closed and moving erratically under her eyelids.

Her eyes flutter open, and her hands move. I watch the pattern, losing track of the weaving pattern and focusing on the hold I have on the sheets. She's working quickly and not so gently, and I have to clamp them in my hands to make sure she doesn't tear them from my grasp. When she finishes, the sheet looks like the braid Quin usually wears in her hair. She takes the pillowcases, keeping them married together, and works the braided sheets into the slits. I lean forward, watching her work it through the two layers of pillowcases.

"I will take that end, start grabbing water," she instructs. I follow her directions, glancing at her as she twists the braid around her waist and the diagonal across her back.

"Did you just make a backpack?" I ask.

"Pretty much, it should work for a while until we can get to my storage. I made a carrier for Warner out of a sheet, and he didn't fall out, so I am pretty sure it will work."

"It's genius," I praise, smiling widely as I lean to have another look at it.

She shakes her head, then turns her back to me so I can see the pillowcases waiting to be filled.

"How many?" I ask, scooping up a few loose bottles.

"I guess we should keep the weight lower than 20 pounds, each bottle contains 16.9 oz or 500 grams. So 18 bottles would weigh 9000 grams, which comes out to 19.8 pounds," she calculates.

"18 bottles it is," I agree, placing them in the pillowcases. "How is 20 pounds your magic number?"

"I am not sure how well the pack will withstand our journey, and with approximately 20 pounds, I can be about 87% sure that it will hold together for a few days if I did it right," she explains. I place the last bottle in, then grab the band of my watch and loosen it.

"Knife," I request. She hands it back, and I make two slight cuts four inches from the top on the front and back top of both pillowcases. Then I push my wristbands through and re-latch them as tight as I can. "Secured," I announce.

She turns her head to look at me.

"I just closed the top." I shrug, then grab my pack and move toward the open window. I glance up when I hear her watch click and see her looking at it.

She had taken a picture of the backpack to see what I had done. "That was a great idea."

"Have to keep up with my intelligent wife."

She blushes and then moves next to me. We look out the window, and I find that braving the horde in the house sounds more ideal now.

CHAPTER THREE
RORY
"FIRE IN MY EYES" BY FIREFLIGHT

"I WANT us to be very careful exiting onto the roof," I remind Sterling, looking out the window. "If you think you're going to fall off the tree, I want you to use your arms and legs to secure yourself, and focus on your balance."

"Focus on you, baby, I will follow," Sterling reminds me, tightening his backpack straps.

With a nod, I step onto the roof, holding on tight to the windowsill, then stretch for the tree before releasing the window and jolting to the trunk. I grasp the tree with a sigh and then straddle it. Finally, I back down a few feet with my eyes on Sterling. He steps out of the attic as I had but reaches the tree without lunging. I sigh with relief, then climb down further before an abomination comes into my line of sight about ten feet below.

I look up toward Sterling, who is closing the distance between us silently. Then I shift, pulling Dean's knife from my pocket and swinging my leg off the tree. I twist and drop from the tree, the knife in both hands, as I crash down atop the abomination. I hear a strange growling noise above me and glance up. Sterling is climbing down, his face tinged red. I move to the bottom of the tree, keeping an ear out for approaching abominations. He reaches the bottom, slides off, and turns to me.

"Are you okay?" I ask, looking him up and down for injuries.

"Did you fall?" he growls.

"No, of course not."

"What happened to staying as safe as possible?" he asks, his hands flying up in exasperation and a scowl pinching his face..

"I used two hands to kill it," I say with a duh tone, shrugging my shoulders.

His jaw tightens, but the sound of movement around the side of the house reminds me of our situation.

"Come on," I whisper, grabbing his hand and pulling him to the path. I move soundlessly and flinch when he snaps a branch under his heavy footsteps. We reach the gulch and then the other side with no incident. We slow as we near Dad's. "Do you smell that?" I ask quietly, scanning the dense woods around us.

"Yea, it's a burnt smell."

Voices catch my ears, and I freeze, my hand resting on Sterling's chest. He frowns, and the pop of gunfire causes us to hit the dirt. I crawl forward, peering through the grass and trees toward my dad's house. The roof looks charred, and half the house looks like a fire had consumed it. I catch sight of men on the deck using Davin's grill.

"When will Moore be back?" I hear a female voice ask. My eyes shift from Mick and Dietler's faces to Chevon, who walks out of the sliding glass door.

"You know he is too old for you, dollface," Bryar announces, standing up from the table and walking toward her.

"You're just jealous, Bryar," she flirts, caressing his cheek.

"Everyone except Andrew has had a go with you, what is there to be jealous of?" he challenges. My eyes lock on Andrew Heartclave sitting on a chair at the edge of the patio. "I could untie him and give you a chance to have a go with him as well," Bryar offers.

"I am tempted to say yes so I can watch Chip kill you like he did

Rory," Chevon counters, swaying her hips as she stalks toward him. I reach over and touch Sterling's hand as he tenses.

Andrew makes a loud noise, pulling against his restraints. I watch Mick look over with concern. Dietler turns away from the grill and focuses on Andrew now. "Take out the gag," he orders.

Bryar moves and pulls the gag from Andrew's mouth, then shouts as Andrew sinks his teeth into his finger.

"When Rory and Davin find out what you've done to this home, you'll all be sorry," Andrew threatens, struggling against his restraints.

"Big words for a geezer," Dietler goads, flashing him a wicked grin and swigging from the beer can in his hand.

I nudge Sterling and gesture for him to fall back. We crawl back silently till we are clear of the sight of the house. "We need to free Mr. Heartclave. I don't think Mick will act against us. We should move on them before Chip returns."

"Agreed, what's your plan?" he asks, glancing back toward the house.

His acceptance makes me smile. "I want you to break some windows with rocks if you think they hear me. I am going to sneak around to the shed and come up behind Andrew to cut him free."

"What if they fire?" he asks.

"Then we bug out and regroup. If all goes as planned, when I get Andrew clear, I want you to shoot the propane tank," I instruct, pressing my gun into his hand.

He nods, taking the gun. "If they close in on you, I will use this to protect you."

"Agreed, just be confident in your aim. You're the best shot I have seen in this whole town. Don't waste a bullet that won't take someone down," I remind.

He pulls me to him, kissing me. "Be safe," he murmurs against my lips.

"I will use both hands," I tease, caressing his face. "Stay low, Wolfie," I add, then pull away before we can distract each other.

CHAPTER THREE

Making a wide circle around the property, I avoid making any noises I can. I come up behind the shed, listening to the banter on the porch. Something presses against my leg, and I glance down to find a small cat purring against me. It escapes into a hole in the back of the shed. The snap of a branch causes me to raise my fists defensively and glare in the direction the noise came from. An abomination tramps out of the woods, and I freeze, but it veers away from me and toward the commotion of the deck. I look down at where the cat had disappeared, wondering for the first time if the cats were the deterrent for the abominations, or if it had just not seen me.

"Another one!" I hear Dietler announce.

"Ignore it, or we will run out of ammo," Bryar warns.

I smile at this, then hear the crack of gunfire. The three morons move noisily to see if the abomination is dead, and I race for the patio, sliding under the deck. I hear a crash of glass and listen as the feet move to the other side of the deck.

"Did you hear that?" Chevon asks.

"It sounded like glass," Bryar admits.

"What if it's another horde?" Dietler asks, racing across the patio searching for signs of abominations.

"Then we go inside and let Andrew feed them," Bryar replies.

I pull a bottle of water from my bag, open it, then peek over the deck floor toward the BBQ. Mick's eyes land on mine, and he freezes, but I just smile, gesturing for him to move. He steps to his right, eyes moving pointedly at the house. I throw the water bottle at the grill. It hits the roasting cat and then splashes onto the grill. The smoke is worse than when Quin had ice teaed it months ago. I cut Andrew's hands free from the binds and then reach for his feet. I have to duck back down as Bryar stumbles over, the rest of them screaming in confusion.

A cat wriggles next to me. "Sorry, kitty," I whisper, grabbing it by the scruff of its neck and standing back up. Bryar's jaw drops, and I fling the cat at his face. I quickly cut the bindings on Andrew's ankles, yank myself up on the rail of the patio, and grab him under the arms, pulling him backward over the rail. I hear the crack of gunfire, and Dietler drops to the deck, his gun sliding across it from his hand. Mick snatches the gun and vaults over the rail, landing next to me and Andrew Heartclave.

Chevon screams, and I grasp Andrew's arm, dragging him to the shed as fast as I can. "Chip!" I hear her scream as we slam the door to the shed. I push Mick and Andrew to the floor as bullets rip through the walls. Cats flee through the hole in the back.

"Mick, kick out the back, get Andrew out!" I demand, shoving them back.

"Where are Dean and Davin?" Andrew barks.

"What the hell is going on?" I hear Uncle Chip holler.

My blood boils at the sound of his voice. I move to get to my feet when an explosion from beyond the door causes me to hesitate.

"That's my man!" I cheer, steeling myself to make my next move.

"Here, Rory," Mick offers, holding out the gun.

"No, use it to protect yourselves," I argue. With a kick, the door to the shed slams open, and I cover my face with my arm as the heat from a roaring fire greets me. Sterling appears in front of me and moves inside the shed to help Mick with Andrew.

I hear Chevon screaming and spot Chip struggling with the door to the house. "Hold the water, meet me at Davin's," I warn, yanking off the bag and racing from the shed. Sterling protests behind me, but I run faster. Rebounding off the tree, the fire licks at my legs as I land on the deck and sprint toward Chip. Chevon screams when she sees me. I have a second to register her singed hair and charred skin before smashing Chip through the glass door. We skid to a stop in a heap on the floor. I throw a punch, clocking him in the face.

I yank his gun free, flinging it out into the fire that is rapidly devouring the patio and moving into the house. "Now you die."

Chip's eyes focus on me for a second, then I throw myself aside as a second explosion blasts from outside. I look at the oven and then get to my feet. With a twist of the gas knobs, I salute Chip, then sprint toward the front door. I aim for the stained glass window beside it, throwing my shoulder forward.

The force of my body shatters the glass, and I tumble across the porch, then through the rail as a tremendous blast echoes over me. I cover my head with my arms, forcing my legs to move. I finally find my footing and run from the massacre onto the road. Pausing, I turn back, watching the house collapse in on itself. Sterling, my brain screams as I look toward the woods that would lead me to Quin's and then at the road that would take longer but be less exhausting if I didn't meet opposition. I see the first sign of abominations on the road and move to the woods. My skin aches here and there with pain, and I cough, trying to expel the smoke from my lungs.

"I need to go back," Sterling's voice announces.

"She said to go to Davin's," Mick argues.

"That's right, Davin's house we go," I agree, moving through the brush to join them.

"Holy shit, Aurora," Sterling growls. He hugs me, and I wince.

"Let's get the glass out before we celebrate, my love."

He pulls back, looking me over. "I am so pissed at you."

"That hug said something totally different," I tease lightly. "Let's go, I am assuming y'all are lost?" I ask, glancing at the men.

"I didn't know Davin had a house," Andrew admits.

"He just acquired it before everything hit the fan. Also, I spotted abominations, and we just killed four people, so we should probably move."

"That and started a massive fire," Mick reminds me, wearily looking back.

"She likes to blow shit up as of late," Sterling sighs.

"I just got all the abominations away from my house," I say, shooting him a grin.

Sterling shakes his head, keeping pace with me as we push through the woods to Davin's house. I slow as we reach the property, no noises greet us from ahead, so I step into the yard, looking at the pergola with the dark twinkly lights from the rehearsal dinner. The chairs and tables are scattered around the lawn. It is as if time has stood still here, the only difference is the lack of power and the clear sign that the weather has continued to befall the area.

"We need to collect all the food and supplies we can and get Andrew in the back of the box truck," I direct.

Sterling hands me the water bag, and I sling it over my shoulder and then step onto the patio. The images from that night blast into my brain. His proposal, our dancing, the heat of his body against mine.

"You alright?" Sterling asks.

I look up, realizing I stopped mid-stride. "Yeah, memories."

A brief smile breaks through his frown, then he pulls me toward the backdoor. He yanks at the door and then sighs. He snags a large rock from the planter and smashes the glass in the door, reaching in and unlocking the house.

"It's no fun when you don't tackle the door," I tease.

"It's less painful," he argues, pulling me behind him. We pause as horrible smells reach us. "Dead?" he asks.

"Food," I argue, turning the corner to see all the perishable food swarming with flies. "Okay, we better make this fast," I gasp, covering my face with my shirt.

"Candles, non-rotten food, drinks, and the keys are in their room in the bedside drawer," he instructs.

"I will get them. There are heaps of grocery bags in the bin over there." I point toward one of the kitchen cabinets.

We separate, and I dart down the hall to Quin and Davin's room. Dead rose petals litter the floor, crushing under my boots.

I push the door open. The heart of dead petals rests on the bed, and a bottle of champagne sits on the bedside table in water with a big box of chocolates next to it. Collecting the keys first, I stash the box of chocolates with the water, snatch the bottle of champagne, then move to the bathroom. I yank the towels from the bars and the toilet paper from the holder. I scoop up the candles around the bathtub. Then I move back to the bedroom, shoving everything into a

CHAPTER THREE

pillowcase along with its pillow from the bed. I grab the other pillow, swiping the dead petals from the comforter, then throw the blankets over the pillows, grabbing the entire stack before moving back to Sterling, who has collected at least seven bags of food, drinks, and candles.

He spots me, and we move to the front door. We step out front, gasping in the fresh air. We move to the box truck, the backs open, and Andrew is sitting next to Mick. He looks bad now that I have slowed down to take in his appearance.

"Where is Davin?" Andrew questions the moment we step up to the open truck.

"He is safe with Quin," I reply.

"Where?" Mick asks.

"The old mines," I admit, setting the blanket of supplies in the back of the truck.

"Why there?" Andrew asks.

"They have food, weapons, and safety. It was his best option," I supply.

"We should go too," Andrew announces.

"I am not allowed to go there," I admit.

"Why," Mick asks.

"The person in charge might hate me more than Chip." I shrug.

"You both could try to get in. They need trade workers, and you can be with your new grandson," Sterling suggests.

"Grandson?" Andrew asks, his eyes wide with disbelief.

"Yes sir," I agree.

"Can we have a few bottles of water?" Mick asks. I nod, pulling the bag off my shoulder. "Which entrance?" he asks.

"Go up the back road, and you can't miss it," I instruct.

"Will you be okay out here alone?" Andrew asks.

"She has me, I will make sure my wife stays safe. Well, as safe as she can be while running into the fire," Sterling admits, looking at me pointedly.

"Why did you save us?" Mick asks, tucking some of the water bottles in a pillowcase and slinging them over his shoulder.

"Because no one deserves to be a prisoner, and you need to make better choices about whom to side with. Next time I won't spare you with a warning," I warn.

"Next time? What happened before Mick?" Andrew asks.

"Tell him on the way, you need to get there before lockdown. Tell no one but Davin that you saw me, or they might deny you safety," I warn.

They nod. "Wait, where is Dean?" Andrew asks.

Mick stops, looking back at me, and I look at the ground.

"He was bitten," Sterling says.

"Did you put him down?" Andrew asks, his voice cracking.

"Yes, sir. We said a prayer as well, so hopefully, Warner will look after him in heaven," Sterling explains.

"He saved one of my sons. I am sure he will save Dean as well," Andrew sobs.

"I am sorry," I offer.

"Don't be, you were a great friend to him, you made him a better man by challenging him. You owe me no apologies, Rory. Just look after yourself. Thank you for the rescue and for incinerating the sheriff," Andrew says.

"Be well, Mr. Heartclave," I respond.

Mick waves, and they walk down the road together, Andrew clutching a few water bottles to his chest. Part of me thinks we should take them with us, but I know keeping it just me and Sterling is for the best, and all I can do is hope they make it.

"Better go get the water before the fire spreads to your place," Sterling reminds me with a sigh.

With a nod, I agree, pulling the door shut and latching it. I move to the passenger side and pull myself up into the truck. Sterling gets in, sticks the key in, and starts the engine. I stare out the windshield, thinking about Gus and the hours he spent watching me through this very glass. My body aches, reminding me I am still here, and that he hadn't won, no matter the horrors that seem to cascade on us one after another.

I smile as we pass Dad's burning house. The pain is worth Chip being dead. Worth losing an ancestral home, worth smiling till I take my last breath.

CHAPTER FOUR
STERLING
"LET THE SPARKS FLY" BY THOUSAND FOOT KRUTCH

I DRIVE to our home one last time, trying not to look at the raging fire or the decimated home of my wife's father. I stare ahead at the road, relieved that she is okay, bewildered that the men we saved were already off on their own, and a weird sense of accomplishment battles within me. With a quick glance, I see Aurora has a smile on her face, her head resting on the headrest as she stares ahead.

Turning on our street, I pull into the driveway and around the house, wheels squishing the dead abomination in the backyard as I turn and back up to the cellar. I turn off the truck, pocketing the keys. With a glance at the door that leads to the back, I slide it open and step back, moving everything toward the front of the truck. The passenger door closes, then the back door rolls open. I jump down, helping her open the cellar doors.

I see her roll her shoulders and then turn the light from her watch on. We grab cases of water and then walk back up to the truck.

"How about you move these forward and watch for trouble?" I suggest.

"Okay."

I glance at her and then move to get more water. After ten trips, she spots the first sign of the fire getting closer and abominations moving our way. I close the door and latch it, moving to the driver's seat. I lock my door and look back as Aurora messes with the door.

"Good to go," she announces, taking her seat next to me.

I start the truck and pull around the house, past the driveway, and onto the road, heading away from our cul-de-sac. "How are you feeling?"

"Sore, but nothing bad. I am sorry I ran into the fire, but I couldn't leave with him at our backs," she explains.

I sigh. "I know, and I knew when we made our pact that sometimes we would both stretch the bounds of our agreement, but you know I am only mad because I love you."

"I love you too, and I think you're sexy when you're mad at me. However, I don't enjoy making you mad, I am just glad you understand that who I am is sometimes outside the norm of human safety."

With a chuckle, I slow the truck as we pass a burned-out car.

"Turn right, try to get to the 220, and head North," she instructs, pointing to the right.

I make a right, swerving around an abomination stalking down the street. "Can you get me some water, baby?"

She moves, grabbing the bag and pulling it to her, then sets a box of chocolates on her lap and opens a bottle of water. "Here you go," she offers, holding out the bottle.

I take it, drinking deeply, then set it in the cup holder. "I would do anything you want for one of those chocolates."

She giggles as I maneuver around cars blocking the turn to the 220. "Let me give you road head, and you can have a chocolate."

My mouth falls open in shock at her request, I glance over at her. She pops a chocolate in my mouth with a mischievous grin. "Sing me a song," she redirects, sitting back.

"What song?"

"Our song, I know I have left an unpleasant taste in your mouth with the way I sang it last, but you can make it right again."

I smile at her. "At least you finally sang in front of me, so I take that as a win. Even if it was a distraction for the dead to go for you instead of me."

Her soft laugh brightens the cab briefly before it's cut off by a gasp. She sits up, looking out her window at Maggie's a street over, smoke still funneling out of the ruin of the building.

"Was Maggie at the mines?" she asks hopefully.

"I don't think so," I deny, looking at her sad face. "Wash some of yourself up while I sing to you, so we can make sure you have no injuries that your brain is ignoring."

She nods, moving to the back of the truck, returning a moment later with a towel. "Is there another entrance onto the 220 ramp?" I ask, slowing down as cars jumble together in our path.

"Take the off-ramp," she instructs. I turn the wheel and then slam on the brakes as a car blasts past, narrowly missing the pileup. "Shit," Aurora swears, turning to look. "Go now, they are turning around!"

I step on the gas, maneuvering the truck up the off-ramp. She twists in her seat as the car gains on us. I push my foot to the floor, but I know all I am doing is wasting gas. This vehicle is not meant for a high-speed chase.

"Who is it?" I ask, swerving to cut off the car. A horn blares, and the truck lurches forward as the car crashes into the back of it. I clutch the wheel, keeping us steady.

"Asshole is trying to run us off the road!" Aurora growls. She cranks her window down and then reaches behind me to retrieve her gun, checking the ammo. She tucks the gun in her bra strap and then grasps the window. Pulling herself out to sit on the door, she grabs the side mirror and leans out to see around the back of the truck. I grab her ankle, trying to control the truck with one hand at a speed it isn't used to of 85 mph. I glance at her, keeping my fingers locked on her firmly. She pulls the gun from her bra, releases the mirror, and uses her hand to support her aim, followed by the sound of gunfire. I glance in my side mirror, and the car jerks to the left, clipping a car and smashing into the divider on the side of the freeway.

I shove my knee up to the steering wheel, slamming on the

brakes and grabbing Aurora's legs. We screech to a stop, and I throw the truck into park, pulling her in the window. Her hair is windswept, and the gun is white-knuckled in her hand. She pulls the handle and kicks at the door. I scramble to follow her as she storms from the truck. She crosses lanes, the gun drawn, but probably out of ammunition. I chase behind her, my long strides helping me reach her before she reaches the overturned Toyota Prius.

The sound of a groan causes Aurora to stop short. I sidestep her, moving to the driver's side door and wrenching it open, looking down and inside the car at a man who looks vaguely familiar. Not placing his face, I look at Aurora and shrug.

She leans down. "Jessie?" she asks, her face flushing with a fresh wave of anger.

The man turns his head, blinking at us as if just realizing that we were there. He screams in pain or panic, struggling to free himself from the seatbelt. The latch comes free, and he struggles against the airbag, then crashes down on his head. I back up as his legs unfold from the vehicle, and he slides across the broken glass and pavement to get clear of the wreckage.

He rolls to his side, his chest covered in blood. "You shot me," he gasps.

"You tried to run us off the road, you idiot," Aurora responds.

"If I knew it was you, I would never have done that, I just needed supplies," Jessie gurgles as blood flows from his mouth.

"Honking a horn and asking is too hard?" I ask.

His eyes lock on me, then roll back to Aurora. "Rory, help me," he begs.

"No, you could have killed my husband and me with that reckless stunt," she denies, and with an about-face, she turns and walks away, back to the truck.

"She married you?" Jessie stammers, gasping for air.

"She did. Good luck with the sunburn your abomination is going to get out here," I warn, reaching in the shattered back window for a backpack laying on the ground. "Thanks for the pack," I call, turning to walk away.

"No! Come back!"

I keep walking, reminding myself that this is his karma for making the choice to try to take out our truck. I'm just glad they did not build his car tough enough to cause major damage. The broken tail light would only help us on our journey.

I climb into the truck, shoving the keys in the ignition.

"All I could think of is Quin and Davin's accident for a moment there, and then that scum bucket rolled out of the car, and I had no pity," she explains.

"Other than almost falling out of the truck, it was a great shot," I compliment her, putting the truck in drive and steering across the slight dip to the other side of the freeway and speeding up.

"You would never let me fall," she sighs, setting the gun in her cup holder. After pulling the towel up, she splashes it with water and wipes at her face and arms, not so gently. "Did you end him?"

"No, I wished him luck with his sunburn as an abomination."

She bursts into laughter, snorting, covering her face with the towel.

"If I believed in hell, I would have a slide waiting for me at the end for finding that so freaking hilarious," she gasps.

I roll my eyes at her, focusing on the road ahead. "So we are heading to Brooks, how do we get there?"

"When we hit 84, turn left," she yawns, wiping her forearm tenderly now as she pries the glass out of her skin.

"Oh, here," I offer, holding up the pack.

She beams and takes it, pulling it open and abandoning her injury. "Ew," she complains.

"What?" I ask, keeping my eyes on the road.

"Porn magazines, lotion..."

"What?" I press.

"You don't want to know," she admits. I glance over at her, her face is pinched, and she looks thoroughly disgusted.

CHAPTER FOUR

"Aurora, what is in the bag?"

She sighs and hands over two photos. I glance at them, and they are stills from cameras where I am assuming his store is. In the picture are Aurora and Quin sitting on the couch we had eventually delivered to our home. I look at her, confused, and see she has a notebook in her hands. Setting the pictures of her and Quin in my lap, I reach over for the notebook. I feel her grip, hesitant to release it to me, but I pull it to me, glancing at the first few lines.

I met the most delectable woman today, Rory Moore. Her brother is a police officer in Enigma and told me about her being single. I admit when I was considering what a female Heartclave would look like, I did not know she would look anything like Rory Moore. She must be adopted, her ass is truly sublime. I fantasize about spending hours cheek-deep. Her demanding voice, subdued by our burning passions...

I stop reading and look over at Aurora. "I am going to turn around and pop his skull with the tires," I growl out through gritted teeth, moving my foot off of the accelerator.

She laughs and reaches over, taking the notebook and flinging it out the window. "We need to get to Brooks so we can both eat and sleep soundly for tonight," she argues gently.

"That sick bastard," I complain, my knuckles whitening on the steering wheel.

"Just be happy you're not a speed reader," she gags, taking the pictures and frisbeeing them out the window.

"I should have had him investigated after his behavior at the house."

"We had no reason to think he was still hooked on his idea of me."

"Then I should have beat his ass, I know Dean would have backed me up."

"Dean would have definitely backed you up," she agrees with a small smile.

"Clean up, baby, I think your hair is singed as well," I warn.

She gasps in response, and she pulls the visor down to examine herself. "Well shit, I don't regret mutilating Chip's carcass with gas-powered kitchen decimation, but why my hair?" she complains.

"I am guessing it's when you did that twist-flip thing onto the patio."

"See the safest way onto the patio, and I burned off some of my hair," she teases, pulling a small matted patch..

I roll my eyes, focusing on the road.

"Chevon looked extraordinary from the first explosion," she continues, using her knife carefully to trim the burned hair off.

"I was pretty stunned just how big that propane blast was, what was the second explosion?"

"Davin keeps the backup tank under the patio, I forgot it was there," she admits.

"And the third?"

"I cranked the gas on the stove," she explains, very pointedly not turning to look at me.

I look at her, and the truck jolts to the right.

"Eyes on the road, love."

"You cranked the gas? What if it sparked faster than you fled?"

"Well, the explosion would have expelled me from the building through the window I crashed through anyway," she guesses.

I shake my head with disbelief at the ignorance of her own safety.

"I am fine, the house, however, not so much, but Dad won't be able to return soon anyway," she shrugs.

"You terrify me sometimes."

"Told you that you were scared of me," she counters with a dark smile.

"Brat, I meant your actions terrify me sometimes."

"Is that why you said no to the road head?" she asks. "Too terrifying for you?"

"Minx," I respond, shaking my head but unable to not grin in response.

"Probably not my best idea with the demolition derby grease

stain trying to crash his Prius into us. We don't need any teeth marks there."

I laugh at that, and we fall into a comfortable silence. I debate pulling over and making love to her in the back of the truck on that blanket she gained from Davin's house. We reach the 84, and I slow down, cars block the turnoff, doors flapped open, and blood stains the road around them, and off the side of the road, I spot at least five abominations alerted by the sound of the truck.

"You said left on 84, right?" I ask, turning to look at Aurora.

She jolts awake at my words, her eyes scanning the scene before us. She yawns, unbuckling, and pulls Dean's knife from her pocket. "Cut the engine in case it's an ambush," she warns.

I scan the cars, and the only thing I see moving is the abominations. We open our doors, locking them behind us, and drop to the pavement. I pick up a pole from a car jack off of the ground.

"We have eyes from the woods at three o'clock," Aurora whispers, looking at the oncoming abominations.

"Let's deal with these first," I reply, not looking at the directions she's indicated. I use the pole to slow the closest abomination, and Aurora darts forward, driving Dean's knife into its head. These abominations must have been out in the elements for a while. Their skin is saggy and crispy looking. When we move to the next one, Aurora grabs it by its outstretched arms, and I slam the pole into its head. I vaguely hear voices, but focus on the next abomination. This one, we slam onto the pavement next to a car.

"Got this?" Aurora whispers.

I nod and try not to watch her dart away. I smash the abomination's head down, then stand back up, the sound of footsteps approaching sets my nerves on fire. Moving the pole as if to whack the last abomination, I turn, striking out at the person advancing on me. The pole connects with a bat. I drop the pole, find my balance, pivot on my foot, and throw a punch into the man's face.

"Roger!" a woman screams, stepping from the tree line with a rifle in her hands.

I put my hands up, catching sight of Aurora directly behind her. In her next breath, Aurora has her blade pressed to the woman's neck, and I dive out of range of the barrel, rolling to grab the bat. The abomination falls on Roger, who, in his delirium from my punch, screams as reality tears into his chest.

"Drop the gun," I hear Aurora demand.

"Kamron!" the woman bellows, then screams. I look around the car to see the woman drop the rifle, and now it is in Aurora's capable hands. She spins, leveling the barrel at a man's forehead as he emerges from the woods behind her.

"Hello, Kamron," Aurora greets.

I stand up, looking at the sword in his hands, wondering if he has any proficiency in using it. "Drop it," she warns. The man's eyes swing to me, and he drops the sword. "Officer, can you detain this man, please," Aurora requests. I glance at her hold of the weapons, her finger sitting steadily on the trigger.

"Yes, ma'am," I agree, but I do not advance my eyes to connect with another pair as the body that possesses them barrels toward us. Aurora shifts, a bullet exploding from the chamber, the advancing man's head exploding. Kamron jolts for his sword, and I smash my knee into his face. I grab the sword, slashing at a nearby abomination, its head cutting clear off, the body taking two more steps before it collapses on Kamron's chest.

Kamron holds his face screaming now, but as the butt of the rifle crashes against his skull, silence slams down around us. I knock the man out, but he is still breathing. I look toward the woods, expecting more.

"We need to collect their supplies and gather some fuel from these vehicles," Aurora orders.

"Sounds like a plan, we need to stick together, though," I counter. She nods and steps to my side, her eyes examining the sword in my hand.

"My Wolfie seems to have been holding back mad sword skills," she grins, winking at me.

I laugh, kneeling to check the man's pockets, freeing his back of the sword's sheath and a pair of keys from his front right pocket. I sheath the sword, then grab Kamron's arms and lug him up and into the trunk of the nearest car. Aurora leans over, slicing the escape line and tossing the handle into the grass. I tuck his limbs into the trunk and slam it shut. Then I follow Aurora back to the truck to get Jessie's backpack.

CHAPTER FIVE
RORY
"INFRA-RED" BY THREE DAYS GRACE

WE MAKE quick work of the cars at the blockade, emptying the gas by puncturing the gas tanks with a Phillips screwdriver and collecting the gas in this silicon baking square Sterling pulls from the bottom of his bag. We then trek off the road, in the direction the group had come, and find a small camp with four sleeping bags on the ground.

"Let's make sure the bags are empty, then fill them with supplies. We will deal with organizing it later," I suggest, moving toward the bags.

"Sounds good," Sterling agrees, stepping in the other direction, his eyes scouring the trees around us.

We shake the bags out, then I move to gather the can goods, hesitating at the ice chest. I push it over with my foot, uneasy about opening it. The ice chest falls to its side, its contents spilling out, but I am now staring at a hole that was directly below it with a metal ammunition box underneath.

"Sterling," I call, kneeling. I flick my knife out, poking the lid of the metal box and prying it open. I frown, reaching down and plucking a gallon-size zip-lock bag from inside. Inside the bag is an assortment of watches, jewelry, cash, and car keys. I look down in the ammo box, pulling out two knives that I attach to my belt before pulling out a box half full of rifle ammo.

"We should keep the bag to barter with. If people are only focusing on material items, we might be able to trade for food or weapons," Sterling suggests.

"How do people like this survive?" I sigh, pushing the bag into the sleeping bag.

"The ruthless will surface before the good people who are waiting out the storm."

"Oh great, sounds like our journey will be eventful," I sigh.

"Speaking of, let's hurry so we can make it to Brooks before nightfall, I don't like the idea of driving with or without the truck's lights on."

I nod, moving to look at the contents of the ice chest. I lift a three-fourths full bottle of cheap vodka from the ground, open it, and sniff at it.

"Dumping it?" Sterling asks.

"Naw, we can use it for cleaning or first aid," I respond, putting it in the sleeping bag. Collecting two bottles of water, I leave the unlabeled mason jars that could honestly be anything lying on the ground. I sort through the woman's clothes, tucking a few shirts that would fit me into the sleeping bag before moving to a pile of empty handbags someone had been using as a pillow. I reach down, unclipping any of the straps that will come free, then turn to Sterling, who is watching me curiously.

"All set," I inform him, twisting the open end of the sleeping bag and picking it up. I reach down and lift the empty bag, walking back to the road. He follows me with half a bag of supplies in each. We circle the truck before approaching, not wanting to be caught off-guard. I leave the bags with Sterling and unlock the driver's door before climbing in, locking it behind me, and moving to the back. I pull the shell casing from the door track and lift the door open.

Sterling hands me a bag, then grabs another, pushing it in. We get the bags on board, and then I put my hand out for him. He flashes me a grin, takes my hand, and steps up and into the truck with my help. I pull the door shut and re-secure it. I turn to him, knowing by the warmth of his body next to mine that he is still standing behind me.

His lips meet mine, his beard tickling my face. His hands pull me to him, one on my side and the other on my ass. The tang of sweat mixes in with our heated kiss, and I gasp for air. "That's not the noise I want to hear you make."

"Then we better get to Brooks, might want me to drive so you can refuel," I gasp, kissing him again.

"Sure, I can be the navigator."

"That's not as good as offering me road head," I tease, untangling myself from him. I grasp his belt with one finger, then lean down and whisper, "I will see you soon," with a cheeky grin. Then, standing up, I walk toward the cab of the truck, taking a seat in the driver's chair and buckling up.

Sterling takes the passenger seat, buckling his pants; I grin at him. "With just a whisper," he sighs, sitting back.

"Buckle up," I warn, starting the truck.

"Have you ever driven a box truck?"

"Nope, but I am pretty good at watching you, so I will learn."

"Would you like me to feed you lunch while you drive?" he offers, rifling through his backpack.

"A granola bar or similar would be okay, and we can have dinner later."

"Okay, and a water," he offers, holding both out for me. I take the water, downing it, then pass him the bottle back and take the fig bar he is holding.

I hear the empty bottle crinkle. "Don't crush it, we can refill it."

"Baby, we have hundreds of bottles," he reminds me, crushing the bottle.

I sigh and nod my head, speeding up as we reach the next stretch of road that seems clearer.

"So we are on the 84?" he asks.

"Yes, sir, usually it's a three-hour drive from Enigma to Brooks, depending on weather and accidents. We will turn onto the 92, then the 250, after that the 55 and the 33, and finally the 119."

"So our arrival time depends on all those roads being clear?" he asks, staring out the windshield at the desolate highway.

"Yes, so I am estimating it could take about 7 hours if we keep stopping like we just did."

"As long as we make a plan before getting out, we should be golden, right?"

"Ideally, we also have to anticipate the truck making it as far as it can after Brooks, depending on tires and other aspects of it getting us out of West Virginia," I say.

"Virginia," he corrects.

"No, we are in West Virginia by now, or nearly there," I argue, pointing at a mile marker as we whiz by.

"So after Brooks and sleeping, then what?"

"We will look at the maps in storage. I think we need to avoid all the towns and cities, and if we loot, it needs to be on the outskirts. I don't want any repeats from Chattanooga."

"I agree, so we will head for my place near San Antonio to start?" he asks.

"Yeah, that makes sense with winter coming."

"What are our chances we make it before the weather hits hard?"

"There are too many variations to affect an accurate probability rate." I shrug. I steer around an abomination walking down the road. Then I slow at the sight of rocks littering the road and proceed slowly as Sterling leans out to look at how close we are. "37 inches, turn to eight o'clock with a three-millimeter press on the gas pedal," I whisper.

"Are you mathing the rocks?" Sterling asks in disbelief, craning his neck to see them down below.

"Mathing is not a word, but I am working the numbers so we don't take any damage that is unnecessary."

"Your brain is amazing," he sighs, sitting back and looking at me with adoration.

I shrug, adjusting the wheel as we make it past the last boulder, the tires grazing the side of the road. I speed up away from the rocks, determined to make it to Brooks as quickly as possible.

As we turn on the 92, the sky begins to darken above the trees. I glance at my watch, which reads 2:04 pm. "Shit," I swear.

Sterling jolts awake. "What's wrong?"

"There is a storm pushing in. I didn't mean to wake you."

I hear him yawn. "Well, let's stop for a bathroom break, and we can check the tire tread."

"Should I check if you need to go?" I tease, grinning but not looking over at him.

"That's so weird," he chuckles.

"Weird, maybe, accurate, very," I laugh, slowing to a stop. "Let's take turns."

"Ladies first."

I turn the truck off, pocketing the keys. We both exit the truck. I have the baseball bat in my hand, and Sterling has the sword sheathed on his back. We lock the truck and meet in front of it, and I catch his gaze, leading him off the road into the trees. I hand him the bat, then step around a tree to relieve myself.

When I finish, I take the bat and wait for him to go, a sound reaching my ears from the road.

"Scooter, a truck!" A woman's yell floats toward us.

I feel warm liquid on my leg, and I move. Sterling had turned to listen, losing focus on his task. I stifle a laugh at the look of shock on his face.

"Kathy, get back on, them things are comin'!" Scooter yells.

I move closer to the road, staying in the tree line. Spotting two people, a man and a woman, who mount a moped and, with a whirring sound, take off down the road. Thunder causes me to shrink back for a second, then my eyes land on abominations heading up the road.

"Sterling, we need to go," I demand. I feel him next to me, and we bolt for the truck. I slowly draw the bat back and swing it hard. The abomination sprays fluids from its head and then falls away. I swing again at another one, then kick it in the chest to get past it. Finally, I unlock the truck, pulling myself in. I kick an abomination back and pull the door shut. Once it latches shut, I lunge to the other door, unlocking it for Sterling. I stick the key in the ignition and lock my door.

"Go!" Sterling yells. "Aurora now!" he demands in a muffled voice.

I slam on the gas, my eyes searching my mirrors for him. A few hundred yards ahead, I hit the brakes, then spot him rounding the truck. I let out a breath of relief, and he hops into the passenger seat, shutting the door behind him.

"What the hell," I breathe, smacking the steering wheel.

"I didn't mean to pee on you," he begins, failing to stifle the laugh that slips through his lips.

I have the truck moving already, and I try not to look at him as I chuckle. "I wasn't talking about you marking your territory, what happened out there?"

"There were so many, so when I had enough space to move, I hopped on the back of the truck."

"What if you fell?" I ask, unable to look over at him as I navigate the road.

"I hope you know I'm rolling my eyes at you, daredevil."

"You do know that both sides of that sword are sharp, you can swish it forward, then pivot and swish back," I instruct.

I hear the sword being pulled from its sheath and focus on the rain that's been released from the dark clouds above us. "Who taught you to swing a bat like that?" he asks. "And where did you learn about swords?"

"Davin was a ballplayer, remember, and the swords from the last guy who peed on me," I joke. With a glance at him, I see his jaw slack, his eyes on me, and I snort with laughter. "I am joking, you're the only man I would let pee on me."

He laughs now, and I sigh.

"A book called *RC Anabella The Fallen*."

"God, I love you, I will have to thank Davin someday," he admits. "We need to find a copy of that book."

"Oh, for our recreational time?"

He laughs in response, and I slow down for the next turn. The roads are slick, the wipers barely cutting it.

"I will tell you the story if you start singing for me again," I offer.

"Deal," he agrees. "So what were the people on the road driving? Why didn't we hear it coming?"

"A moped, lime green," I inform.

"They are running from this shit on a moped?"

"Better than on foot."

"Not in this weather," he argues with a shake of his head.

I turn the headlights on to help me navigate the wet world outside. Something outside catches my attention, and I slam on the breaks, the truck hydroplaning about fifteen feet across the wet pavement. I turn into the spin and look out my window at the gleam of green, a body laid out next to it with an abomination feasting on its innards. I sigh, steering the truck away from the wreck and backing up so I can get back on the road.

"Maybe I should drive," Sterling offers, his hands latched tight to the armrest of his chair.

I glance over at his pale face. "Take a nap."

"I think ice and snow is your territory, but rain and survival need to be mine," he argues but sits back.

I ignore his jab. "Can I have water, please?" I request, causing him to chuckle.

"See, for your survival," he says, handing an uncapped bottle to me.

I drive us as carefully as I can through the storm, clutching the

CHAPTER FIVE

wheel to keep the truck on the road as the wind kicks up. After making a right on the 119 a few hours later, I pull to a stop, the cab rocking in the wind that is swooping through the underpass I stopped us under.

"Sterling," I say, watching his eyes flutter open.

"Hey, baby," he greets. Then catching sight of my face, he wipes at his eyes and sits up. "What's wrong?"

"We are nearly there, and I know I won't be able to back up for the life of us, also..." I ramble, swiping the hair from my face.

"Yes, I get to drive," he interrupts, unbuckling immediately.

I smile, thankfully.

"Is it weird that you asking me for help turns me on?" he asks as I climb over him to switch spots.

"You're sure it's just not my ass being that close to your face?"

He laughs, but the thunder drowns him out. He leans forward, squinting out of the front window. "So you need to go up three streets and make a right, then down six more, and it's on your left. It's a hairpin turn, and you'll stop in front of a security gate."

He turns the lights off and creeps the truck forward. The wheel jerks as the truck gets slammed by the wind. "Now I see how you got your workout, and why you're glistening with sweat."

"I don't glisten unless you cause it, this is just sweat," I respond, pulling the front of my shirt up to wipe my face.

His beard twitches as he grins. "I assume this storage unit is on the outskirts?" he asks, maneuvering around a car crash at our first turn.

"Yes, sir," I agree, looking into the growing darkness for signs of life. The storm would help hide our arrival. We pull up to the gate, and Sterling looks out at the dark keypad, then over at me.

"Stay in here, as soon as the gate opens, I need you to pull in, then I will shut it and get back in," I instruct. He nods, and I roll my window down. "Roll this back up after I get out."

He puts the truck in park, leaving it running.

I pull myself out the window and then up on top of the cab. I brace myself against the solid truck behind me, measuring the distance to the top of the gate, the wind speed, and then assessing the risks.

Pushing up, bracing against the rain, I get to my feet, then launch myself toward the gate. I clear it and land with a flop on the pavement, sliding on my stomach. I push myself up, gasping and spitting dirt and water, before moving toward the bottom corner of the gate. With a click of my watch, the light illuminates the blood coming from my mouth now. I probe a sore tooth with my tongue as I yank a black cap from the base of the gate. I pull a knife from my belt and jam it into the keyhole, then down. The lock gives, and I twist the knife, disengaging the lock and breaking my knife. A hot sear of pain lances through my hand, but I reach down with the other to release the valve.

I grab the gate and pull it open with my right hand, pulsing as I do. Sterling pulls the truck in, and I walk the gate back to its position. I re-engage the valve and push the cap closed on the open lock, then dart for the truck, reaching with my left hand, open the door and climb inside. Finally, I slam the door shut, swiping the soaking wet hair from my face.

"Pull up past this building, you'll want to back up to the door to the building," I explain. When we don't move, I look over at Sterling, who is looking at me with concern. "You can help me grow back when we are safe inside."

He nods, following my instructions, backing us right up to the door. "Is the key with your motorcycle keys?"

"No," I reply, pulling my dog tags out where a small key and my house key are attached. "Turn it off, leave nothing up here," I instruct, grabbing the trash and realizing that blood is dripping everywhere now.

"Shit," Sterling swears, looking around for something to stopper the blood.

"It will deter people from trying to steal it," I supply, moving to the back.

He pulls the keys out, checks the doors, grabs the water bag, and shuts the door behind us. I click my watch on and step over stuff to get to the door. I slip the casing out and then pull it open. We stare at the side entrance to the storage facility and the bumper of the truck snug against the building.

"Nice parking," I admit as I lean down, place the key in the lock, and push on the door. The door swings open into complete darkness. The light above the door inside beams to life, and I smile.

"Power?" Sterling asks.

I step forward, but he tugs my shirt, making me pause, and then he jumps down, putting his hand up for me. I reach for his hand, and he moves, grasping my sides and lifting me down.

"What do we need out of the truck?" he asks, looking back.

"Just some water. Do the keys lock it from this side?" I ask, watching for lights or movement ahead..

"We will find out," he replies. He pulls the door down, latching it, and then locks it with a smaller silver key on the key ring. He turns back to me after pocketing the keys, and I pull my bat from the water bag and step further into the storage hall. Another light turns on as I step further, light bulbs beaming above me and turning off after we pass.

"How do they have power?" he asks, staring at the lights above us nearly entranced.

"We upgraded the building about a year ago with generators."

"Who owns this building?" he asks, walking beside me.

"Shell corporation, we have it run by townees."

"It's yours?" he asks, raising an eyebrow.

"No, Sprocket's," I admit. He looks over at me and then bonks into me as I stop at my door. I look at my bloody hand and sigh, then reach up, pressing it against the dark pad on the wall. The door clicks, and I open it up. The light inside beams, and I step in, turning to look at Sterling's stunned face.

CHAPTER SIX
STERLING
"MYSTERY OF THE INVISIBLE" BY VERIDIA

MY CONCERN over her hand has my focus until the door fully opens, and I glimpse what Aurora thinks is a storage unit. But, in fact, looks more like a supply room for a Marine. I suppose that is accurate, and I remind myself that with her job, she would need some place to tuck away from it all. Her hand caresses my chest, then she grabs my shirt and pulls me inside.

"Wow," I breathe, unable to hold my attention on any part of the room before something else catches it.

"It's nothing much, Quin's been here before. It seems like a lot now that we don't have much."

I shake my head, looking around at the boxes of MREs, the closed safe that is at least as tall as her. Another wall has camping gear.

"Can I have your screwdriver, please?"

I pull my pack off and open the front pocket and hand it over, turning to look at what she's doing. I watch her pull a lever down and then grab the door, rolling it down.

"It won't lock us in?" I ask.

"I turned off the pad for now," she explains, gesturing to the lever. She sticks the screwdriver in the door's track to keep it shut. "The light might stay on for another five minutes, so let's move some stuff around," she directs, moving to the MRE boxes.

"We need to get your hand cleaned up first," I argue, sliding my arm from my shirt to use it as a bandage.

"There is a first aid kit on top of the safe."

I hear a box thud to the ground but reach up for the first aid kit, after righting my shirt. "We should have brought in the vodka."

"We have rum, so that will have to do."

I glance over, and she points at a crate full of rum. I raise an eyebrow at her, and she laughs.

"It was a gift."

"You got a whole case of rum as a gift?" I ask, moving over to examine her hand.

"Yeah, I had an Op in Barbados last year, the Prime Minister's daughter was abducted, and he didn't want to get the crown involved because he was worried they would hurt her if he did. I owed him a favor for allowing Sprocket and me asylum at one point. Sprocket is not allowed on the land ruled by the Monarch," she explains while watching me bandage her hand up.

"Why is Sprocket banned?"

"If I was to make a guess, she killed someone important. I personally would be more curious about the taste of rum from its birthplace, it sure did sting well, so I am guessing it's sublime."

"Why don't we share some? I know it breaks Davin's rules, but it's just us, and we need to relax before we head out tomorrow or the next day."

"Let's toast to Davin," she agrees, walks to a box labeled camping, and fishes around for a second, then pulls out two metal cups. She hands them over, then moves two boxes, revealing a small sofa beneath. The lights blink out, and she turns her watch on, taking a seat. I sit down next to her, handing her a cup and filling them halfway with rum before setting the bottle on the floor.

"To Davin," I say, holding my cup up.

"Hope you're surviving being locked up with Quin," Aurora

adds, tapping her cup against mine. I smell the rum and then look at Aurora, who has just downed the cup. "Trevor had the lot tested, and it was not poisoned."

I smile, then down the drink.

"We should eat something."

"Okay," I agree, lunging at her neck.

She giggles, squealing as I capture her hands gently. I replace my teeth with my mouth and tongue. Her giggling eases, and I release her hands, running my palms up her body. This was my sanctuary, her body, her spirit, her responsive nipples as I yank her shirt up and her bra down.

I hear her moan and slide my hands down her pants. An urgency fills me, the one that started after the world died. My need to connect with her, to control something in this uncontrollable world through love instead of fear. I pull her pants off, trailing kisses down her legs. I return to her face, catching the glimmer of her green eyes in the dancing light of her watch. Her lips parted as she breathes, her body responding to every touch of my hands.

The feel of her surrounding me completely is as close to heaven as I have ever been. Her screams reverberate around the dark room, flowing through me, causing me to grind up harder against her. I would never get enough of her, not if we had sex every day for the rest of our lives. I would never tire of the way she makes me feel. Her lips find mine, fingers dragging through my hair until we are left panting together in a tangle of limbs.

"Can you handle another round?" she whispers, her finger running down my chest hair down my abs then following my happy trail.

My legs are now covered in a cold, sticky mixture of us. "You bet your sexy ass," I reply. "Grab a blanket so your breasts don't freeze on the concrete."

"No, I like the idea of you pounding into me on an unforgiving concrete floor," she denies. I watch her move, I feel lonely as I slide from her warmth, and she takes a seat on the floor. "Master?" she teases.

"You first this time," I promise.

"Together was amazing, so stop fighting it," she whispers as I crawl to her.

"You just want the count for tonight," I growl, kissing her.

"I want the count always," she moans.

"I love you," I promise, adjusting her body and moving behind her.

"I love you too," she pants.

I wake in pitch blackness. Most of my body is ice cold. I hear a thumping sound that must have woken me and reach for the warm body nestled next to me. My hands slide over her naked, smooth skin, her breathing even; she's asleep. I listen, straining through the oppressive silence for even the slightest noise, and just when I give up, a loud thud crashes against the door to the unit. Aurora stirs, sitting up, her hands moving.

"Baby, that's not your weapon," I hiss, frozen in place as pain screams through me.

She giggles, releasing her death grip.

I move to sit up, reaching around in the darkness for my clothes. The thud rattles against the door again. Aurora's watch beams to life, and I see my pants sticking halfway out from under the couch. I grab them, then yank my boxers to me, pulling them on. Climbing to my feet, I put my pants on, and Aurora hands me my shirt. I look at it, and she winks at me. "When did this come off?" I ask.

"Like magic, you took it off as you lunged at me," she giggles.

"I must have wanted your hands on me," I smile, then flinch as the thud rattles the door again.

"I am pretty sure it's just an abomination, we raised the dead."

"So we ignore it for now?" I ask, glancing at the shaking door.

"Yup, ready for food?"

"Yes please," I yawn, stretching.

She moves to the camping box, pulls out a lantern, cranks the bottom, and then sets it on the safe, casting a glow around the room. She turns off her watch light and opens a box that reads MREs. "I only have the kinds I like, so hopefully, you'll find a tolerable flavor."

"As long as it's not the Gumbo ones," I sneer, wrinkling my nose. A smile breaks out across my face at her laughter, before I step over to look at what she has. Beef Stew, Pepperoni Pizza, Chicken Pesto Pasta, Pork Sausage Patty, and Beef Ravioli.

"Anything interests you? Just remember, it's better than starvation," she reminds me.

"Didn't we talk about these on our first date?" I ask, taking a Pork Sausage Patty pack. She nods at me, then sits cross-legged on the floor with a beef stew MRE, so I sit next to her. She pulls a knife from her side and opens it. "Where is your other one?" I ask.

"Broke it opening the gate, that's how I cut my hand," she admits, opening her MRE and handing the knife over so I can use it.

I open mine, dumping it in a pile in front of me, then checking the date on the wrapper.

"They should be okay, bought them 2 years or so ago," she offers.

"Two years or so?"

"I try to keep my computer brain mellow to not overwhelm people with the vast amounts of useless knowledge I possess," she shrugs, opening an oatmeal cookie.

I grab my cookies and open them, looking down at the Statue of Liberty and eagle-shaped patriotic cookies. They happen to be Davin's and my favorite MRE cookies. "I love your brain, I think it's miraculous to remember everything. I can tell that there are downfalls, but I have to be the luckiest man in the apocalypse."

She scoffs. "What are you eating?"

"Patriotic cookies, want to try one?"

"Sure, want some oatmeal?"

I take the piece she offers and hand her an eagle, and she smiles at it. "Thinking about your dad?" I ask.

She looks up and nods.

"They make me think of Davin."

She giggles, taking a bite. "Because they are pale and short?"

I laugh, shaking my head. "When we were overseas, this guy wouldn't eat them, so he kept throwing them at Davin and told him to fatten up."

"What did Davin say?" she asks, nibbling on her cookie and watching me.

"He would say, 'Thanks MoonPie, more rations for the men who work the hardest.'"

She laughs, rolling her eyes.

"So he would pour them on his tray and split them between us, like we were in kindergarten," I explain with a smile.

"Not getting enough calories?"

"I think it was the heat; mind you, I worked out twice as much as the rest of them, so it could have been that."

"Sexual frustration in the heat of the Middle East is no joke."

I laugh, covering my mouth so the cookies don't fall out.

She prepares her flameless heating bag and sticks her beef stew and cherry cobbler packs in it.

I do the same with my pork sausage patty, then set my corn muffin top aside and grab my apple turnover, putting that in the flameless heater bag and setting it aside to heat. "How do you know I was sexually frustrated?" I ask, opening a pack of crackers.

She smiles. "My brother proclaimed that you're a sex addict, no complaints, mind you. My nympho brain is more than happy with that character detail, also, you guys had four women in your unit, and Davin said they were all into the same guy."

I nod. "And you know I wasn't that guy because?"

"Davin would have bragged about his best buddy hooking up with all the women in his unit?"

I laugh, nodding. "Very true," I agree. "He used to brag about you."

"All lies," she replies, taking a bite of her steaming beef stew.

"You used to beat him racing your bikes when he was back home, you helped him ask Quin to prom, voted valedictorian for your graduation, enlisted and passed Marines training, elite job, and you never took his crap?"

"He bragged about me not taking his crap?" she asks, pausing with her fork almost to her mouth.

"He told this guy to man up, his sister wouldn't have reacted that way. She would have thrown me on my ass."

She laughs, then takes a bite, "I miss Davin."

"Me too, but maybe we will see him again, who knows."

"I could pass on a Quin reunion, though," she sighs, after swallowing her next bite.

I laugh at that and take my pork, setting it on my corn muffin and drizzling it with maple.

"What are you doing?" she asks.

"I got to work with what I have." I shrug, taking a bite.

She scrunches her nose adorably, and I try not to smile while I am eating. "Keep the toilet paper and matches to take with us," she reminds me, leaning against the couch with her cobbler.

"We should keep the drink mix as well. I know you're hardcore about water, but these could be a lifesaver to the right person. Also, mixing it up with flavor is never a bad idea."

"Says the man who denied me whipped cream and strawberry coulis," she sighs, trying to hide a mischievous grin behind her next bite.

I cough, laughing. "Do you think you would have respected my honor as a man if I would have agreed to that?"

"Hell yes!" she cheers. A loud thud again causes her to cover her mouth.

I chuckle, sitting back and looking at the crackers distastefully; I hadn't eaten this much in a while.

"Full?" she asks.

"Yeah, I just feel bad wasting food," I admit.

"They will still be stale crackers tomorrow." She shrugs, putting her unopened items in her MRE bag and opening a moist wipe to wash up. I follow her lead, and she takes my bag from me and stands up to put them in the MRE box.

"I have to admit I am slightly grossed out that it tasted so good," I sigh, stretching.

"Lack of food does that to a person, seemed like the sex was doing it for you as well. I have never heard you make some of those noises."

I grin and blush. "I don't know what it was."

"The acoustics, my loud self, just does it for you."

I nod. "That you do, and that makes sense."

She moves to the couch, pulling the cushions off as I slide out of the way and watch as she pulls a twin bed from the couch. "Be careful, we would probably break it."

I laugh and watch her move the cushions to replace the lack of pillows. She sits down and then pulls a sleeping bag over, laying back. I get up and sit down next to her, looking at the smirk on her face.

"I so love to scream your name," she sighs, taking my hand and cuddling up next to me.

I caress her hair, staring up at the ceiling as I try to ignore the banging of the abomination against the door. "We should bathe in the rum before we leave," I yawn.

"I am game, I would give you 1000 dollars to shave your beard again."

I laugh, reaching up to touch it. "You don't like it?"

"Oh, I like it, but if I am going to demand road head, I need that smooth sexy face I have grown so accustomed to."

"You're my favorite person in the world."

"Mine too," she agrees. "Good night, my love."

"Goodnight, my brilliant wife," I respond, closing my eyes, focusing on her hand on my chest, her face on my shoulder. Her breath evens out as she drifts into sleep.

CHAPTER SEVEN
RORY
"ALL I SEE IS DARKNESS" BY ICON FOR HIRE

WATER RUSHES PAST MY EARS, all other sounds muted by the roar. I hold my breath as the water presses in on me. My face hits a rock, and my mouth aches, but I can't scream. I can't cry because if I open my mouth or lose my focus, I will drown. My face breaks the surface of the water, and I gasp for air, screaming. I catch sight of the riverbank; it's empty, no help is within my reach. Something pushes on my chest, and I fight harder to stay above the water. I let out a scream, freezing cold water filling my mouth, then right as I feel like I am about to drown, the water vanishes, and I feel muscular arms wrapped around me.

"Aurora!" Sterling yells.

I gasp for air, my eyes opening to pitch blackness. *I'm dead*, my brain thinks wildly. I can hear his voice in the beyond's nothingness.

"Baby, breathe," he demands. His chest vibrates against my back, his hands grasp me, and his arms wrap around me. "Deep breath in."

I drag in a breath, my mouth trembling.

"Now breathe out," he urges.

I let go of the breath I have just gulped in and feel my pulse slowing.

"Baby, I need you to sit up and turn on your watch."

I move to sit up, his arms untangling from me. When I reach down and turn my watch on, I expect it not to work, but then the storage unit's interior materializes out of nowhere, basking in the light of my watch. My mind races, and I remember where we are; we are in Brooks. We are momentarily safe. I wipe at the sweat drenching my body, then pause as blood gleams on my hand. I look at my shoulder and then over it at Sterling, who is using his shirt to cover his nose, blood pouring down his bare chest. "Sterling," I gasp, moving toward him, but he flinches away from me.

"I think it's broken," he grumbles.

"How?" I gasp, then freeze, looking down at my hands, the night terror running through my mind in a flash. "I am so sorry."

"It's fine, can you get me something else for the blood?"

I get to my feet, my legs still trembling. I push the MRE box aside and grab a provisions box, opening it up and grabbing a single towel and a box of tampons. After tossing him the towel, I open a tampon, take my knife out, and slice the strings free. I put my knife away and bring him the cotton rectangles.

"Do you know how to reset it?" he asks, his voice muffled by the towel and blood.

I stare at him wide-eyed. The truth is, yes. I know how to reset a broken nose. Panic fills me, I had hurt him without meaning to, badly, I might add.

He takes my silence as a no and releases the towel, grabbing both sides of his nose and jamming it back into place. His eyes roll, and I grab his shoulders, steadying him. "I'm okay," he mumbles.

I hand him the cotton and then move to grab a bottle of rum and some ibuprofen from the first aid kit. I open the bottle and hold it out with the pills in my other hand.

He takes the pills first, then the bottle of rum, his nose packed with tampon cotton. "Is this scented?" he asks, pointing at his nose. I turn to the wrapper and then back, nodding. I hold up the wrapper and watch his eyes focus on it. He bursts into laughter and then groans.

"Let me see if we have an ice pack," I offer, turning back to the first aid kit. I find one near the bottom and pull it out, reading the instructions carefully. I activate it and hand it over.

"Can you turn on the lantern? Your watch light is making me dizzy," he requests, placing the pack on his face.

I turn my watch off, then stumble and crash against the safe. I grab the lantern and crank it, light basks the room, and I set it back down.

"Thank you," he sighs, laying back on the cushion.

I move forward, taking the bottle before it falls, then back away, taking a seat next to the door on the floor. I sit there watching him, his mouth is open, and he is covered in blood. Part of me yearns to crawl back into bed, but the logical part of me reminds me I could hurt him.

Wetness coats my cheeks, not even realizing the tears broke free. I pull my knees up to my chest and force my eyes to stay open, greeted by the raging river when I fail, but unable to not look at the love of my life lying in his own blood. I push on my loose tooth, and the pain makes my eyes open back up. This is my penance. I have to sit here and see what I have done, to remember the way he flinched when I moved toward him.

The door smacks hard against my head, the abomination must smell blood. Can they smell? I wonder for a moment before Sterling's groaning cuts my attention back to him. I look at the rum, wishing it could assure a dreamless sleep if I got blackout drunk. Setting it aside, I take the towel that is stained in Sterling's blood and splash it with dark liquid. I scrub all of the my skin I can see. It helps me stay awake, and it rids me of the salt from my sweat, tears, and Sterling's blood that is caked on my shoulder.

When I am done, I set the towel aside with the rest of the rum. The chill helps me stay awake as my moist skin dries. I should do something, like looking for the maps or loading my weapons, but all I can do is watch him sleep. At some point, I must start dozing. The water doesn't surge over me this time, it's blissful darkness.

"Aurora?" I hear Sterling call, I blink, but the world stays black.

CHAPTER SEVEN

The lantern must have turned off, and I consider if I had actually been asleep or if I was in some cold state of in-between, my brain refusing to surrender to the sleep it needs.

"Aurora? Where are you?" Sterling asks.

I open my mouth to reply, but the abomination in the hall slams into the door behind me, smacking it into the back of the head. "Son of a bitch," I swear, punching the door hard, the noise even louder. I shake my head from the impact, then look around as the room lightens around me.

I flex my hand, moving for the screwdriver.

"Baby, what are you doing?" he asks, taking a step toward me.

"This thing is driving me crazy," I growl, wrenching the door handle up.

"Give me a second, and I will help you," he offers. I look over at him, watching as he brushes at the dried blood on his chest, his eyes black. Shame fills me, and I turn toward the door. I punch it again, this time screaming. The door thuds back, rattling on its track.

"Is it keeping you awake?" he yawns, moving to my side with his sword.

I yank the screwdriver free, and he pulls the door open about three feet. The main light beams on, and I stomp on the abomination's hand and then throw myself forward, my knee connecting with its head. Before it falls, I drive the screwdriver into its brain, then pull it free and kick the abomination away from me with both feet. I slide back, grabbing the door and yanking it back down.

"I had a sword," he reminds me, his tone disapproving.

"Go relax and take care of yourself," I sigh, replacing the screwdriver. I move to a box nearest me, open it up, and look inside, then push it to the floor to look through another box.

"How about you lie down and try to sleep, and I will go through the supplies? After all, the best trained me."

I sigh, knowing that sleep is essential to his survival when we leave. "If you get tired, let me know, and we can switch."

"Sure, is that the rum you used to clean yourself up?" he asks.

"Yeah, there might be some towels or rags in the box I just knocked over," I admit as I move past him, not looking at him, and take a seat on the sofa bed, staring at the safe.

"Are you okay?" he asks.

I nod, not looking up.

"I don't believe you, but we can talk after you rest."

I fall back on the bed, staring up at the ceiling.

When I wake, I am relieved to have had dreamless sleep and feel rested. Sterling is sitting on the floor surrounded by maps and his crackers from yesterday's supper. I stretch and get up.

"How did you sleep, baby?" he asks, glancing up at me but keeping his finger on the map.

"Blissfully without dreams."

"Good, with these maps, it looks like we should get as much sleep as possible."

I crane my neck, and as he looks up at me, I can feel my jaw drop.

His eyebrow raises as he takes in my expression. "What's wrong?" he asks, twisting to look behind him.

"I...I..." I stutter. Tears spring from my eyes, racing down my cheeks as I gasp for air. I see him get up, rushing to me in panic.

"Baby, breathe, what is it? Are you hurt?" he asks. I feel his hand on me, searching for something that could hurt me. "Aurora, what is it?"

"I am so so so sorry," I gasp.

"For?" he asks.

"You don't have to pretend I didn't fuck up!"

"Fuck up? Aurora, what the hell are you talking about?" he asks.

I click my watch and hold my arm out to him. He glances at the watch and then back at me. His eyes snap back to my watch.

"Wow," he gasps. "I look like you after that fight with Dean way back in Enigma."

I feel the laugh bubble out of me, but the tears do not slow. Instead, I make this strange strangled llama sound and cover my face. I feel his arms wrap around me, and I try to go very still. I know how his force field works when he is worried about hurting me. This is different, I actually hurt him. "Worst honeymoon ever," I blubber.

I feel him shaking next to me with mirth.

My lip pushes further, pouting as the tears slow.

"I love you, baby," he proclaims, grinning at me.

"I love you too," I whisper back.

"You know, if we were on our honeymoon right now, you would wear nothing but a negligee the entire time," he says, leaning back to watch my reaction.

"You would let me fight and kill abominations wearing nothing but scraps of lace?" I ask, trying not to smile.

His smile spreads wider. "Where would we have gone?"

"The entire world is closed. So the airport parking lot?" I guess.

"That doesn't stop Rory friggin Karter, she had a privately chartered helicopter take us to a rooftop resort. The help wasn't great, but it was secluded," he says. I stare at him as he talks. "You being you had to work out and might have strained yourself a few times, but nothing we couldn't work out in the bedroom. One night I even drank too much, and you tried to be Captain America," he continues. "We went on a strange excursion where you did some banister diving, and I explored mysterious closets. Then we tried another resort, and you missed the flight, but you caught up, and we had a bonfire, then a road trip," he concludes. "I forgot to add all the mind-blowing sex."

"And the big KAPOW," I sigh.

"KAPOW?" he asks, raising an eyebrow.

I show him a fake punch. "KAPOW."

He bursts into fresh laughter. "You are my favorite person who has ever existed." His amusement is infectious, and I feel the corners of my mouth turn up. He takes my hand and kisses my knuckles.

"So you found a route for us?" I ask, trying to focus away from his injury.

"I think tentatively, it supplies us with alternative routes, if something is closed and avoiding major cities. So I am thinking we can take the 50 to the 16 to the 33 west and then the 2 and back to the 33 to bypass the 77," he explains, tracing the route with his finger.

I look down at the map, examining it; I have in the past driven through West Virginia. "We should play it all by ear and use your plan as our main course, except I think we should avoid the 50 West, maybe try the 20?" I suggest, tracing my finger along that road.

He leans closer, squinting at the map.

I stand up, pulling my knife from my belt. "From where we are," I explain, carving an X in the paint on the wall, "if we head out to the road we came in on, we can turn left and go out of the neighborhood and West toward the 20." I finish dragging the blade to create a map of the surrounding area.

"Sounds like a plan," he agrees, studying my drawing while munching on a cracker.

I glance over at him, and he is beaming up at me. I try to smile back, but his injury makes it forced.

"We should eat actual food, and then go through everything to take things with us."

"Shouldn't we stay for a few days?"

"All it will take is for someone to notice the truck out there. I don't think that staying too long in one place will be a very good idea," I sigh, turning to the box of MRE's.

"So you want to wait for tomorrow morning?"

"If we are going to do mornings, it should be predawn pack the truck and out by sunrise," I suggest.

"Sounds good, do you want us to only bring essentials?"

"Probably, why, what did you have in mind?" I ask, glancing around.

"If we might be in the truck for weeks or months, it might be a good idea to bring the couch bed."

"I don't know, let's see how much gear we have, and then we can consider it," I sigh, not so keen on the idea. Honestly, I don't even want to sleep here another night, but leaving at sundown would be a bad call. It's too dark out there on the roads, with too many problems and low visibility.

"Okay, so all the maps should go, and I found a backpack at the bottom of a box," he announces, holding up a green bag. It has Moore stitched into it, my eyes lingering on the bag for a long moment. "How about you tell me about this while we sort, then we can eat?"

"Tell you about what? The backpack?" I ask, abandoning the MRE's and moving to take the backpack.

He nods and picks up the maps, tucking them into the bag. "I got it after training when I started my original position for asset recovery," I explain. I watch him repack the MRE box and look over at me expectantly. "During my first mission, I almost lost it in the Middle East."

"Your first mission was in the Middle East?" he asks, dragging another box over to us.

"Yeah, back then, we were having problems with units missing soldiers, and at first, they thought these soldiers were MIA or deserters. But after careful investigation, we found some soldiers were hardcore lifers, young males, who all seemed very dedicated to proving themselves to their commanding officers," I recall. I can feel his eyes on me as I move to the safe. "I started at one of the three bases that the men had been through within their tour to gather intel, the men had a few habits in common. Workout regimes, food preferences, and training remarks on their files. But it came down to why would a soldier leave a post unseen if they were not intentionally walking away from their responsibilities?"

"You came to Egypt," he breathes.

I glance over at his stare and nod, frowning.

"I was there before I got reassigned to Davin's unit. It was brief, and I remember that the whole place was on high alert. One of my friends was one soldier who was MIA, and I had an interview with my commanding officer about it."

"Bensen or Gerret?" I ask.

"Gerret," he whispers, the paleness of his face causing his black eyes to look even worse.

I glance away, knowing that telling him about this isn't altogether legal, but that at the end of the world, what was the purpose of keeping secrets from someone I trust?

"Well, if you remember, Gerret had an itch for gambling and smoking. Honestly, those were the only things every single soldier had in common on impeccable records that caught my attention. So I interviewed every single smoker on base, and then every soldier who had been part of the gambling as well; this happened at each base. Must have been after you stopped smoking," I recall with a small smile. "So we soon found out that sometimes soldiers would gamble with the locals and try to buy cigarettes instead of waiting for the packages from home when they ran out."

"That sounds accurate. Last time I saw Gerret, he was hounding me for a cigarette," Sterling informs.

"So I went out to the local area and tried to buy cigs or to find a gambling ring. Unfortunately, I got nothing, but then it was only men who were missing, so the soldier who volunteered to escort me became my bait person. He was mic'd up and went back through the areas we knew that the two soldiers from your base had last been posted. Soon enough, they propositioned him, an old man who wouldn't even speak to me. The soldier followed the man, and I shadowed them both. Luckily, I was armed because he was too far away from me, and he didn't heed my warning to slow down. I think he wanted to crack this case open; he wanted his friends back. A gaggle of men swarmed him, they had him subdued and dragged him into a building within moments," I explain. I glance up, and he is frozen, watching me.

I open the safe and then turn back to him. "I was able to follow, taking a few of the lookouts out. Of course, I knocked them out, and in hindsight, it might have been a bad call. I made it into this room that was underground, and I was able to tuck behind some stairs and request backup, but his radio was on the wrong channel. I still don't know how or why, but he was on my channel instead of on his assigned one," I admit, looking into the safe and avoiding his gaze.

"Shit," he breathes.

I swallow. "As soon as they knew they had an intruder, they were swarming everywhere. I was hidden well; it's lucky I was so tiny back then. I stayed where I was, waiting for backup. When the gunfire started, I crept out and stayed in the shadows. I made it to this room with a weird metal bar. I had a lock pick, so I could open the door, but as I opened it, one man returned. He was confused. I wasn't dressed as a soldier, but I was obviously a white woman, and he let his guard drop for a second. In the end, I returned with one injured soldier and the bodies of the missing 2 from your base."

CHAPTER EIGHT
STERLING
"UNBREAKABLE" BY FIREFLIGHT

I STARE at the side of her face, and I can see her anger and pain in her profile. "We also had a prisoner who we pulled information out of, and located the remains of the other soldiers and rounded up anyone involved."

"All of them were dead?" I ask, clutching the side of the cardboard box, staring at her in shock.

"Tortured and murdered for no information. They served their country like warriors," she sighs. I watch her pull a gun from the safe, and after I move closer, she hands me a shotgun, and I check it out. It's in pristine condition, and I carefully lean it against the wall, then turn to take another shotgun from her. This one is clean but has an engraving on the butt. I look at it, reading DH. With a smile, I set it with the other, I miss my best friend. I wouldn't trade my situation now or being with Aurora for anything, she helps ease my mourning for all the friends we have lost, and the countless lives of those we don't know that have died because of this new world.

"Sterling?" Aurora calls, holding out a long case that had been fitted at the back of the safe behind the removable gun rack. I take the case smiling, set it on the bed, and open it gently. A small piece of paper flutters out, and I grab it, flipping it over.

CHAPTER EIGHT

Whisper - You can do this!
- Amin

"Who is Amin?" I ask, curious.

She flushes crimson. "An ex."

"He gave you a sniper rifle?" I ask, pulling the weapon out gingerly and checking its sights.

"He figured flowers would die, and the only thing he wanted dead were the people they trained me to kill."

"So, he is an assassin?"

"Not sure. We were both poached for the job around the same time. He got a partner in South America to work with, and I was placed at first with Sprocket, then they changed me back to my regular job because I was not up to par," she says. "They gave me 4 months to answer, so I ran the clock out and then took leave. In that time, I rescued countless people, people that might be dead now because of an agency that values death over life."

"Well, we can help people now," I remind her, setting the beautiful weapon back in its case.

"But will helping other humans hinder our chance of survival? I am not saying everyone we have met has been bad news, but you have to admit we have had some shit luck with survivors."

"Other than the guys at the gas station, who else did you meet? Anyone decent?"

"One guy, he lives outside of Chattanooga in the middle of nowhere. We found the house when Quin mentioned that I should have shared you with her. Luckily, it had power, or we wouldn't have spotted it. It was filled with cats and a dead body," she explains.

"An abomination?"

"No, she died and stayed dead."

"How?" I ask, accepting a box of ammunition from her.

She shrugs. "The abominations didn't even try to follow us into the building."

"Was it raining?"

"No."

"The rain seems to make them distracted or more docile or something."

"Yeah, I have seen it. But this was different, it happened behind the shed at Dad's, too, before I saved Andrew," she explains. "The abomination just turned and walked away."

"Well, we know that you're not a deterrent, unfortunately; that would be pretty cool though," I supply, with a laugh.

"The only thing that I can think of that both places had in common is the cats."

"You think the abominations are allergic?" I chuckle, smiling at her to help ease the frown lines on her forehead.

She shrugs. "Maybe it's the smell?"

"Of the cat's blood?" I ask.

She shrugs again.

"Well, if we find a cat, we should collect it to run some experiments because if we can figure out what is keeping the abominations away, maybe we can keep them at bay in large groups," I suggest, taking the last of the ammunition and stacking it next to the sniper case.

"Sounds like a plan," she agrees.

I look down at the rifle, it shining up at me like it wants to stay unboxed. I look up as she tucks ammo in a green metal ammunition box. "Do you think we should leave some stuff in case we come back this way?"

"No weapons left behind, I think we will need them."

A thud from beyond the door makes me pause. Aurora reaches for the lantern, clicking it off, and I move so I can feel her next to me.

We listen intently. "How does this place have power?" a muffled voice asks. We hear a thud, and the door rattles. "Shit, it's a zombie!" a voice yells.

"Dude, it's dead, so someone must be around somewhere," another voice responds.

"Let's check every door, then we can start cutting locks and move the entire neighborhood in here," the first voice presses. "Watch your step."

The door rattles, and I move to step toward it, but Aurora's hand presses against my chest, stopping me. The noise of rattling doors fades, and Aurora's watch beams to life.

"We should pack and go," she warns.

"We have to rest, or we will be at risk."

"If we wait, we could be looking at a whole slew of people, not just two," she argues in a whisper.

"But there is so much we should bring."

"The sofa should have wheels, we can unlock them, stockpile what we can on it, and push it to our door," she considers.

"But they will know where we are because of the lights," I remind her.

"If we take out the lights, then we won't be able to see them. I think this needs to be a sprint to the exit. If I fire any gun in those halls, I am going to lose my hearing again, and I can't risk too much more to them after last time."

I am surprised she is admitting that it's a risk, then I find myself nodding. We knew coming here was a risk, and while leaving is not ideal, at least we will have more supplies.

"Okay, let's pack fast and quiet. It's lucky they came today and not yesterday when your screams reverberated off the walls."

"It's possible they know we are in here, that whole discussion could have been planned."

"That's a stretch," I say, caressing her arm gently to soothe her.

"Whatever, conspiracy or not, we have to be prepared for an ambush when we leave this room," she argues, pulling away to pack.

"Okay, so let's hurry," I urge. I watch her for a moment longer, but her eyes never meet mine. I am worried that she hasn't had enough rest and can only hope that she can sleep in the truck after we leave.

We start packing, and when we finish about two hours later, I am looking at the sofa with two boxes packed tight with MREs, atop those are weapons, ammo, and the case of rum. I have the maps secured to my chest, my bag over my shoulder, and my sword on my back. I look at Aurora, who has been oddly quiet. She has a shotgun on her back and a gun in her thigh holster, along with another gun in a chest holster. My eyes linger on the straps of this holster, then trail up to her impassive gaze. She has a laptop bag hanging on her left side as well.

She averts her eyes, and I frown. She is scanning the area for anything else we may need, but we have left no weapons or food behind. We prioritize the best we can. I watch her hand grasp the screwdriver silently but pauses. I can hear her breath hitch as she strains to listen, then she glances at me.

"We go left, then right, and then left again, and we are at the door. You will need to unlock it, grab the couch and lift it. When you have your side up, I will push it up, and you can cover me if you need to," she instructs.

I nod, we have been over this a few times, but I know she's worried about an ambush. I watch her pull the screwdriver noiselessly from the door track, she hands it to me and then shoulders her shotgun. Grasping the door, I glance at her, she nods, turning her watch light off. We slowly push the door up just enough for the supplies to roll under, and we duck. We leave it open, and she takes the lead walking ahead as I push the couch.

The clip of the wheels on the cracks of the pavement is maddening. We make it to the first turn, the lights in front of her storage locker already out behind us. She peeks around the corner, then gestures for me to follow her to the right. She posts up at the corner, and I push the couch behind her. We hear a far-off thud, and I pause. I feel her hand on my ass pushing me.

"Move," she warns.

I slow as we near our last turn, and she squeezes past and steps down the hall. The lights greet us, and we can see the closed door a hundred feet away, its hinges gleaming in the hall light as we approach. I feel her move past me and focus on getting the couch to the door instead of what she's doing. She is back at my side in a minute and I am opening the door as she vibrates with anticipation next to me.

I wrestle the door unlocked, then up. Turning, I grab a few of the boxes sliding them on. "That's not the plan," she hisses, her eyes locked on the corner.

"The boxes will fall if I tip the couch," I whisper back. Her fingers slide into my pocket and see her shotgun dip as she reaches for her satchel. I set the last box in a dim light appearing at the far end of the hall, then grab the couch and heave it up, setting its wheels in the truck and climbing up to pull it in. I hear a clicking noise and then a strange hissing sound.

Aurora grasps the couch with one hand, her shotgun slung over her shoulder, but her body twisted toward the lights beaming to life down the hall. A high pitch squeal pierces the air. I see her throw something, then grab the couch and shove it toward me. I move, grabbing her arm, and I yank her in. Bright colorful fire shoots down the hall toward whoever is approaching, their screams nearly inaudible over the sound of the fireworks.

Aurora slams the door closed, and I jolt for the driver's seat. I fall into the driver's seat, slamming the key in the ignition and yanking it into drive, glancing up at the darkening sky, then around at the people staring at the truck from the pavement outside the cab. I slam my foot on the gas and flinch at the thud that comes from the back of the truck.

Guns rise around us, and I put the pedal to the floor. "Get down!" I bellow, ducking as I head straight for the gate. I spot a pickup just beyond it, and I jack the wheel.

"Around the back," Aurora demands, crawling up next to me.

One man, not startled by our escape, raises a gun, and I duck again as he pulls the trigger. I flinch, but the bullet ricochets off the window.

"Mother fucker! It's bulletproof!" Aurora screams, slapping the floor.

I race the truck to the back gate. This one doesn't look as sturdy, but the dirt road behind it is not very inviting.

"It has advanced suspension if it's bulletproof, just go!" she screams, pulling herself into her seat and wrestling the seatbelt on.

Fear floods my senses; the truck, the gate, and the uneven dirt all scream pain for my wife next to me. This is not how I want either of us to go.

"Why did he call you Whisper?" I demand, grasping for a distraction.

I glance at her, and she looks at me, dumbfounded by my question, her forehead creasing as her eyebrows pinch together in a beautiful frown. The front of the truck smashes through the fence like an iron through shortening.

The truck lurches up, and I grasp the wheel, willing it to stay on all four wheels.

"Hard right!" Aurora demands. I follow her directions, my fingers fumbling for the headlights. They beam to life, and I catch sight of an abomination before it's swallowed by the hood of the truck and thuds beneath our undercarriage. With a lurch, we screech onto the asphalt, and I look around wildly for signs. "You want directions or my history?" Aurora smirks, holding on tight.

I shake my head at her. "Directions then history, I had to distract myself. I am not as fearless as you."

She laughs, snorting as her hands cover her face. "Second right, then the next left after that. Then stay to the right, and try not to slow down too much. These fuckers might follow us," she directs. "Fearless," she scoffs.

I raise an eyebrow, staring straight ahead, waiting for her to continue as I maneuver around stopped cars.

"Let's just say I am very good about coming and going unheard."

"That's a lie, I have heard how loud you can be coming and going," I tease, with a grin, glancing at her flushed face.

"I meant during ops, perv. And no one has ever made me scream as you do."

My smile widens at this, and I am momentarily annoyed that I can't pull the truck over and remind her how true that statement could be.

CHAPTER NINE
RORY
"ENEMY FIRE" BY BEA MILLER

AS HE MERGES onto the 19, narrowly missing a flaming vehicle, the truck accelerates South. I open the glove box, pulling at the side, and as the panel pops free, I see a USB slot. I rifle through the insurance and registration that I am sure are falsified if I examine them hard enough, then unbuckle and move to look under my seat. I find nothing but continue to search, moving under the dash and then toward Sterling. I run my fingers over the rubber mat that lies flush against the floor between our seats.

I move to its edge, closest to Sterling.

"Baby, if you do what it looks like you're going to do, I won't keep this truck on the road," Sterling announces, his voice husky.

I giggle, then find a nub on the corner of the mat. "This is a company truck, I am looking for this," I explain, prying up the rubber mat to find a metal hatch with a keyhole. I pull at the latch, but it's locked tight.

"Holy crap, the lock pick set from your safe is in my back left pocket," he informs.

I smile, then reach across him, sliding my arm around him and gliding my fingers into his back pocket. My ear presses to his side as I reach, and I can hear his breath hitch slightly. I feel the metal at my fingertips, and I hook it, fishing it free from his pocket. I pull away, sliding my arm innocently across the front of his pants. The truck sways, and he lets out a deep breath. I chuckle, leaning down to the lock, and unfold the lock picks, fitting the lock with the perfect size pick, and make quick work of the floor lock.

The latch pops up. I fold the picks back up and tuck them in my pocket. Grasping the latch, I yank the hatch open. I pull out a manilla envelope, a flash drive, and a company-issued 9mm. I check the weapon and place it in the glove box, then shut the hatch, pressing it to re-engage the lock, and take a seat. I push the flash drive into the waiting slot and shut the glove compartment, then flip the folder to look at the front. It reads: "Classified Master Sergeant Aurora Moore ACTIVE" across the front. My brow furrows with a frown, and I flip the brads back and open the envelope, reaching in. I expect to see the paperwork that I signed. Instead, I pull out a thick fill and a smaller envelope. I set the file in my lap and open the smaller envelope.

I pull out a stack of photos, the first one is my headshot from Basic. My frown deepens, flipping to the next; this one is after training and before my first mission. I tuck this to the back with the other and look at the next one. It has a picture of me when I was hired by the company.

"Are those pictures of you?" Sterling asks, breaking my racing thoughts.

"Yeah, basic, after training, and hired at my first position," I list, flipping to the next picture. I freeze. It's a picture of me and my father in New York. I look at the next one, which has a picture of Sprocket shaking my hand. I freeze; they had been following me when I went on my quick leave to visit him. I had known that running into Sprocket wasn't a coincidence, but did she know they were clicking pictures? Sprocket would never allow them to take her picture. She was a shadow, while I was just a whisper.

"Who's that?" Sterling asks, glancing over before his attention returns to the road.

"Sprocket," I sigh.

"They took a picture of an assassin who, from what you have said, is not a team player?"

"I was thinking the same thing, I don't think she knew about this.".

I flip to the next shot and see a picture of me and Amin, we are sitting at a cafe in Dubai. I remember this day. He was mad that I wasn't taking my training seriously with Sprocket, and he had heard about the helicopter maneuver from the flyboy. I realize now that it's weird he would talk to someone I had recently been hooking up with. I study his expression, his head tilted toward the sun; he knows we are being watched. At that point, we shouldn't have had any communication, but I needed to release the stress.

"You don't look amused, see that frown line I was telling you about," Sterling teases, gesturing at the picture.

"That's Amin I am talking to."

He glances over curiously. "That's the side of someone's face."

"Because he knew we were being watched," I conclude. His eyes shift to mine, and I move to the next picture. I feel my hands shake now, my eyes lingering on the dark picture, they have taken it around a car at the drop-off zone at the airport in Texas. In it, my hair caressing my shoulders, my hands planted on the hood of a taxi, my face angry. I realize my mouth is open and close it, tracing my finger over a startled-looking Sterling, tiny in the background.

"What the hell?" Sterling asks, the truck swerving slightly.

I jam this photo to the back, then gasp as I catch sight of a picture from inside the airport in Saint Louis. I am sitting on the ground near a window with my mouth partially open. "Shit," I breathe.

"What's wrong?"

I flip faster now, dropping the pictures to the floor. Sprinting from the plane in the Appalachians, driving away with my motorcycle. Sitting with my family at Quin's birthday dinner, walking out of the boxing studio with a black eye, in full uniform with Pearson and Hewett, sitting on the back of Davin's truck with hordes of people celebrating behind me, my house, a picture of my garage from the backdoor. A picture of the broken taillight, a picture of the flowers, and a mask. I pause at the last picture. It's of me and Sterling dancing at Rocks, but his face is crossed out with Sharpie. This is why no bugs were found at the house because I was being surveyed. Sterling reaches over and takes the picture in my hand.

"How many pictures did he have?" he asks, crumpling this one up and launching it out the window.

"Too many, I feel so stupid, how did I not notice sooner that someone was watching me?" I question myself.

"I am pretty distracting," Sterling says, trying to cheer me up.

"What would he have done to you if you had been home that night?" I counter. I feel his eyes on me but ignore them and grab the file, opening it to a two-prong file with my company ID picture with my name and agent number across the front.

"Read it out loud," Sterling insists, swerving around a stalled-out car.

I swallow, folding up the first page and looking at the company seal at the top of the page, then I read.

Agent Gus Walters, your assignment is to shadow Master Sergeant Moore, and you must stay out of sight at all times. Change your appearance often and DO NOT ENGAGE! Her unredacted file is attached for your complete understanding of the seriousness of this situation. Moore is an ASSET to our establishment and as such has full unwavering abilities to torture and torment any and all information out of you if you are discovered. Your mission is to watch and report, keep all your findings on your flash drive, and review often so that you can completely understand all aspects of Agent Moore and her whereabouts during her vacation.

Agent Moore is a full-functioning member of our trained assassin team, and while she has yet to take a life, proceed with extreme caution, some things that she is capable of are worse than death. She is extremely intelligent and stays very isolated, do not let her solo behaviors deter you from your goal of not being seen. We expect regular reports sent to HQ every three days with an update.

Corporal Allen

I stop reading and look over at Sterling, noting his frown before flipping the page and beginning to read my unredacted file:

We have selected Master Sergeant Moore for our Asset Recovery division. She shows exemplary processes in locating lost people and property. Her IQ of 190 puts her in a league of her own, with a photographic memory and sharp moral standards, she is a prime candidate for this position working with our most intelligent handler, Trevor Savant. Savant is working on an experiment to keep our agents connected at all times with their handlers, both through open communications and vitals.

Moore has passed all prerequisites with outstanding scores. We have cleared her to begin work immediately at an annual salary of $147,000, with full benefits and housing. We will reevaluate this within her one-year term.

Sign-on bonus dispersed of $10,000.

A change to Moore's contract marked on her one-year assessment is $150,000 with full benefits and housing.

A change to Moore's contract marked on the 4th month of her second, one-year term for $40,000 for hazard pay and included in the family separation funds in the amount of $1,000 a month. (This change is due to incident 1545284 HQ disruption.)

We have requested Moore for evaluation after the incident on 1545284. She is being offered a promotion to our

CHAPTER NINE

elite task force. Moore shows promise and has proven that her ability to recover assets is merely the tip of the iceberg. We have closely monitored her since the 1545284 incident and have since had a run-in during Operation R18 at a Russian nightclub with 5 heavily armed Russian intelligence officers. Hostels were subdued.

Moore has declined the position and has been offered a counteroffer for her salary. We have sent another agent to work closely with her to help her make the only right choice.

Agent Amin has reported that Agent Moore's moral values won't be up for sale. He recommends after working near her for one year that we train her for the position that we want her for. He says she needs a push for a big change.

I stop reading and stare at the paper. My eyes scan the report, and it has more salary data and more setups. I swallow hard, closing the file.

"Was that all? Didn't you say Amin was your ex?" Sterling asks.

"Yeah," I reply, my head spinning. Amin had worked his way through my carefully constructed walls, he was playing me the whole time. "We need to go back!"

Sterling looks over at me and shakes his head. "We both know how that would end up."

"They deserve it," I growl, the papers in my hand crumpling in my grasp.

"We made a pact and going back would break that," he reminds me gently, slowing the truck to fit carefully through two cars blocking the road.

"If we ever run into Amin, I'm going to dislodge his tongue from his face," I grumble, crossing my arms and sitting back.

"Deal. I will even hold him down for you so he can be alert for the process," he agrees.

I fight the smile that's pulling at my mouth, glancing at the file, then shove it in the glove box with a huff. I feel my eyes prickle and I look out the window to my right at the darkness of the world around us. My bosses paid the last two men I was with before Sterling to sleep with me. They were friends on a mission. A searing rage replaces the feeling of sadness.

"I should look at a map, not reading that bullshit," I deflect, trying to refocus.

"We are almost at the 33, you should sleep for a few hours before you take the wheel," he argues.

I sigh, sleeping doesn't sound like a good idea with how full of drama my brain is right now. I reach up and turn the radio on and switch it to AUX. "This is Gus Walters reporting for Moore duty. I have completely read the file and affirm that I will follow any and all directives set forth. The subject has arrived in her hometown, which is noted on page 33 of her dosser in Enigma Valley, Virginia, in the Appalachian Mountains. The man I saw her fraternizing with at the airport met her at her house at some kind of party, add a question to HQ if another agent is on this case," Gus says before the recording cuts off.

"Creep," Sterling growls.

"Gus Walters here again. We are on day three, the subject has regular deliveries to her home address but does not seem to reside in the home, even though she answers the door. Today, two men showed up, and the warning from HQ was validated. I have never seen someone kick so hard and so high. I have received your intel that the man she seems to be with constantly is not, in fact, a member of the organization," Gus concludes.

"No shit," Sterling snarls, jerking the wheel a little harder than necessary.

"Gus Walters here," Gus begins.

"Is he reminding himself what his name is?" Sterling interrupts, nostrils flaring.

I smirk, listening. "The male in question has been identified as Officer Sterling Karter and seems to work with Moore's family in the

CHAPTER NINE

Sheriff's station. After your call today, I have been provided with clearance to dig deeper into Moore's situation to see if there are any ways to pull her back in for a new mission requested via Strafford."

I push the power button. His voice is causing my brain to replay every instance that he could have seen or met me. I cringe at memories assaulting my brain. Leaning back, I take a deep breath, trying to suppress the overwhelming search. The small, subtle hints of him nearby surface, his delivering a package to me on various occasions and calling me beautiful. I really had let my guard down, or did I ever really possess the ability to look out for myself? Gus wasn't the first person who was put in my atmosphere that I had not noticed. He was by no means as detrimental to my self-worth and abilities as the thought of what information Amin had shared with our employer.

I was mad about Flyboy, but he never got much information, he just got lessons on how to make sex a better experience for a woman. I grab my water, polishing off the bottle.

"Want to talk about it?" Sterling asks, glancing over with unease vibrating off of him.

"No," I whisper. I stare at his profile, wishing I could set up the bed in the back and still see him. Even in his battered state, I can't help but stare at him, I treasure what we have together. It is real and incredible. Our relationship was never about learning how to please one another. It was solely on building a solid relationship and learning what made the other tick. My memories bring me back to our first date at the airport, Sterling had been an immediate acceptance into my existence while both Flyboy and Amin had spent countless hours acclimating to my high intelligence and intensity.

I drift into dreams of airplanes, of Sterling and I simply leaving the world behind and flying around endlessly in our suspended perfect universe before the world crashed to its knees. Its people succumbed to the debilitating effects of a virus that is infectious and deadly at an unforeseeable rate, but even in this flying paradise, they are there on the wings of the plane, twitching and rattling, moving ever closer to the window. The window disappears, and the wind wipes at my face, taking my breath with it. I watch the decomposing fingers grasp the window frame as it tries to force its entire head and shoulders into the airplane. Next to me, Sterling is asleep, his head resting on mine. The fingers caress my arm as the rattling grows louder.

    I gasp and sit up, my hands grasping onto the armrest of the seat and the cold dashboard of the truck. Sterling glances over and I shake my head, willing the fatigue to melt away. The sun is rising and my agitation grows. Why had he let me sleep so long?

CHAPTER TEN
STERLING
"FIRE N GOLD" BY BEA MILLER

I YAWN and slow the truck, glancing over at Aurora, whose abrupt wake-up startled me. Her current behavior concerns me. I know she is processing the information we learned last night, but I also know that she tells me everything.

"Where are we, why did you let me sleep so long?" Aurora asks, rubbing at her face and popping her back as she stretches.

"We are still on the 33, not too far from the two. We need fuel and a restroom break," I explain, before slowing the truck to a stop, turning it off, and looking over at her as she stretches again. She makes a small moaning noise that I have become accustomed to, and it's incredibly adorable.

"Okay," she agrees, running a hand into her hair before catching on a knot and snarling as she frees herself.

I keep my door locked, pull my sword to me, and follow her out of her door.

"Bathroom first, then fuel," she yawns, rubbing her head slightly.

I snag a bottle of urine from the floor and jump out of the truck. I turn, catching her glistening green eyes full of curiosity watching me.

"I had to pee." I shrug, tossing the bottle to the ground. Her eyes track the bottle and then swing back to me.

"I wonder if I could do that," she considers, biting her lip as she thinks.

I grin at her. These moments I am incredibly thankful that my wife is so technical and not concentrating on how gross many others would find peeing in a bottle. "I think it's something to attempt when not stuck in such a small space for the foreseeable future."

Her smile blossoms across her face, and she shakes her head, leading the way away from the truck. I check the door and follow her into the woods. We stay close together, relieving ourselves before trekking toward a rest stop that we had passed just before we pulled over.

Aurora's hand presses firmly against my chest, and I halt. She has a finger pressed to her lips. I follow her line of sight, bending slightly to see. Hundreds of abominations rattle around the overloaded parking lot, tents scattered around between cars. I feel her pulling me away, and we make our way back to the truck silently.

"How much fuel do we have?" she whispers.

"Maybe 15 miles, we can check that car while we are here."

She glances across the road at the car. "Can you hot wire it?"

"Sure, why?"

She grabs my hand and pulls me with her. She lets me go, climbing over the median, and we circle the car before trying the doors. The back door opens, and she slides in to unlock the front. She searches the car while I pull the driver's column free and get to work. The engine sputters, then purrs to life. I stand up and smile at her, then look down at her hands. She has a shredded seat cover in one hand and a chunk of broken concrete in the other.

"Check the trunk while I secure the wheel," she directs.

I move to the back seat, pulling up a latch and folding the seat down, and squinting into the trunk. I back away as something shifts within, then pull my sword out and feel a hand on my shoulder. "Leave it," she argues.

"But what about its soul?"

"It will be taken care of in a moment."

I sheath the sword and watch her shut the back door. She picks the chuck of concrete up off the ground.

"When this moves, we should probably hide out in the truck for a while before going back over there," she explains.

I step back, watching her as she shifts the car into drive, and it rolls forward slowly. She steps to the side to jog next to it, then launches the concrete into the car and springs back to me, passing me, vaulting over the median, and booking it to the truck. I follow her quickly, my focus on the car that's speeding down the opposite side of the freeway back toward the direction of the rest stop.

I unlock the truck, and she climbs in, grabbing my hand. I pause to watch the car scrape the median blasting down the road. It reaches the turn, and I make out its impact before the thud of the crash reaches my ears. Her powerful hands pull me into the truck, and I shut and lock the door behind me. She moves to the back, and I follow her. She moves the boxes off the couch and grabs water, taking a seat. I watch her cross her toned legs, leaning back, her green eyes traveling up to my face.

I smile when our eyes lock, and I shut the center door and pocket the truck keys. I trip slightly, catching myself on the corner of the couch. She giggles, and I reach for her gorgeous legs. They are warm and strong under my fingers.

"Careful," she warns me, grasping my forearms as if to steady me.

"Are you hurt?"

"No."

"How long do we have?" I ask, trailing my hands up her legs.

"Maybe an hour," she breathes.

"I think we can manage that."

"Sterling, your face."

"Then don't look at me, I need you," I growl. I unbuckle my belt and pull it free, pressing it into her hand, my mouth trailing up her neck. I can hear her panting now, and I know her body is screaming with need. "Tell me how I can have you. That makes you feel comfortable with my face. It's pitch black. You can't see me."

"Bend me over so I can't hurt you by accident," she pants. I grasp her hips, move to her mouth, and kiss her deeply. It smarts, but the taste of her lips has me straining against my pants.

"Are you sure?" I ask, hesitating.

"Please," she begs, her ass bucking back against me.

I unbutton her pants, and dropping to my knees, I free them from her legs, leaving them bunched at her boots. She struggles to get free for a moment, then stills as my hands grasp her hips. I rise to my feet, pulling her up and twisting her around so her back is to me. I wind my hands around her and up her shirt, sliding across her breasts masked in her bra.

A fresh wave of need overwhelms me, and I fight it back, knowing we don't have time for me to take her again. I listen to her breathing, and I can tell she wants more, but I pull her onto my lap on the couch.

"I need more," she gasps, her body trembling in my arms.

"We are out of time. We need clothes or we will never refuel today," I mumble, trailing kisses across her shoulder.

Her watch beams to life, and every ounce of my being wants her splayed out on the sleeping bag on the floor with me pinning her down and encompassed in her serenity.

"You okay baby?" she asks.

I snap out of my daydream and focus on her face. "Way more than okay, love, my brain still has you beneath me."

Her cheeks dimple, and she grabs a towel from our supplies. I reach down and tug my pants up to my knees. I stand up, my eyes locking on her as I peer down at her. Her eyes move, scanning my face before a frown line appears on her forehead.

I smooth it with my thumb, then kiss her forehead. "I love you, baby."

"Even though I hurt you?" she whispers, her lips trembling.

CHAPTER TEN

I fasten my pants, staring at her face as she looks at me, her eyes soften and she looks pensive.

"How do you think you hurt me?" I ask, confused.

She reaches up, her finger gliding feather-light over my nose and the shiners I am undoubtedly sporting.

I grab her hands, bringing them to my lips. "That was an accident."

"Still."

I tuck her hair back from her face and lean in, kissing her, and note now that she doesn't respond like usual. "I love you always and forever, I am your ride-or-die, baby."

She wraps me in a hug, and I pin her to me. After a moment, she sighs and pulls back. "We better go."

"Yes, ma'am, you distracted me. What is the plan?"

"I am sure that was all your doing," she smiles.

I follow her back to the front, grabbing the half-full gas jug. She scans our surroundings, then leads me out her door, which I secure, and then to the back of the truck, where I deliver the remaining fuel into the tank and then follow her into the woods. We make our way back to the rest stop. This time, she doesn't stop. She leads me behind a car where we squat down.

"So I will clear inside, you gather fuel?" she asks, rubbing her hands together.

"Sounds like a plan," I agree. I pull the silicon pan from my bag and drop it to puncture the fuel tank. Aurora plants her feet on either side of me and moves to search the car from above me. I know she's protecting me, so I make quick work of it and slide back up and to her side, looking at a purse she has acquired that she's stuffing small items into.

"Next car," she whispers.

I follow her, and we repeat the process; we continue till the jug is full. We head back together, and she leaves her bag of goodies on the side mirror as I drain the jug into the tank. We make our way back to the rest stop. The longer we spend, the more abominations we begin to see. After filling the jug again, I gesture for her to move back, and we make our way back to the truck. I step out of the woods, heading for the gas cap.

"We can take that for you," a voice offers.

My head snaps to the right, and Aurora's foot reacts faster than my brain. She kicks my bottle of urine and it flies at the man, pegging him in the face and exploding on impact. Aurora drops to her knee and sends two bullets into the head of the flailing, pee-riddled man. The man next to him dives away urine-soaked and frightened.

"Fill the tank, Sterling," she demands.

I move and add the fuel. I hear a shuffle to my left so I spin, putting my back against the truck and holding the jug in place with one hand.

Aurora pivots, her eyes widening, and she ticks her head to the right, signaling me to get in the truck. I pull the jug out and move for the cab. "Down!" she hisses.

I drop, rolling under the truck, and as I do, gasoline covers the asphalt. The blast of a much bigger gun and then I see a body drop at the back of the truck. I scoot away from the gasoline and pull myself out. Aurora collects the man's shotgun and moves toward a man who is getting his bearings back. He passes the dead guy covered in piss, looking livid. I pull my sword free and his eyes bulge, and he backs up a step.

"Sterling, in the truck!" Aurora booms.

I snarl but comply, unlocking it and climbing in.

She keeps her gun trained on the man and follows me, locking the door behind her. "Go now, the horde is coming."

I glance in the mirror as I start the truck, catching sight of the flaming abominations on the road. I pop it into drive and step on the gas pedal, leaving the man standing on the side of the road, staring in horror at the abominations bearing down on him. He doesn't run, and as we watch in the mirror, he falls to his knees in fear.

But to our shock and amazement, the herd veers around him. The moment is short-lived, the first flaming abomination who steps into the gasoline causes a flash of fire that knocks the man off the road and out of sight.

"It's the urine," Aurora breathes next to me.

I glance at her.

"Urine deters them, that's why they don't like cats or the cat house I found because it smelled like cat pee," she explains, her eyes sparkling with discovery.

CHAPTER ELEVEN
RORY
"TAKE IT OUT ON ME" BY THOUSAND FOOT KRUTCH

I DRIVE THROUGH THE DAY, trying not to jostle Sterling, who is sleeping in the back. He told me a thousand times to wake him if I have a problem. However, for the last stretch, since I took over, it's been pretty easygoing. Abominations, broken-down cars, and small fires are seemingly starting to become part of my norm. I am most nervous about the bridge crossing, from what I see on the map. If we can't cross here, then it's an extra hour one way or the other to try again. But I want to avoid getting too close to Parkersburg or New Haven, which is permitting that the bridges are still crossable.

I take a longer, less direct route toward the bridge, and even from here, I can see some sort of blockade on both sides of the bridge. People mostly, a few cars, but nothing unmanageable. I pause, considering my options, then decide to try the bridge and ask for passage. After all, we have a bulletproof truck that I could use as a battering ram. I chew on the inside of my lip as I contemplate my decision, growing more and more nervous the closer I get. I check that the doors and windows are secure and slide the shotgun under my seat.

I slow as I near the barricade. It doesn't look very organized. A large piece of plywood leans against a car and reads, 'Trade to pass'. I slow to a stop, my eyes locking on steel gray ones, the face beneath them smiling kindly. I wave through the closed window, and he gestures to the sign. With a quick nod, I grab my makeshift bag full of water bottles and pretend it's heavy. Holding up the bag for him to see, he frowns, but I reach in and pull out the water, shaking it like the prize it is. He beams and nods vigorously. I slowly roll the window down, just enough to shove the bag out. He takes it and gestures to the others in his group to let me through. I roll up the window and glance at the gray-eyed man.

He has a small sign he is holding up to me. 'Be careful ahead,' it reads. I nod, and he holds up the bag, nodding at me and yelling, "Thank you!"

I proceed onto the bridge, waving back at the people waving happily at me. I stay at 20 miles an hour until something catches my eye, and I brake hard. Putting the truck in reverse, I back up and crane my neck to look at the road. Road spikes gleam up at me, and I snarl. I grab the shotgun and crank the window down three inches.

"Sterling!" I warn.

I fire the shotgun with one hand. It connects with the release mechanism of the road spikes, and the spikes retract.

"What happened?" I hear Sterling call.

I roll the window up and proceed, reloading the spent shell one-handed and clutching the warm barrel between my knees as I steer. I slow as I spot another road spike laid out before I crank the window down, take aim, and fire.

I catch sight of a person moving toward the truck from my peripheral vision, then I feel their weight as they pounce up onto the running board of the truck. I yank the shotgun in, dropping it in my lap and cranking the window closed on a dark hand that reaches in after the barrel. A scream alerts me, then another shake causes me to glance over at another man trying to open the passenger door. I slam on the gas, swerving with a lurch, and jerk the truck toward the edge of the bridge, where the truck scratches against the concrete barrier. The man is yanked sideways and collides with a concrete pile. Blood explodes outside the window, and Sterling appears next to me.

I steer us back into the middle of the road. "Take the wheel, plow through!" My order is just out of my lips before I unfasten my seatbelt and yank the shotgun with me. He takes my vacated seat, and I grab the door handle to the passenger door and push it open. The man screams, grasping the mirror. I yank the door closed, and when he doesn't fall free, I crank the window down and blast him off the truck. I can see his body fly back past the concrete guide and into the air over the open waters of the Ohio River.

"I gotta break!" Sterling warns.

"No, punch it!" I argue, dropping the shotgun and unholstering my 9mm. "Aim for the back of the green van ten to one. It's in park, with no E brake."

"And if the E brake is on?"

"Then this might hurt," I admit.

I wrap the seat belt around my waist, and grabbing the oh-shit handle, I lean out the window, leveling my weapon at the human barricade about 100 feet in front of the car barricade. Humans scatter, but the ones who take aim or fire at me, my bullets connect with their brains. I brace, swinging back in the cab as Sterling barrels through the blockade, swerving to stay on the road. I roll the window back up, wincing at a pinch in my right arm. With a glance down, I stare dumbfounded at the crimson stain on my sleeve.

"Shit," I swear. I move toward the back of the truck, sitting on the swaying bed and yanking the first aid kit from a box nearby.

"Are you bleeding?" Sterling asks.

The truck slows, and I growl, moving back upfront with the first aid kit.

"Keep driving!" I order, sitting in the passenger seat.

"You need help."

"It's a graze. Just keep going. When we are sure we are not being followed, we will find a place to hide out for the night."

"Dammit, Aurora! Fuckin avocados," Sterling growls, the truck picks up speed, and I turn my focus to my arm. "We could have barreled through without catching bullets."

"Well, one, that's no fun, and two, they deserved it. Think about how many unarmed innocent people they have most likely taken out of commission or robbed of supplies and let them starve to death. I tried it your way at the first roadblock," I counter, adding pressure to my wound.

"First roadblock? What happened to waking me up!"

"I had it handled," I reject.

"Aurora, I have to be able to trust you, or I won't be able to sleep," he growls.

"Then trust me that your presence appears aggressive sometimes, even when you don't mean it to."

"How bad is your arm?"

"It's just a graze," I respond, belting in.

He lets out a breath of exasperation. "Why are you so stubborn? I saw the blood so honestly, how bad is it?"

I look over, his eyes are on the road, his knuckles white on the wheel. "I am stubborn because I know my limits. Some nerve coming from a man who looks way worse off than me and acts like it never happened."

"It was an accident," he growls.

"Like this happened on purpose?"

"Yes, you putting yourself out a window puts it as an asked for injury!"

"So is your face for sleeping next to an assassin so, you're welcome!"

His jaw drops, and I jerk out of my seat, fighting the seatbelt, and go into the back to change my shirt and finish dressing the graze, which, to my luck, is merely a flesh wound that will clot over quickly enough. For good measure, I splash some rum on it, hissing in pain as it lights the wound on the proverbial fire.

After I clean up and am less pissed, I make my way back up to the front, take my seat, and buckle in. The silence is debilitating. It numbs me, but I take solace in his demeanor. His body language has calmed, and his focus is on the road. I look out at the green landscape and looming clouds. I spot a sign that reads Racine and a sign for a truck repair shop up ahead.

"Pull off up here," I request, pointing to the exit.

"We are not far enough. What if they have followed us?"

"Please pull off here," I repeat. His jaw twitches, and I know he is not happy. "To the left, the right is the direction that a right-handed shooter would take."

He crosses over and takes a left onto a frontage road. The ground is low, and we would have more cover to the right, but I do not want to be found so easily. We drive for another 15 minutes, and I strain to see through the murky gray. Eventually, we hit a fork, and Sterling looks at me. I point to the right, and he turns onto Tornado Rd. Up an incline, I can see the freeway. Ahead, trees line the road, and I feel better about our choice.

Rain begins to patter on the window, and I squint ahead. "I think that's a church," Sterling offers, pointing to up a road to our left.

"Too many people looking for saving at churches," I deny.

About a mile ahead, I spot a sign that reads campgrounds tucked in the brush. "What do you think?"

"If my opinion matters, the dirt road is too risky with the weather, and the creek down there has a possibility to flood if the storm gets as nasty as a few days ago," he responds, slowing to a near stop.

"Good point, keep going."

He pushes down on the gas and propels us further down the road. After another 15 minutes, as the storm intensifies, I become nervous. Visibility sucks, and I know that turning our lights on only makes us a target.

"Look!" Sterling announces, pointing to our right. The freeway is parallel to us once more, and I swear. I spot a turnoff, and Sterling slows, and we stare down a dark gravel road that passes under the freeway.

"Perfect, tuck under to the right."

He follows my instructions, my door is pressed up to the wall of the overpass. "Bathroom, then sleep?" Sterling asks.

I nod, following him out the driver's side door. I click my watch on so we can see, and my eyes catch on the blood that bathes this side of the truck. Guilt seeps through me, but I clench my jaw and turn toward Sterling. He is watching me closely as I pass him, moving to the front of the truck. I look out into the pouring rain, knowing that however uncomfortable I am urinating in front of Sterling, it would be far worse to brave the rain and get sick later.

"Go first. I will keep a lookout in the other direction," he offers.

I watch him turn, and I quickly lower my pants and squat down. As soon as I finish, I walk to his side. He moves to the front of the truck without a word. I wait for him to finish, then glance at him as he pauses next to me.

"You have first shut-eye," I remind.

"I would like to look at your arm and then lay down together."

I look up into his face, and I can see how much he wants me to agree with him. "Let's get in out of the weather to look at it," I partially agree, then led him back to the truck, where he unlocks it for me, and I climb in. I walk to the back, take a seat on the bed, and look around for the medical kit. Sterling walks through the dividing space from the cab, holding the first aid kit and pulling the door closed behind him. I grab the lantern and wind it up, setting it on a box.

Sterling takes a seat next to me, and reaching over, he carefully unwinds the bandage. I watch his face so I can see his expression when he realizes I wasn't under-exaggerating. He reaches for the cut, and his eyes flicker up to mine.

"I am sorry," he sighs.

"Why?" I ask, frowning.

"Because I just assumed that you were holding back the true damage, and you were honest. But I was already mad about you not waking me sooner, and I admit I forget that a problem, in your opinion, is probably much bigger than an emergency for everyone else. We need to be awake at the same time, baby, it is making us cranky and puts us at risk if there is a problem."

I stare into his eyes. "I don't want to sleep next to you."

"Are you that mad at me?" he asks, his head tilting.

"No, I think it's hot when you get mad at me, even if I am annoyed."

"Then why do you not want to sleep next to me? Do I smell that bad?"

I chuckle. "Your natural scent is riveting." I glance up to see him watching me, patiently waiting. I click my watch and turn on the camera and move my arm so he can see himself.

"Would you like me to shave? I can take care of that when we find supplies," he promises.

"That's all you see in this reflection? Facial hair?"

He shrugs, looking again, then looks back at me.

"The shiners, Sterling. I do not want to lay next to you and put you at risk of another injury like before. We are lucky I didn't murder you," I growl.

"So your force fields are up because you don't want to hurt me?" he asks.

"Learned from the best," I remind, staring into his green eyes.

He runs his hand through his hair.

"But unlike you, that was, in fact, my fault."

"How about I tuck you up into a sleeping bag? It is pretty cold. We can both use one, and we will tuck your arms in," he suggests.

I sigh.

"Baby, I sleep better with you. You have, in the past, told me the same thing. With that being said, we both need good sleep," he reminds me.

"I do not know if I can sleep if I am worried I will hurt you, but I guess we can try. I just wish you had your handcuffs."

"Let's try is better than no," Sterling agrees, getting to his feet and grabbing the sleeping bags. I wrap my arm back up and pull my clothes off. I climb onto the bed, aware that Sterling is watching me with extreme intensity. Then I lay back, resting my arms at my sides. I watch as he moves gently, placing the sleeping bag over me with one hand as the other zips the zipper up. I can see his eyes travel up my body, and as they meet mine, I know what he is thinking.

"We won't both fit, and I don't want to hurt you," I deny.

I can see his grin flash before he tucks the blanket over my head. I hear him chuckle and then pull the blanket down. Even with the bruises, he is a picture of the perfect specimen. His kiss is quick, and he lies down next to me. I do not dwell on the fact that he feels like he is winning; instead, I memorize the moment as one of the playful times. As the man I love accepts that I can be mean and grumpy and he can make me comfortable and wanted without the need for sex.

I stay awake just watching him. We stare at each other until his eyes flutter closed, and while I am still so terrified that I will unintentionally hurt him in our sleep, I crave to un-tuck my arms and ask him to hold me. To rest my head on his chest and listen to the ebb and flow of his breathing. If the world is over and this is all that's left, while it's a travesty, I can take this moment and immortalize it in my memory. While the world burns and bites, I am here with this perfect imperfection.

I feel my eyelids fighting to close, and I take soothing breaths to let myself sink into a much-needed sleep, but for a few seconds, my brain fights me. It wants to continue to take its pictures, count his breaths, and trace his lips with my mind.

CHAPTER TWELVE
STERLING
"WELCOME TO THE MASQUERADE" BY THOUSAND FOOT KRUTCH

I WAKE up when I hear a whimper. The pitch black of night surrounds us, and I listen intently, waiting to hear the sound again. Aurora whimpers next to me, causing me to turn toward her, reaching over gently. Her body is still secure and cozy in the sleeping bag.

"Sterling," she whispers in her sleep.

"I am here, baby," I soothe, stroking her hair. A small gasping sound escapes her before she seems to calm down. I continue to run my fingers through her hair as I drift back to sleep, careful of the tangles. When I wake again, it's because of the rattling of the truck and my need to pee. I blink, tracing my fingers over Aurora's arm that is flung across my body. Then I tilt my head, trying to see her face, but her hair strewn across my chest, and one of her legs tangled with both of mine. I can feel her right hand clutching my shoulder from beneath me.

I sing our song; it's hard for me at first because I can only remember her voice reverberating around a warehouse, belting the words like they were weapons. As I reach the end of the chorus, she stirs, rolling to look at me. When I quiet, her cheeks dimple.

She smiles at me happily. "Thank you," she says in a cheerful, sweet tone I know she uses when she is exceptionally shy or sweet. I see her brow crease, and she flexes her hands, following them with her eyes.

"You escaped," I soothe, running my fingers down the back of her hands.

"Well, lucky for us, you are in one non-blooded piece this time," she sighs.

"That I am, unfortunately, we should get back on the road," I remind, kissing her head.

"Is it still raining?" she asks.

"Not sure, let's check," I urge, untangling myself from her. She follows me to the divider, to the cab, where I pause. I open in a crack, peering out into the daylight glowing in the cab. Nothing moves beyond the glass, so I let myself into the cab and take a seat, examining the soaked world around us in the morning's light. I see no movement or signs of human life near or around us.

Aurora plops down in the passenger seat with her curious, intelligent eyes raking the area. "We should shower," she insists. She moves back to grab some towels, and I frown. When she appears again, she pauses, looking at me.

"Showering?" I ask. "I thought that time is pressing?"

"I smell, and if I don't get my hair clean, I am cutting it all off with a knife. This may be our last chance for a long time," she argues. "Your welcome to stay here and watch if you prefer."

I follow her, not because I think she's right, but because I don't want her to sheer off her hair, and I have to admit that being cleaner would be nice. My current smell is like stale rum and mouthwash. I bring my sword just in case, knowing she has at least two guns holstered to her. I watch her walking toward the edge of the overpass, her head moving as she clocks the area. When she feels secure, she steps into the rain and walks toward the tree line. I follow her, looking back over my shoulder at the truck.

When I reach her, she has stripped down to her underwear and stepped out from under the protection of the trees, where she takes a handful of grass using it on her skin like a loofah. I stand there watching her dripping pale skin, goose flesh assaulting my arms. I grab a low branch to steady myself. Her hands rub down the length of her body, and I shift uncomfortably, aware of my raging hard-on trying to break the zipper on my pants. We wouldn't be getting clean if I was plowing her into the wet earth at her feet.

Her dazzling green eyes connect with mine, and I close my mouth, realizing it's open and I am all but drooling. She holds a hand out to me; I release the branch and step closer, transfixed. My fingers touch hers, then my mouth suckles at her hand. Her gasp makes me smile. My mouth burns up her wrist, and I graze my teeth over her arm. The rain pours down on me as I go. I pause at her bandaged shoulder, my eyes searching the bloody gauze. I feel her hand on my face, then she pulls me to her.

Her mouth meets mine, opening slightly to invite me in. I grasp her to me, her naked skin slick with rain. One of my hands slides up, grasping one of her breasts, the fabric of her soaking bra hiding her nipples momentarily from me. I pull the fabric aside, tracing her cool breast with my fingers before capturing her hard nipple between my fingers. Her moan tugs at every nerve in my body.

"I need you, Sterling," she pants, her hands trying to free me of my wet clinging clothes.

I don't need to hear that twice. I lift her and then drop to my knee, laying her on the grass.

"Where is the screaming coming from?" someone shouts.

"I don't know, but by the sounds of it, we won't be able to save her!" someone yells back. I freeze, my chest pressing against hers as we both stare toward where the voices are coming from.

"Shit," I swear. I pull out of her, rolling to her side and yanking up my pants, then zip them up. I glance over at Aurora's clothes hanging on a branch of a tree, then focus back on the voices coming

CHAPTER TWELVE

from the road. Part of me berates myself for not finishing, my soaking wet gorgeous wife, still panting next to me.

"We need to get them out of here," Aurora says.

I push myself up, peeking over the high grass. I spot two men standing near the overpass. They are at ground level, but if they had been up on the road, they would have easily spotted us.

"I see two," I whisper.

"That's it?" she asks. "Are they armed?"

Before I can respond to her first question, I push up again, peeking over the grass. I squint slightly at the back of one man who I can see is talking to the other. I don't see any guns, but I hesitate to say no.

"Not that I can see," I admit, lowering myself.

"Do they look familiar from yesterday?" she whispers. I shrug; I have no clue. She rolls her eyes, rolling to her stomach, and then she gets to her knees to look. She ducks down, shaking her head at me. "I don't think they were there."

"I am going to stand up, we can't stay out here and risk getting you sick," I warn. I see her face fill with anger, but I stand up. "Hey, fellas!" I call over, raising my hands to show that I mean no harm.

"Where did he come from?" one man yells.

"Is that a sword?" the other asks.

"I was looking for a water source and got turned around," I yell over, noticing that they don't pull any weapons. I freeze as a group of men walks up behind the two, then glance at Aurora and shake my head once. She snarls, but I snap my gaze back to the heavily armed men now flanking the two bewildered men.

"Drop your weapon!" a man bellows.

"It's sheathed, and I need it to protect my wife," I argue, the presence of the sword comforting on my back.

Gun's lower. "Wife?" a woman's voice asks, peeking around the group.

"She was washing her clothes, and we got distracted. We sure are sorry if she scared you," I announce, lowering my hands to clasp them in front of me. I smile apologetically when I hear a response of chuckles. Aurora crawls around me and then rises slowly.

She waves, a hand up in the air. "Hi," she calls in a meek voice that doesn't suit her.

"Can we move to get her clothes, please?" I ask.

"Turn around," the woman barks. The men turn around, and I feel Aurora's fingers on my belt loops, pulling me back as she moves back to the shelter of the tree.

"Take my gun and strap it to your calf," she hisses. I frown but follow her lead.

"What kind of dipshit would wear a gun like this?" I ask.

"The kind who doesn't know much about them and has the only goal to protect his fragile woman," she replies.

"You are anything but fragile," I scoff.

"She is an alpha, so me and my big girl britches don't need to challenge her until absolutely necessary," she sighs, pulling her pants back on.

"So I get to baby you?"

"Treat it as foreplay, because next time I get my hands on you, I am blowing your mind," she teases with a wink, yanking her shirt on.

I can feel the heat rise on my face and the ridiculous smile making my cheeks sore.

"Come, Wolfie," she whispers, leaning into me and tucking her other gun in the back of my pants.

I wrap my arm around her and lead her back into the tall grass. She has her boots clutched to her, and she stays like a scared creature glued to my side.

We approach the group, and I can hear her counting. We turn toward our box truck, and my jaw drops. The gravel road is spotted with sleeping bags and tents, and they parked vehicles out the other direction on the road. I feel Aurora's nails on my back and pull her closer. She does not like all these people being here.

"Are you okay, sweetheart?" the woman who Aurora told me is their leader asks.

I feel her nod, then hide her face against my side.

"She looks injured," a man growls.

The woman moves to get a better view. "We have medical supplies, what happen to her? She isn't bitten, is she?"

Her men take a step back, and I shake my head. "We were ambushed, and a bullet grazed her."

I watch the men with guns clutch their weapons tighter.

"You let this happen to her?" the woman asks.

I tense, anger flooding me.

"It was my fault. I thought if we talked it out, they would let us pass, but my husband saved me. He had to take their lives, but I am sure God will forgive him," Aurora interrupts.

I look down at her, split by my agitation at the woman and in shock that Aurora just spoke of God as if she were a person of faith.

"Praise God," the woman smiles, her fingers grasping a cross I hadn't noticed she was wearing. "Excuse my questions, we have learned the hard way that this world is full of dangers. We are from Wellston's. The looters decimated the town, and the people lost control of the fires while trying to stay warm."

"Shouldn't you be heading South or West then?" I ask.

Aurora pinches me, and the woman's eyes grow.

"I have friends in West Virginia," she responds.

"Well, this road will only leave you to the shoot-out road barricades over the Ohio River," I explain. I watch her eyes dart to the men nearby who look put off. "Maybe they moved on?"

"Maybe," she replies.

"Are you a minister?" Aurora asks.

"No, sweet girl, just one of God's true believers. My name is Joyce."

"Nice to meet you," Aurora responds, politely.

"And what are your names?" she asks.

"Aurora and Sterling Karter," Aurora responds.

"Samuel, can you grab these two some chow?" Joyce calls.

"No thank you, we have to get moving while the weather is tame," I respond.

Joyce looks at Aurora, not acknowledging that I had spoken. "Can I have a word with you, Aurora?"

I frown, looking down at Aurora, who shrugs and cuddles closer to me.

"Joyce, the next storm is rolling over. It doesn't look good!" Samuel interrupts, walking over, holding two unlabeled cans in his hands.

"Samuel is a meteorologist," Joyce explains. "Show me what's going on, Samuel."

Samuel thrusts the cans against my chest and then turns to lead Joyce over to the far side of the overpass.

"We should go," Aurora whispers.

"I agree."

We turn, coming face to face with a man standing directly behind us near the truck. Aurora moves behind me, and I frown at the man.

"Didn't mean to startle her. Look, I am trying to help. You should just listen to Joyce, let her talk to your girl and then she will just happily let you leave. It doesn't look like you need any more bullet holes in this thing," the man warns.

"If she is dangerous, why are you with her?" I ask.

"Because my girl wants to be," he responds. "Let me go find you a can opener."

I frown, then feel Aurora tug at me to turn around. I turn to see Joyce stopping, her eyes falling on the cans I am holding. "Samuel, these are not pop tops!" Joyce announces. "Men!" she sighs to Aurora.

"How is the weather?" I ask.

She smiles, delighted that I am taking stock of her opinion over a meteorologist.

"It doesn't look good, I think our biggest concern is flooding and tornadoes," she admits.

"The river is that way," Aurora says, pointing in the direction we had seen the river yesterday.

"We should be okay for now. If the water rises, a sentry will let us know, and we will move along." She smiles. "Let's not worry about the weather, Aurora. May I talk with you in private?"

Aurora looks up at me, and I smile. "Your call, baby," I say, knowing that any sign of negative feedback could set this woman off. I don't care if they shoot up the truck, I only care if they take a shot when we are out in the open.

"We won't be long, just girl stuff," Joyce explains, not waiting for Aurora's response. She takes her hand and I flinch, expecting Aurora to punch her. But Aurora lets herself be led away, over to a large tent in the middle of the others, where she disappears inside. I run my finger over the key to the truck in my pocket; I do not feel comfortable opening the cab with Joyce's men watching me so intently.

"Anyone find a can opener?" I ask, holding one can up with a smile.

The man who had given us a warning about Joyce appears from behind the truck, holding out a hand crank can opener. I open one can and then the other, setting it on the truck for Aurora, and then take a seat on the ground, examining the contents of the can and taking a sniff. I am pretty sure it's dog food, but I also remember eating worse when I lived on the streets before boot camp.

I pull Aurora's knife from my pocket and glance at the clean blade before using it to scoop out some of the dog food, ignoring the eyes on me. Samuel nudges the man next to him. I ignore the stares and the hush of people watching me take a bite. The tang of the dog food isn't great, but I know it won't hurt me, but did these people know that? I smile politely, taking another bite. Oh, Aurora is going to be pissed that they gave us animal food, and then watched with amusement as I ate it. I ate all of it, figuring the test was to see if we were really that hungry and if I had a bad temper.

CHAPTER THIRTEEN
RORY
"CHAIN OF ABUSE" BY THREE DAYS GRACE

JOYCE LEADS me by hand to her tent. They may not think I notice, but I'm aware of the quiet, watchful eyes of the woman nearby. I've met women like Joyce before, women who think they are the alpha and that everyone is lesser than they are, but something about Joyce is slightly different. It's in her body language, the shifting of her eyes, the way she talks and pronounces her words. My brain thinks psychopath, but my eyes see a victim. I have a strange feeling I am dealing with some sort of sadist, and that has me curious. Joyce sits cross-legged, and I follow suit, keeping my meek facade firmly in place.

"Aurora, I want you to know that this tent is a safe place," she assures me, and while her words are honey-sweet, her eyes gleam with control. "Do you understand what I mean?"

"I think you mean you won't hurt me when we are in here," I respond, knowing full well that my physical safety is not what she's talking about.

She smiles, taking my soft voice as a roll of submission. "Not exactly, it means that whatever you tell me will be treated with utmost honesty and integrity. You see, Aurora, God put me on this earth to help young women like yourself," she explains. I stare at her, not speaking, and she grins wider now as if I am caught in her spell. "I would like to ask you a few questions. Do you think you can answer them honestly?"

"Yes, I can answer questions honestly," I agree, pouting slightly so she grows more comfortable in my presence.

"Good girl," she praises. She reaches toward me and I withdraw on instinct. "You poor thing, someone has hurt you in your life to not trust the hand of a friend."

"Someone has hurt me," I agree, not adding that she is not my friend nor that I don't let almost anyone touch me.

"That man out there, is he really your husband?" she asks.

I smile. "In the eyes of the lord, he is indeed my husband," I reply cheekily, knowing she will eat up the line.

"Very well, are you happy with him as your husband?"

"Yes?" I respond, confused by her question.

"Are you sure? He is a gentleman to you? He doesn't make you do anything you don't want to?"

"Yes, I am sure. He is the very best to me than anyone ever has or will be," I respond, trying to keep the sincerity of the answer but also not let my overindulging brain use all its big fancy words.

She looks slightly put off by my response.

"Did I say something wrong?" I ask.

"No, Dear, it's just that the screaming we heard wasn't what I would have thought was from passion."

"To be fair, I didn't know anyone was listening. I do not make it a habit to have sex around other people," I explain.

"You say sex and not making love, why is that?" she asks, staring at me.

"Are you a psychologist?"

"Why yes, I am, how do you know that?" she asks, her eyes widening slightly with surprise. I shrug, hiding the pleasure I get for pegging her vocation at some point in her past. "What did you do for work before the world ended?" she asks, her eyes searching my face.

"I was unemployed. I had just gotten a job offer working on identifying areas that needed to be surveyed for rock slides," I respond honestly.

I see her head crease slightly. "That sounds like a very masculine job for such a beautiful woman."

"We all have to work," I shrug. "My brother was the boss, he just wanted me to have a job so I could use my talents."

"Looking for rocks?" she asks.

I laugh. "Rocks on the road, silly," I respond, mimicking Quin's annoying titter.

"Sounds like your brother thought little of you, how did your mother take this behavior?"

"My mother died when I was eight," I respond.

"How about your father? How did he take your relationship with your brother?"

"My daddy died when I was in high school, his husband wasn't all that okay with his behavior until he started dating my sister, and now they get along great," I respond, blinking my eyes innocently at her as her jaw drops.

"Thank you for answering my questions," she dismisses, flustered by my story.

"I am going to go find Sterling," I inform.

She is too flabbergasted to respond, and I exit the tent smiling with amusement. A few women nearby watch me carefully. A man squints at me, and I smile sunnily at him then proceed to Sterling, who is sitting on the ground next to the truck with an empty can in front of him.

I take a seat in his lap, laying my head back on his shoulder.

"Welcome back," he greets.

"Why do you smell like dog food?" I ask, confused.

He nudges the can with his boot. "It's Pedigree, no expense spared."

I lean back, looking into his serious face. "Why did you eat it then?"

"It would have been rude not to. It's really not as bad as some of the food while deployed." He shrugs. "You're about to lose your temper and blow your cover, my fragile wife."

"PDA is not acceptable in gatherings such as ours," Joyce announces, standing outside her tent.

"See you soon, lover," I whisper to Sterling, who smiles as I get up, grasping the open can as I do. "I hadn't meant to offend anyone," I pout.

Joyce smiles, opening her mouth to respond.

"But your DOG Samuel has offended me," I announce.

I hear a gasp, and Joyce's face falls.

"I really thought that you made so much sense, Joyce. Like you could see right inside my head and understand me," I whine, moving closer to Samuel.

"Samuel offended you? But he is the truest to me and to God," Joyce reasons.

"Samuel is a dog, why else would he have served us dog food?" I ask, batting my eyelashes.

"I had no—" Samuel begins.

"I was talking to Joyce, not to you," I deny, smirking at him. His jaw drops, and I grab a handful of dog food and shove it in his mouth. Then, dropping the can, I grasp his nuts, pushing him back against the wall he had been leaning against. I grasp his gun, spinning around to the onlookers. "Joyce, you have shown me the light!" I announce. "I bow wow to no man, woman, or God. You are a revolutionary. What you said about the world being scrubbed free of the filth of the heavenly followers, and while killing your group at first sounded like an insane idea if that shall bring me penance for the sins of my skin, and the sins of my family, then I guess I must listen to you!" I yell, lightning dancing behind me in the raging storm.

"I never!" Joyce yells, as men turn their guns on her.

"You see, Joyce here is what some might call a sadist. She lives off the misery and pain of others, she sucks the soul out of your burning desires, and then all that's left is an abomination, no better than the dead ones walking," I announce.

"Y...You liar!" Joyce bellows.

"You are correct. I did lie, but just once. Oh heavenly Joyce, please forgive me for I have sinned. I was not exactly unemployed when the world fell, I was still a pawn in the game of men, that game you so fear, the one of control," I admit, closing the distance between us.

She is gaping at me now, a small knife clutched in her fist.

"You see, Joyce," I whisper. "I was retiring from being an assassin that wouldn't kill, and then, well, oopsy daisy, I slipped up. I really thought your words were so well delivered for someone who has to have spent years locked up in some asylum," I explain, louder now.

"How do you know that?" she yells.

The few followers who hadn't yet turned on her start backing away.

"You keep reaching for your medical bracelet, you have track marks on your back left shoulder, you have a God complex, and the need for confined spaces with no one directly behind you. You probably eat like a cheetah on fire and don't play well with others, unless they are the woman you talk into your blankets in the dead of night where the eyes of sin close for your experiments," I embellish.

"You bitch!" Joyce roars.

"Indeed." I smile. "You have three options, you can decimate your flock as planned, you can walk away and take who's left with you, or you can let me and whoever wants to follow leave before you take away any other liberties."

"Kill them, you won't do it," Joyce calls my bluff.

"I won't, but they will," I insist, pointing behind the group toward their vehicles. I run to the truck as it roars to life.

"Shoot her!" Joyce screams.

I round the truck, but they fire no shots. I pull myself up into the truck, slamming the door shut behind me, and Sterling steps on the gas. He is laughing hysterically as he drives us up the gravel road and up a wet incline, away from the chaos. One tire spins as the truck lurches up the hill. I grasp the seat belt, wrestling it on. Sterling turns the brights on and maneuvers the truck around the next curve, trying to keep the truck from overturning. The road winds through the trees, and just when I am growing concerned that we would need to back out toward Joyce and her group, the road flattens out and heads West.

Headlights beam in our side mirrors, and I sigh. "Pull it over."

I see him look at me, but I raise an eyebrow just staring at him. He slows and stops in the middle of the road. Cars stop behind us, and a few swerve around stopping in front of us. We couldn't risk wasting gas to outrun them; this would have to be a gunfight, and my money was on us.

The car doors of the stopped vehicle in front of us burst open, and a woman hops out, throwing her fists up in the air, screaming in triumph. I frown, watching as she dances in the rain. The woman from the passenger side flings herself out of the car as well, her voice piercing our bulletproof glass.

I look at Sterling perplexed, he just watches, looking in the mirror as people race up next to the truck, fist-pumping, cheering, battling the storm's thunder into oblivion. Sterling's face turns to mine as we watch the group dance around us. I can hear someone screaming, 'Freedom!' I crank the window down slightly so that the man who warned us about Joyce can press his face in.

"Lead the way, your majesty, we got your back!" he crows into the cab, then hops down yelling, "High hoe Exp's truck away!" The woman from the vacated vehicle in front of us jumps back in, pulling out of our way.

"Did I just inadvertently become a cult leader?" I ask Sterling.

He laughs, turning the truck on and driving us further down the road that eventually deposits us and the five cars following us back onto the 33. I yank the map out, beaming my flashlight at it, and then look for a mile marker or a freeway sign. We catch sight of a sign for a town ahead called Rock Springs, so I scour the map. The city is tiny on the map, and I can not see a way to bypass it. The 33 turns North at Rock Springs, so to continue West and get further from this storm, we would need to take the 7.

"Stay left up here," I warn as the signs for several turnoffs appear in the darkness, illuminated by our headlights. The gas light chimes and flashes on, and Sterling swears. I squint out the front window, growling before unlatching my belt and cranking the window down, the cold air blasting my tired eyes open. I pull myself out the window, my eyes searching the signs, holding on tight as Sterling swerves around stalled cars.

I catch sight of a billboard illuminated by lightning, then slip back into the truck. "Slow down and turn right up here."

"You want off the freeway?" he asks, following my directions.

"Yep," I sigh.

Our lights sparkle on the front of shiny, wet, brand new vehicles at the car dealership shadowed in the darkness that greets us as we pull off. I point ahead, and we follow the road to the back entrance.

"Use the truck to pop the chain on the gate," I urge.

He listens, and I grab his sword.

"Stop at the back awning, I will shut and secure the gate," I direct. I hear some kind of argument, but I am already out the door in the beating rain waving the cars in. When the last car passes, I pull the gates shut, yanking the chain to make it look secure.

I turn toward the cars, and a scream pierces the storm. I run toward them, shielding my eyes from the glare of the headlights. I can see a woman in a car under a large awning, trying to pull her door shut as several abominations shove their withering dead limbs through the gap between the door and the car.

"Come on!" I scream, advancing. The abominations' heads swivel to me. "Bring it on!" I coax. I run at them, bringing Sterling's sword through their necks like butter. More move toward me and I spin, kicking one back and then cutting it down. Sterling appears by my side with a bat. I hand him his sword and spin the bat. "I am at 4!"

"That a challenge?" he asks.

Before we break ranks and charge forward, I see his sword flash in the glare of the headlights. Blood spraying into the air before I bring my bat arching up into the jaw of a nearby abomination. I connect my boot with the next one, kicking it back before rebounding off the front of a car to crash down on top of it.

Its head cracks between my bat and the cement, and I move on, my muscles gleaming in the rain. It feels good to use my strength. All too soon, I blink, finding myself standing in a pool of blood breathing heavily as my eyes search the darkness for signs of movement. I bring my wrist to my chest. "Flashlight on level 5."

My watch beams at the glass entrance to the back of the dealership. I see nothing moving beyond the open doors. Turning to check on Sterling, I see him rinsing his sword in the water runoff from the roof. I glance out at the small crowd of people staring at me. "If we want a safe night, I need volunteers to move cars to block the glass while a few of us clear the building," I call out to the silent people.

"Or you guys can sleep in your cars." Sterling shrugs, stepping up next to me.

"Me and Colt will take the second floor to clear," someone announces.

My eyes shift to the voice. "Thank you, please check every corner, we don't want to have one straggler taking out this entire group."

I see strange glances pass between people. "Andy and I will clear the first floor," the man I had met with earlier offers.

"Wonderful, thank you, please call out if you need backup," I agree. I watch the strange looks spread around again. "Is anyone comfortable moving cars?"

No one answers.

"Okay, no problem, I will go move the cars to make a blockade for the front, we should move our vehicles in and turn them off for the night," I direct.

"I can start moving cars, but what are we blockading against?" a woman asks.

"Humans," I inform.

She frowns.

"I just pissed off Joyce, and if she grew a pair and comes after all of you, it is my duty to keep you all safe until you decide to travel in a different direction than us."

The strange look again is shared around me.

"Is there a question or a problem?" I ask, twirling the bat on the front of my boot.

A few people shake their heads and then they all move, my knuckles whiten on the bat handle momentarily then relax as most of them pass me to deal with the building.

"Let's rinse off in the rain," Sterling insists.

I let him pull me to the side, and we walk out from under the awning into the pouring rain. I tilt my head up, welcoming the rain as it rids me of the sickly blood splattered over my body. A truck nearby catches my attention, it looks eerily like Davin's police truck did.

Sterling turns, looking over. "Does that look mean I can't talk you into the back of that truck to finish what we started this morning?"

"If it's open, nothing would stop me from warming you from the inside out," I reply.

He smiles, his teeth flashing under his beard in the light of my watch. He approaches the truck carefully. Reaching out, he looks back at me. He pulls the handle and the door pops open, the cab glowing in greeting.

"Mrs. Karter," he offers.

I walk over, reach up, and pull myself in, then turn to reach for Sterling's hand. Instead, he presses his belt into mine and grins as he climbs in, pulling the door shut and extinguishing the light.

CHAPTER FOURTEEN
STERLING
"DESTINY" BY SKILLET

WE CLIMB out of the steamed-up truck, walking toward the building, ready to assist however we need to. I only feel slightly guilty that I have pulled her away, but we made it quick. I make my way toward the people moving around the entrance. "We cleared the building, can you check the cars to see if they are where you would like them?" a woman asks. I look over at her, but her eyes are glued to Aurora, who steps up next to me.

I watch Aurora follow the woman, considering her words about being an alpha personality. I guess I haven't noticed because she is so submissive to her family. Even in our relationship, she always tries to make sure we are communicating, but I never felt that she had the most control. But seeing her here with these people, it is like she is radiating it. I now understand how she had moved up in the Marines as quickly as she had and gotten a six-figure job by age twenty-two.

I watch my wife from a distance just basking in that word, wife. I feel so content in my relationship that I have tuned out reality. My eyes shift to the survivors with us, some milling around wide-eyed and scared, others scavenging for food.

"Okay, let's get our cars moved in so we can't be spotted from outside," Aurora announces.

The crowd turns toward me. They file out, starting their cars with no questions about why and pulling them into the building. I look at Aurora, watching her move toward a detailing waiting section. She walks fearlessly through a door. Her watch illuminates the surrounding walls. I follow her without hesitation. It is my duty to keep her safe, even when she may not think she needs it. I glance around the darkroom, realizing we are in a large garage.

"Can you pull the truck in after I get this door open?" she asks.

"Of course," I agree, watching her move, the deep darkness of shadows cast by the glow of her watch making me nervous. I watch as she unhooks a chain from the wall and then flinches as the noise of the chain grading on the metal grate of the door reverberates around the room. Nothing moves in the room, and I feel slightly foolish for being so scared. The door rolls open and I shield my eyes from the headlights of passing cars entering the main building. I step forward, tripping on something. I look down, making out the dead abomination at my feet. Next to it, I see a gleam caught from a passing light. Crouching, I reach out and pick up an aerosol paint can. I set it on the workbench and then move carefully toward Aurora. With my hand, I graze her back as I pass, the slight sign of affection causing her to beam at me with her beautiful smile.

I get into the truck and pull it into the garage, Aurora shuts the door, and I get out ,looking at the workbench. "How long are we staying?" I ask.

"Depends on supplies, if there is a place nearby to do a food run, that would be great. But I am guessing 2 days max, let the storm dissipate. I think we should share 2 cases of water," she adds in a hushed voice.

I nod, glancing at the truck. "I will bring them in, in a moment. Grab the map and let's see if anyone knows the area," I suggest.

She nods in agreement. I open the truck, and she climbs up, grabbing the map. She backs up and pauses, standing on the footstep so her eyes are level with mine. I watch her eyes gleam in the dim light of her watch. I feel her breath on my face, then catch movement as her mouth turns up in a smile.

"I love you," I promise, reaching forward to caress her face. She nuzzles into my hand and then sighs.

"I love you too, see you in a while with the water," she agrees. She kisses me quickly, her eyes shifting over my shoulder. "They're waiting for me," she sighs, hopping down. She steps over the slain abomination and out of the detail workshop to go talk to the others. I take the flashlight from the door of the truck and shine it up at the truck. An idea strikes, and I move to the workbench and grab a can of black paint. I spot another and a few brown cans. I turn back to the truck, eager to get the bright purple letters hidden under the paint. I have to take a break when the fumes become overwhelming. That's when I grab two cases of water and make my way back into the main building.

Everyone is sitting in a circle with Aurora in the middle, her watch beaming from her wrist. "So we have a tentative plan, half of us need to do a food run, the other half will connect vehicles with keys and gas up as many vehicles as possible," Aurora announces. I step past someone, setting the water next to Aurora. "Here is our contribution to the group for the next two days," she announces.

I glance around at the wide eyes staring at the water. I move out of the way. The attention is unnerving.

"A leader who shares supplies makes me nervous," someone announces.

"A leader that doesn't share sounds worse," I respond. Many people chatter in their agreement, eyes sweeping over to register my words.

"I think the best thing to do is hydrate, eat if we can find some food in here, and then get rest, so at first light, we can start getting to work. Please sign up for a team, we want them even as possible," Aurora announces.

"I can help split people up," someone offers.

"Alright, I will do the food run, and Sterling will gas up vehicles here," she announces.

I frown, and I can see her gaze sweep over me with slight apprehension. I watch her rise, and she moves toward me with a fake smile on her face. She nears my face, securely set in a what the hell expression. She glances behind her as people move toward their vehicles.

"What happened to communication?" I whisper.

She turns back to me and sighs. "If you come with me, then the truck is unprotected."

"So what, if I am here, then you're not protected," I counter.

"I am pretty sure I can protect myself."

"You know what I mean, splitting up is not good, look what happened last time," I remind her, trying to keep my voice level from rising.

"This time we know exactly where the other is located. If something happens and the other isn't where they should be or we hear distress, we will know how to get to the other person. This time we have vehicles to run down the abominations if we get another horde."

"For such an intelligent woman, sometimes you make the strangest choices. What if you guys run into other people, what if you get hurt or captured or killed?" I question.

"You are a police officer, you know what clues to look for, and you also know that no one is going to take me down easily," she reminds me.

I stare at her, waiting for her to answer all my questions.

"You made a deal with me. We promised that if something was to happen to either of us, the other had to continue to fight till the end."

"I am aware, but why risk splitting up?" I growl.

"I don't trust that we won't come back to all the cars ruined or gone, and no supplies to survive," she responds.

I could see in her stance that this was a losing battle. "You know we only discuss things when they don't go your way," I press. I knew it wasn't a 100% genuine statement, but I need her to open up to me and realize that we need to decide together.

"What is your alternative?" she asks.

"I haven't had a chance to think about it."

"Sometimes things have to happen hard and fast." She shrugs. She gives me a mischievous smile, and I shake my head, biting the inside of my lip to not succumb to her flirtatious diversion. "I think you're hot when you're mad, you're the one fueling this fire," she sighs when I don't respond.

"Let's go eat, so I can think this over," I suggest, throwing my hands up in frustration.

"Sure," she agrees.

I turn and pause, finding a woman standing directly behind me, smiling.

"I found some food to share since you shared your water," she offers.

"Tamera, wow, thanks," Aurora accepts, taking the unmarked cans.

"I think they are ravioli, but I'm not completely sure," Tamera explains. I look wearily at the cans and then back at her smiling face.

"Thanks," I add.

"Don't worry, it's not dog food. We left all that for Joyce," she admits with a smile. "Would you like to sit with us?"

"That would be wonderful, thank you, Tamera," Aurora agrees. I follow, taking a seat in the detail waiting room. I nod to the two men sitting across from me in greeting.

"I am Regan, and this is Billy," the man Regan introduces.

"Sterling," I respond.

"I can't believe you ate that whole can of dog food like a boss," Billy chuckles, he winces as Regan elbows him.

I smile, listening to Aurora chuckle next to me, "At least it was name brand. Some of the cheap stuff is ridiculously nasty."

Laughter fills the room, and the tension loosens in my shoulders. While I still don't trust these people, it is nice to be around people who have lowered their guard.

"Dude, how do you even know that? Been hurting for food since this all started?" Regan asks, holding out his half-empty can of pasta.

I pop the lid off the can in my hands, shaking my head. "No, we do okay usually, but years ago, I lived on the streets in Texas. You eat what you have to in those situations." I feel Aurora's eyes on me but fish out a ravioli with my fingers and pop it in my mouth.

"Texas is pretty far away, man," Billy admits, breaking the awkward silence.

"Yeah, my best friend lived out in the Appalachians, so I moved out this way to have a fresh start."

"Not many jobs up in the Appalachians, it's been rough the last few years with the economy, and now, well, you know, life in the apocalypse slamming down around us," Billy responds.

"He got a job at the police station," Aurora adds, as I take another bite.

"Did the police have any heads up on this?" Regan probes.

"Nah, it came out of nowhere," I respond.

Regan looks crestfallen, and Billy shakes his head.

"I told you, Regan, everybody thought it was a new strain of the flu, people were sick for a few weeks before the travel ban hit," Billy reminds.

"People were sick?" Aurora asks.

"Oh yeah, I worked at a tire shop, and we had people coming in hacking and coughing, people were calling out, and then one morning it was like, everyone was told to stay home," Billy informs.

"Where are you from?" Aurora asks.

"Just North of Parkersburg in Vienna," Billy responds. "How about you?" he asks.

"We are from Enigma," she responds. I look at her, noticing the small cress on her forehead.

"What you said to Joyce," Tamera whispers. I glance at her, and she stares at Aurora. "Did you work for the government?"

"I was on a sabbatical to visit family and attend a wedding," Aurora explains. "But yes, government work."

CHAPTER FOURTEEN

"You didn't get a heads up either?" Billy gasps. "This must be a terrorist attack," he hypotheses.

"It's global, that's all I know," she admits.

"Global?" Tamera gasps.

Billy and Regan shift, staring at Aurora in disbelief.

"That's insane, so there is no escaping this?" she asks, her breath coming now in quick gasps.

"Sure there is," Aurora argues.

I watch all eyes turn to her, then look over at her determined face.

"We fight our way out of this," she declares.

I smile, taking her hand. The others don't look so sure, but all I care about is that she is holding on to hope for surviving all this. I reach the bottom of the can, slurp the sauce from the can, then whip my fingers on my pants.

"It's time!" someone calls from somewhere across the dealership.

I tense, my hand fisting by my side.

"Are you guys coming?" Tamera asks, getting to her feet.

"What are you guys doing?" I ask, trying to keep the concern from lacing through my words.

"Nightly ritual time," Tamera announces, with a grin.

I glance at Billy. "It's not religious and usually ends in a massive orgy. It's pretty fun, you're both welcome to join."

"Joyce was okay with that?" Aurora asks, bewilderment filling her face.

"Sure as long as she had the first pick. I suppose you're the new leader, would you like the first pick?" Billy asks.

"No thanks, I am good, really tired actually," Aurora denies, with a fake yawn.

Billy looks at me, and I shake my head. "Not my scene, but thanks for the invite, have fun," I respond with a smile, trying not to laugh at the shocked look on Aurora's face.

"Have a good night," Tamera says, as she walks away taking Billy and Regan's hands.

I stifle a chuckle, glancing at Aurora.

"Let's go rest, I am currently very happy we are parked in another part of the building," she whispers.

I set the can down and follow her through the door. She pauses, her watch light sweeping across the truck.

"Camouflage," I admit.

"Great idea," she yawns, pausing so I can unlock the truck. We climb in, and I lock the door behind me. We shut the divider door and make sure that the back is secure before we lay down. Aurora tucks herself in tight, and I lay behind her, playing with a lock of hair. I lay awake for a long time worrying, battling with exhaustion. What if Joyce came back during the food run? What if a herd of abominations blindsides them? I finally drift into a fitful sleep, my dreams haunted by the demise of the woman I love.

CHAPTER FIFTEEN
RORY
"SECRET WEAPON" BY DISCIPLE

STERLING'S BEHAVIOR over the next 24 hours becomes stranger than ever before. I try to understand that it's because we have not been apart since we were reunited, but I also can't get why he seems so worried. I am fully capable of looking out for myself. My soul has to be dark as squid ink by now. I watch him fuss over the paint on the truck; the weather still isn't great, it has been off and on downpours, and the survivor's food is running low. I walk toward Sterling, preparing myself for a possible argument.

"Wow, it's near unrecognizable," I compliment, stopping next to him and looking up at the black siding.

"I think so too," he agrees, smiling up at his work.

I trace his face with my eyes. One of the guys lent him a razor, and he shaved his beard off. He looks so handsome and for a brief moment worryless. I shuffle from one foot to another. "How long till the paint dries do you think?" I ask curiously.

He shrugs. "Not too long now, why what's up?" His stance changes as I smile weakly at him. "You want to take the truck on your food run?" he asks with a sigh.

"Yes, it makes the most sense. We can take out our supplies and store them below out of sight." I shrug. I watch his jaw tighten, and if his piercing eyes hadn't been fuming with anger, I probably would have tried to jump him right then.

"Don't look at me like that," he snaps, averting his eyes. "You're going to do whatever you want no matter what I say, so give me 20 minutes, and you can run off to get supplies."

"Sterling," I begin. He punches the side of the truck as he walks away, not pausing to look back. "You messed up the paint." I sigh then make my way back into the dealership. "Get ready to roll out!"

Cheers blossom from the people in my group. "Everyone else is on gas duty. We need to fuel up the cars we are taking only, then use whatever fuel holders we can find for extra gas to take with us," I announce. Another cheer bristles around me, and I help people collect the empty bags we had squirreled free of other items so we could carry the loot we hopefully find.

I check weapons, everyone has something, either pieced together or found. Tamera pops up with a bow and arrow and holds it out for me. I glance at it, smiling at her. I have seen her practicing, and she wants to teach me once we get to our next location. I don't tell her that I have memorized her stance and calculated how much pressure she must put on it based on her physical capabilities.

Normal, I remind myself, glancing at my boot to check my knives. I give Sterling 20 minutes, then make my way back to the details garage. Plastering a smile on my face, I look around the garage, the smile slipping off. I look up into the truck and then walk around. The back is open and mostly empty. I spot a case of water on our sleeping bags and the couch. Then I look around, spotting the keys to the truck on a workbench next to Sterling's sword. I walk past them and over to the metal stairs that lead down below. I squint in the darkness, pausing as a flicker of fire catches my attention.

"The keys are on the workbench, take my sword so you can keep yourself safe," Sterling responds, not removing his gaze from the flame. The lighter clicks, and his face disappears into the shadows. It clicks again, and I can see his handsome face in the glow.

"Sterling," I begin then pause. "We will be back no later than three. We don't want to be caught out in the dark during the rain." I catch a nod before his face is succumbed to darkness again. "I love you," I announce, then stomp up the stairs and snatch the keys and sword. Lunging up onto the back of the truck, I yank the door down, then grab the chain to the door and heave it down, pulling the huge metal doors up. I jump into the air and drop to the ground to get the damn door up faster.

Why am I so angry about him being angry at me? I shake my head as I secure the chain and move to get in the truck. I crank the key, the engine grinds, and I growl with frustration. With a low growl, I check the mirrors, then back the truck out, clipping the building. I stop when clear and roll my window down, waving for the others to jump in. Two cars follow me as three people join me in my truck, we have split up the entire group 50/50. So I have fifteen people on the run with me.

I drive carefully on our dedicated route, I had promised this to Sterling, so he would feel just a little better about separating. I shake my head to get him off my mind. My eyes flick around our surroundings. The rain has let up, but the ground is wet, and the next turn is half-flooded. I stare at the road estimating the half I can't see and keep as far over as I dare without going into the mud. Getting stuck would not be a great thing to do, I'd never live it down.

We spot no people on our way, though, we do come across a few straggling abominations but beeline to our destination. We pull up out front, parking a distance away in a deserted parking lot. I get out, followed by the others, with a glance at the two vehicles parking ten spaces away on each side. We had discussed this, I had explained that visitation would be best in case abominations happened upon us.

We approach the building in a long spread out line, I glance from left to right. I know that protecting them is important but keeping my promise to Sterling is more important. I unsheath his sword, breaking ranks as we near the door.

"Stay back," one of the men calls, a brick hurls past me, smashing through the glass door.

I cringe, sending him a nasty look as I step forward, pulling the door open easily. "Smooth," I lie, turning toward the dark interior. I hear a curt reply as he passes me. I slam him into the door frame hard, his yelp of pain greeted by my sword at his throat. "If you're willing to sacrifice any of us, then you can die first," I threaten.

"I'm sorry," he gasps, his eyes terrified.

The musty smell of piss floods up between us. I shove back, turning to the dark store, flashlights already swinging in every direction. I grasp the sword with both hands. "Flashlight on, level five," I dictate. My watch beams to life, and I ignore the stares. I am staring past the checkout stands, my eyes on the abominations staggering forward. They are clustered, probably due to the crashing of broken glass. Getting in and taking them out quickly without risk is off the table now. A gun raises in my peripheral. "Put it down, or you'll call the rest toward us," I hiss. "You have weapons, use them." My sword cuts through an abomination, freeing its snapping head from its twitching body.

Tamera charges up next to me and kicks the head, watching as it soars up and smashes through a banner that reads Summer Sale. "Touch Down!" she bellows, before lunging at another abomination as it nears. I follow her, yanking it back when it gets too close and letting her take it down.

"We should go!" someone yells.

I grab a shopping cart, ignoring the memories that blast into my mind of Sterling and me at the grocery store. I clutch the handle then ram it forward, throwing my weight behind it, my sword acting as a bayonet as I plow through a group of abominations. "Fight," I rally, then grin at the others as they take up shopping carts and rush toward me. I jump up onto the checkout belt to avoid being run over, stomp down on the hand of an abomination, then bring the sword slashing at its head. I step up onto the shelving out of reach as I take in the chaos of my surroundings.

My eyes lock on an abomination that is inches from locking its teeth into the man who had broken the glass and brought on this small horde. For a moment, my brain wants me to let it happen, then my humanity crashes down around me. I jump to the next register, my hand snatching BBQ prongs from an overturned bucket near the bagging station. I drop my sword and crawl forward using both hands. I grasp the tongs and throw myself at the two. The man's grunt of surprise, then the rattling ceases as the tongs shoved into the abomination's eye sockets pierce its brain.

"God, that was hot," the man grumbles. I frown, moving to untangle myself. He grabs my face and smashes his chapped lips against my mouth. My hand clasps on his throat, and I yank myself free. I pin him down to the ground, his eyes bugging in shock, his lips gasping for air.

"Rory, get off, it's just Holden!" I hear someone scream over the blood pounding in my ears. I feel myself being disengaged, my nails dragging across his throat.

"Rory, what happened?" Tamera asks. I glance at her and then pull free from the hands holding me.

"Next time he puts his hands on me, none of you will save him," I threaten, spitting on the ground and walking past the dead bodies to take in the store. I ignore the commotion behind me, bringing my watch up to look around. I right a shopping cart and push it into the darkness. A few people scuttle after me. I pause next to a camp display and grab a box with a lantern in it that says try me. Then I tear the box open, pulling the lantern free and turning it on, rolling it away from me.

"Good idea," Tamera agrees, joining me as I rescue more lanterns from their boxes.

Soon the store is dimly lit with lanterns, and we begin to gather carts full of supplies, lots of dry goods. I roll my eyes at the cart of toilet paper.

"Gotta stay clean," Tamera says, smiling.

"Use a washcloth, the paper's just going to remind you that you can't shower regularly." I shrug.

We walk with the group toward two rolled-up doors. I slow my pace as my eyes trail across the dark parking lot, I glance at my watch to check the time. The sound of crashing glass causes me to draw my sword, spinning to the sound. I hear a thud and gasps, and I spin back toward the doors. Holden kicks a large ice chunk toward his friend. My attention flickers to the parking lot as large pieces of hail pummel the near-empty lot.

"Back up," I call ahead, trying to shout over the deafening sound of the hail on the building. I sheath my sword and cover my ears as the sound gets louder. I glance at Tamera, but she has moved to the door to look out. I abandon my cart. "Tamera!" Lightning smashes into the ground outside the store, and I halt. Suddenly chaos replaces the howling winds. Ice chunks fly toward me, and I duck. The roof of the building groans, and the far wall rips free from the ground.

My feet are swept out from under me, and my face connects with the cement floor. I grasp at the floor, my hands sliding over the smooth cement as I am dragged backward. I roll to my back and then shield my face as a large fluorescent light kit from the ceiling falls toward me. Managing to sit up, I try to move out of danger, my eyes registering that the back of the building is gone, that I am being dragged toward spinning winds. I grab a bollard, the yellow paint gleaming under my grasp. I try to hug the barrier, pulling myself closer to it. Screaming catches my ear for a brief moment, and Tamera's hands slip on the edge of the building.

I yank myself up, hugging the bollard now, my eyes on Tamera. "Tamera hold on!" I scream, the only thing I can hear is the building smashing to pieces around us. My eyes hyper-focus on her hands as her grip gives out. I let go of the pole with one arm and grab her arm before she can be whisked past me.

"Rory!" she screams, trying to grab hold of me. My hand slips on the bollard, I struggle to regain a hold and keep Tamera from being yanked away. A huge chunk of ice smashes into the yellow paint, and I squeeze my eyes shut, tucking my face down as splinters of ice ricochet toward me. My hand burns, and as I adjust to pull myself closer to the barrier, melted ice and blood impede the friction my fingers need to hold on.

A sense of weightlessness overcomes me. I brace as the forklift and my body collide but clutch onto it, looking down at Tamera. She grabs hold of the large machine, her hand grasping mine now. I see her lips moving. I know she's asking me what to do, and I open my mouth to try to respond, but I am greeted with the warm spray of her blood before her lifeless body spirals backward toward the vortex. The machine shudders beneath me, the object that had smashed into Tamera zips out of sight.

The machine jolts beneath me, and my eyes search the area around me. I catch sight of someone hanging from a shelf unit, their leg caught in the prongs. I spit blood from my mouth and pull myself toward the body, If I can reach it then I could pull myself up and take safety in the shelves, they look sturdy. I feel the forklift begin to slide, and I move faster.

I jump, kicking off the forklift, and manage to grab one of the man's hands. My eyes register his face, it's Holden. His hand doesn't respond to mine; there is blood seeping from beneath his hair and down his face. I use my other hand and pull myself up his lifeless arm. I stare at the bars of the shelves, at his twisted leg, wondering if it will hold our weight and if he is about to turn into an abomination. I hear a loud scraping sound and glance over my shoulder as the forklift tilts and then smashes to its side, moving across the floor toward the tornado. *I need to move faster*, I urge myself, knowing that the forklift could soon come crashing back toward me.

I unsheath my sword with my one hand and hold on tight to it as I claw into Holden's shirt, trying not to get yanked away. I stab the knife through his back, jamming it all the way through so I can use the handle to pull myself up. Holden lets out a scream of pain, but I keep climbing, my hand finally reaching the shelf's iron support. I yank my sword free, sliding it between two supports and leveraging my way onto the shelf.

The sword snaps under my foot, but my body clings to the shelf. I twist through the rungs, wedging myself to protect as much of my body as I can. Holden's screams can not be heard now, all that surrounds me is the screaming of the wind, the groan of twisting metal, and the thunderous sounds as the building collapses around me. I graze my finger over my watch and type furiously:

```
STERLING, I LOVE YOU. REMEMBER OUR
DEAL. WE ARE FOREVER, BABY, I SHOULD
HAVE LISTENED. I AM SO SORRY. LOVE
YOUR TRUE WIFE, AURORA.
```

CHAPTER SIXTEEN
STERLING
"SAVE ME" BY SKILLET

"STERLING!" I hear a male voice call from upstairs.

I get up knowing she's not due back for another hour and a half, part of me lightens, hoping she's back early. I walk up the stairs, popping my head up and looking toward the open door. I roll my eyes, wondering why no one has shut it. A loud thud catches my attention, halting my forward movement, and I instinctively duck, then throw myself toward the chain as chunks of ice ricochet off the ground toward my head. I free the chain and dive for the door to the dealership.

"Take cover!" I bellow.

But my words are drowned out by the crashing of glass. All around the showroom, the windows are smashed to smithereens as hail the size of oranges smash through the glass walls. I dodge back into the detail room, a few people following. I move to the back door, yanking it open to see how bad the storm is. My eyes lock on a funnel cloud descending to the East.

"TORNADO!" someone screams.

"Get below!" I order, letting the door slam shut and racing with the others to the stairs. I try to take a headcount, but it's too dark, and the screaming of the wind and smashing of ice on the roll-up door is clawing at my ears. We crash into our stockpile of water, my eyes locking on the stairs. *I have to go after her*, my brain demands. My body jolts forward and hands grab me. "I have to go!"

"The others will find shelter, you can't fight a tornado!" Regan yells. I look up at the dim light above us, praying that someone is telling Aurora the same thing. Praying to a God I know she has little faith in, that she is safe.

As soon as the banging from the hail stops, I venture up the stairs. The five people who have been huddled below with me follow wordlessly. I look around the detail garage which looks no worse for wear, then walk toward the backdoor. I pull on the handle and then back away from the door, which is completely blocked by a blood-spattered forklift. A stifled sob breaks my concentration, and I move toward the showroom. It's like walking back into a war zone.

Glass is everywhere, and ice chucks lie around the room, one of them melting in a pool of blood. Cars have smashed windows and large dents. The showroom and supplies that were caught in the storm are destroyed. I hear cries for help, and the people with me move into action to help their fallen friends.

"Watch for the dead," I warn, receiving a glare from Regan. I move, looking for a vehicle that had been spared the severity of the storm.

"What are you doing? We need to help," Billy says.

"We need transport to check on the other half of the group," I explain, making sure to say the rest of the group instead of just Aurora.

"Shit Tamera," he gasps. "We had the keys stored over here," he urges, leading me over to a massive battered desk where some other supplies have been spared by being stored underneath. Billy grabs a bag ,yanking a hatchet from the side. He unzips the bag, pulls out a hunting knife, and hands it over.

I take a few pairs of keys from him, pressing the lock button to locate the vehicles outside the building. The damage inside should have prepared me for what's waiting outside, but the site is heart-stopping. Panic pulses through my veins, I need to find Aurora. We pass large hail chunks and broken glass, searching for a vehicle that has been spared enough to make it the three-mile trek. I am tempted to just start running, that's what she would do, and the idea that she's not here yet makes me even more nervous.

Billy finds a car on the opposite side of the building that he can get to start and out the gate. I jump in and direct him down the specific path Aurora had designated. I look all around. How long had they been gone before it hit? How far did they make it, and were there any diversions from the plan?

"Shit," Billy breathes. I look toward where the building should be and my heart stops. The world stills, and before I acknowledge what I am doing, the car door is open and my feet are thundering on the pavement.

"Aurora!" I scream, skidding to a stop next to the overturned EXP truck. My eyes lock on the twisted black metal. Billy rushes past me to the smashed cab and then looks back at me, shaking his head. I yank at the doors, scrambling back as the sofa bed bursts out, smashing to the ground at my feet. My eyes search the empty truck to no avail, and I am forced to turn to the demolished building. My eyes search the debris of the building, the wreckage of other cars and bodies, and so much blood washing down the road as the rain starts again.

Abominations begin to rise from the rubble. But this time, it's shock that fills me. The faces of people who followed us blindly are shattered and rattling.

"Tamera!" Billy yells.

My head snaps toward him and to the girl Aurora has befriended. However she died, it did not look quick or painless.

"No!" Billy shrieks in dismay.

I look beyond her for Aurora. *She is not as strong as my wife*, I remind myself, ignoring the pang of guilt at the loss of yet another human life. "Free their souls," I demand as abominations draw near. I kick one back, its head bouncing off the truck.

"Sterling, don't, these are our friends," Billy warns, his fists pulling at his hair as fear takes control of his body.

"Your friends are gone, their souls are trapped in these shells. So save them so you can see them someday in the beyond," I order, slamming my hunting knife into the jerking thing's temporal lobe. Part of me wonders why I didn't refer to it as heaven or hell, but I have little time to dwell on it before Tamera's husk is upon me. I shove her back, spinning to find Billy, but he is falling back.

"Aurora!" I bellow.

"Come on, man," I hear, but I am not a coward. I made her a promise to survive, but I also made a promise to always be there for her. I would never stop searching, I would only run after I found her. My rage consumes me, letting her training overpower the fear in my brain. Tamera drops, and I scream Aurora's name again as I drop the next one. I lurch away from another who has gotten too close, my foot skidding as something metal slides under my boot. I glance down, trying to keep the distance between me and the abomination. My eyes lock on the broken blade of my sword. I feel myself breaking even as I fight back against the abomination. I spin, staring down at the blade in shock. The sound of an engine catches my attention. The sedan we arrived in speeds away. I glower after it for a moment, then have to move away from another abomination. I climb up on the rubble of the building.

"Aurora!"

My eyes search what's left of the building. I make my way deeper into the mess, finding blood pooling from an abomination pinned between blue steel shelves and an enormous chunk of what looks like the ceiling.

I hear a noise, and I freeze, glancing at the trapped abomination. I frown, leaning closer to it, examining the wounds on the back of its shirt. The wound is a slice, and the skin beneath is just barely visible. It looks like a sword made it. I look past him through the steel pillars, part of the roof rests heavily above as I search a shelf nearby that is riddled with blood. I move further into the darkness, hesitant at first. A scream fills the air, and it's like nails clawing at my mind. I jolt forward.

"Flashlight level 10!" I instruct. To my extreme relief, Aurora's watch beams to life ahead on the ground. I smash into the abomination rattling next to her, yanking the hilt of my sword from its neck and bringing the broken stub of it crashing into the thing's head.

I turn to Aurora, her eyes are closed, her breathing shallow. I press my finger to her neck, trying to calm myself. Her heart is racing, and I take a moment to run my hands over her skin, looking for bites carefully. The wounds I find are mostly superficial and not abomination made. I pull her up off the ground and into my arms, making my way back out before the rubble can shift and flapjack us beneath. As we exit, I squint into the sun, wearily watching the abominations a few hundred feet away. I could not carry her back the three miles. I would need my hands to fight off the rattling beasts who will surely be drawn in by the scent of her blood.

I have to set her down unmoving and unresponsive on the pavement. I turn a shopping cart over and then lift her, setting her inside it. From under a car, I rescue a bat and move back to the cart. She looks small and defenseless in unconsciousness, and the three-mile walk makes me worry about what injuries she may have. I scan the parking lot again but see no other viable options. I take out the approaching abominations and then push the cart back toward the car dealership.

When we reach the dealership, the sun is setting and the usable cars of the other survivors have bugged out. I roll her into the garage, yanking the door shut and securing the door to the dealership before clearing the shop and its sublevel. Pleased that our water and supplies are still there, they must have left in a hurry, without searching for our stuff. I grab a blanket we had rescued from Davin's and bring it up with a few bottles of water so I can get her out of the shopping cart and have a better look at her. Her unresponsive behavior on the trip home concerns me. I worry it is another head injury and that her brain can't handle more trauma, but even as that dark thought consumes me, I take her hand and bow my head in prayer.

CHAPTER SEVENTEEN
RORY
"GET WELL" BY ICON FOR HIRE

DAD LAUGHS, causing me to smile at him as I follow him out of the restaurant. I'd let him pay, because this was his day with me. I watch him stride ahead, proud of him for taking on an administration position at the new location for the plant. The gray in his hair has doubled since I had last seen him, reminding me that life was too short to be away so often. I can close my eyes and imagine Daddy standing by his side, but I don't. Dad was finally moving past his grief, and I need to focus on that, on his happiness, not my warped brain's fixation on what's gone.

"So it's only a matter of time before Davin proposes, and I suppose if I haven't scared him off yet, then he is worth keeping around," Dad sighs.

"Quin doing better on the new meds? Have they stopped fighting?" I ask, keeping pace beside him as we stroll down the street. We reach the corner of Madison and E 41st. "You turned us the wrong way," I announce, smirking over at him.

"I have been to Manhattan more times than you have, I know where the Metro is," he argues. Then he looks up at the street signs and sighs. "Which way do we need to go?"

I grin.

"Moore!" my blood freezes as her voice rings in my ears. I turn quickly, knowing my ankle weapon is too far. I am engulfed in blonde hair and a firm embrace. "How the hell have you been?" Sprocket crows, releasing me from her hold and extending her hand to my Dad. "Hello, sir, I am Moore's friend, Sprocket," Sprocket announces.

Dad's look of shock turns into a smile, and he takes her hand. I wince, but they release hands, and Sprocket twirls a long lock of hair around her finger.

"Dad, Sprocket and I work together," I say, shooting her a look.

"Dad? Oh look at me thinking you found yourself a sugar daddy," Sprocket teases.

Dad blushes and chuckles. I make a face, and Sprocket boops my nose playfully. "On our pay, you might have to," she stage-whispers to me.

Dad looks at me with concern. "Very funny, Sprocket. Dad, she's trying to teach me to loosen up, be normal and all," I lie, glossing over her remark.

Sprocket laughs and Dad smiles.

"Well, don't loosen up enough for a sugar daddy," he advises, shaking his head.

I roll my eyes. "Great to see you, Sprocket, we best get going, see you at work."

"Need directions?" she offers, ignoring my hint to walk away.

"Yes, please," Dad agrees, with an easy smile.

"No," I respond, letting ice lace in my voice as I frown at her.

"Don't be rude, Moore," Sprocket directs. "Turn right here, make your next right, then up one block on the left," she directs.

I open my mouth to rattle off the street numbers and buildings on the route but swallow my response as Sprocket hooks her arm with mine and pulls me toward the crosswalk. Dad hurries after us as Sprocket's fingers dig into my arm.

"You need to get out of the city," she warns, her lips grazing my ear.

"Sprocket, I don't work for you."

CHAPTER SEVENTEEN

She releases my arm, spinning happily to my dad. "Safe travel home, Mr. Moore," she says, then walks back up 41st.

Dad passes me after a quick wave. I watch her hair sway as she all but skips away. I glance at my watch and then turn to catch up with Dad as he turns at the *Chick-fil-a*.

"You know, Dad, why don't I call us a car?" I offer.

"Not after what your friend just said, you need to hang on to your money," he teases. "The Metro is perfectly safe during the day, Rory," he urges.

I look up at the sign as we descend into the underground. I hate the subway, not enough escape routes. It's like I can feel her nearby making sure we are leaving, so I refuse to look around. Dad buys our tickets, this time because I am too focused on being invisible. We enter the railcar, and I make my dad take the open seat as I stand holding the pole. I smile as he pulls his phone out, then glance away to the door dividing us from the next car, and I freeze, staring into Sprocket's wild eyes and her too-big smile. The car lurches forward, and I snatch the poll, then look back to where Sprocket was a heartbeat ago, but she's gone. The shriek of metal on metal surrounds me, and the subway races to its next stop.

My eyes fly open, all I can see is water. I gasp, waiting for the river water to fill my lungs. My fist connects with solid glass, and I yelp in pain.

"Quin?" I groan, grabbing my pounding head.

"Aurora, you're awake," I hear Sterling's voice say. His strong, warm hand touches my arm, and I look toward his voice.

"Sterling," I gasp, lunging at him, my fingers grasping his chest. He is here, he is real. "Where are we?" I ask, my eyes leaving his face for a moment to look around the darkness that surrounds us.

"Few Miles from the Mississippi River, not too far from Jefferson Barracks. I figured we could get medical help there. If nothing is left, then on to Fort Leonard Wood," he explains.

"Are you hurt?" I ask, running my hands lightly over him.

"Aurora, you barely survived a tornado!"

"But you're okay?" I ask him again.

He sighs, "Yes I am fine, but you took a beating. We need to get you some help, I am honestly surprised you're still in one piece."

"We can't go toward the city," I argue.

He frowns.

"We need to go to the 3 and go South."

"I know we agreed on Texas, but it's so far. You won't believe the mess I have seen this week," he argues.

"Week?"

"About that, give or take a day. Haven't slept much, and you've been in and out. You were talking to Sprocket," he admits.

I look down at my watch.

"In your head," he adds.

I look up, shaking my head. "Find agent 1487542." The face swirls, then pulses.

"Who is that?" he asks.

"Sprocket, we need to go to Costa Rica."

"Are you sure?" he asks.

"She's been trying to protect me longer than I knew. She will have this figured out, she might already be at her own bunker."

"Let's head South, and we can talk about it on the way," he agrees.

I nod, sitting up and reaching for a seat belt.

"In the morning, Aurora, it's too dangerous at night without lights, and I'm beat."

I release the seat belt, moving back to him. "Where is everyone?"

He pulls me against him. "Dead, turned, or gone."

My brain reels, what had I missed, where did all the gone people go? I hear Sterling's breath even out before I can ask another question. I cuddle into his sleeping form, trying to ignore the pulse of pain in my head.

I am pulled back into unconsciousness. This time I have no control as my body moves. *Is this what it's like to be an abomination? Had I turned in the truck? Is this what I think is happening while my body eats flesh and destroys the world?* I wonder, panic filling me.

My hand comes up and wipes at my brow. I realize how sweaty I feel, so strange versus the chill of the truck. I look down at the grime on the back of my pale skin, annoyance pooling within me. My brain reminds me of what I remember, even as the feeling of sore muscles and exhaustion creep over me.

The extra training had been hard, all the secrets surrounding it irritated me and concerned that my trainer had been the most dangerous assassin our agency had ever collected. I watch the tall, blonde woman scarfing down her rations like she is worried that I, with my considerably shorter 5'7 frame, slim but strong, was going to take it from her. I look at my own rations, the response from my stomach is startling. It's like I remember being hungry, but my actual body knows better and is demanding I feed it.

I remember debating if eating the MRE was worth it, or if I could somehow talk myself into a shower, then eating. The door bursts open, and I draw my weapon, my chair flinging backward, clattering across the floor until it collides with the wall.

"Stand down, Moore, no more training today. Time for a debrief," Corporal Allen barks.

I feel myself hesitate for a heartbeat, reading the man's body language and noting his lack of weaponry. I try to warn my body to not take him as a weak man, but I am powerless. My memory lowers my gun but does not re-holster. I snatch my MRE and move forward, depositing it before Agent Sprocket. May as well keep the deadliest in her good graces, I consider, ignoring Sprocket's grunt of approval. I step into the hall, my eyes mapping my surroundings, my brain capturing everything in mini bursts.

"We will go ahead to Bay 14, your handler is waiting along with your competition for a promotion," Allen grunts.

"I do not want a promotion," I growl.

"You're not always right about everything," he scoffs.

I ignore the pompous man, stepping away from him, letting my mind locate the path in a blink. I stalk through the halls, not letting signs of fatigue show from my stride or emotionless face.

"Moore, this way," Allen directs, turning down another hall.

I ignore him, knowing that my way is 25 ft and 7 inches shorter, and with my stride, I could make it there faster than if I took his preferred route. I turn, bursting into the dressing room. Men scatter, not bothering to cover their nudity but to avoid me, the feeling of power ruffles deep in my belly, and I try to push it back. I may not be a murderer like Sprocket, but they fear me. I blink, pushing through the next door.

I halt at Bay 14, my eyes scanning the room, catching with Trevor's, who signals to holster my gun. My jaw tightens, but I follow directions.

"Agents, you were all chosen for different reasons: your abilities, grit, and lack of weaknesses. One of you, however, has outperformed every test, outmaneuvered every obstacle, this agent is the epitome of what we seek in an assassin," Allen drawls. "Moore." He gestures over to where I stand, scowling.

"You're shitting me, I have been here for years! Working harder than anyone. My kill count is amazing, and you're going to promote her?" Agent Grant bellows.

I open my mouth to argue that I do not want a promotion. That I will never be a murderer, but before my angry mouth can produce words, Grant's gun is drawn. I lunge forward as the rest scatter, the gun's blast deafens the room for a moment. The bullet tears through my side, but I can't feel it. *Had I felt it when it happened?* I wonder. I disarm the man as I turn into him, my shoulder catching him in the sternum before I sweep my leg out, taking them from beneath him, slamming him to the ground.

"Throw him in the brig till he cools down," Allen barks.

I let security take the subdued man from my grasp, getting up off the floor. My eyes dart to Allen. "Pass," I inform. With an about-face, I stride away ignoring his loud objections behind me, letting the pain burn now, reminding me I am alive. That no matter what others think, I am not insignificant in the grand scheme of things, and I would not kill. So, I have to leave.

My eyes flutter open and the pounding in my head returns with full force. The phantom pain of the gunshot eases, and I reach down my fingers finding the scar.

"Are you okay?" Sterling asks, caressing my arm lovingly.

I nod, then glance around at the truck interior around me.

"Aurora?" he says.

"Yes, I am okay," I respond, trying to roll my neck and shoulders to ease the pain in my head.

"Please don't do that," Sterling warns, his hand grasping both of mine and lowering them down.

"Do what?" I ask, staring at the side of his tired face. I look out the windshield and frown at the sun waning in the distance. "How long was I asleep this time," I sigh, with annoyance.

"First, you have some butterfly bandaids I had to procure for your head, and I do not want you ripping them out. Last time you were awake was late last night, do you remember talking to me?" he asks, without looking away from the road.

"Yes, I was worried you were hurt," I respond, flipping the visor down to look at his handy work. "Are we on the 3?"

"Yes, we are on the 3," he informs, his fingers drumming on the steering wheel, giving his cool tone away to the nerves he must be feeling.

"So catch me up, you said everyone was dead or gone?" I press, pushing the mirror up and twisting in my seat to look at him, noting his once again fluffy face.

He glances at me, his shoulders drawing up as he takes in a deep breath. "After the assholes you left with me chickened out, when we reached the store, they took off," he explains.

I quirk an eyebrow at him, slightly affronted by the malice in his voice. He must have left the static in the air cause he glances over and frowns at my intense look. "They didn't take any of our gear or anything, we got lucky there. Unfortunately, I had to drain tanks to get this beast full. Speaking of the next car I see, we should stop and give it a go."

"I didn't leave you," I choke out. My head pounds, my heart feels like it is pumping through molasses, and a chill washes over me. That feeling from the dream like I am no longer alive sweeps over me. The sound of the wind fills my ears, I clutch my watch. Focusing on the time, the date, my grounding spike to remind me that time is passing.

Hands on my face bring me smashing back into reality. "Aurora, focus," Sterling urges.

I gasp for air, my eyes darting around. The truck door is open, the weather is windy and fierce, and Sterling is standing outside the truck grasping my face.

"You okay?" he asks, his eyes darting between my own.

"I was stuck," I breathe, blinking wildly.

"Stuck?" he asks with a slight frown.

"In the tornado, I didn't mean to break my promise of being safe, I would never intentionally break a promise to you," I blubber, letting tears overwhelm me.

"I am not upset with you. My anger is at the cowards, not you. Never you," he assures, caressing my face. "You have fought like hell to keep your promise, you are here now, with me."

I nod gently, my head still aching. "How bad was the head injury?" I ask, my eyes catching on a movement behind him. "Abominations," I warn, grasping the front of his shirt, yanking him into the cab with me. I slide back, annoyed at my sluggish, stiff body. I yank myself over the center console and into the driver's seat.

I reach for the key, my hand sliding over the empty ignition. Sterling jolts next to me, kicking the rattling bodies back as he tries to close the door. I snatch the screwdriver off the dashboard, preparing to help, when my brain finally takes over. Finally, I stab the screwdriver into the ignition and twist. The truck roars to life. I grab Sterling under one arm, yanking the truck into drive. I slam my foot on the gas pedal. The truck peels out, my hand clutching the wheel as I

CHAPTER SEVENTEEN

maneuver us forward and back onto the road. The door slams shut, and Sterling swears.

"Watch the gas, Aurora," he warns.

Moving my foot from the pedal, I stare ahead. "Are you good?" I ask.

"Yeah, they didn't bite me," he informs, patting his legs down.

A warmth of relief washes over me, but my focus needs to stay on the road. After miles, we pull over next to an abandoned car to drain its gas. When we have all we can, Sterling takes over driving again. I can tell by the way he watches me, he is anxious. I have never in my life felt so drained. *I need a vacation from this apocalypse,* I think as I stare out the window, watching the trees flash by.

CHAPTER EIGHTEEN
STERLING
"WHATEVER IT TAKES" BY IMAGINE DRAGONS

IT HAS TAKEN WEEKS, but the Texas state line is now whizzing beneath our tires. We have agreed to try for supplies in areas of Texas I know before pushing South to find Sprocket. Part of me wants to argue that we don't need anyone. I just hope that when we get to my condo near San Antonio, that we will find somewhere safe to haul up for the grunt of winter. I glance over at Aurora, who is studying the map intensely next to me. Color has returned to her cheeks, and she grows stronger every day. I look back at the road, glancing at the gas gauge, which is almost on E again.

The last nine cars we passed had been dry, and their interiors picked clean.

"Are you sure about going to your old place?" Aurora asks, running her fingers across the map.

"Yes, at the very least, it should be empty, and we can hunker down to rest."

"Okay, you said it was on Canyon Gulf, right? It's good that it's not right in the city," she sighs, tracing her finger across the map.

"The condos are enclosed in a gated private security entrance," I supply, a small smile pulls at the corner of her mouth, but I avert my attention back to the road.

"How many access points?" she asks. I hear her shift, and I know she's watching me.

"Six on the first level, two doors lead outside, one into the garage, the rest are windows."

"And upstairs?" she asks, folding the map up.

"I don't know eight or nine windows, we can see out front and back," I respond.

"So you have neighbors on the sides, do you know any of them?" she asks.

"On one side, I had neighbors, and I knew them."

"Positively or negatively?" she asks, tapping her chin as she thinks.

I grin, my wife is way more observant than I give her credit for, I realize. "Are you profiling me as my younger, less settled down self?"

"Of course not, you didn't have me with you to wake the dead," she recalls cheekily.

I laugh, the moment warming me. The truck chimes, and I sigh, the amusement seeping from me in an instant.

"Let's roll on fumes while I pack up in here, it's still pretty early in the day. We can start off on foot after you eat something."

"As long as it's you, I will agree to your plan," I supply, grinning as I stare ahead at the road.

"Smart, limbering up before taking off on foot is an excellent plan," she purrs.

Turning my head to look at her, I freeze, her teeth grazing my ear lobe. I shiver, trying to focus on the road, willing the gas to run out faster than necessary. She pulls away, and I hear my pack open. I let out a chuckle, knowing that she is holding up her end of the bargain by packing.

It feels like it's been forever since we last had sex, here in this very truck, in fact. I try to focus on the road, knowing that if I draw attention to us, this opportunity to have my face buried between her thighs might not happen again for quite a while. After a few more miles, I start to wonder if the dash light was merely a suggestion and that the truck would run on fumes for another 100 miles. When I feel it sputter, the dread I knew should wash over me is overshadowed by my need and my nearly naked wife splayed out on the seat next to me, her fingers running across her pale skin.

I let the truck roll off the road and toward some trees for cover. No way in hell is my girl setting a foot closer to San Antonio tonight. I shove the truck into park and wrestle my seat belt off, lunging at her, the truck erupting with her laughter. I take heed of the bruises that mar her skin but don't hold back. It is as if I have never laid hands on her before. My hands feel rough on her naked body. I suckle kisses from her neck down her chest, across her quill tattoo, tracing my tongue across the letters scripted under her breasts and then down.

A goddess, I am married to a goddess; I think, studying her pink cheeks, her lips parted and my name vibrating in my ears. Those eyes open, locking with mine as she slows to a stop.

"You are so beautiful."

She doesn't roll her eyes like she would have months before. She smiles instead, glancing out the back window to the tarp covered bed of the truck.

"We should stay in here," I insist, gesturing to the looming storm clouds.

"We rest, wash, and head out tomorrow," she agrees.

With a nod, I cradle her in my arms as she cuddles against me, her sweaty naked body glistening in the warm truck. I touch her hair with my hand, carefully not letting myself dwell on the injury I know hides beneath. I close my eyes, letting my body relax, comforted by the weight of her body on mine.

We are woken by the rumble of thunder. *Texas,* I remind myself, yawning. Thunder in Texas is nothing like anywhere else in US.

CHAPTER EIGHTEEN

Aurora sits up, her face turning up to look at the sky. I can tell she's remembering the tornado by the way she flinches when the rain assaults the windshield. I stroke her back, silently reminding her I'm here.

"We should wash up," she sighs. I see in her body language as she begrudgingly follows her own directions.

I stretch, my body sore from sleep, but remind myself this could be some of the best rest for a while. I follow her out of the truck, scanning the thin trees around us, looking around wearily for humans. The rain would mellow the abominations, but humans never stopped. Glancing at Aurora, I smile, watching her tilt her head up, welcoming the rain. I reach into the truck, slipping my hand under the tarp and fishing around till I find a gallon ziplock bag with some toiletries we had acquired back in Arkansas when I had left the truck long enough to search for food alone. Opening the bag, I pull out a worn bar of soap and a quarter bottle of shampoo. Two luxuries we would not be hauling to Costa Rica. I quickly scrub myself down, knowing that the rain could blow over pretty quickly. Squirting shampoo into my hands, I notice the feeling of being watched. I spin toward the woods, knowing how vulnerable I am butt naked with my hands lathered with bubbles.

"No one's there," Aurora soothes.

My eyes lock on her, and I bring my hands up to wash my hair, watching her stare shift following every movement. By the time I can rinse the shampoo from my head and beard, I am uncomfortably hard watching her pull her hair up and letting the rain push the bubbles down her gorgeous body. I watch her lip hitch and her eyes gleam with primal need. Smiling, I pull her to me, tilting her chin up to meet my lips. Her hands clutch at me, one on my shoulder and the other on my ass.

Thoughts of our second kiss in the rain outside Maggie's trickles through my brain, every kiss with her feels new. Her arm tightens so I lift her, pressing her against the truck. One of her legs hooks around me, waiting momentarily as I position myself, then slam into her. Her scream greets me, but it's drowned out by thunder. I could live the rest of my life like this, wick deep in the love of my life, worshiping every ounce of her as God plays the drums in heaven above us, giving us our time away from the apocalypse and dangers that lie ahead.

CHAPTER NINETEEN
RORY
"IODINE" BY ICON FOR HIRE

MY WATCH WAKES us at 4 am. The mugginess is clinging to me, making me feel like my excellent shower in the rain was in vain. I yawn, slipping out of the truck. This has become my morning routine the last few days, to step away to relieve myself and regain some of my hygiene normalities. We get pretty lucky finding partially used toothpaste and deodorants, but when we are scavenging, it hasn't always been our focus. Though, I know it needs to be. Recently I got lucky to find a decent razor for myself, never in my life have I ever felt so furry.

I look at the trees carefully searching for a Maple or DogWood. I snagged a few leaves from a low branch of a tree, then squat to take care of business. When I'm done, I rise, turning to kick dirt over out of habit and pause. "Shit," I swear. I stare at the blood staining the dirt, then check out my clothes, swearing when I see the stain of blood on my underwear. All of my sweating, and I ignored the feeling of dampness. I had one change of clothes, but I wasn't wasting perfectly good clothes. I open the water bottle I brought along to clean my hands, scowling that I would have to waste more, and hoping that some water from last night's rain is trapped in the tarp for cleaning.

As I make my way back to the truck, Sterling glances up and then goes back to his pack. We have agreed to fit as much water and food as possible. I pass him, peering into the back of the truck. I know what I need isn't here before starting my search. But I search anyway, trying to reign in my frustration. I move a few broken cases of water, a blanket, and three MREs that must have escaped the one Sterling was packing. I fling them over my shoulder, crawling across the truck bed and pushing aside the nearly empty bottles of shampoo and conditioner.

I let out a frustrated growl, glancing up as movement catches my attention.

Sterling is leaning against the truck, watching me intently. He smiles when my eyes connect with his. "Everything okay?"

"We don't have any tampons or pads," I explain, chucking a loose water bottle away from me . "How could I not have brought them?"

I feel him watching me as I climb out of the truck. "I swear I did, but now I know they are not here, I just don't know when I would have thought. Oh, blood-stopping demon sticks, let's not bring these!"

"You brought them, unfortunately, they were unsalvageable after the tornado," Sterling explains, his smile faltering.

I look up at him, shock flushing through me. He shuffles with his pack, and I feel like an asshole. "I wasn't blaming you, I am just annoyed that I couldn't remember."

He looks up and smiles. "I know, and you are human at your core, so get used to not knowing everything. Here, take this," he offers, holding out a plastic package he must have requisitioned from an MRE. It holds toilet paper, matches, toothpicks, toothpaste chews, gum, salt and pepper, and a sugar packet.

"I was only human the day of the tornado until I woke back up. I do not claim that title anymore," I deny snarkily, looking for the opening of the package.

Sterling chuckles and watches me open the pack to take out the toilet paper. Using this to slow the bleeding would not be comfortable, but it would give me some time to find a tampon in someone's purse or at an abandoned home. My mind wanders back to the tampons at the gas station and then to Quin, safe and sound, back with Warner and Davin. I glance at Sterling, who has gone back to securing his pack. I insert the tightly rolled toilet paper, wincing at the uncomfortable sandpaper texture. Then I rise, drop a toothpaste chew in my mouth, mash my teeth, and use my tongue to scrub it around my teeth.

Sterling approaches, his expression assumed. I spit the white foam from my mouth, and he raises an eyebrow. I offer him the second tablet, and he takes it.

"Are you not supposed to swallow?" he asks, dropping the chew in his mouth.

I watch him with a smile for a moment. "I am particular about what I swallow."

He laughs, and I step aside, foam spraying from his mouth. I grin and walk away to finish preparing to leave. I drag the tarp over the grass and fold it down, using a bungee cord from the truck to attach it to my pack. I stretch before pulling my harness on. With a glance at our measly supply of weapons, I slide a hatchet into my harness, then examine the bat and the two knives we have. Finally, I open the glove box and pull out my 9mm. I check it, knowing that it has no ammo, before tucking it into the back of my pants.

"I thought you hated when people do that?"

"When they are loaded, it is not the smartest thing to do. But it makes us look not so prepared and, if I need to scare someone off with it, then it will be handy," I explain. I lug my pack on my back. "We should stay on the road looking for some supplies in cars for a little while."

"Sounds like a plan, let's go," he agrees, adjusting the straps of his pack.

I glance back at the water we have to leave behind, then polish off another bottle as we step up next to the road. Leaving any water behind sounds like suicide, but there is just too much to carry.

Sterling is looking at the map as he walks the road before us, deserted. "Where do you think we are?" he asks.

"Texas 8. I think we have passed the 3108 and 2101, my plan is to get to 3009 and head west that way we have a water source for a while, then when we reach the 3378, we will go south to the 98, then reassess. It is a little close to Red River Army Depot, but we need to be within some distance of supplies if we need them."

I watch as he traces the route as I speak, then study his face as the distance we have to go to avoid people settles in.

"What about the snakes and gators?" he asks.

I scoff and then look over at his concerned face. "This far north?" I question.

He shrugs. "Leeches, ticks, definitely snakes, and spiders."

"Well then, we stop overnight at homes along the way, if there is no safe place, then we push on."

"And if we find a car before the turnoff?" he presses.

"Then we will make our way south the same turnoff." I shrug.

He seems to take this as a challenge, but as we get further down the road, even I am getting annoyed with the lack of vehicles to scour. The toilet paper is grating against me as I walk. It has only been three miles, and it is as if I have a cactus lodged up there.

A rustle from the bushes to our left causes us to pause. A white mass of hair and teeth lurches from the bramble of branches. I swing my arm back, but Sterling's hand slams into my chest knocking me back. The animal's body collides with him, sending them both ass over tail into the middle of the road. A fit of snarls and yells breaks the silence. My boot connects with its sturdy side, swinging my ax up over my head, following it as it lets out a whimper, then hits the pavement.

"No!" Sterling demands, his hands grasping my own, stopping the descent of the arching ax in its downward pursuit. His green eyes burn into mine, making sure I connect his words to my actions before releasing me and turning to the animal that I can clearly see is a very large white dog. "It's okay girl," Sterling says.

The dog snarls, baring its teeth, then whimpers as it tries to rise.

"Whoa." Sterling calms, his hands coming up slightly, his shoulders drooping as he tries to calm the animal. "You must be hungry."

"No shit, it just tried to maul your face." I hiss, thumping my ax on the ground.

"Shh," Sterling warns, dropping his pack and pulling a bag of jerky out.

I glare at him but heed his warning, annoyance raging inside me, steaming from him giving our food to an animal that has just drawn blood. I move to try to check Sterling for injuries, but his hand comes up to halt me. The other reaches toward the snarling dog holding out a piece of jerky. He tosses the piece toward it, and the animal flinches back, then still growling, its nose turns to the food. Slowly, nose still twitching, it leans toward it. Its big brown eyes angle up to Sterling.

"Go ahead, girl," he coaxes, wiggling the meat at the dog.

A rattling breath reaches my ears, and the dog's behavior shifts to one of terror. A loud scraping noise grinds from the brush. The dog tries to rise again, but I step toward the brush, ax raising as I draw closer. Edging closer, I can make out the form of an abomination, glancing back at Sterling, who is comforting the animal. I move down to the fence of barbed wire that the abomination has become embedded in. Slashing the ax down, I release its soul and then glance past it looking for more. I squint slightly at a blue building just visible beyond the trees.

Moving back to the road, I drag my ax through the tall grass to rid it of the rancid blood. Sterling has the dog in his lap, running his fingers across its ribs while it tries to lick his ears.

"You have a way with the ladies," I say, crossing my arms as I watch him.

The dog growls at me, but I watch Sterling. "You kicked her really hard."

"She drew blood on you, and you shoved me. I think we are all even," I respond dryly. He looks down like he's mad, causing anger to simmer deep in my belly. "Let's get off the road," I direct.

He looks back up, but I turn toward the direction of the house and then follow the road to the right. There has to be a driveway nearby. I walk down the road, glancing back to make sure he is following. A scowl claims my face when I see him carrying the blasted dog a good 100 feet behind me.

I try to rein in my temper, ignoring the chafing pain of the toilet paper tearing into me. I spot the silver of the mailbox before noticing the dirt road ahead. Then follow the road with my eyes to a metal chained gate that blocks vehicle access. Every part of me wishes to have a rifle right now. Stepping onto the path, my hand tightens on the handle of the ax.

"Any way to undo the chain?" Sterling asks.

I ignore his question. Something tells me to walk the other way and search elsewhere. The grating of the toilet paper pushes me to check the chain, but the ominous feeling of eyes on me prickles my skin. I grasp the Master lock in my hand, checking to see if it will just open. When it doesn't, I adjust my ax so that it can bludgeon. I grab the shackle of the lock, loosening any slack, then slam the back of the ax down on the lock, then again. The shackle releases, and I shimmy the lock open. I unwrap the chain and then push the gate open to let Sterling pass. Closing the gate after he passes, I re-wrap the chain, and slide the lock on, not fastening it.

Taking the lead, I ignore the dog's growl as the blue house comes into view, my eyes searching for movement, or some sign of life. The building is a second story, a doghouse out in the yard and an old barn a few hundred feet to the left. Gnomes spot the front yard and an old pickup truck is parked out front. Nothing moves from the house, not even a flutter of the curtains.

Glancing at Sterling, who is still carrying the damn dog, I let out a breath I wasn't aware I was restraining. "We need to clear the house, then set a timer."

"Can't we crash here to give her some time to heal up?" Sterling asks, looking around at what looks like a tranquil safe place.

"I don't want to be here longer than 45 minutes, something is wrong."

He sets the dog down in the grass and then steps up next to me.

"I've got right, you take left, then we will go up," I say, stepping forward.

We move up onto the wooden porch, ignoring its whines as we flank the door. Sterling's eyes meet mine, and I nod. He grasps the doorknob, and to my surprise, it swings open easily. We press into the room looking beyond the farmhouse tchotchkes and the wood-laden walls. We break in opposite directions, a bearskin rug muting my footsteps as I move through the dining room and around into a white-washed kitchen, spotting a back staircase and an open back door. Glancing out the back door, I then move toward the staircase, looking down a hall where Sterling steps out of a room and signals that it's clear.

We move up the stairs, the creaking of the wood sending us up quickly. We check the two rooms upstairs and the bathroom but find no one. Making our way back down, I stare at the back door, which is still ajar. I move toward it as Sterling heads toward the front of the house.

A quick scan of the back patio and yard, my eyes linger on the barn before pulling the door shut and securing it. Setting the timer on my watch, I move down the hall, finding Sterling has disappeared. Glancing into a small room, I continue down the hall to a restroom. Trying the tap, a gush of cold well water rewards me splashing down into the basin. Kneeling to open the cupboard below the sink, searching for something that would help me, knocking over stacks of toilet paper and rolled towels before slamming the cupboard shut and lurching for the medicine cabinet.

Glancing at the bottles of prescription medicine, ointments, and bug spray before snagging a first aid kit and shutting the cabinet. Leaving the bathroom and turning toward the front of the house, I step into a living area. Sterling is on the couch with the dog, soothing it. She looks like she's a reflection of my inner anxiety about this place.

"What should we call her?" Sterling asks, stroking the dog.

I stare at him, waiting for him to explain why he thinks it needs a name. "Do you not remember Darkness?" I reply, raising my eyebrows to accentuate my point.

He scowls but doesn't respond. one step forward, and she's snarling at me again.

"Call her druga žena," I suggest distastefully, with a step back.

"What language is that and what does it mean?" he questions, his eyes meeting mine.

Smirking, I take a step back further. "It means the other woman in Serbian."

His laugh doesn't help my mood, neither does the dog's angry stare. Glancing at my watch, I backtrack from the room and to the stairs, moving up them quickly. Reaching the bathroom, pulling open the doors, and pausing, a large pink box is shoved in the far back. Pulling it out with a sigh, I look into it, hoping it's been updated or added to, but unfortunately, it's packed with about 75 pads. The toilet paper reminds me it's a better option than my current one.

Dropping my pack on the ground, I shove as many as I can inside before moving to the toilet to rectify my torturous situation. Freeing the paper from its entrapment, I force myself back to my feet, admitting that the pad is much more comfortable even if it isn't ideal. Snagging another first aid kit, I scour the room searching for weapons, batteries, and flashlights. Empty-handed, my attention goes downstairs to the kitchen, where I throw open every cupboard, pulling any food out and shoving a cracker into my mouth as I go.

When nearing my 45-minute limit, I deposit my spoils onto the coffee table before Sterling, who, much to my annoyance, is still with the dog. "Clean up your cuts, I am going to go check out the barn for anything to use as a weapon."

"I can probably hot-wire the truck if we can't find keys. Any signs of dog food?" he asks, not getting to his feet.

"No, and you can try if it has gas."

His eyes lock onto mine, but with an about-face, I am heading down the hall past the kitchen and out the back door, my eyes focusing on the barn. It is also blue but not as well-kept as the house. Slowing as I near, I make a circle around the building before entering through the backdoor. Bringing my watch up to activate the light, a large body smashes into me.

The wood wall behind me stabs into me as the air rushes from my lungs. I shove the body back, but it's massive. My brain finally connects with the lack of rattling. "Get off me!" My nails dig into whatever flesh I can find. I thrash, trying to dislodge the person from me. A grunt is my only response, but I have enough room to kick out, my foot connecting with a solid leg. Then a cry of pain as my fist finds its mark. A large hand clamps down on my neck and the ground falls away.

"People who try to steal from me don't live to tell about it," an angry male voice announces. I grasp the sausage-like fingers, prying them apart in whatever directions they refuse to go. My knees hit the ground as the man yells, and I gasp for air. Charging to my feet, he pulls a revolver from a ratty side holster. Taking in the man's haggard appearance, he looks feverish, his face red and angry. His clothes are a mix of torn, bloody, and soiled.

The gun levels at my face, his finger on the trigger.

A growl from the door causes my attention to briefly move from the muzzle to the dog.

"Get out of here, you dumb bitch!" the man roars, his angry, fevered face swinging toward her, spit flying from his lips.

The dog advances, its hackles raised.

"Juliet, get back!" the man yells. His gun swings toward the dog as its teeth latch onto his leg.

Moving quickly, I crash my fist into the crease of his arm, unlocking his elbow and grasping his hand with the gun in it, and shoving it under his chin as he pulls the trigger. Blood and brain matter shower my face, hair, and clothes. I spit the iron taste from my mouth, prying the gun from the dead man's hand before kneeling and checking his pockets.

CHAPTER TWENTY
STERLING
"OUT OF HELL" BY SKILLET

AS I'M FINISHING up pulling dog food from the bottom of the pantry, I hear a gunshot pierce the air. Dropping to the ground, panic floods me. Where is Aurora? Listening intently, all I can hear is a strange scraping sound growing closer. Moving toward the door, I grab a kitchen knife off the counter. The noise grows louder, the sound of gravel under paws. Cautiously, I peer out the back door, spotting the big white dog moving to enter the house. Her hair is coated in blood. Rushing past her, I raise the knife defensively, running for the barn.

After rounding the front door to the barn, I hesitate, the darkness is overwhelming. Shoving back the doors, I let the light in, then jump back as Aurora appears, a gun trained momentarily on me.

"Are you okay?"

Her hand comes up. "Stop, he could have been infected, I need to rinse off and then we can search the barn before we leave."

"Let me help you."

"When I get rinsed off."

Stepping back and letting her pass, I watch her as she moves to the house. She has blood dripping from her; it's in her hair, on her face, and staining her clothes. We make it back to the house, and she moves to the downstairs bathroom.

"Juliet, come!" she orders.

Frowning at her, I look down in surprise as the dog follows her into the restroom. Moving to the bathroom door, I watch as she picks up the dog and sets her in the tub first.

"Find some towels so you can dry her."

I turn to the small bedroom and move to the closet where I'd spotted towels earlier. Grabbing as many as possible, my next steps bring me back to the restroom. Aurora is leaning over the tub, washing the dog gently with shampoo. When she finishes rinsing her, she backs up.

"Out, Juliet."

The dog jumps out of the tub and comes to me.

"You must be Juliet." Her tail goes bonkers behind her. Kneeling, I towel her dry, my eyes straying to Aurora as she climbs into what must be cold water. She shivers and her nipples pebble, the dog shakes, spraying me with water. I watch the soap run down her skin, aware of the bruising but appreciating the slick traveling down her firm, toned skin.

"While that look is incredibly enticing, it would be best to leave as soon as possible."

I nod and flash her a grin before rising to my feet. She is right, we need to get going. I began to collect all the essentials we have gained, packing them tight into an old overnight duffle while Juliet eats the spilled kibble off the floor. I turn when I hear Juliet's nails move on the tile to see Aurora lacing her blood-stained boots behind me.

She has fresh clothes on, and her hair pulled up in a high ponytail dripping down her back. She is gathering everything from the house and moving her way back toward the barn without a word. Juliet follows between us, breaking off to inspect the dead body on the ground as we approach.

"Unchain and open the far door as wide as you can."

Moving to the door, I use a penlight to locate the end of the chain and quickly unwind its hold on the large doors before shoving them open, letting light wash into the barn. A gust of clean air spirals dust and hay from the floor. I glance at Aurora who is stalking forward, knees bent, a bowie knife clutched in her hand, eyes gleaming, her nose wrinkling slightly, showing her tension before she bolts. I jerk my weapon to the ready as a hidden door on the floor slams open, dust assaulting me. Before I shield my face, then move quickly forward, realizing Aurora is no longer in front of me.

Panic seizes me for a heartbeat before I spot her down in the room below the barn. The knife she is clutching now resting on her thigh as she stares toward a far wall. The rasping growl of the dead bubbles up to me, dropping next to her. I frown at the abominations chained to the wall, moving up to Aurora's side.

"It's his family, the decomposition of their flesh suits can't hide the bone structure from those that match the people in the photos upstairs."

I glance over, watching her analyzing stare. "Why would he put them down here?"

"To keep them safe and close? Hopefully, they didn't die down here. Let's look for anything useful and head out."

"I would hate to be kept safe like this, I would rather have my soul released," I admit, then move to search the sleeping bags around the room.

"Find peace," Aurora whispers behind me.

I glance back, then look back to my task, listening as she drives her new knife into the brain of each abomination one after the other. My hand brushes something stiff in the sleeping bag, and I hope it's a weapon of some sort. I push back the fabric to uncover a thick leather-bound notebook.

"Ready?"

"I didn't find much, just this." I hold up the notebook, and she takes it, and I smile for a moment, watching her as she opens it carefully.

"July 3rd, 2019. Early this morning, the blasted national alarm went off on the TV, radios, and on Ruthie's cell phone, warning us to lockdown and shelter in place. Of course, I had to go get Juliet from the vet, so we locked down as soon as I made it back from town. Can you believe Jeddah has us in the cellar below the barn instead of in the house? Gracie's already coughing her head off, probably some kind of allergy. I will need to talk him into letting us ride out this lockdown inside the house. It feels like we have been stuck down here forever. I snuck to the house for my favorite blue dress. I know the color will cheer us up, and Mama has started coughing with Gracie. She's too old to be out here with a cold." Aurora reads.

I look over at the abominations. None of them look like a mother, but I can see the teen girl and the grandmother's lifeless forms. With a glance back at Aurora, I watch her flip to the next page, her eyes dart across the page.

"Shit." Aurora shoves the book into her bag and then moves to exit the room, pulling herself up out of the hole. I follow her, watching her intently. "We need to go, there is a military installment nearby, we need to get some distance."

"It said that in the book?"

"The girl, Gracie, had left her phone at home the day the alert happened. The mother talked about how mad Jeddah was about him finding out she had been sneaking to see some man from the base. I think she was almost 18. I guess that's how she got sick so fast."

"We can take the truck a few miles away before we take a break for the night. Shat are we going to do about the dog? We can't leave her here."

She looks at me with a slight smirk. "I will not argue with you about Juliet, let's see if the truck starts before you get your hopes up." I watch her walk back into the house to collect our supplies. I drag my eyes away from her ass and move to the truck. Reaching for the handle, I am not surprised to find it locked. I look at the cracked window, the corner of my mouth lifting. I move to the back of the truck, opening a small toolbox in the bed and pulling out a large flathead screwdriver.

I use the screwdriver to wiggle the window down a little, then grasp hold of it and lift it to try to pull it from its track, knowing that the old truck should allow me to wiggle the window down.

The window edges down, and I smile. The glass slips from my grasp and drops into the door with a crash. Before I even process what I did, a snort of laughter draws my attention.

"Smooth," Aurora says, walking up and tossing our bags in through the now vacant window.

With a quick tug, I pop the lock and open the truck, trying not to let her amusement distract me from my goal. I look under the steering wheel to see what I am dealing with, then glance up as she raps her knuckles on the window on the passenger side. I climb in, reach over, and unlock the door, then move back to wrestle the wires I need free. The truck rocks, and I look over to see what she's doing only to be met by Juliet's wet slobbery tongue on my face. I groan, moving away from her and focusing on connecting wires.

"Juliet, back."

The dog chuffs at her, then jumps out. The truck rocks again, and I swear.

"Are you doing okay?"

"Yeah, I almost got it," I say, glancing toward the door next to me to spot her.

"Focus on your work, I was just admiring the view."

"It's a pretty piece of land they had here..." I swallow whatever I was going to say, my hands going still. Her fingers claw my ass, moving up under my shirt and then sliding across, then toward my neck. I duck out from beneath the steering wheel, craning my neck to look at her.

She has a mischievous grin on her face, her body pressing against me. "I think I need you to take me like this later."

"As long as you're the one bent over the seat, you got a deal." I agree, connecting the last wire, and rewarded by the thundering growl of the truck's engine. She growls playfully and releases me, moving around the truck to get in before I can start something that will keep us here all night. Instead, I climb all the way into the truck and shut the door, glancing in the mirror at Juliet, who is laying in the back with a large bag of dog food and what looks like a few gallons of gas in strapped-down red cans. I glance at Aurora, who rolls her eyes at my glee.

I put the truck in drive and turn the beast around to lead us back out onto the road. It will be nice to ride for a while instead of walking, even if the breeze through the cab would get bitter the later it got. I turn onto the paved road, taking a left so as not to backtrack and then speeding up on the straightaways where I can see ahead. As I reach the third blind hill with no cars in sight, I admit I have started to feel more comfortable. We crest the hill, and I slam on the breaks, Aurora's swearing warning grinding out next to me.

Ahead, down the long stretch, about a mile up, is a barricade lit with barrel fires and many trucks.

"Turn right," Aurora hisses, checking her weapon.

The wheels of the truck skid on the dirt road as I push the limits of the truck's agility on the turn. I stare ahead, maneuvering it faster down the winding road.

"Shit, they are coming. Sterling, drive faster."

I try to oblige, but the road is unforgiving, and Juliet's whimper of distress causes me to growl in frustration. I slam on the brake as we reach the back of a large building. My eyes search for an exit. I jerk the wheel to the right and pop up on the curb, avoiding a chain across the one-way road. I glance at the building as I burst around into its front parking lot. Noting that it's a school, I beeline it out of the parking lot and, to my extreme displeasure, back toward what looks like the main road on the back side of the barricade.

"Let's take the go bags and run."

Before I can respond, a bullet ricochets off the hood.

"Down!" I yell, not slowing the truck. The front left fender connects with a man with an automatic rifle before I have it back on the main road and screeching away from the chaos blossoming behind us.

"We need off this road, one blockade could mean many more people. All of them could have those weapons."

"Find a road then."

"No, just pull over and we run. We can make it into the woods and disappear."

With a glance in the rearview mirror at the vehicles driving over the hill behind us, I then glance at her.

She slams her fist on the dash.

"Find me the next turnoff."

"Next hill you stop, park across the road, and we bail."

I do not argue, knowing that sacrificing the truck would help cause maximum damage and distract them from following us for a while. I crest the next hill, slamming on the brakes, and we bail.

"Juliet, come!" Aurora calls.

The dog bounds behind us as we reach the trees. A resounding crunch behind us sends us to the ground as we scramble to cover the dog disappearing ahead of us. With a quick glance, I see one car smashed against the front of the truck just as another vehicle slams into the back. Aurora tugs me deeper into the thicket, and I follow. Down an incline through thick tree coverage and then we pause at a twelve-foot wide river babbling away in front of us.

"We can wade across." I offer, then look over at Aurora's stony face. "Or not?"

CHAPTER TWENTY ONE
RORY
"ALL AROUND ME" BY FLYLEAF

WE HAVE no choice but to cross the river. I fight with every part of me to stay current, not to be swept away in the nightmares my PTSD wants to ravage through my psyche. Sterling's firm grip on my arm helps ground me, and when we make it to the other side and scramble up the bank to get back into the trees, rage is thrumming through me. We move through the woods quietly and quickly. I have never missed GPS in my life until this moment. Without the roads, I have to rely on the idea that we are heading in the correct direction.

I check my watch to make sure we are at least heading southwest, and I adjust our direction, slowing slightly as Juliet darts west.

"Juliet..." Sterling hisses, but it's no use. She's gone. The foliage grows dense, but we don't slow our pace, the angry voices around us in the distance urging us on. The feeling of the ground under my boots changes, and I skid to a stop.

"Sterling..." The warning is too late. He passes me and then vanishes with a loud thud followed by a crash and a groan. I jolt forward, fear silencing the silent scream from exiting my mouth. My hands grasp a tree trunk, its branches hanging over a steep drop. I realize it's not a cliff, but a man-made wall that buts up into the wilderness that we had been racing through, and Sterling's unmoving body lies on a heap of trash 60 feet below.

I immediately start calculating how he fell, running the probabilities of various injuries through my mind while considering what the safest way to get down to him would be. *He is dead!* The panic in my brain screams, trying to make me react faster. I open my mouth, prepared to call out to him when the sound of voices sends me slinking back.

"This way, I know I heard something!"

Men swarm the alley, and I glance at the brick building they appeared around. A quick calculation tells me it is a good ten stories high. I peek down at the men below, clutching the farmer's gun as one of them wades into the trash and approaches Sterling.

"He has a pulse, where did he come from? I thought we had this sector on lockdown. We need to do another sweep, someone must have dumped him here to bring him back. He can lead us to the others."

I risk another peek down to see them lift him out of the trash. Sterling groans and part of me wants to drop the distance and save him somehow. Instead, I count the men and watch the seven of them carry him away, then silently shift, trying to watch their retreat, but the trees block me from acquiring the vantage point necessary. The panic within me rockets higher now that he is out of sight, but I shove it down, and it burns like bile as I force myself to look around the alley again, letting my brain find a way down that would be quiet, effective, and less likely for me to get injured.

I pause, squinting slightly at a sliver of a shadow. I crawl as far to the left as I can, trying to look at the shadow. What looks like a clear 60-foot drop was actually only partially true. Sterling had been 60 feet down, but a concrete enclosure that must be housing the trash cans for this building cuts the 60 feet down to 50. I consider Sterling must have hit this and rolled off. With a quick scan of the alley, I move to the tree and check its branches' strength. I grasp several, taking a seat on the ledge, and gingerly easing myself off, the

CHAPTER TWENTY ONE

branches creak, and a few snap. I hang as low as possible, my hands burning as I adjust my grip to lower myself, then drop, landing in a pile of trash bags. After a quick 30-foot drop, letting myself roll slightly, my body is airborne for a moment before my boots make purchase, and I duck into the concrete containment with a breath of relief. The side of the overfilled dumpsters read Red River Army Depot.

"Shit," I say in a whisper, knowing that this was going to be an immense problem. I try to formulate a plan to find Sterling, how I could blend into the depot to get to him? Was the area swarming with the dead? Was he even still alive? I jerk from my hiding spot and out into the setting sun. My body presses up against the building before I slide toward the alley where the men had disappeared. Moving silently, I pause, pulling my wrist up to my face.

"Locate warbler." I hiss.

The face swirls and directs me toward Sterling's unseen location. I move forward, staying in the deepening shadows and weaving between the buildings through alley after alley. Until a loud cheer causes me to halt. Voices around the next turn drift down the alley, but to my frustration, I can't make out their words but know that it's many more than the seven I had seen. I peek around the corner toward the cacophony of yells, yanking my head back when a shadow moves further down that alley. When no one approaches, I slowly peer around again, then sigh with relief.

Taking in his lean silhouette and firm jaw, I move forward slowly, waiting to speak until I am three feet away. "Sterling, how did you get away?"

The figure spins to me, and I scuttle back, staring up at a near replica of Sterling's face but one which has aged to near mid-50s.

"How do you know my name?" the man growls, brandishing a knife between us.

"Scour the streets. We will find any others who have made their way into our depot to steal from us. Take the prisoner and get info out of him, if he dies, kill him before he turns!" a voice roars, silencing what looks like at least 70 others who all stare at this man with what looks to be fear and appreciation.

I note the M16 shouldered on more than half the men, but there are no BDUs in sight.

They drag Sterling past the leader, who looks back with a smirk. His eyes are open, and a grimace marrs his handsome face.

A hand clamps on my arm, and I am yanked back from storming into the group. "Do you have a death wish?" the man who could be Sterling's older replica asks.

My fists clench before approaching boots send us scrambling out of view. A large calloused hand claps over my mouth, and I am pulled through a window at ground level and deposited on a cement floor, hands releasing me and closing the window and covering it with a large crate.

"How the hell do you know my name?" the man asks in a fierce whisper.

"I thought you were someone else."

"Liar, who told you my name, girl?"

"Girl? The only reason you're standing and alive is that I can't figure out why you look so much like my husband, so mind your manners, asshole."

"What a line, how much food are those womanizers paying you to pretend to know me, and how did they figure out my name?"

I roll my eyes then pause. "Your name is Sterling? Sterling Karter?"

His gun levels at me, and I sigh, wondering why he hadn't started with a threat. "How the hell do you know that?"

I let out a breath as my hands move through my hair, ignoring the man I now know is Sterling's father. Even if I could get this jerk who abandoned his son to help me save him, we are still vastly outnumbered. Panic replaces some of my brain's focus. Seventy men are too many, I would be easily breaking our pact if I were to take them head-on. I drop my pack to the ground and yank out my map, ignoring Sterling Senior's curious stare, his gun now pointing at the floor.

CHAPTER TWENTY ONE

Unfolding the map, I trace the route we were on and then locate Red River Army Depot. We were a stone's throw away from New Boston, but I don't have time to round up help or abominations. I glance up at Senior, who kneels next to the top of the map, his eyes looking eager now.

"I can give you the map for information on this group." I offer.

"If you're not with them, then why are you here?"

"They have my husband, and he can not die," I say, looking back down at the map.

He eyes my bag, and I sigh. He looks at me doubtfully, and I ignore how much he looks like Sterling. "You know there are like 50 men in there, many of them with M16s and willing to do anything to a woman like you without her consent. You will get both of us killed."

I close my eyes for a moment, fighting the fear to find a way to save Sterling. *"God, it's me, Rory, I know I deserve no favors, but Sterling is a man after your own heart. Please help me figure out how to save him so he can continue to change the world and make it better."* My eyes spring open and tears sting as I force them back. I need help, and this is the way Sterling would request it. I let my eyes search the room, ignoring Senior, who is talking to me again.

"Do they have radios?" I ask, pausing, staring at a black radio laying on top of a crate with a small backpack and a sleeping bag.

"Yes, is that the only question you have for the map?" he asks, reaching for it.

"Listen carefully, you can have the supplies in my bag if you help me get my husband. Seriously, all the supplies. I can always find more. All you have to do is respond on the radio, but I need you to respond."

"They'll know it's me. I am finally free from them, waiting it out, that's what works best for me," he says, sitting on a crate and staring at me.

"Fine... what a coward, your wife would have helped me, no questions asked," I say acidly, fixing my hair so it won't distract me when I make a big move.

"See how much you know, I don't have a wife."

"You used to." I hold up my hand, his eyes locking on my ring. I dart out of the way as he tries to grasp my wrist.

"Where the hell did you get that?"

I ignore his yelling, letting him make himself a target. I owe this man nothing because of his lineage.

The door bursts open as I reach it. The barrel of an M16 swings into the room, but my pace doesn't slow. I've nothing to lose if they kill Sterling. My brain tries to remind me of our pact, but I push down with a surge of emotion. I grab the barrel, slamming it up and back in the face of a fierce-looking man. He yells in surprise and pain, releasing the gun and lurching at me.

"Get off of her!" Senior yells from behind me.

I wrap my leg around the man's, shoving him with my hands and pulling a leg out from under him. He hits the ground hard, and I back away, smiling at him as he gasps for air. I circle around him, picking up the M16, watching the anger battle pain in his eyes as he groans and gets to his knees. He pulls his radio from his belt, bringing it to his mouth with a gleam of self-righteousness.

"Victor, we have company," he rasps.

I check the ammo, then rack the slide and switch the safety to semi-automatic. I level the muzzle at the man's face, cradling the weapon against my shoulder like the expert I am. His lips tremble and he releases the radio, his hands flapping above him. The smell of urine wafts up around him, but I do not take my eyes off him.

"Pick it up, let me talk. If you so much as breathe a warning, I will send two bursts through your skull before the words can properly form on your lips."

His lips clamp shut, and one of his trembling hands reaches for the radio, his eyes glued to mine. Senior hits the radio with his boot, sliding it within reach, then moves for his duplicate, clicking it on and lowering the volume.

"Go for Victor, what's your location, and how many?"

The man's eyes lock on me. "New Boston off of Elm and Lion. It looks like a whole damn cavalry," I say with a glance at Senior, who nods at me.

"That's part of their patrol area," he whispers.

"Make it convincing," I hiss, watching his trembling finger moving for the button.

"Looks like they are moving into the high school, there are a hell of a lot of ems."

My eyes move to Senior, who smiles with a nod.

"Tell him their commander wants to speak with him about food rations for the base," I demand, making sure the weapon is pointing at his head.

"How many is a hell of a lot, you idiot?" Victor asks, his voice sounding agitated.

"Hello, this is First Sergeant Aurora Moore with the United States Marines. We are here to bring supplies to fuel this depot. Do you have able bodies with no infections to come to collect your share? Over," I bark into the radio that I have wrestled out of the man's hands.

"Yes, ma'am, sorry for my tone. Of course, we can come get supplies," Victor responds.

"Make sure you are in uniform or have your ID to sign off on these supplies. I know it looks like the end of times. but you know how protocol is. Moore out. Over."

"Percy, is this for real?" Victor asks.

I glare at the man, and he nods, then remembers he needs to speak when his eyes connect with the radio in his face.

"That bitch is scary. She has men going to get some big trucks. I overheard that they have to be ready to supply us immediately." His Adam's apple rocks as he takes a big gulp.

"We are gearing up, monitor her, let me know if you see any funny business."

I watch as the man sets the radio on the ground, then looks up at me. With a glance at Senior, I calculate which one of these asshats is going to be most useful. "Do you know a way out of here that these dumbasses haven't found?" I ask Senior.

Senior nods, watching me, his eyes looking at the muzzle of the gun still trained on the man before me.

"Where is the prisoner?" I ask the man.

"They do interrogations in the big green building," he responds, shuffling slightly as if to rise.

"Do you know where that is, Senior?" I ask.

Senior's brow furrows, but he nods in response.

The man before me takes this moment to kick out at me. The M16 spins in my grasp, the butt of the rifle snapping against the man's head, sending him to the floor without him making a sound.

"Guess you are on board, we need to get moving. Help me put this dipshit into a crate and lead the way, but just know, if you betray me you will die a slow, painful death."

"That's reassuring," he says dryly.

"I could offer you the moon, but all we need is to rescue my husband, then get out of here, and I will help you get whatever rations you desire."

"You seem so sure that you can save him."

"I know that when you see him, you'll know why, and you won't screw it up this time," I say, hoping that I am right. With quick, measured movements, I move to my pack, tucking the map back in. "Hurry, old man."

"I am not old," he growls, dragging the man toward an open crate.

"You're old enough to be my father." I grab the arms of the limp man and help haul him into a crate.

"You know, some woman would find that attractive."

"Wait till you meet my husband, and you will understand how ridiculous that statement is. Grab your shit, let's go." I urge, moving to the door.

We both freeze as the sound of trucks from outside rumbles through the air. I smile, and Senior looks at me in awe.

"Come on now, Senior, let's go."

CHAPTER TWENTY ONE

"Stop calling me that, you obviously know my name, and when we get out of here, you're going to explain how," he says, stepping up next to me.

"Deal," I agree with a shrug.

Senior pushes the door open, checking if the coast is clear, and I prime the M16, ready to eliminate everything in my path until I find Sterling

CHAPTER TWENTY TWO
STERLING
"PUSH ME DOWN" BY ALL GOOD THINGS

MY EYES FLUTTER OPEN, pain screaming through my body. My heels drag on the ground, unable to find a purchase with legs that are unresponsive to the need to rise from the grasp on my arms. I look up, my head lulling back, eyes rolling, trying to focus when what looks like 100's of men fill my line of sight, the ringing in my ears muffling the surrounding ruckus. The double vision ebbs away but doesn't make me feel any better about my situation. Another pair of hands clamp down on my arms as I start to struggle.

The pain doesn't ease, if anything it worsens as my arms are trussed up above me with a chain, and I am suspended by my arms from the ceiling, my toes just grazing the ground. The pull of unconsciousness drags from the back of my mind, pain taking over my senses.

Pain lances through my ribs, and my eyes shoot open as all the air leaves my body. I struggle to pull in air, my surroundings a haze of dark colors in a dimly light room. Water sloshes into my face, causing a coughing fit to rock my body. Finally catching my breath, a man moves in my line of sight. I jerk my arm to punch him, realizing I am still restrained.

"Good morning, sunshine," the man says, tossing an empty

CHAPTER TWENTY TWO

bucket onto a table nearby. He moves closer, laughing as I pull at the chain. Grasping the metal links, I support all my weight in an agonizing moment, and with both feet, I kick the man in the chest, sending him crashing backward across the floor.

Groaning, I try to relieve some pressure by setting my feet on the ground, but it's no use. The vaulted ceilings of this building, even with my 6'4 frame hanging from my arms, still don't allow me to do anything but graze the floor with my foot. I push down on the front pad of my foot then rise to my tiptoes, attempting to loosen the metal locking my hands in place, but there is no give.

My focus is drawn back to the groaning man rising to his feet, his face flushing in anger and embarrassment.

"I am so much happier you fought, 'cause now I don't have to go easy on you." he sneers, rubbing his sore ass.

"Lucky for you, you have a one-time opportunity not to die today if you release me now," I reply, struggling against my restraints threateningly.

His scoff gives me just a hint of his disbelief before his fist slams into my stomach. "You see, I am in charge here, not you."

With a sharp jolt, I ram my head forward, head-butting him in his face. Pain leeches from a new abrasion on my forehead, but I smile. "Are you sure that's your choice? You're picking death?"

"You bastard, you could have made this easy. Everyone else is off gathering supplies. You could have easily given me information and hung around till they got back, but now my friend here and I are going to make you eat your words."

A low chuckle behind me greets me with a jab to my left kidney and sends me swinging forward to a waiting fist to my face.

"Lower this bastard so I can carve up his face," the man from behind me requests.

"Is that a good idea, Sean?"

"Shut up and lower him down, he already had his fun making you look like a wus, Enrique."

The gleam of a blade flashes, and I tense before taking in Sean's body language as he moves to stand before me.

"Hey, shorty, this will not be your day," I greet.

Anger flares in his eyes, and he pulls a 9mm from the back of the man's pants, the muzzle pointing at my chest. "Lower him down now!"

My feet hit the floor, but as I take back, the weight from my arms agonizing the deep pain that radiates from my right hip, and I remember the fear of falling before unconsciousness had swept it all away. My scream nearly blocks out the sound of a pounding fist at the door.

"On your knees!" Sean yells, his eyes locked on me.

"He only submits to me," a growl announces before Aurora appears, her Gerber soundlessly slashing into the nape of his neck, instantly severing his spinal cord. Enrique's yell sends her into a fury. She launches herself forward, grabbing the man's hair and forcing his face down to her knee before burying her knife into his back and releasing him into a heap on the floor. Her eyes meet mine, and anger fills her face before she silences the man's screams with a quick drag of her knife across his throat, ending his agony. I groan, collapsing to my side, arms catching me before my knees hit the floor.

"Release his hands!" Aurora demands to someone behind me.

Instead, I feel large hands lifting me back to my feet. "On your feet for just a moment, son."

A yell of pain escapes me before I can stifle it, and the man's embrace on me tightens as my hands are freed. I scream as my arms lower, pushing through the pain as I reach for my hip. Aurora moves back in front of me, her eyes full of fear.

"Let's get him to the couch. Sterling, I need deep breaths like when you try to help me calm down, we've got you," she coaches, mimicking the deep breaths we had practiced a while back.

"Sure thing, I got him, move aside," a man replies half dragging half carrying me.

I see her eyes roll, and she slides next to me, her hands moving up

CHAPTER TWENTY TWO

under my aching arms as we hobble 15 feet to a couch across the room.

"We won't be able to run, Senior, we need transportation soon," Aurora demands, wasting no time unbuckling my pants and sliding them down before I am lowered gingerly down onto the couch.

My eyes shift to an older man who moves to secure the open door and then to an open window, I assume Aurora had come through. Pain brings me back to Aurora, her fingers kneading my left hip, which is badly bruised and screaming with pain. She moves to her pack and pulls out some aspirin and an almost empty bottle of water. I accept both, my hands still shaking from the effort of moving my arms.

"We are going to get you out of here. I am sorry, baby, but there is no time to heal or to rest."

"I will be okay, I can be strong like you."

Her smile flashes across her face for a moment, then she's rocketing around the room, collecting anything she can to help us on our escape, including wrestling my bag from a box of supplies. "Stock up, Senior, we have a deal. You can have all of this if you help get my husband and me out of this."

I frown, wondering when she would accept or ask any stranger for help. The man frowns at her and then turns to me, and I freeze, his face itching at the back of my memory.

"Give me the gun, girl, I know how to use it, and it will help us get out."

"No, you're helping your son. Now that we have him, I have no problem alerting this whole place of our arrival. Where can we get a vehicle?" she asks.

His eyes pin on me, and I can see the graying hair almost as dark as mine, his green eyes twinkling behind wrinkles that had never been there before.

"My son?" he whispers, his face draining of blood and his hands falling to his sides.

"I leave you alone for five minutes and you find the man who deserted me twenty-some-odd years ago?" I ask.

"I'm an amazing wife and probably part bloodhound. Who must forgive you for ditching her in a failed attempt to skydive," she says, one of her eyebrows shooting up at me while she tucks extra ammo for the 9mm in her pocket and an M16 mag in her bag. She pulls something else from the dead body before piercing their brains so they don't rise again.

"Wife? You're my son's wife?" Senior gasps, looking back and forth between us.

"Snap out of it," she demands, her face set in a storm of beautiful fury.

"She's my everything. Let's get moving before they come back. We need a car, Senior, so let's go," I demand, gritting my teeth as I struggle to pull my pants back on. I know that getting up is going to hurt and that I have to be as careful as possible until we know if I broke anything. My absentee father is staring at me, but I ignore him and focus on getting to my feet, putting my weight on my right leg. Just standing nearly doubles me over with pain.

My father moves toward me, and I begrudgingly must let him assist me. I ignore his questions about what hurts, keeping my eyes on Aurora, who is stripping the room of anything else and securing my pack on her back over her own. She holds a 9mm back, her eyes locking on mine.

"You two decide who is shooting. If I can get another, I will hand it back, but for now, put on the kevlar," she orders, thrusting it into my arms.

I groan as it's strapped around my chest, then hold myself up against a wall as my father straps his on. My eyes move to Aurora and her eyebrow raises.

"If we find another kevlar, I will put it on. Please don't be mad, love, you know how I operate. Let's move, we are running out of time." Her face tilts up, and her lips move as she whispers.

"Are you praying?" I ask, fighting back a groan of pain as we move forward.

"It's the only way this is going to end well."

Fear trickles like venom through me. Aurora is worried which means this will be bad. I need to stop her, hold her. If our lives end here, I should have her in my arms. Opening my mouth to argue, the door bursts open and the M16 blasts to life, sending two bodies to the ground in a heap. I ignore my father's swearing before focusing on moving forward, the pain all-encompassing.

CHAPTER TWENTY THREE
RORY
"WAR OF CHANGE" BY THOUSAND FOOT KRUTCH

THE PAIN on Sterling's face is just too much for me to endure. These assholes are going to pay for making him feel worse, and then after getting him to safety, I'm going to lay into him about breaking our promise to be safe. My prayer up to God surprises me but feels right. I need support to get them to safety and not break his heart by losing my own life at the same time.

The men on the floor are my green light to switch to agent mode. Anything that moves is getting a bullet to the brain, no point wasting ammunition. I frisk the bodies, sliding an extra clip in my bag, then moving in a crouch to the door, gun to my shoulder, my eyes darting methodically up and down the street.

"Go right," Senior instructs, leaning me that direction before following after her..

I clear left, popping two shots in quick succession, not waiting for the bodies to drop before turning to the right and taking out 5 men huddled together with weapons rising toward us. My boots are silent on the pavement as I go, but behind me, the sounds of Sterling's distress pull at my concentration. A man rounds a corner ahead to the right and a few hundred yards behind him, another two from the left, a head pops over the lip of a building 300 feet away.

CHAPTER TWENTY THREE

The gun pops three times before I swing it behind me, roundhousing the man who has reached me before dropping on him with my Gerber. I silence his screams, hip-checking the M16 and taking it in my grasp to fire off another four shots as I advance down the street.

The crack of the 9mm causes me to slow. "We are good, take the 2nd left and go up to the enormous building marked mess hall on the front in big bold black letters," Senior instructs, his breathing slightly labored.

"Give me the gun," Sterling grunts, reaching for it.

I force myself to not look back as we move, stepping past the bodies on the ground and scooping up a reload. I eject my mostly spent magazine and pop in a fresh one. Before pocketing a few knives and moving on. Voices ahead cause me to slow.

"Sir, are we training or something?"

A radio crackles. "No, you dimwit, we went to retrieve supplies."

"I know, sir, but there is gunfire…"

However, he is going to respond is silenced by a bullet to his frontal lobe. The radio crashes to the ground, and I take out the man next to him without hesitation. We near the Mess Hall, and I slow again, watching the front door rattle. I glance back at Senior, who shakes his head at me and points to go around the building. I hesitate but then catch sight of Sterling's beet-red face, sweat beading on his brow.

I move around the building, glancing in a window as we pass, shivering at the site of naked women, dozens of them walking in the shells of abominations. Anger churns in my stomach as we press on.

"We are taking one of those, the exit is over there. See that huge crane? It is holding up a shipping container filled with bags of cement and fertilizer. They use it to block the entrance they tore down," Senior explains in a strained voice as he supports most of Sterling's weight before setting him down in the passenger seat of a UTV.

"This is your transportation?" Sterling growls, grasping onto the side and biting back the pain, causing his face to darken.

"It will get us out of here, at least as far as camp. We should find a truck there," Senior insists.

"Where are the children?" I ask, my attention diverting to the survival of our next generation.

"Most of them are used as zombie bait or woman bait when they want to satisfy their needs," Senior replies.

"It's official, I miss Joey," I growl before jerking and sending a bullet through a man's forehead about 1,000 feet from us toward the exit to this colossal dumpster fire of an army depot.

"Nice shot, babe, let's go," Sterling urges.

I look at him, nodding once, knowing how much pain he must be in. I climb up into the small cargo bed of the UTV, listening to its little engine crank to life. "Circle around the front of the Mess Hall, then let's head to the exit," I direct.

"But it's a straight shot..." Senior argues, gesturing forward angrily.

"You need to listen to her, or you can stay here," Sterling interjects, clenching his teeth against the pain.

"Where is the 9mm?" I ask, looking between them.

"Right here," Sterling says, holding it up.

I hand him a full clip and then steady myself against the roof, finding my balance and bracing my feet to the sides of the bed to help absorb the bumps and movement below me. The UTV moves forward, and I have to grasp the top rollover bar as we jolt. Sterling hisses in pain, and Senior eases off the accelerator.

"Sorry, it's been a minute," Senior barks, wrestling the steering wheel.

He maneuvers us around the building, and I take out three more men before turning my aim at the chain on the front door of the mess hall. I pull the trigger and send a prayer to God to save the souls of the woman whose abominations whoosh from the building.

"Go!" I demand, spinning to face forward.

Senior guns it, and Sterling's knuckles turn white as he holds on. I line up my next shot with the calculations of weight spinning through my mind. I wait till the last possible second before pulling the trigger, my bullet connecting with the chain holding the shipping container. The chain jerks and the left side of the container swings past my head, then the entire thing smashes to the ground behind us.

I feel the UTV slow slightly and then dart left away from the main road and onto an old trail. "What are you doing?" I demand, holding on for dear life.

"Those men will come back on the main road by now. They are going to be spitting mad about no supplies, and I am not risking any of our necks playing cowboy," Senior growls accelerating down the bumpy trail.

"Pull over!" I yell, slamming on the roof.

We skid to a stop, and the furious man turns, fuming at me.

"I need 15 minutes, and we need to take cover, not lead them away."

"You want to stand and fight?" Senior gasps, turning the UTV off and rising to his feet.

"I don't want a bullseye on my back when someone tracks us."

"They hurt my son. Shouldn't he be your biggest concern?" he counters, anger filling his features as he gestures wildly at me.

"My husband is military. He knows what risks we take not cleaning house," I snarl my finger caressing the trigger of the gun in my hand that is pointed at the ground between us.

"Military?" Senior asks, looking to Sterling in surprise.

Sterling growls in frustration, ignoring the question. "What do we need to do, Aurora?"

"We need to park in the thicket, Senior needs to camouflage the best he can while checking the 9mm and the M16, and you'll also keep hold of what little supplies we have. While you guys do that, I am going to cause a distraction, then come back this way. I am going to lure a few in, get our hands on another decent weapon, and clean up this mess," I explain, clicking on the safeties and handing over my weapons.

"I do not want you to do this alone." Sterling frowns, accepting the weapons.

"I am not alone. Anyone that follows me this way will get taken out by you or Senior. We have to be sure they don't follow. This is our only chance at the upper hand."

"You know our pact," he reminds, pressing the guns on Senior.

"The one you dropped 60 feet over a wall, yes I do, and if it's too risky, I'll sneak back, and we can go with no resistance," I bargain.

"Fine, no unnecessary risks."

"You two hurry here. I'm going to create a Venus fly trap real quick," I say before handing over almost all my gear except for the full front pockets of my jacket and the Gerber at my waist.

I sneak back to the road, checking to make sure the coast is clear, before scurrying around to find some branches that are long enough and spry enough for this simplistic but deadly trap. With a quick check for people, I take the unsuspecting branches into the road, winding them at one edge to cause tension before surrounding the base with rocks. I move ahead a hundred feet and create another one on the other side of the road, keeping toward the yellow center line. When the branches are ready to be set off by a tire running them over and causing them to spring apart, I gingerly weave the end of the branches' whippy twigs and leaves through the ring of a grenade. Then I follow the same careful work on the other three branches before tiptoeing off back into the woods to check on Sterling and Senior.

I'm pretty impressed when I near their location and raise my hands up, speaking just loud enough for them to hear from the formidable hiding place.

"No sign yet. You guys did great."

"He is good at disappearing," Sterling says, shooting Senior a dirty look.

I avoid Senior's eyes but notice the flare of anger that darkens his ears. We would have to check that temper if he was sticking around. I glance over my shoulder, the sounds of traffic from the road reaching my ears. I hold up a finger and signal for them to hide. Sterling pulls Senior into the nearly invisible UTV.

An explosion from the road causes me to drop slightly as the chain reaction of the other three grenades breaks the forest's serenity. I sneak back to the road, staying low and silent. Pausing within the shadows of the trees, I take in the carnage of four vehicles. Bodies litter the ground, but others are moving, shrieking, and panicking. I catch sight of a man toward the front, his uniform sets him apart from the rest in mismatched fatigues. He is bellowing at the ten or so men still on their feet, demanding answers. I emerge from the woods slightly, keeping one arm on the tree beside me.

"Run! They are coming!" I scream at the men on the road, then yank myself back toward the trees. "No, you blew them up with no warning. Let me go!" I scream before disappearing into the woods.

"After her!" a man yells, breaking into a jog, gun raised.

I slow my pace so that they will see me turn ahead but then sprint past Sterling and Senior's hiding spot, tucking around a tree across the path and out of sight.

The M16 shreds the men to pieces, then immediately stops. I run toward the bodies, falling to my knees grabbing one gun, and turning my back in the direction of the road. A rush of footsteps behind me tells me that only one person is approaching.

"Why did you have to kill them? They could have helped us!" I scream into the woods away from Sterling and Senior's position. I bring the gun up, shaking it with my hand as I grasp Gerber in my right hand, the gun with my left finger on the trigger. "Fire, dammit!" I swear at the weapon, listening as the boots move closer behind me.

I turn my head back, making my eyes as wide as I can. "Please, how do I use this? Your men didn't deserve this."

The man lowers his 9mm and reaches toward me. "Set it down, cupcake, I will protect you. It looks like your friends took off."

"They were not my friends. All they wanted was my body. You're not like that, are you, mister?" I ask, lowering the gun and reaching toward his hand.

A wolfish grin spreads across his face, and the madman below his facade beams at me as if trying to devour me here and now. His hand clamps down on my wrist and yanks me to my feet.

I let out a yapping sound, playing the timid roll for one last moment before burying my Gerber into the man's chest. Yanking my arm away, I grab him by the belt before he can fall and drop an unpinned grenade down the front of his pants, then shove him away and dive for a tree.

"Down!" I bellow, covering my head.

The man explodes, penis first, in a blast of blood, bone, and vengeance.

CHAPTER TWENTY FOUR
STERLING
"EVERYWHERE" BY MICHELLE BRANCH

THE LOCATION we have selected for the night is not as comfortable as I have been hoping for. But at the end of mankind, I suppose counting one's blessings and being content that you and the one you love are alive is supreme over all else. I adjust my position on the long booth I am laying on, trying to find some comfort but just causes my hip to grind back with pain.

I try to stifle my groan with the table linen that is in a makeshift pillow under my head, but my attempts are in vain. Aurora's eyes flash open in the beaming light of the moon, and my father, who is standing sentry, turns to look my way from his perch on a stool near a fake ficus in the corner. The room is a shamble of overturned chairs and long stained blood puddles that mar the glass-riddled floor. It must have been tossed and picked through a dozen times. But, of course, whoever had come and gone wasn't Aurora, her ever-present ingenuity and clever skepticism of others foraging has been our savior for dinner tonight. Some just cook pasta smothered in anchovies and black olives.

"Anything I can do to make it better?" Aurora asks. Breaking me from my thoughts, her hand slides into mine.

"I could do with less padding under my ass."

"I can't do that. We need to elevate it and ice it, but I am at a loss there. We need to reduce inflammation," she sighs, rubbing at her eyes.

"We could give him some ginger, that's what his mother took when she was pregnant to reduce swelling," my father says, swinging his leg back and forth as he watches us, concern creasing his brow.

Aurora looks over, and he averts his eyes. He is scared of her, that's easy to tell, but his voice sounds strange. She looks back at me and nods thoughtfully. "That might help a little. The best thing would be to reduce your mobility and let your rest. We don't know how bad it is, let alone if there is a fracture."

"I can go foraging for supplies, maybe I can find medication," my father suggests, rising to his feet.

"Maybe when we get further from the city. I mean it's possible we didn't get all of them, and it would be great if we could find a van or a covered truck to travel in so we could raid a house and pillow him until we can get to his house and lockdown for a while."

"How can you plan that far ahead? We don't know what will happen." my father asks, knocking the barstool with his leg as he paces.

"Looking forward helps us to stop looking backward; that's at least what my daddy taught me when my mother died."

I felt his eyes on me but kept mine on Aurora, who shrugs and settles back down on the floor. Her hair slides off the bench as she lowers herself onto her pack. My fingers yearn to run through it, to caress her body, and worship her with my touch. I can almost feel her heat on my fingertips, ready to slide deep when her voice full of rage makes me wake with a start, the pain crashing around me as I try to rise to defend her from whatever problem she might be facing.

I squint at the sun streaming in through the broken windows of the restaurant then fall back on the booth, hissing in pain. I look down to where she should be lying but am greeted by the soft wag of Juliet's tail. With a frown, I try to figure out when she got here and then not seeing Aurora my heart races. With all my strength, I try to get up but only manage to slide to the floor screaming out in pain this time, Juliet scuttling out of the way. I shift to my good side, pain like knives dissecting my hip, causing me to growl as I drag myself across the floor, smacking the broken glass from the floor.

Running footsteps screeching to a stop cause me to look up at Aurora's stormy face. Her jaw drops, and she falls to her knees, glass crunching beneath her.

"What is happening?" I ask, my voice harsher than intended as I fight the pain back.

Air rushes into her mouth, tears spilling from her eyes, her lips trembling as she crawls to me. Her hands tremble as they reach my face, one caressing my cheek and one running through my hair. She presses herself to me, my face smothered against her breasts, her chest heaving as sobs rip from her. Juliet moves slowly toward us with a soft whimper before laying down and resting her head on my leg.

I pry her arms back and look into her face with concern. "What happened?"

She shakes her head. "It sounds stupid now."

"Nothing you have to say is stupid," I soothe in a gentle tone, caressing her soaking cheek.

"Your father took off."

"So? He is pretty good at that. Why would that make you cry? One less belly to fill," I reason, ignoring the pang of disappointment.

"No, I thought you turned. I thought I lost you," she whispers, her lips quivering as tears drip from them.

It's my turn to stare at her in horror, her trembling body next to mine, a mere shell of her powerful essence. "I look that bad this morning?" I ask, trying to lift the mood.

"A little. Why are you on the ground?"

"I was having this amazing dream about you, and then I heard you swearing, and when I woke up, I couldn't find you. So I was trying to help but couldn't get to my feet," I admit, shifting uncomfortably.

"I'm sorry, I ran out to see if he took the UTV, cause the M16 is gone. I left Juliet with you."

The sound of an approaching vehicle stops the stream of profanities from bursting from my mouth. Aurora jolts from my embrace, grasping an overturned table and dragging it to me; the sound is loud as the heavy wood scraps the floor. Before she barricades me from sight, a large van stops in front of the shop, so close the exit and broken windows are blocked.

"Go out the back!" I demand, unable to move further.

Her fierce eyes meet mine for a second before she moves to stand before me. If we die now in a hail of gunfire, at least it will be with her glorious ass as the last thing I see.

"Sorry that took so long," my father's voice announces before cutting off with a groan. Aurora's fist clocks him, sending him falling back into the now-open van. Juliet rises to her feet, teeth bared as she steps over me, backing up my furious wife.

I raise an eyebrow, staring at the back of the van filled with pillows, blankets, and a box of food. "Aurora, stop. Juliet, heel," I say before either of them can tear him apart.

"You left," I say, shaking my head.

"I figured Aurora wouldn't want to leave your side or let me go off alone, so I didn't ask. I figured I would be back by dawn, but I got hung up on the ginger," he explains, holding up a sealed package in his hand.

Aurora's jaw clenches, and I can tell she's torn between how mad she is and also the relief she feels knowing that everyone is okay.

"If you're going to be her father-in-law, you will have to be less afraid and more communicative," I say, ignoring her dark look over at me. "Can either of you help me so we can get going? I am sure all this ruckus will call the dead."

They both move toward me, and Juliet backs away. Their hands reach down to haul my ass up off the floor. I stifle a groan, trying to put pressure on my good side.

CHAPTER TWENTY FOUR

"You should only make that noise when I am..." Aurora stops, and I look down at her pink cheeks, her eyes locked on my father.

He is listening intently, his face swelling from the impact of her fist.

"When I get better, you can show me what your wonderful brain is thinking," I assure her. Smiling before a hiss of pain escapes my lips, she leads me to take a seat. "Senior, just a heads up, my wife is obsessed with me, and I with her. We are used to being alone, so sometimes, we forget social norms. Also, this is Juliet." I shrug after they shut the door, and we settle in. Juliet sits on the opposite captain's chair, her tail thumping like she has not a care in the world.

Aurora giggles, and my father tries to smile but reaches for his face. "I've never decked a Karter, you have a sturdy skull," she praises, reaching back to pet Juliet and sending me a wink.

"Thanks, you hit like a wrecking ball. Don't worry about embarrassing the old man. It's good to see young love again, plus you remind me of Sterling's mother. She, too, was a spitfire, but thank God she didn't hit as hard as you. Who taught you to throw a punch like that?"

Aurora doesn't respond but drives us out of the tiny strip mall.

"She was trained in her uncle's boxing studio since she was in 3rd grade, then when she joined the Marines, I am sure she got some practice in. After that, she was in black ops where she honed her skills. I am just glad she doesn't hate you, or you wouldn't have been standing. Once I saw her uppercut an abomination into the next century."

I can see her eyes roll from the rearview mirror, and I grin. "It's not even her best quality."

"Well, she shoots like it's breathing to her," my father acknowledges, shifting uneasily.

"Oh yeah, she's great at that too, but definitely, there are other things she excels at."

"I have a photographic memory; that's what he is talking about," she interrupts, shaking her head and sending me a look in the mirror.

"Nope, not that either. Think deeper."

Her face flushes, and she laughs, snorting and covering her face with one hand while keeping the other on the steering wheel. "There it is, the cutest laugh in the world."

"How long have you been married?" my father asks, turning in his seat so he can see both of us.

My eyes meet Aurora's in the mirror again, and I smile. "I proposed on July 3rd," I say. I lay back on a pillow, thinking back to the stunning dress she had worn to the rehearsal dinner and the epic lovemaking of our last night before the world fell. My arousal is uncomfortable, and I have to force myself away from my current train of thought.

"How long were you and my mother married?" I ask, eyes darting up to my father before focusing on my hands.

"We still are married; just because she's gone doesn't end that," Senior sighs, leaning against his seat and staring up at the van ceiling.

"It just ended your responsibilities to father me?"

His jaw tightens, and his fists clench, his face filling with anger.

Aurora's hand claps on his neck. "Breath, Senior, and be very careful how much you want to throw at him when he has the right to not speak to you at all."

Senior's anger focuses now on Aurora for a moment before his brow relaxes and his hands release the tension. "I am still your father, even if I screwed up in the past. We are still blood."

"Blood is good at clotting problems, but it's also what can drain us of life when we lose too much," Aurora says, breaking the staring contest between us.

"You lost your mother as well?" Senior asks, rubbing at his neck.

"I did. My mother committed suicide with pills when I was little while I was home alone with her. How did Sterling's mom die?" she asks, her eyes moving back to the road and accelerating around a semi-truck.

Swallowing back emotions, I listen intently, waiting to find out what had really happened, my fingers caressing Juliet's soft white hair.

"An undiagnosed aneurysm. You see, Scarlet was working for a catering company trying to work her way to owning her own business. At the time, I was between jobs due to major layoffs so she started taking extra shifts so that we could keep saving for our endeavors and feed our family. One night she took a great paying gig in the Southside. We argued about it, but she won like always, she was so passionate about reaching her goals. After the event, she was driving the catering truck back toward the shop when she was carjacked. Scarlet was not one to just obey, so of course, she fought back.

"The call from the hospital the next morning was to come to collect her, so I dropped Sterling at school and went to get her. I hadn't slept, and when I got to the hospital, I could tell she, too, had a very long night. I wanted so badly to find the hoodlums and take them out. But of course, violence wasn't the answer, and instead, I brought her back home, and she stayed home healing. While I tried harder than ever to get back into any worksite, to take any job. Eventually, I contacted her father and asked for a loan, but he still hadn't forgiven us for getting pregnant before we were married.

"Scarlet was very mad and still in pain with constant headaches; she kept striking out. Eventually, I snapped and pushed her back. I will regret that push for eternity. She made me a much better person than the young man I was becoming before I met her. I took a walk to cool down, and when I came home, Sterling was tucked into bed, and my wife was sprawled across our bed. She was just gone... The autopsy said the cause of death was some kind of aneurysm, and they concluded it was probably because of the severe beating she took when she was attacked," Senior explains, his chest heaving as he fights back sobs.

I stare up at the ceiling of the van, my stomach rumbling, my heart hammering in my chest. He hadn't caused her death. That to me was what mattered in this story.

"Then why did you drop me at the state?" I ask, smacking the door angrily.

"What state? I brought you to your grandfather, I was a mess. Your mother was everything to me, and I did everything I could to keep myself from dying along with her. Your grandfather had money and resources, and, above all, you were his blood, so I knew he would look after you. It surprised me when you didn't withdraw your college money at 18, but at that point, your grandfather had lawyers keeping me away from him," Senior explains. "I never meant for him to keep you, I just needed to be mentally secure for you. But he never let me take you back."

"I don't know my grandfather, I was raised in foster care. Mostly lived on the streets after I was 14 until I almost got pinched for grand theft auto, and I enlisted in the Air Force, where I met my future brother-in-law and the best friend I could ever have hoped for."

His eyes bore into mine now, his mouth slightly open as he stares at me in shock.

"I am adding someone to my list, Sterling," Aurora interjects, her hands tightening on the steering wheel.

"We should eat something, I think we all need substance," I redirect, trying to change the subject back to ultimately the only thing that needs to matter at this moment, and that's our survival.

CHAPTER TWENTY FIVE
RORY
"I AM AN OUTSIDER" BY THREE DAYS GRACE

I SNACK on the small provisions we have allotted for this morning, keeping my eyes peeled for places we can raid. With a few extra magazines and someone to protect Sterling until he is better, my eyes swing down to the gas gauge, then over at the cars on the overpass jammed together, unable to bypass a military barricade. I pull us to a stop under the overpass, a small smile curling my lips at the memory of the last underpass we had been under. With a glance at Senior and Sterling's sleeping forms, I cut the engine and wait to see if anything creeps up around us, my eyes focused on the mirrors.

A grunt from the back catches my full attention, my head snapping back to look upon the men again, relief skirting through me as I find sparkling green eyes staring at me, pain clear but also no signs of darkness. Juliet's tail thumps him in the face, and she whines to be let out.

His brow furrows, swiping at her tail while trying to see my face, but I glance away, catching movement near the window. My fingers grasp my Gerber, and my foot connects with the door, popping it open and sending the abomination flailing backward. I charge forward, dispatching the abomination before rounding on another. My boot connects with its face with a crunching sound that causes gurgling instead of a rattling groan. Juliet latches onto its arm to take it down. The van door shoots open, my Gerber lodging in the next skull before rounding toward Senior. His stance reads fight, but his eyes scream hide before he blinks rapidly, looking around wearily.

My arm jerks, sending the Gerber flying at an abomination closing in unseen to his right. "You need to secure yourself before others," I lecture, then retrieve my knife from the dead carcass at his feet. "Don't be a hero!"

Sterling rolls his eyes at me from his propped-up position in the van.

"You're family. I can not let my son go through a loss like I did."

"Your son has a God he prays to. Don't take on the shadow of someone you can't contain."

Senior turns to Sterling, exasperated. "Is she always so cryptic?"

"My wife is a Marine and a retired agent of the US. She's also more intelligent than I could ever understand. That's why I stand beside her. I had to learn to trust and understand that she is stronger, faster, and more precious than myself," Sterling says, looking over at me fondly.

"But ultimately, his faith is that God will help us overcome," I interject, ignoring his sweet face and focusing on the withered scowl of his father before looking back at him.

Sterling's eyes meet mine, and he puts his hand out for me.

"If your God hadn't intervened, you would be dead. My plans to get you back were failing. Ask your father; it was this black hole of darkness," I say, moving into the back seat next to him.

He touches my face gently, the corner of his mouth hitching with a crooked smile. "He is not just my God, you prayed to him, and he heard you. Thank you for your faith in me, that you could reacquire your faith in God."

"But, I can't have faith, not after all the bad things in life. I was always so good, and he still took away everything."

"Have you ever considered that all your trials and heartache could be, in part, a way for you to be here now, surviving in a world overrun by the dead?"

"Even if I wanted to find forgiveness, it's too late. I have taken human life, and while I know it was usually to survive, killing is still the worst sin you can commit. He will never forgive me."

"You're wrong, God sees everything. Just because you tried to pretend he didn't exist doesn't mean he didn't do everything he could to bring you back to him."

"Sterling, I love that you think that..."

"Don't turn your back on this, just sit here and bask in the miracle for just a moment. One of God's children has returned to him, and he, in turn, helped you save me. He even brought my father to aid you in the mission, a man I haven't seen in 20 years. You can't blame that on coincidence."

"Maybe you're right. It's scary to think about the idea of someone controlling me, though, even if that someone is God."

"But it feels right, doesn't it? To know your choice was the right one with no regrets?"

"Yes, to be honest, I don't know just yet if it's you I believe so hard in or him."

"That makes sense, join me tonight as I pray just this once, and I won't push again."

"Of course, but until then, I need to get out and scavenge for gas, then we need to find a place to park for the night."

"I can go get gas, we can find a hose around here and siphon some tanks," Senior offers, looking around.

"Screwdriver?" I ask Sterling, getting up.

"It's at the bottom of my bag. They didn't consider it important. Go with him and teach him the right way so he doesn't end up killing himself with gas consumption."

"He can stay here and have your back, I will move faster alone."

"Why don't I just go alone?" Senior asks, scratching his head.

"No!" we both respond.

Senior looks slightly amused, but his body language is showing me his underlying annoyance.

"You shouldn't be alone," I tell Sterling, ruffling his bead.

"Neither should you, and he needs training. If he is planning to continue with us, I will sleep. It will be fine, just leave me the keys," he argues, his jaw set and eyes yelling at me to argue with him.

"You're stubborn," I growl, fetching the keys from the ignition and handing them over.

"Wait till this hip heals, and I will show you stubbornness," he challenges playfully, watching me lock the doors before pocketing the screwdriver. "I love you," he says with a smile.

"I love you too. If someone comes, I want you to hide the best you can, and if the doors or windows are breached, then aim for the back of the neck or the brain. Remember my ears in the stairwell, gun acoustics in vehicles suck."

"Yes, ma'am."

"Juliet, stay!" She chuffs at me and squats next to a dead abomination to pee.

Senior closes the door, then looks at me expectantly. "You both know I don't drink the fuel, correct? I've known how to siphon a gas tank since before either of you was born."

"Okay, so you know you can acquire a cough, shortness of breath, chemical pneumonia, chemical burns, or unconsciousness up to the very valid risk of asphyxiation? Also, you can tell the difference between the years of the vehicles so that you know which ones have the new rollover valves and which don't?" I question, leading him up the incline toward the packed road above us. "Do you have a weapon?"

He holds up his gun, and I scowl.

"This is a loaner," I inform, handing over my extra knife from my belt before hopping off the guardrail and darting to the nearest car, popping the trunk with a light-clicking sound. The car's interior is free of blood, which is a feat of its own. Unfortunately, the car is nearly OCD clean, with no half-full water bottles or lighters to be found in here. Popping open the glove box causes me to pause. Beneath the registration and insurance papers is a smaller compartment.

Senior opens the passenger door, looking at what I am examining. "I will pop that open so you can start with the gas on this vehicle."

I shrug, checking the back seat before sliding out and moving to the trunk, which is oddly void of items, not even jumper cables. Finding the flap, I pull it back to search for a tire iron. Frowning at the small mickey mouse tire, I reach down to its odd angle and pull away the cut remains of a tire, finding small tight packages secured with black duct tape.

"Drugs?" Senior asks, saddling up next to me.

The trunk clicks, and I turn to him, holding it closed even though I know it's latched. "What was in the glove box?"

He holds up a satellite phone and a small 9mm hellcat. "Are we taking any of that with us? I bet we could trade it for whatever we need?" Senior asks, releasing the phone and gun to me with his eyes on the trunk.

"If you value your opportunity to get to know your son, you pretend you never saw what was in the trunk and help me find something to put the gas in," I threaten before checking the gun to find it fully loaded with one in the chamber. I flick on the safety and tuck it in the back of my pants before holding the power button on the phone. I have no one to call, but my curiosity about the satellites still working outweigh the absurdity. So I click contacts, pausing when I find only one saved number labeled with the Number One. I click the call button to auto-dial the number.

I am rewarded by the sound of ringing, then a deep voice answers. "Go for Lucas."

Clicking the power button, I shove the sat phone in my bag and move to the next car. I quickly dispatch a woman trapped inside the back seat and pop the trunk. Anything inside the car is a waste, as the entire vehicle's interior is coated in blood and gore. In the trunk, a large duffle full of clothes sits next to a stack of photo albums. Rifling through the duffle, I pull out several shirts that Sterling or I can wear. They would float on me and be tight on him, but a clean shirt is a clean shirt at this point. The pants are a complete loss, but I keep all the socks and remove the bras and panties, leaving them behind and pulling the bag free of the trunk.

"Aurora, will these work for gasoline?" Senior asks.

I scowl at how loud he just asked, and look toward him to find him standing on the side of an overturned truck holding a five-gallon jug. Beaming, I race forward, dropping the duffle and springing up to clamber up, ignoring his waiting hand.

"Help me with the other door," he says.

We yank at the dented door, and it wiggles, but the angle is strange.

"Let me try something," I request. Dropping, I grab the support of the metal shelves, then slide my feet back to the door before lowering my chest down, my ass poking up in the air. Bending one knee, I push with my arms and legs, a scream ripping from my throat before the door slammed open. Senior hauls me up by my belt before I can land on my face. Back on my feet, we stare down at six 5-gallon jugs full of water and two empties just in the first row.

"If we move some of these cars, we can get the van up here. It will make it look less suspicious and save us some time hauling stuff down," Senior says, looking around.

I look out at the road, nodding at his idea before spotting six abominations wandering our way. "Start moving the cars."

"No, we can take them out together," Senior argues, reaching out to grab my arm.

"Remember what Sterling told you about listening to me? Try that. I will call you if I need your help," I deny, staring at him as he pulls his hand back.

"You know that you're not my leader and that your safety is more important than my own. I do not want my son to feel the pain of losing the woman he loves."

I shrug, taking two quick steps back and then lurching forward, soaring off the truck into the back of a pickup truck, my feet sliding slightly, shins hitting the side before my Gerber embeds into an abomination's skull. Stepping to the right with a tug and a thrust, I dispatch the next, releasing a breath before my feet hit the pavement and my muscles urge me on. With a shove, one abomination stumbles back as I dispatch another, then with both hands on the Gerber, slam the blade into the fourth's skull. My foot connects with a metal pipe on the ground, clearly some part of a vehicle. Kicking it up with my boot, I catch it in my now free left hand and slam it into the chest of the fifth abomination, my Gerber puncturing through the rotten eye and then the skull of the sixth.

Senior skids to a stop next to me with my extra knife in his hand.

"Come on, old man, let's move those cars." I walk away, ignoring his look of astonishment.

Moving the cars takes more time than it should, but we have taken our time to be strategic with where we drive or push them so we can have some warning if any abominations are drawing near. The cars surround the overturned water delivery truck, blocking it in and providing resistance for the mindless droning to be diverted around us. We walk down and climb in the van; Sterling's brow raises when he sees our empty hands, but I start the van and put it in drive.

"How did it go?" Sterling asks, looking carefully at each of us expectantly.

"Your wife sure is a force to be reckoned with. Honestly it's intimidating," Senior whispers, leaning over.

I roll my eyes, grasping the wheel as the van lurches up the incline, slowing as we approach and calculating the space and angle before throwing the van into park. After locking Senior's door and the driver's door, I slide over to the passenger seat and then out into the new secure area for the night. Opening Sterling's door, he grimaces at the harsh light of the sun before grinning at me.

"We should find something to hold all this water so we can drink it," Senior suggests, scanning the areas around us.

"You found water?" Sterling asks, his tongue sliding across his dry lower lip.

"Your father did." I parkour off the van up onto the side of the water truck, pulling a five-gallon jug out and smiling over at Sterling. Senior carefully maneuvers himself out of the van before reaching in and offering Sterling help to sit up. While they readjust, I lower the jug onto the hood of a nearby car. I rescue another jug, setting it on the hood before moving back to the open door and wrestling another one out.

"Here, hand that down this way," Senior, offers raising his arms up.

I lower it down to him before moving to rescue the rest from the truck.

CHAPTER TWENTY SIX
STERLING
"OPEN YOUR EYES" BY BEA MILLER

AFTER REQUISITIONING five-gallon bottles of water, which we drink our fill of before cleaning ourselves the best we can, my father and Aurora use the bottles to hold gasoline that they leach from all the cars they can until the van and six of the five-gallon jugs are filled and stored upright in the back where they have pulled the back seats. They then take the remaining water jugs still filled with the precious life-saving resource and stack them on their sides until we run out of space.

Aurora secures the jugs with one center captain's chair and a few thin blankets and ratchet straps she found in the back of a station wagon while pillaging the cars around us for anything she could find that could be useful. She has even acquired a storage bag for the top of the van and some painkillers to help ease the pain in my hip. Part of me wishes we can stay in this haven of safety for a few days, but within 24 hours, we are back on the road toward my old house in San Antonio.

Aurora's tense and worried attitude is only cushioned when we spend time together in the evenings trying to stay warm while I pray for our safety and health. While praying is not new to me, it has been a minute, especially since it was a ritual with Davin and Quin in the various condos back in Chattanooga. Now, with Aurora's warm hand clutching mine, it is becoming something I look forward to every day.

On our fifth day on the road, we have to adjust our load, the gas and water dwindle, but we are unwilling to leave behind the jugs; knowing that they can be refilled gives us hope.

"Sterling, do you know a way around New Braunfels? The map is water damaged halfway through the city," Aurora explains, squinting at the colorful smudges of the water-soiled map.

I reach up for the handle and force my body to sit up, pain lances through me, but I look instead at the map. "I know the main freeways, but not the back roads. The land is pretty flat. We will have to cross over at least two bridges because of the Guadalupe River and the Comal River."

"Are you worried about the bridges because of the one in Tennessee?"

"I can't believe you're not worried about that. I am also concerned about the overpasses and ambushes."

The van slows, and Aurora pulls the map her way, then smiles. "Cushion up, Sterling," she warns.

My father turns to see if he can assist, but I ignore his curious look and pad myself the best I can. "All set," I say when I am finished.

Aurora's finger traces across the dashboard, and I smile, waiting for her to process the math she's doing. Senior looks at her quizzically, then back at me with concern. I shake my head at him to keep him quiet.

"Slow and steady," she sighs, cranking the wheel and pressing gently on the gas as she moves us on the railroad tracks leaving the 2439. I look to the right, catching the sign for the 1102, then tug the map back toward me, letting my finger follow the tracks south. They weave through the town, staying away from the most populated areas. Surely parts of it will give us more cover than the road will. The van bumps slowly down the track, and I catch Aurora's eyes on me, judging by my discomfort.

"I will be okay, just drive." My words are even and direct, but a lie. I know rations are low and pain is bound to happen. With this knowledge, I accept medication from my father without a word as we bump along. Settling in to watch Juliet, who can sleep through anything as long as the vehicle is moving.

We eventually stop on the tracks under an overpass, Aurora looks exhausted, and hunger is eating at all of us. We all ate our rations with no gusto, the stale crackers and too-sweet granola bars grading on our taste buds after two days of nothing different.

"I am going to scope out the houses nearby. Need anything other than food and sanity?" my father asks, pulling the strap of a duffle bag over his head.

"Tampons, candles, blankets, pocket heaters, hand sanitizer, soap, shaving supplies, pain meds, and first aid kits. Top our list."

I look up at her, frowning at how short the list is, knowing that she has a million other things she wants to add and wondering if she's holding back to not overwhelm him or just because she's ready to pass out and sleep for a week.

"You got it. How about you, son?"

My gaze stays on Aurora, and worry tugs at me before I glance at my father, who is waiting patiently for my response. "Blue cheese."

Aurora chuckles, scrunching her nose in disgust, her tongue popping out of her mouth at me as she shakes her head.

"That's gonna be a ridiculously nasty treat for your wife."

"I only needed her to smile, Dad. I am good. Be careful out there, and take Juliet with you."

He smiles and exits the van, pole in hand, watching the dog he is gradually learning to trust clear the door before locking it behind him.

"You okay, baby?"

She nods, her eyes fluttering open before she yawns. "I could use like three cheeseburgers, 24 hours of sleep, and like seven orgasms."

My laugh makes me wince, and I'm thankful her eyes are closed so she doesn't see it. Her head tilts back as she slips right into unconsciousness. I silently tug the map from where it's stored between the seats, opening it slowly, the crinkling of the paper cacophonous in the silent van. I lean forward, gritting my teeth against the pain, my fingers brushing the top of a pen on the floor. Suppressing a grunt, I snatch the pen up and fall back breathlessly against my seat, glancing at Aurora's sleeping form.

I look down at the map, noting where my father's sloppy circle marks our location. I turn the map, squinting at the town I have only visited a handful of times, but only ever from the highway and never for a long period. If it hadn't been for the water park, Schlitterbahn, I don't think I would have a single time ever come out this way. I'd been twice, once with Davin, and another time with Victoria's twit friends. I mark the park on the map and then trace my way toward the freeway, marking what places I know we may find along the way.

I stare at the few locations, trying to be brilliant like my wife and find a place where we could scavenge for food before reaching my old place. Eventually, a headache blooms, and with a sigh, I set the map aside, drinking deeply from my water bottle. I let my mind's focus shift and pray. It's something I am doing with Aurora, but the panic in my rumbling stomach is a prayer I want to have alone.

God, thank you for helping us to survive this end-of-world chaos. Please help us find sustenance and provide us some insight on safe travel so we can take a break from running from winter and get healed up. God, I know many others are asking for your grace, and I pray for them as well, for their safety, health, and avoidance of our path forward. God, please help us locate food and provide us with a clear path back to my house. Please take these hunger pains away and know that my faith and love are true. It's in your son's name, I pray. Amen.

I keep my head bowed as I let the prayer replay in my mind, trying to memorize the words and let them become absorbed in me so that God will know how much I need this. Sleep must have tugged me under because the next moment, I am jumping at the sound of a rap at the window where my father stands, glancing back over his shoulder.

Aurora wakes, reaching for her gun that hasn't been on her thigh

CHAPTER TWENTY SIX

for a long time now. She unlocks her door and crawls over to the passenger seat.

"Hey, sorry it took so long, but I found quite a bit before it got sketchy."

Aurora looks at her watch and frowns. "Three hours is too long to stay in one place, we need to keep going. What did you find?"

"I found some canned food and some dry goods. As well as some medications to go through. I found some random tampons in various houses and some candles that were part of some shrine. Can you believe how many people have switched to sprays? I got a few clean blankets. Much of the other blankets were soiled with bitter fluid. I found a variety of soaps and some first aid items. Oh, and a pair of walkie-talkies. Who knows what kind of range they will get, but I grabbed them anyway. Juliet found herself a rabbit and a new ball."

"We should eat, we all need our strength, and we will have the energy to find more," I announce, looking at the bag of food.

Aurora's eyes shift to me curiously. "We can't starve."

"We also can't keep running with no fuel for our bodies, well, you two can, but personally, my body needs the fuel to heal." I watch the worry float across her face and feel bad about manipulating the conversation. All I want is to make sure she will have the strength to make it back after her next run.

"I agree with Sterling, we all need the calories to keep up our pace, and he needs to get better as soon as possible. Who knows how long it will be till we have to flee on foot?"

Aurora's eyes flick from my father to me and then over to Juliet, her muzzle coated in dried blood and gnawing on a tennis ball. I catch her gaze, and she sighs. "As long as we eat on the go, we are drawing way too much attention out here."

My father smiles, handing over the large duffle overflowing with supplies. Aurora pulls out the blanket and hands it back to me. I shift painfully, moving the dirtiest of the surrounding ones that Juliet is always next to, and hand it to her, wincing at a bump in the road. She rolls her window halfway down and shoves the blanket out before her window races back up to close.

She focuses on the duffle again and hands me back the medications and first aid items, which I store in the old canvas bag near my feet with the rest of our medical supplies. She passes back the candles next, and I set them in a box on the floor near Juliet's chair with our camping gear. Finally, she pulls out a can opener after tucking the toiletries under her seat.

"Good call on the can opener, Senior," Aurora praises.

"It would be a special kind of torture to bring food back with no way to eat it. There are a few forks in there somewhere as well," he says.

I watch her fish around for the forks before setting the can opener and forks in a cup holder and pulling some cans out of the bag. One large can of tamales, two cans of refried beans, a can of broccoli cheddar soup, three cans of mixed fruits, and one can of enchilada sauce. She leaves the dried goods in the bag, and I figure they need to be cooked.

"So we each get a can of fruit, and we can circle the other cans around until they are empty. I am thinking beans and enchilada sauce bites first, followed by tamales and soup bites next, then we can cleanse the palate with some fruit?" she offers.

Senior gives her a look, but my hunger outweighs any judgment I would have had a few months ago.

"Has to be better than MREs," I agree, smiling.

Aurora chuckles, opening the two cans of beans and plopping forks into them before passing one to me and one to Senior and opening the enchilada sauce. I quickly take a bite before handing Aurora the can back and accepting the sauce, taking a sip before swallowing down the concoction. To my surprise, it is pretty good even without being heated. Aurora watches with amusement before I smile, and she tries it the same way, trying not to spill the enchilada sauce as she sips and passes it to Senior.

CHAPTER TWENTY SIX

We finish the cans like this and then take our time with our fruit. I am not sure if it's the food itself, how long it takes to eat, or just not feeling the hunger pains, but it is one of the best post-apocalyptic meals to date.

CHAPTER TWENTY SEVEN
RORY
"CHAMPION" BY THREE DAYS GRACE

AFTER AN ASSORTED BUT oddly satisfying meal, I pull the map to me to double-check that the railroad tracks will lead up to the midpoint of the map, and from there; hopefully, we have gained a new map. I pause, looking at the writing on the map, then glance back at Sterling, who is staring out the window, his face set in a determined, frozen state.

"You okay, Sterling?"

"Yeah, just focusing on a full belly and the scenery makes the bumps easier to take."

Senior slows the van down, and Sterling sighs, rolling his eyes.

"Did you write on the map?" I ask, staring down at the doodles and messy writing.

"Yeah, when you were napping. I wanted to contribute somehow, I marked just a few places that I've been to with Davin and Quin a few summers ago."

"What is Schlitterbahn, a butcher?" she asks.

Senior and I chuckle. "It's a water park. From what I remember from the GPS, it is like central North New Braunfels. If I am not mistaken, we shouldn't be too far from it at some point."

"That would be a great place to forage."

"Really?" Senior asks.

"Yeah, think about it, they have loads of food at those places, and it was the Fourth of July weekend when things started falling apart. We should find plenty of sugary snacks and processed desserts, but also we could find more water, pop, and chips. We should also be able to gain a bunch of first aid items and flashlights. There might even be a stand with those little brochures that have maps of the area."

Their silence tells me they think it's a bad idea, but I am already formulating a plan. The river on the map is my only hesitation. I couldn't risk another river mistake. I have to figure out what our best choice will be. The map marks an open area near the circle, and I turn back to Sterling, who is opening his mouth with an argument in his eyes.

"What's right here?" I ask, pointing at the map.

"I think it's a golf course, why?" he asks.

"We can plan to meet up at the edge of the map. On the golf course, you guys will be able to spot trouble from a mile away out there, or maybe there will be an overpass or something to take cover under." I empty the duffle as Sterling shakes his head. "Before you argue, I am running on full fuel and lots of sugary fruit, I will be fine, and I can keep one of these walkie-talkies on me. Our fallback location, if there is trouble, can be over next to the bridge over Cormel River. There has to be another overpass over there."

"Why are you talking like you're going in alone?"

"Because unless I find a sweet haul that is safe for the van, then you're staying with your dad. He won't let anything happen to you, and you'll protect him, and Juliet will keep her ears and nose ready as well."

"You're not taking Juliet either?" Sterling gasps at me, surprise overshadowing the anger I know is about to spew from his lips.

"There are so many problems with this plan," Senior interjects.

"Good thing you're not in charge then, and you agree protecting Sterling is a top priority. In the future, if one of us is hurt, he will protect us the same," I argue.

"Aurora, we are a team, you don't get the final call!" Sterling's loud voice causes Senior to look back at him with rage.

"You do not speak to your wife like that!"

"Whoa! Looks like you all need father-son time to talk through this and that there is the Schlitterbahn resort, and the bridge is coming up, so slow the van down. You guys can talk while I get supplies and not waste any more daylight."

Senior slows the van down, and Sterling growls in frustration.

"I love you, and we have a promise I will keep. I'll be back before nightfall. Remember, if the golf course has issues, then go to an underpass near the next bridge. Keep your walkie on, the batteries look good on both."

"I love you too, I am not happy about this," Sterling grumbles, crossing his arms.

"You can spank me later."

Senior flushes, and I point at Juliet. "Stay with Daddy." I wink at Sterling and check our surroundings and my knives before hopping out of the van and racing for the cover of the trees. The branches slap at my face and arms as I move, careful to stay at least ten feet from the river. It doesn't look as dangerous as the one I fell in before, but I still feel panic just looking at it.

I slow my pace as I reach the buildings towering above. I stay in the tree line as I circle around the building, not daring to move closer and expose myself to the possibility of humans and abominations alike. When I reach a metal wrought-iron fence, I put on the speed and clamber up it and pounce from the top, landing in a crouch silently on the other side. Ahead is concrete and a metal barrier that stops people from entering the water to the right. I creep up to the back of a building, peeking around. I spot a few abominations about 150 feet away.

I sprint to the next building, crouching low as I pass a window and moving toward the direction where I can see the tops of the water slides in the distance from the guardrail. I duck into the tree line, moving down the incline carefully, then climb over another gate, dropping on the pavement before diving for cover. My shoe slips on something, and I glance down, snatching up a weathered park map. I frown, turning it in my hands as I study it. I flip it over and nearly groan, there is more than one Schlitterbahn water park, and I will need to find a ride to figure out which one I am at.

With a quick peek over the trash can, concealing me from any prying eyes, the nearest sign reads Gator Bowl. I creep forward, eyeing the direction that should take me to the medical building. My eyes catch on the movement ahead, and my motions halt, eyes scanning the torn posters, wrecked awnings, deflated pool tubes, and flipped-over chairs. Slinking to the right, my steps silent, my Gerber slides from its sheath with a slight whisper of metal. Two quick steps, and with one hand grasping the abominations shirt, my Gerber sinks into its sun-crusted skull.

I catch the body as it drops, lowering it to the ground silently. Then I look it over quickly, frowning at the olive green rag of a shirt torn open at the abdomen where its oozing insides show me a cavity where its guts used to reside. I pat down its pockets, pulling free a pocket knife, which I slip into my pocket before moving to its feet. I glance at the boots and then sigh, untying them and wrenching them free before tucking them into the duffle. Checking my surroundings, I silently advance to the walkway that should lead me into the main part of the west section's resort side entrance.

With a quick sweep around the corner, I map out my next path and then double-check the map. I scan the walkway, which is wide enough to be a road. The large brown gate to the left is padlocked shut from the inside. A tube pickup stand blocks my view straight ahead toward the main gate, but my current focus is on a building to my right. The first aid sign glimmers above a closed door, teasing me as an abomination slugs past aimlessly.

While killing it would only take a moment, the ground littered with trash and dead leaves would cause a commotion I am not ready for. With a quick glance at the ground, I dip back and snag a few rocks from the planter with the dead tree. I look back at the abomination, shifting the rocks in my hand, ready to chuck them. My fingers falter on the uneven synthetic surface of one rock, and I look down at it, realizing the rocks are hand-painted with little fishes on them.

    I smile, then send a rock flying toward the gate, where it connects with the wood with a thud before clattering to the ground. I throw another two, these pinging off the metal support beams of the gate. The abomination moves toward the sound, and I scoop up more rocks, shoving them in my pocket before darting to the first aid building, my steps quick and precise. Dropping to a crouch, I reach for the doorknob, sending a silent prayer that it's unlocked. To my absolute astonishment, the knob twists easily, and I stand up instinctively, reaching up for a bell or chime that may announce my entrance. My hand slides over a small box that looks like a mag strip to announce guests electronically.

    Closing the door behind me, I drop back into a crouch, moving through the small waiting room and toward a counter, pausing at the site of a shoe beyond a bright-colored curtain. I clear behind the counter, my Gerber clutched in my hand as I creep forward. Taking a risk, I stand up; it looks like whoever or whatever the shoe belongs to is sitting or laying on the ground on the other side of the curtain. I reach with my free hand up and slide the rings from the curtain silently across the bar.

    I focus on the direction of the only known threat, stepping forward. One abomination lies on its back, a leg tied off with a tourniquet, pool shorts, and a t-shirt covered in blood. I gently end its suffering, my eyes taking in the story of the blood trail; it screams at me of a scared young man bitten and scared who came in through a back entrance to find aid and died while trying to tend to his wounds. The door is latched and has dried blood smeared across it. The keyboard from the computer dangles off the desk, the monitor's face is dark, and everything else on the desk is untouched.

    Other than what the man needed to survive, he had taken nothing else. I move quickly, drawing the curtains on one window completely shut as I take anything I can that could help us, leaving behind anything saturated in blood. I pull some towels and a life preserver from a bright red duffle before shoving the bag into my own just in case I find enough to fill my bag. Carefully, I move to the window, checking outside for more abominations, spotting three further away to my right. My concentration pulls to the closest building a few hundred feet away. The sign above it reads 'The Wave Gift Shop.' Checking the map, I find out that to get there, I'll need to pass two heated pools, which must be the dark masses on the ground littered with overturned umbrellas and chairs and debris of food wrappers and deflated pool tubes of various sizes and colors.

The stick of an overturned umbrella taps the door next to me as the wind picks up. I snatch it and duck down to stay out of sight. Testing the weight of the umbrella in my hand, I glance toward the abominations milling about to my left. Shifting the umbrella to shield myself from being spotted by the abominations, I stay low to the ground, shuffling toward my next destination, slowly pausing and listening for anything moving closer. Passing the murky pools, I hesitate near a large trash can. The straight shot it looked like I had from back at the first aid building is only an illusion. Ahead of me, sloping sides and stagnant water stretch to my right and left, the only crossing points are footbridges, one closer to the abominations about 50 feet to my left and another about 200 ft away, just visible through a few trees and ripped banners.

My brain calculates the jump to clear it; it isn't impossible but would definitely draw attention to anything nearby. But the bridge would expose me to things I can't see from this vantage point. I check the map, squinting down at the tiny picture. The jump would be easy enough, but throwing the packs over first would be ideal. I pull the lifeguard bag out as quietly as I can, scanning for danger. When I don't see anything alarming, my attention shifts back to what I'm doing as I jam my duffle into the bag, thankful it isn't full. The red bag makes me more visible, but its thick coated canvas material is water resistant, and I can't risk ruining the medical supplies.

If the guest service building wasn't on the other side of the gift shop, I would change my route, but I need a map of the area, so getting across is my only option. I continue forward after a quick check for the locations of the abominations, then move to the edge of the ride, reaching up to unclip the chain barrier, and glance at the planter on the other side. I am tempted to wade across but decide against the idea at the thought of the squelching sound my boots would make on the other side and the thought of the unknown bacteria in the stagnant water.

I grab the sides of the duffle, rising slightly, and heave it across the water and into the planter, dropping back behind the umbrella and listening for the telltale sound of rattling. When nothing nears, I check my surroundings and back away from the water, giving myself an extra five feet of running space in case my weight calculation fails me again. I rise to my full height and then bolt forward, focusing on speed and strength. Then, at the last second, I spring, soaring over the ride's seven-foot girth, my boots snagging on the planter, sending me rolling across the pavement and crashing into pool chairs. I scramble to my feet, snatch my duffle and book it to the gift shop. My luck runs out when I collide with two solid, locked glass doors.

A splash behind me tells me the attention of the abominations has drawn one of them into the water. Dropping the duffle, I spin, pulling my Gerber, checking for threats. More abominations are ambling from further down the walkway where the restaurants and restrooms should be. I look for something to help me open the door and then spot the displaced brick I must have torn free when I collided with the planter. I sprint forward, lifting it into my arms, risking my safety by sheathing my Gerber and running back to the gift shop. Finally, I aim high at a window near a support beam a good five feet off the ground.

With both hands and all the thrust I can muster, the brick soars at the window and, with a resounding sound of breaking glass, enters the store. I pull my knife and sink it into the skull of an approaching abomination before kicking another back and grabbing the duffle, throwing it up into the broken window before dropping and swiping my leg out to take out the abomination behind me. I slam my blade into its head, then with a quick check at the seven abominations making their way toward me, I run at the building, rebounding up the support beam and grasping the window. Broken pieces of glass pinch my hands, cutting into them, but I force the pain away and roll into the store, crashing down into a mountain of stuffed animals and shattered tempered glass.

I freeze, staring around the store, waiting for someone or something to materialize from the shadows. I look up at the broken window where sunshine beats in at the colorful walls and ceiling above me. Then with a glance behind me, I realize the tempered glass is tinted to keep the store cool, and the abominations outside can not see me through the glass doors and windows. I carefully move, checking for injuries and pulling a unicorn from beneath me before finding my footing and climbing out of the stuffy mountain.

I locate my duffle and secure it over my shoulder before looking around. Setting my watch, I give myself five minutes to clear the store and another fifteen to loot it, knowing that I have to get back to Sterling as quickly as possible. The store is empty of any people or abominations. I leave a door marked employees only for last and move a chair in front of it before turning to the store. I collect candy bars and food items first, chugging two bottles of water before snatching up some sunscreen and a first aid kit from behind the counter. Then I move over past the neon clothes sporting the water park's logo to the darker colors, pleased to catch sight of the name brands. I pull five shirts from hangers for each of us, all in various shades of black, gray, and brown. I find some one-sized adult socks that I stuff into my bag before pulling a few packs of hair ties and then smiling at a rack labeled: Did you forget me behind?

I dump toothbrushes, deodorants, disposable razors, toothpaste, and boxes of tampons into the red duffle, making sure my original black one is empty before moving for the door at the back and taking a few bottles of water with me. Water is heavy, so I only keep five with me, knowing that leaving behind the rest of the bottles could ultimately leave us with no water. I have to be able to make it back to the others, and being weighed down with all the water could be detrimental.

I open the door with my Gerber back out in my hand. The hall that greets me is much brighter than the store, telling me that if the sun can get in, then things can see me from outside. I dodge to the nearest window, glancing out to the abandoned water park's murky waters nearby. On the other side, I'm greeted by the wooden fence. I stay toward the side that looks out to an open area and move past the windows, quickly checking to see if I have alerted anything and avoiding an emergency exit.

When I reach the door at the end of the hall, the blood trail on the floor disappears. Glancing at the door, it reads guest services. I pause, pressing my ear to the door listening, then readying myself as I pull it open. The room beyond is dark, with splotches of light throwing off my eyesight. With a click of my watch, I beam it into the room. Blood pools on the floor next to a large counter. I move into the room, my attention drawn to the door and windows, all with shades drawn and the door barricaded by all furniture that must have once been placed around the room. Brochures and maps litter the floor, but nothing moves. I do a quick sweep, concluding that whoever had been in here must have left out the emergency door.

I drop to pick up the brochures, shoving them into the filling red duffle. I would have to check them out later with the guys, hopefully somewhere safe. Next, I move to the shuttle counter and duck behind it with my flashlight, triumphantly pulling an old Texas road atlas from under a box of wristbands. I tuck it gently into the red duffle before zipping it up. A loud thud causes me to freeze, my Gerber gleaming in my watch light as I stare around the room. Another thud directs me to a window, and I move cautiously forward. I pull the shade aside, gasping at an abomination mere inches away, its gnarly sun-roasted face directly in front of mine, a sundress drenched in blood adorning its body.

I release the shade, backing away. The duffle on my back hits the shade on the next window, causing it to snap up to the ceiling, its cord whipping up. I attempt to grab it, but it slides from my grasp, vibrating with a resounding ping as it spins at the top. I back away, my heel catching on to something. I yank my boot free, trying to hide from the sun and abominations on the other side of the glass before me. The shade in front of me slams up as the cord untangles from my boot, causing a chain reaction. The front of guest services fills with sunlight, and I freeze, taking in the sight of thousands of abominations filling the parking lot. They move around tents, luggage, and unmoving bodies. They move like a wall. The sounds from the building I am standing in have drawn their attention, thousands of dead eyes on me. I move slowly back toward the door that will lead me back into the hall.

When the first body collides with the glass and bounces off, I jolt from the room, slamming the door shut and racing for the emergency exit. Bursting out into the sun, the sounds of rattling and groaning fill the air, and I look to my left. The banners on the gates swaying in the breeze show me the horror beyond closing in on the gates. I give up my attempt at stealth and choose to beeline it to the closest food locations before escaping this place, preferably the quiet way I came in, before following the tracks to where the guys would be waiting.

I race past a few abominations and swerve around palm trees and debris before reaching the front of the first restaurant called Gatorgrill. I yank the doors open, and once inside, I lock them behind me and clear the restaurant, which looks mostly untouched. Unlike outside, the elements and abominations haven't ravaged this area, the smell from the kitchens, however, is disturbing. Rotting vegetables and meat mixed with the stale smell of the room cause me to gag slightly before I refocus on my mission and rush back, clearing the area before moving any can goods I can find into the black duffle. I take a cleaver with me, sheathing my Gerber. I find a canister of fuel for tiki torches and put them in plastic to-go bags before putting them in the black duffle. I acquire two more first aid kits and dart out the back door to the BBQ stand right next door.

I follow the same routine, aware that I am more in the open now. Finding water, I take a long drink, then leave it behind to race to the footbridge to check the stores and food places across the way before I can consider going back. I loot the gift shops in under ten minutes each. The noises I am making are reckless, but I am running out of time. I find packaged food and dried pasta in the next restaurant and take as much as I can, allowing myself more water before moving back to the entrance to check my route back the way I came in, about 300 ft to my left beyond a dip-in-dots stand.

But what I find beyond is an onslaught of bodies moving like a wave into the park, falling into the water before being replaced by other bodies pushing forward. Swearing, I run for the back door, checking that nothing is within range before running past a sign that read Polywog Pond and darting toward trees. After jumping a metal handrail, I turn toward the direction of the horde, backing away slowly as I watch for any sign that they spotted me.

I let out a sigh of relief, checking the zippers on the bag. The rattle to my left causes me to fling the butcher knife into the face of an abomination and back away three steps. On the last step, my heel finds no purchase, and the bags pull me backward. I throw my arms back to catch myself on the ground, but my hands hit a hard wet slippery surface, my head smacking hard before I am dragged backward down a waterslide, the water beneath me moving quickly.

CHAPTER TWENTY EIGHT
RORY
"GLADIATOR" BY ZAYDE WOLF

GASPING FOR AIR, panic courses through me until my brain takes over, and I stand up, forcing the duffles with me as the current tries to pull them down the next slide. I shake my head, thankful that the hit wasn't toward the front and that it wasn't a river I had fallen into like a dumbass but a water ride. It makes no sense to me how I didn't hear the water before when it was all I could hear as I was sliding backward down a steep slide that people used to pay good money to ride down in a raft.

I let out a frustrated growl and climb out of the pool, unamused at my soaking-wet entirety. My hand drops to my knife, and I let out a sigh of relief that it's still there, safe and sound in its sheath. I move into the trees, trying to decipher where I am before pausing and looking back at the water. If it's flowing down, then it has to be river powered. Without electricity, there are no other alternatives, so from what I remember, this slide goes nearly to the other side of the park.

I walk alongside it and then catch sight of a footpath the employees must have used to get to their stations. The sound of my boots on the concrete grate at my nerves, and I contemplate removing them so I can gain some stealth but nix the idea when I catch sight of the debris on the path ahead. I choke the sigh that comes from my mouth back with a gasp as I dodge behind a tree, catching movement ahead.

Peering over, the shivers from the cold water transform into fear. Hundreds of abominations fill the kiddy area further ahead. I scurry to my left back toward the slide, backtracking up the hill slightly to stay in the forest's cover. I step into the wading pool to cross the ride. A loud splash next to me sends water splashing up into my face, and an abomination thrashes in the water at my feet. I step on it and plunge my Gerber into its head, a sound further up the slide causing me to look up as another two abominations hit a bump in the slide and collide before racing each other toward me. I force my feet to move as fast as I can, taking loud plopping steps to free myself from the water as quickly as possible. I roll onto the ground beside the pool and then push myself up, stifling a groan. The weight of my water-logged clothing and bags is like dragging a dead horse through sand.

I move away from the ride, praying that the path ahead will give me some hiding spots so I can make it out of this mess and back to the van. The water slides ahead and above me give me an idea of where I am in the park. Heading for the slides, I know that the park's outer wall is just beyond them, and if they do not overrun this part, I may get out and make it around to the golf course.

I reach the tree line, spotting abominations far left at the top of the hill and to my right, quite a bit closer. I dart across the path, my body protesting the resistance of the wet clothes. Dropping low, I move as quickly as I can, lugging the duffles along. They scrape the wood fence, and the responding rattle and groan from the other side tells me that over the fence is no better. I close my eyes and then open them, staring ahead at a tall lighthouse with dry slides that lead steeply into the air.

Dropping the duffles would give me more strength, but we could die without the supplies inside. Fishing out a water bottle, I down it and then focus on the path I know I need to take for any possibility of making it out of here alive.

"Never give up; always keep going until the very end," I whisper, looking at my ring gleaming at me from my left hand. Moving forward, my soul reaches out for Sterling's before blasting from my hiding spot and across an open space toward the ride with a sign that reads 'Hillside'. I shoulder through the abominations in my way, jumping over a handrail and nearly wiping out as the momentum of the bags spins me sideways.

I growl through the discomfort and scream as I leap over another pole, clamping my arms down on the bag before sprinting up the face of the slide, my slick boots causing loud squeaks as they lose purchase. My hands grasp the sides of the slide, and a scream rips from my mouth as I yank myself up, my shoes wedging to the side as I force my way up to a curve in the slide that inclines hard left and then switches back hard right.

When I reach the top, my feet carry me into the women's restroom, and I press the door shut, gasping for air and flashing my watch around the room for danger. Finding none, I move further into the bathroom to the other door, shaking off the lethargy my body is fighting before pulling the door open and spotting the gate. I bolt for it, yanking the duffles off and yeeting them up and over before heaving myself over. My feet land neatly on the other side in a heavily wooded area, the sounds of the thousands of abominations behind me less concerning now. I lean over, gasping for air, my muscles burning.

A branch snaps to my left, and I reach for the duffles, criss-crossing their straps over my head and down my back. An abomination staggers into sight, and I swear, moving toward the direction I should find the golf course. The sound of breaking wood behind me sends my heart back into overdrive, and I rush to get away from the relentless herd pressing in around me. The river greets me at the bottom of the next slope. I stare down, then look left to where it is being directed into round drains under a bridge. My foot catches on a branch as I move toward the bridge, unconcerned about being in the open.

I yank the walkie from my pocket, turning it on, holding my

breath as the lights flash to life. "Sterling, Senior, do you copy?" I ask, not slowing my pace.

Static is the only response I get before changing the station and calling again.

"Sterling, 911, copy!" I growl into the receiver.

The smell of smoke and then the clouds of it wafting at me cause me to hesitate as I cross the bridge. There is no time to hide and question; hundreds of people are scattered across the golf course, the barricade across the road is easily passable, and the men standing guard, calling out with concern.

"RUN! They are coming!" I scream before laying on the speed and sprinting past the first men and down the road. They ignore me as the horde emerges at the other side of the bridge behind me. Bringing the walkie up to my mouth, I stifle a cough, the setting sun not helping visibility in the haze of smoke. The yells behind me tell me that some are fighting and some are dying. I push on, guilt chewing away at me relentlessly to bring me to my knees.

"Sterling, do you copy!" I scream, lungs burning, feet thundering on the road.

Lights ahead darting back and forth warn me of humans ahead with flashlights. I take the path left toward the overpass as pain pulses through my legs.

"Sterling, go! Now drive!" I scream into the walkie, the incline slowing my pace slightly as humans race up the other side. When I reach the corner, the sound of an engine blesses my ears for a moment. I look down and then vault over, landing hard on top of our van, clutching onto the cargo bag.

The van slows, and I scream, "GO!" With a jerk, the van shoots forward as bullets and rocks fly by us. I slam my fist on the roof. "Faster!"

The cargo strap I am clutching snaps. My other hand grasps my knife, slamming it into the top of the van to the hilt, holding on for dear life as the cargo beneath me shifts the bags, trying to choke me and yank me free as they rip at my body. I make a crude knot with the broken strap on the handle of my blade before sliding to the passenger side. The only safe place for me now is inside, so I slam my hand down on the window and wait to feel it open before ripping the duffle free and jamming it through the window. I lower myself down, wrestling the other one in with me.

Ignoring the looks of horror on Senior and Sterling's faces, I stumble to the back, pushing Juliet to the front atop the bags. I yank a blanket with me, sticking my fingers into the holes Juliet has torn into it and shredding the blanket apart, then I shovel items, moving them away from the back doors and dragging one five-gallon jug 3/4 full with gasoline to me.

"Bridge ahead!" Senior announces, panic filling his face.

"Aurora, what happened?" Sterling presses, reaching for me.

I ignore him. "Do not slow down, it's all or nothing. Gun it!" I demand. After shoving the blanket into the hole and down into the gasoline, leaving part slightly dry, I unlatch one door, and it flaps open wildly. My eyes take in the racing humans behind up the thousands of abominations overtaking the golf course before looking back at Sterling, his face pinched with shock, and fear floods his eyes.

"Give me your lighter," I order. "Senior, pedal to the metal now!"

I light the fabric, watching the fire race down before throwing the jug out onto the middle of the bridge. It bounces once, then as it goes to slam down again, it explodes. The giant Molotov cocktail rocks the bridge as I scramble for the door. The van hits the end of the bridge with an enormous thump as we hit a corner of the train tracks, sending us bouncing and swerving before the van bounces hard. My body flies up, and all I see is the ground reaching up to smash my face in. A hand on my belt, and a scream of agony tells me Sterling has caught hold of my certain demise and is attempting to pull me back in. Panic like no other fills me, and I scream for the death of the railroad, for him to stop trying to save me and let me die and for him to be out of the agony I can hear tearing from him. Senior skids to a stop, and I land on my ass in the van, the door slamming shut.

I spin around, my body rejecting the quick movements, but I

ignore the pain as I see Sterling laid out cold on his seat, his breathing ragged and body limp. I check his racing pulse, tears stinging my smoke-blazed eyes, rasping gasps wrenching from my guts as the sobs rake over me. Senior drives again, no words spoken. Eventually, I pass out, the fatigue dragging me into the nightmares where I am trapped not by the water but by his scream of pain which rebounds around my brain, holding me down as my imagination kills Sterling and tortures him in every way possible.

CHAPTER TWENTY NINE
STERLING
"INFECTED" BY STARSET

"WHAT THE HELL are we supposed to do now?" Senior screams, causing my eyes to flutter open. "It's been days, we need to find a doctor!"

"No, we need to follow our original plan. We have to be close to his house by now, and from there, we can take a step back and reevaluate. Consider what he would want," Aurora argues, her hands flying up as she her voice escalates.

"What are we arguing about?" I ask, my mouth feels dry, my stomach roaring at me to be fed. Aurora's beautiful green eyes connect with mine, but I am not greeted by her beaming smile but by a look of shock, her face gaunt and haunted. Her hand reaches for me before she pauses, snapping it back and pushing her way out of the van's passenger side door.

Juliet whines low, her tail thudding as her big brown eyes stare at me. I reach over and pet her, scratching her behind the ear before looking out the tinted windows to find Aurora on her hands and knees about ten feet away.

"Son, how are you feeling?" Senior asks, twisting around in his seat.

I shrug. "Hungry as always, very thirsty, some discomfort. What is she doing, and why isn't she being vigilant?"

"She's been going through a lot of self-deprecation this last day and a half since you passed out. I haven't seen her eat, and she hardly sleeps."

Anger simmers in my gut, and I unfasten my seatbelt and open the door, taking hold of the handle. I grit my teeth, waiting for the grinding pain that has been relentless since my fall, but instead, I am rewarded with dull pain and weak muscles. My legs shake, and I have to press my back to the van to stay upright.

"Aurora, get up!" I demand.

"Thank you for saving him. I do not deserve your mercy, but I will repay it however I can. It's in your son's name I pray, amen," she concludes, before turning her head to look back at me. Her eyes travel up my legs to my face, before she stumbles to her feet. I capture her hand as she nears and yank her to me, ignoring the tremble in my left leg and the pain from my hip. Her lips crash into mine, and I secure her to me with one hand caressing her lower back as the other cradles her face. Her kiss is hesitant at first, then hungry.

Breaking the kiss, I release my hold on her slightly, staring into her eyes. "You made me a promise," I whisper.

"I came back."

"Not that promise, the promise that if something happens to me, you fight like hell to stay alive. Not eating is not keeping that promise." Tears slip down her cheeks, and I wipe them away. "Let me pee, and we can have lunch while you explain to me what you two are fighting about."

"Do you need help?" she asks, glancing down.

"No, I am feeling a lot better; pretty sure we relocated it. We have some great teamwork."

She shakes her head at me, trying to hide the tug of her mouth that threatens to make her very grumpy expression lighten. I turn away from her to relieve myself, knowing that she is keeping a lookout. When I finish, we both get into the van, and Juliet bounds at me before I pull the door shut. I look around, having not noticed her leave, before pulling her in and closing the door.

"Hey, girl, you've been keeping these two out of trouble?"

Her tongue flops to the side as I scratch behind her ear.

"You should eat, son."

I look up at my father to find a large pan of black beans being passed back to me. "Beans?"

"Found them at the water park."

My attention moves back to Aurora before taking a bite. "So, are we going to discuss the water park or what you guys were fighting about?" I ask, ignoring the heated stares coming my way and choosing to eat one bean at a time to curve the ache in my belly at how hungry I am.

"The water park was a nightmare, but I made it back," she assures me, glaring over at Senior.

The tension between my father and Aurora is like a dense fog suffocating the vehicle and, in turn, us from communicating effectively.

"You both know that whatever the problem is, we can settle it quickly. All that needs to happen is that one of you needs to tell me what you're both so angry about."

"We were arguing about you," Aurora sighs, shaking her head and sitting back.

"Me? Did I say something in my sleep that you thought my father shouldn't have heard?" The slight smile they both get pushes me further. "Or Dad, did I say something my wife didn't want to hear?"

This time both of them crack a smile, and Aurora shakes her head.

"We were arguing over where to take you," my father reveals, rubbing at his exhausted face.

"I thought we were going to my old place?"

Aurora raises an eyebrow at Senior but stays silent. This is a quick tell for me; that I am on her side without trying to take sides.

"That was the original plan, but after you passed out and

wouldn't wake up, I started recommending we go to one of the FEMA camps to get help," he explains.

"Hell no to that. Even if something was very wrong, which obviously it is not, the deal is to keep going and keep alive and as safe as can be. Aurora and I have a pact."

"You have a pact that even if the other person is in dire straights, you'll move on without deferment to the plan?" he asks, scowling.

"No, we have a pact to keep ourselves alive and well as long as possible if something happens to either of us. Dad, that means we carry out the plan agreed upon before the other was taken down."

"So that's it. You automatically agree with her without even hearing her side?"

"Usually, I admit, though, I am miffed at her behavior before she came back to the van. I disagree with her actions when she took the water park on all by herself. But honestly, what's done is done, and she brought us food. So mission accomplished. So how far are we from the house?" I ask when neither of them fills the awkward silence and avoid looking at each other.

"From what we can tell, we are not too far, but with you asleep, we were not sure. Here, check out the map," Aurora offers. She opens up an array of maps that have been smorgasbord together out of many sources. I look at her, and she beams with pride.

"Show me where we are now," I request.

She points just north of a thin line that must be the road that runs parallel to the tracks. I look at the map, catching site of a street I know.

"We are about 20 minutes away from my place on a normal day. So maybe an hour or two, depending on delays and trying to stay unnoticed."

"Really?" Senior asks, leaning over to look.

"That is much closer than I thought. Show us where it is," Aurora requests.

I point to the map where the street I live makes an enormous circle that encompasses the condos in a tall, black gated area up on a hill away from the city. I had chosen it because of its proximity to the police station they had assigned me to and the incredible views from the upstairs windows.

"So if we get off the tracks about 3 miles up and take Hamonder over to Trickster Ave, we could go up and maybe cut through the park?" she asks, tracing the route.

"No, there are too many bronze statues to dodge and man-made ponds. But we could skirt behind the police station here and go up Blance. There is a minor road that cuts over to the community gate from there; it's usually used by service vehicles."

"Sounds like a plan," Senior agrees, nodding.

"Let's do it," Aurora agrees with a determined smile.

"If the police station isn't overrun, we might stock up on a few things as well," I suggest.

"If it's that close, maybe we will scope it out now and come back later," she counters, biting her lip as her eyes scour the map.

"Makes sense to me," I agree, looking again at her exhausted features.

The van jolts forward, and we rumble down the tracks. I am surprised by the lack of discomfort, my pain level is about a four, but after this last few days of torture, a four is just amazing. I smile reassuringly at Aurora when she turns back to check on me, then clean up the area of the van I can reach from my seat.

Aurora glances back and pauses. "Too much mess for you to handle?"

"I am sure it won't hurt anyone if I just clean up while you guys navigate and drive."

"Doesn't it hurt to move like that?" she asks, watching me intently.

"No, I have a dull ache, but whatever we did must have made a tremendous difference. I am being honest, Aurora."

Her expression of disbelief causes me to laugh.

"You know, every time you argue with me that you're good, and in the end, you are, and I am just overthinking it? This is one of those times in reverse."

Her eyes roll, then her attention darts out the windshield as the van skids to a stop.

"Your turn," Senior offers.

I frown, looking at the small horde outside the windows. Aurora opens her window and pulls herself up onto the roof, and Dad slides into the passenger seat, yanking the seat belt on and rolling the window back up. Aurora slides in the driver's window after kicking an abomination in the face.

"There are fifteen," she relays, rolling up the window.

"Not bad, Sterling, are you buckled?" Senior asks, glancing back.

"Yes?"

Aurora cranks the wheel to the right, throwing the van into drive and mashing down the gas pedal. The van whips to the right, the back fishtails and shudders in the tight turn.

Putting up a hand, I catch myself before the momentum can send me face-planting into the window. The van screeches to a stop, and I find we are facing the same direction we were initially.

"Did you learn a new abomination slaying trick?" I ask Aurora, with an amused smile.

She grins in the rearview mirror and then drives forward easily, following the path I recommended without checking the map again. We pass the station about twenty minutes later and find that attempts to burn it down have assaulted it but doesn't look overrun. Fear seeps into every pore. What if my house is burned down too? Will we find another place to lie low or will we end up having to continue on as we have been? Before I can overthink the situation, we crest the hill that leads to my complex. The fence is open, and the street is quiet, other than a few abominations milling around.

"Let's secure the gate, and we can deal with whoever's inside on our terms without welcoming others," Senior recommends.

"I agree, they look manual. What do you think, Sterling?" Aurora asks, looking back.

CHAPTER TWENTY NINE

"Sounds good."

She drives us in, and Senior hops out, running back to the gate to pull it shut and drop the can bolts. I twist back to face Aurora, who is surveying the area and looking for abominations closing in or people.

"It's 9618," I direct when Senior is back in the van.

"You have a garage? Is there room to park there?" Aurora asks, looking at the unit.

"It should be empty, the realtor was very adamant about the garage being spotless to help sell the place. There is a key to the garage hidden in the pot of flowers on the front stoop."

Aurora parks the van and takes down an abomination. She exits the vehicle, sprints to the plant, then digs around for a moment before looking back toward the van. I unbelt and open the door ignoring my father's protests. I grab a bat from the small pile of weapons and use it to smash in the skull of an approaching abomination. Before walking around the van, catching a look of shock and worry from Aurora.

"It's not in there?" I ask, looking at the mess of potting soil on the ground and on her hand.

"No, get back in the van."

"Make me," I argue, winking at her before turning to the garage. I approach it, listening intently. My attention is drawn to Aurora as she takes out another abomination and then moves to my side. "If the key is gone, it's possible someone could be here. Maybe the realtor?" I reach down and twist the garage handle, and it moves easily. Hesitating, I glance at Aurora, who trades her knife for a handgun. Senior steps up next to her with a shotgun, and I pull the door up, taking a big step back, holding up the bat, ready to swing. The garage is dark, a silver Mercedes Benz crossover gleams from within, and an abomination thrashes inside the car with blonde extensions barely holding onto its head.

"Victoria..."

CHAPTER THIRTY
RORY
"DISCONNECTED" BY VERIDIA

HER NAME HISSES from his lips in utter shock. Pushing aside all the ill will I have for what is left behind by the woman who not only tried to steal Sterling away from me but also treated him so horribly while they were together, I move to the vehicle after clearing the rest of the garage. The doors to the SUV don't budge, causing the handle to refuse to help me gain entry to the car.

"Do you guys know this woman?" Senior asks, joining us in the garage.

Sterling doesn't respond, he stares at her as he'd looked at Dean, but I know this is different. Dean was a new friend to him, not a person who had been nearly consistent in his life for years.

"We need to release her soul so she can be at peace. Then we can move her car. We should probably let the air clear for a few more minutes in case the CO_2 levels in here are high. By the look of it, she had the car on and hadn't gotten out yet. She must have been hurt before she got here... Unless she used the carbon dioxide to induce..." My eyes shoot to Sterling, then past him at an abomination moving within range.

Senior looks toward where my attention focuses and moves past Sterling to deal with it.

CHAPTER THIRTY

"I am sorry, Sterling," I say, setting my hand on his shoulder.

"Is there any way to find out if she chose this?"

"If we can get the car open, we could pop the trunk or check her phone. Many vehicles on my trek had signs of the choices their owners made, showing they were trying to survive, or run, or something."

"The back passenger door never locks properly, it might still be unlatched if she was in a hurry," he admits, his hands trembling slightly.

I move around the car, sliding between the car and the wall. This handle gives immediately, and the door pops open. The putrid smell within the car streams unseen as the fresh air pushes through the car's open door. From this angle, I can see that the car was left off, but the keys are in the ignition, which means we can easily move it from the garage. Instead, I stay to the far side and hit the unlock button. The vehicle stays silent, and I sigh, squeeze into the back seat, and pull the handle on the opposite door. Climbing back out to get a fresh breath of air, I glance at the empty back seat in wonder.

"Would you be okay if I take out the abomination, Sterling?"

"Yes."

I am much more gentle than I probably should be, but take no risk of being bitten. My blade pierces her crusted skull and ends its movement. "Rest easy; he is safe," I whisper before sliding out of the back seat and taking in the locked jaw and piercing gaze of my husband. I move forward and hug him. "She's in a better place now."

His body heaves against mine as a sob jerks through his body.

Leaning back, I look up into his face. "Nothing is wrong about being sad right now," I assure him.

His eyes dart down to mine, then back at Victoria's lifeless shell, then back at me; a look of fear fills them. "You're not upset?"

"No, you had a history with her. It would be weird if you didn't care."

His arms tighten around me, and I feel his tears falling onto my head.

"Hey, guys, we should get the van in and hunker down for the night," Senior suggests.

"Sterling, why don't you go sit on the steps to the garage door while Senior and I strip the vehicle and move the car. We can take care of her body once we have rested."

"No, I want to help."

"Okay, Senior, are you good at the door?"

"Yeah, for a while longer," he agrees, turning to look out at the neighborhood.

"I will move her body out onto the side of the townhouse, and then we can move the car out after it's clear," Sterling says. He moves forward, opens the driver's side door, lifts the corpse out, and walks out of the garage with her.

I move to the driver's seat, popping the trunk and opening the center console and glove box. I reach into a pile of receipts and pull them out, flipping through them quickly, looking at the dates and times: July 3rd, 10:34 PM, July 4th, 02:45 AM, July 4th, 05:12 AM, July 4th, 8:01 AM, July 4th, 10:57 AM, July 4th, 2:14 PM, July 4th, 5:39 PM, July 4th, 9:11 PM. Each receipt varies with the amount of gas but always has some sort of caffeine and snacks. She must have left the party and driven straight through. By the time she got here, she would have been exhausted, but beyond that, she could have met several carriers in that time period, especially if she went inside to pay every time versus paying at the pump and moving along.

I put the receipts back, pushing through the trash, where I find her purse, which I pull free to sort through later. I find pepper spray in her glove box, along with a bunch of makeup. Sliding out of the car, I see Sterling walking back into the garage, but I move to the trunk. The trunk has gas station snacks and two rolling suitcases. Sterling pulls everything out, and we throw the car into neutral, pushing it from the garage and out of the way. Senior pulls the van into the garage, leaving us minimal space to move, but we pull the garage door shut using a tube of lipstick to bolt the track from allowing the door to rise.

CHAPTER THIRTY

After kicking in the door, we take on the townhouse quickly, noting that nothing inside is disturbed. The staging furniture looks dusty and creepy in the low light but untouched. We decide to take the master bedroom to set up our supplies and bed areas. Then we create a rotation for night watch, leaving one of us at the window facing the street and the other two resting near a window that looks down at the tall fence and grass that runs behind the properties.

In the suitcases, we mostly find clothes and beauty products. In the front pocket of her purse, I find a picture of Sterling, dressed in a white suit and holding a glass of wine, standing next to another man that I pay no attention to. Sterling looks a few years younger, he is smiling and gorgeous, but his hand is clenched by his side.

"That was my birthday a few years ago, and that's Jake with me, the guy Victoria cheated on me with," Sterling informs.

"Why is your hand clenched like that?"

"I didn't want a party; not really my thing. I wasn't used to having so much going on, and I was still having some severe problems with PTSD."

"I bet the vibration from those speakers didn't help ease any of that, especially when the bass dropped," I sigh, admiring the picture of him dressed up.

I feel him staring at me, but I stare at his handsome face, wishing his smile was meeting his eyes like when I met him. We find Victoria's phone, which, surprisingly, still has a charge. She must have had it plugged in when she got here and not plugged it back in when she waited for morning in her car with the music playing to help her not focus on how scary her trip had been, mixed with the uncertainty of being locked out of the main house.

"Why did she come here instead of going to her place?" Sterling sighs, running his hand thru his hair.

"Where does she live?"

"About 45 minutes south."

"Well, by the time she got here, she was probably exhausted. She drove straight through, and when she met the locked door to the house, she probably figured she would sleep here and leave in the morning. She probably wasn't feeling well by then either, and I am guessing she was too weak or ran out of gas trying to cool off in the night."

"What told you all of this? And if she doesn't have the key, then who does?"

"She had receipts from her gas stops. She took the 40 here, it's a good twenty-hour drive through the heart of the country. I don't understand the extra food in the trunk. If she was well when she got here, I'm certain she would have eaten it, but why put it back there?"

"She would always buy double snacks when driving long distances so that if she broke down, she would always have food with her until help arrived. It was something her dad taught her after her older brother suffered from malnourishment as a child on a road trip to visit her and her mother in California."

"Her being sick explains why there is no water left. When you get the virus, you feel like water is the only thing that can ease the pain."

"How do you know that?" Senior asks, glancing over from his perch at the window.

"Because when I had it, I went through at least a case of water, and mine escalated over hours. Instead, this seems like a 24-hour change after a bite, but now that everyone turns when they die, it makes it harder to calculate," I explain, with a sigh.

"But you survived, so there is hope."

"I guess so." I shrug, then lie back to get rest; this next week is going to be rough. The plan is simple enough: wait until someone finds us or until our downtime has given us time to recuperate. It's risky to eat all our food but being strong enough to take on each home in the gated community would pay off if we planned it out.

CHAPTER THIRTY

We have enough supplies to make it into Mexico and as far south as possibly Xalapa, Mexico, edging us closer to Sprocket and warmer weather than what is blowing into Texas. Sterling is still not sold on the idea of Sprocket, electing instead to find somewhere safe and full of natural resources. The discussions all end the same way, with everyone agreeing that warmth and movement win over all else. The supplies will deplete before the end of winter, but even if we stay in Texas, we can't be sure of surviving the strange cold seeping through every access point in Sterling's townhouse.

Leaving the area provides further challenges, avoiding the city and making our way toward the 37 reminds me about the places that we will have to avoid. The first leg of our journey should take about 18 hours to a week at most in an ideal world. Juliet whines, rolling on a bag of dog food that we have stored under her seat.

"She doesn't like her food schedule," Sterling says, looking at her with concern.

"Maybe she will start catching things to eat in between." I shrug, reaching back and petting her soft white hair. She has really taken to the condo, jumping across the couches and bounding up the stairs and into the blankets like a puppy. Her sad eyes don't cause me guilt; instead, I throw the blanket from my lap onto the dog in surrender. Juliet's tail beats on the chair, and her playful growls cause Sterling to chuckle.

"So we have been avoiding the conversation about how you think we are going to cross the border into Mexico," Senior reminds us, resting his chin on his hand and waiting for a response.

"Depending on the situation, we can't guess if the gates will be manned or not. Need I remind you this is global?" I ask, annoyed by this persistent question.

"Are you sure?"

I ignore his question, knowing only what Trevor has told me, and while that might not be nearly enough, it is also all I have to go on. Either way, we will soon find out. I think part of me is really hoping he is wrong and that we can negotiate our way into a better situation.

Even if that means offering myself up for testing to the government of Mexico, allowing them to take the win in the cure department, and allowing Sterling and Senior to have a safe, secure location to live.

I let this idea dance around my mind, like an ultimate goal, which when we reach the border shatters like stained glass and assaults my heart. The entire area looks as if it's been bombed. Hauntingly, nothing moves around the burned-out cars and scorched ground within at least a 1000-foot radius.

"Well, looks like someone made us a clear enough path. We can stay left of that VW and move along to that row there that doesn't look like it was operational. Not sure if it's wise to stick around, in case there are radioactive materials from whatever happened here," Senior suggests, fear evident on his face as he stares at the aftermath of what must have been horrendous.

I don't respond, choosing instead to sit and take in the skeletal remains of entire families huddled together behind what used to be their vehicles. Even if supplies had survived this slaughter, they wouldn't be worth the risk of disturbing this massive graveyard.

CHAPTER THIRTY ONE
STERLING
"UNTRAVELED ROAD" BY THOUSAND FOOT KRUTCH

HER FINGERS PRESS against the glass of the window, eyes shimmering with unshed tears. I hear their brief discussion, but her trembling lips tell me that finding the border in this state is nothing she was expecting. She sits back in the chair after a long moment, a single tear traveling slowly down her cheek. If I'm not mistaken, a look of defeat pinches her beautiful face.

"Aurora, what is it?" I ask, reaching around the seat to rub her knee.

Her, eyes focus on me, and I see her expression clear.

With a sigh, I pull the lever and lower the back of the seat so it's reclining down in front of her. I twist onto my stomach, ignoring the difficulty of this maneuver on my hip, and lay on the seat, staring into her hard green eyes. "Don't block me out."

"I am not blocking you out."

"That's not true, and you know it. We have survived this thing together, and the look on your face moments ago is one I have never seen, and I promise that if your face is changing emotions, I see it. So, instead of me pulling it out of you, I'm going to stare at you until you break the silence and spill it."

Her arms cross, and one eyebrow hooks up in amusement.

I rest my hand under my chin and bat my eyelashes at her, flashing her a smile. Juliet licks the side of my face, but I don't budge. Aurora grimaces slightly but continues to watch me.

"You know that this is in no way a type of torture for information?" she asks, her eyes skimming across my body.

"I am aware." My focus doesn't shift.

"So you're going to just sit there and stare at me?"

"I'm not just staring, I am undressing you with my eyes."

A grin breaks her stern look into one of playful flirtation.

"Now that I have expressed my inner thoughts, it's time you share yours with me," I explain, tilting my head.

"Mine are nowhere near as interesting as yours."

"That's not what your face said when you were looking out the window."

"My face betrayed me, you're lucky I know you like it so much," she teases, scrunching her nose slightly.

"I love your face, please tell me why it looked ready to shatter."

"I guess I was holding on to some sort of hope that Trevor was wrong and that Mexico's government was still standing so I could speak with officials and provide them with the opportunity to find a cure, and you both would be safe. Not like giving my freedom over but working with them to solve this problem that I hoped was national, not actually global."

"So you were hoping to save the world by helping create a cure?" I ask, my brow furrowing.

"I guess."

"Maybe we will be able to someday; let's never give up hope on that, but until then, you need to remember all the good you have done and will do to protect the innocent." I take her hand, kissing her knuckles. I ignore the doubt in her eyes, choosing instead to show her the commitment I have to who she truly is.

"How's your hip?" she asks, reaching carefully toward it.

"Honestly, not as much range as before. I think I need to be working out more."

CHAPTER THIRTY ONE

"More like working me out more."

Her steamy comment is interrupted by my father slamming on the brakes. "We might have a situation," he announces, nostrils flaring as fear consumes him.

I pull the latch and get to my knees to turn around, the scene outside the windshield causing my jaw to drop. Part of the bridge has been decimated by some sort of explosion.

"Trade places with me, Senior. Sterling, I am gonna come up there and sit on your lap. If I hurt you, please use your arms to lift me to a more comfortable position," she warns, then scurries up, her ass resting in my lap perfectly.

I groan, holding her to me so she won't move. My response has nothing to do with pain. Her breathing hitches slightly, and she squirms in my arms. I take a moment to nuzzle her neck before she growls and moves to the driver's seat. Her nipples give her away as she takes a deep breath to calm down.

"I don't think it's my face you are focusing on."

A grin spreads across my face, catching her amused glance before her attention returns to the road. The road looks terrifying ahead, damage beyond this first spot is evident further ahead. I am surprised that the bridge is even still standing.

"Buckle up and secure Juliet."

"Seriously?" Senior asks, buckling in, then securing Juliet's sheet harness.

I follow her directions immediately.

"Aurora, do you think this is wise, maybe we can backtrack and go to another crossing?" Senior asks, his hands shaking as he threads the last part of the harness into place.

"The bridge is a little over 48 feet, the damage here is not to the halfway point, which means the chance of stability on the other side, if brief, should be tolerable."

"Tolerable?" Senior and I ask in unison, while he clicks Juliet into a sheet-made dog harness and attaches the buckle to secure the device.

"Just hope that the damage ahead is better than the damage that will be behind us. Isn't that what you just told me, Sterling?"

Before I can answer, the van roars forward as we pass the first hole as far to the right as she can get from it. She jerks the wheel and the van veers to the far left, speeding up as we approach the next break in the road. We blast by it and then feel the brakes shudder beneath us, Aurora's focus dead ahead.

The van creeps forward and her adjustments of the wheel are calculated. I look ahead and then frown, squinting slightly. "Babe, that's not the road," I warn, my ass clenching the seat.

"No, it's the top of a semi-truck trailer that is 8.5 feet across, and this vehicle is about 5 feet wide, so we have two outcomes here: we make it over or we have a more even drop to the bed of the semi and hope we can back out. The rest of the bridge on either side is nothing but rubble below."

My eyes go to the rubble, and my heart hammers in response, catching sight of cars overturned and the drop that really will hurt if this doesn't work.

"Wait, that's a big drop!" Senior yells, reaching for the door and his seatbelt.

"We can survive it with a probability of 47% depending on what's in the truck, hold on either way."

"No! Shit, Aurora don't!" Senior bellows, spit flying from his terrified lips.

She white-knuckles the steering wheel, pressing on the gas slightly and maintaining a speed of 22 miles per hour. With a thud, the front wheels drop 4 inches onto the semi-trailer. Senior gasps behind me, and my fingers hold on to the handle on the door for dear life. The van continues on at a consistent speed until we hit the far side of the 56-foot trailer. The left front tire dips, and Aurora drops the transmission into Low and floors it, pulling us free from the hole as all-wheel drive kicks in, and we jolt painfully up onto the other side of the freeway.

The van comes to a halt a few hundred feet later on the side of

CHAPTER THIRTY ONE

the road. The wheels kiss the dirt as we stop. Senior yanks open the door, throwing himself from the vehicle and vomiting into the brush. Juliet whines in her restraints.

"Well, that went better than statistically possible. Let's check the map and make sure we know where we go from here," Aurora says, looking for the map as she unbuckles.

I hand her the map but don't respond, I'm pretty sure my stomach is back in the broken top of the semi. Aurora jolts next to me, and the blast of her gun brings me back to myself. She has her arm extended behind me, gun pointing out the open door. An abomination drops to Dad's right. Another, without hesitation, lunges at him. I open the van door, getting caught in the seat belt in my haste.

Senior screams, then suddenly Juliet barrels into the abomination, sending it heels over ass through the bush over a slight drop off. I free myself and move to my father. He gives me a thumbs up, covered now in dirt and vomit. I move toward where Juliet has fallen, Aurora appearing at my side as I reach her. Juliet's standing on the abomination's back, growing at its unmoving corpse; its head is cracked open on a slab of concrete that has a fence pole jutting from it that connects to the rest of a fence meant to keep people from entering the field beyond.

"Come, Juliet!" Aurora demands, smacking her leg.

Juliet squats and pees, then she turns and makes her way back to us.

"Sterling, can you drive while I clean up, and we don't attempt vehicle suicide in the meantime?" Senior asks, heaving again.

"You're welcome for the bullet," Aurora responds, climbing into the passenger seat.

"Take your clothes off quickly and get in and dress in there. You know you have to watch your back everywhere. Are you sure you're okay?" I ask, looking him over.

"Other than shitting my pants and being covered in vomit, I am fine."

I stifle a chuckle and move around cautiously to the driver's side to get in, pulling the seat belt into place after locking the door.

"Now that you're trapped again, you need that road head to relax?" Aurora asks with a grin.

"Absofreakinlutely!"

Senior jumps into the back down to his underwear, and Aurora turns back around, her nose scrunching up slightly. The smell that follows him slips into my nose, and I glance at Aurora, who rolls her window down. Juliet makes a hacking sound, and Aurora snorts with laughter.

"Think that idea will have to wait, won't be able to breathe out of my nose," Aurora says, plugging hers dramatically.

I chuckle, waiting for Senior's door to secure before starting the van and putting it into drive.

"We will take this road from the 97 south to the 101 and then to the 108. Our goal today should be Tampalache or further," Aurora explains.

"How long does it take on a normal non-end-of-the-world day?" I ask, scouring the road for danger.

"About 6 ½ hours."

"Sounds like a good plan, is that where we plan to rest?"

"And raid, if possible."

"Let's keep the stunts to a minimum, please," Senior requests, holding his head and leaning back in his seat.

"I said something similar once when she went all parkour and saved some kittens," I laugh, glancing at Aurora as she shakes her head and smiles.

"Tell me about it?" Senior asks, dropping his hands and relaxing a bit.

Aurora explains, and I focus on making our way back to a steady speed and avoiding the broken-down cars that spot the road, determined to make it to Tampalache.

CHAPTER THIRTY TWO
RORY
"SOLDIERS" BY OTHERWISE

OUR STAY in Tampalache is worth the stop, which means we are successful in gathering many more supplies, eating our fill, and hydrating to our heart's content. The town itself is overrun, and we are fortunate enough to find a restaurant on the outskirts. The building is a giant red eye-sore at first but quickly becomes our haven for the evening and come morning while driving through the town we see hundreds of abominations milling around houses. What is the most terrifying is the variety here. Men, and women as always, but also children. This whole time we had only met two abominations that were not older teens or adults.

We moved through the town as quickly as possible. Guilt pulling at my heart to leave these remains in this condition. There are just too many to safely begin dispatching them and releasing their souls so I mentally add the town to my list to come back once we have established safety and are ready to venture out to take back the land.

"Aurora?" Sterling asks.

I blink furiously and look over at his concerned face. "Sorry, I was thinking about the future."

"Good things, I hope. We have been in this van mostly all day, except for bathroom breaks. Now that we have made it to Xalapa, I think we should sleep and then scout tomorrow. Maybe drive closer and check out some bodegas," he recommends, shifting uncomfortably.

With a nod, I glance out at the darkness that presses so completely around the van, realizing that the light I am seeing anything by is a flashlight wedged under a seat, aiming at the back of the van.

"We need curtains for the windows. Some kind of fabric or something. Are we ready to clear the area to use the restroom and make dinner?" I ask, rolling my shoulders.

"We were thinking cold canned food after relief and staying in here when not on duty. A fire might draw survivors, and while we want to help, how can we? Also, we would want to do it on our own terms, right?" Senior asks, squinting at a can in his hand.

"Good point, alright, you guys start with pee breaks, and let's get Juliet squared away. Then we can make a plan over dinner of what we want to do tomorrow," I agree.

I pull out a few cans, making sure our calories will be decent, especially after overindulging last night and this morning without extra space for supplies. I open each can, leave the lids slightly attached, and set them on the dashboard so they won't get knocked over, then when they return, I take my turn walking into the darkness. I don't dare turn my flashlight on, but I do not go far, and Juliet stays close and seems unstressed so I trust I am safe enough to go to the restroom near the back of the van. Once I'm done with my business, I make my way back inside, taking my seat in the front passenger seat, cross-legged, so I can look at Sterling and Senior who glance my way with identical bushy beards.

Senior pours food out for Juliet and then accepts his rations from me with a grunt of thanks. I pass Sterling his share, and he winks at me, and I smile back.

"So Sterling has been quizzing me on what items we need the most, including gas, fresh clothes, batteries, toiletries, ammo, and weapons," Seniors says.

CHAPTER THIRTY TWO

"Sounds good. Of course, we also want to be looking for medical supplies and maybe some road music, that CD you got in there is getting old," I respond, taking a bite of my food to hide my smirk.

"How did we forget medicine?" Senior asks, his shoulders going slack.

Sterling shrugs, unable to speak with his mouthful.

"That's one of the many reasons he keeps me around. Speaking of, I think it will be beneficial for Sterling and me to take some time to explore alone. As well as finding some maps that take us past here. But let's all stay together first." I advise, taking a bite.

Sterling chuckles, and I know he approves of my plan, and Senior frowns slightly. "You know I can keep up with you guys, right?"

Sterling coughs, covering his mouth with one hand and waving with the other. "No, Dad, we are not challenging that, we just need some alone time to unwind a bit."

"Are you talking about sex?"

"He is talking about multiple orgasmic experiences that can last for hours at this rate," I explain, licking my fork but not looking at them.

"I tried to warn you away from asking, that's what the hand wave was about."

"I am surprised that you both can think about sex at a time like this, but also I guess you're newlyweds, so it makes sense."

"Well, I am very attracted to my wife."

I smile at him and don't let him egg me back into the conversation.

"So, do you want me on duty first?" Senior asks, looking between us wearily like he thinks we will jump each other.

"No, I took the longest nap. I will start off, and we will rotate every 4 hours," I offer, stretching.

"Yeah, I'll go next, and Dad, you can have the last one, you're better in the mornings."

"If you guys insist, I am looking forward to eight whole hours in the backseat," Senior says with a smile.

After finishing up our food, I take up my spot on the hood, not wanting to wander since it's so dark, so I just listen. The night animals come alive around me, and I wish I had bug repellent. We have passed the dryness and into this hilly area. I dislike not being able to see far away or the fact that we are parked on a dirt road outside of a big town where you can't see a problem that could be only 200 feet away because of the way the hills roll. I imagine the terrain I witnessed before we stopped for the night before I had gotten lost in my thoughts.

The four hours slink by, and I climb down silently, waking Sterling with a searing kiss that causes him to wake quickly, his hand snaking into the tangled mess I pretend is my hair.

"Good partial morning, come back to cuddle in four hours please," I yawn, gently nudging him to get up.

"Sure, cuddling is on your mind." He chuckles, stretching and taking the weapon I offer him before letting himself out of the van to lean against the front of the it with a bottle of water, fished from the top rack.

Sleep engulfs me almost immediately, and I don't wake again until the smell of baked beans rouses my senses. With an enormous yawn, I stretch, stumbling from the van, smiling at the look on Sterling's face, and accepting the tin cup of disgusting instant coffee that I know would give me a boost for this morning.

"That was adorable," Sterling admits, watching me intently.

"Better than the faces she's making drinking the coffee, that's for sure," Senior laughs, glancing over.

"I am not a coffee person, I'll leave that to the people of the world that worship the beans of life," I joke, tracing my hand across Sterling's shoulders before taking a spot next to him.

"Well, we can't all be perfect, and to be fair, I love excellent coffee. I miss fresh brew station coffee at this point," Sterling sighs wistfully.

"Station? When I was in the military, we called them depots,

CHAPTER THIRTY TWO

mess halls, or just cafes," Senior says, taking a long gulp of his coffee and finishing it off.

"I mean, from my job after leaving the military as a police officer."

Senior's look of judgment can not be masked quickly, even though he tries.

"He makes up for the police that you seem to despise. My brother and Sterling ended their careers as Sheriff and Undersheriff of a small town in the Appalachians where they were forced to leave because of dead walking. They didn't have a choice but to leave their post because I didn't allow them a say."

Sterling frowns slightly at my tone and looks over at Senior. "Are you not a fan of the police?"

"They let me down when they failed your mother. I admit I have been holding onto that anger for a long time."

"Forgiveness is not for them but for you, holding on to all that anger and resentment just makes it harder on you and ultimately keeps you from connecting with others, including God," Sterling explains.

Senior stares at him, and I finish the nasty coffee before taking a serving of beans and looking around the hills surrounding us, thankful that I didn't see this location before dark last night and that we were not easily ambushed in the night. "So Airforce dudes, you know the whole battle concept of higher ground?" I ask, defusing the tense moment between them.

They nod, their focus swinging over at me.

"I am guessing this location gave us privacy and kept us concealed, however, if a group saw us drive up here, we would be fish in a toilet bowl."

"Toilet bowl, isn't the saying barrel?" Sterling asks.

"I suppose, have you ever seen a fish in a barrel? A fish in a toilet would be easy to catch, and if you can't you could flush it out and end it anyway."

"That doesn't sound fun. What kind of location do you think we should move to for tonight, then?" Senior asks, looking around with wide eyes at the hills.

"I want the high ground. I couldn't see jack last night. At least from a high point, it's possible we can see survivors' fires and avoid those sectors on our explorations."

"Wouldn't a big black van be easily spotted atop a hill out here?"

"Maybe, but if we can find a house on a hill to park next to or behind, it wouldn't look as suspicious and would provide us with the security of not being surrounded completely, giving us some brick to have our backs," I say with a slight nod.

"So let's find a new spot to park first, and then we can move on foot and see what we are dealing with," Sterling agrees, polishing off the last of his beans.

"Let's add binoculars to our watch list," Senior suggests.

"That would be helpful," I say with a nod.

When we finish eating, we clean up the best we can to leave no trace, and Sterling takes the wheel with me at his side. Juliet is unamused at being back inside the van but eventually settles. The dirt road that we are on is away from the city. We can see portions as we move closer past homes that look worn and well lived in. As the houses pass, I realize these houses are the norm for the outskirts of this city. The poverty pulls at my heart but the lack of abominations is concerning.

"How about up that way, the construction looks newer and might provide us with some opportunities to see further?" Sterling asks, pointing up to our left.

The homes on the hill are colorful, and their architecture is unique, yet boxy. As we near, I am surprised by the level of security. Not a single home has a walk-up. The fronts are flush with the sidewalk, with walls, or the front of the homes. Some look like large garages, the whole stretch looks untouched, but they also look unlived in. We drive further up and around, looking for an angle toward the city below.

"Hold up," I warn, bringing my hand up to signal them.

CHAPTER THIRTY TWO

The van slows to a stop, and I get out, checking my surroundings before entering an open lot that looks like it was being prepped for a new home to be placed there. Mounds of dirt and gravel cause me to swerve, my focus turning to the city below and beyond. Xalapa is way bigger than I expected on the map. I calculate what I can see, dread filling me. The sound of an explosion sends me scuttling back to the olive green side of the house next to me. Far away, beyond my line of sight because of the rolling hills of the area, smoke billows from an unknown but large detonation.

Sterling's hand touches my shoulder lightly, his eyes search for signs of danger. "Glad I picked this side of the city."

"That is why the dead are not up here, they are moving toward the sound. If that happens more than once, it would easily draw them in that direction, even in a city I estimate was full of about 500,000 people. Which means, someone is trying to direct them away from the core part of the city, which looks like it's that way to the West."

"Why would someone do that?" Senior asks, watching and listening for another blast.

"To gather supplies easier? Take back the city? To mass kill a bunch of them? Your guess is as good as mine."

"That's good for us, right?" Sterling asks, looking around us.

"Pros and Cons, fewer abominations, more humans, and their warped ideas about what's okay at the end of the world."

"Do either of you speak Spanish so we can practice saying we mean no harm, or we are just looking for supplies, we are sorry?" Senior asks.

"No haces daño, solo estamos buscando suministros, lo sentimos." I recite, looking up and around at the walls of the peach house across the lot, which has a balcony off the back that overlooks the city.

"What other languages do you speak?" Senior asks, looking impressed.

"We can talk about that later, what do you guys think of that place?" I ask, pointing it out.

"We can see if there is a way. I would say we could drive the van back and climb up to the balcony, but I am worried we will get stuck," Senior admits, taking in the hilly lot.

"Let's look, be vigilant," Sterling says, breaking ranks and moving forward.

I roll my eyes as they walk back together to the front. My eyes linger on the back wall that must encompass a small backyard. The guys round the front, and I run forward, scaling the wall and then springing up toward the balcony. I pull myself up and over the warm metal bars, my boots landing with a soft thud on the tile. With a quick glance at the patio furniture, a smile tugs at my mouth. I move to the glass sliding door and find it completely secure. Then I glance around and up at the eve of the building before climbing onto the table and jumping up to grab the ledge, muscling myself up on top of the house. I glance over at another wall that sends the house up to another floor. With a quick look around, I run across the flat graveled roof and launch myself up the wall to the top of the structure before moving to the east corner, where from the front, I see the boxy structure drops again.

I move to the edge and drop to the front of the house roof. The gravel crunches below my boots, and I hear Sterling ask Senior if he heard something. Moving quietly forward, I see Senior scanning the street and Sterling messing with the garage door. I survey my options, knowing that dropping into the entranceway below to the right would get me to the front door. However, the open rectangular window, which is most likely meant to ventilate the home, is calling to me. I measure the width of the trim of the house, which looks bulky and square, as well as sturdy with a brown color I am hoping will hold my weight.

I take the risk, knowing that it gives me the need to aim for the wall for less of a fall. I lower myself down gently this time, testing the trim's stability. My entire foot fits on the trim, and I lower myself carefully. Senior looks up, and his jaw drops. Ignoring him, I creep to the corner and jump down to the wall, grasping onto the house so I don't fall. Shuffling off the wall onto a narrower part of a lower trim, I

CHAPTER THIRTY TWO

pass a window and reach an open rectangular window. Grasping the house with one hand, I pull out my knife and cut through the screen on the window, the sound catching Sterling's attention, and I hear him moving and talking to Senior.

"Dammit, Aurora," he swears, his jaw tightening.

Ignoring him, I slip into the window, enter a bathroom, and I lower myself to the floor, looking around. The bathroom is small and clean. A few items grace the counters, urging me to keep my knife out just in case. I move from the bathroom into a bedroom that is sparsely decorated; nothing within it moves. My next move is out into a hall and down wooden stairs, taking in the furniture and art briefly but mostly looking for signs of someone here or an abomination tucked around a corner. When I find nothing, I search for the garage, eventually finding it and propping open the door so I can pull the emergency release and unlatch the door from the inside.

Senior and Sterling stare at me as the door rolls up.

"We agreed on finding a way in, would one of you like to help me get things set up?" I ask.

Sterling's demeanor doesn't change, but Senior walks over to the van whistling for Juliet, who rounds the corner of a house down the street with something in her mouth. I frown, stepping toward her, a loud squawking screech halting me. I raise my knife defensively, and Sterling moves to my side with a bat.

Juliet pads over, her tail wagging like crazy. The squawk causes us to flinch, but now I smile, the wriggling chicken in her grasp doing all it can to get free of her. Sterling kneels and quickly breaks the chicken's neck, ending its suffering. Juliet drops it on the ground and lets out a playful howl before darting away back in the direction she came, causing a flock of chickens to startle from around the corner.

"Dinner and a place to stay? I can't complain about that. What would I do without my two girls?" Sterling sighs, caressing my back.

CHAPTER THIRTY THREE
RORY
"MY DEMONS" BY STARSET

WHILE SENIOR IS EXPLORING the rest of the street the next morning, Sterling and I take the opportunity to move to the innermost part of the house, which happens to be in the downstairs hallway. The door to the closet slams opens in our haste.

Sterling grabs hold of the coat rod and then grins at me. "Sturdy," he sighs, his minty mouth pressing to mine momentarily while he yanks at my clothes. His hands knead my ass as he presses against me and a fever spikes within me. It's as if at that moment, if I don't feel him inside of me, I'll drop dead. The pulse deep within me will cause me to turn inside out and just be a blob in this broken world.

The feel of leather between my teeth is a brief precursor to the ecstasy my body emanates as my feet leave the floor. My back presses against the back of the closet, my feet brace on the door frame. The moment is fleeting overcome by his presence, him pulsing inside of me, hands caressing every part of me he can reach till suddenly, with a wince, he shifts, grabbing the bar above me and standing up tall. From my angle, I take in his slim muscled build, moaning louder through his belt at the sight of sweat trickling down his chest and torso to mingle with of mess of heat and love. He shifts again, this time swearing, and I can tell he is favoring his hip.

CHAPTER THIRTY THREE

I spit the belt out and cry out his name.

His heated gaze sweeps to my face, and his mouth encompasses mine with primal need.

"I need to be on top!" I gasp, trembling to hold back an orgasm.

He pulls out immediately, and I bite my lip to hide my pout.

"Get on the floor, back to the wall."

When he moves, I can see the strain in his movements and vow silently to make this worth it for both of us and ease some of his discomforts. His moan urges on my own, and while I try to be gentle, I feel his responses getting needy. A scream that stings my throat and causes my ears to ring rips out of me, my orgasm turning me into a breaking crystal statue, my body lighting with pleasure and falling away piece by piece.

Sterling follows me over the edge, causing the ecstasy of riding him out to be all that much sweeter.

"Can we stay right here forever?" he asks, his hands pulling me down onto him, dimpling into the skin of my left hip and right butt cheek.

"In a closet attached, mind, body, and soul, covered in a sweet nectar of love?"

"What I would give for that," he sighs, shifting slightly beneath me.

"We better get moving. I am sure after that last scream, your father will be back soon to investigate."

Sterling chuckles. "Someday, we will be able to fill the world with your screams and not worry about rushing, surviving, or questioning when we will get to make love again."

"Someday, baby," I agree, kissing him.

We untangle, cleaning up quickly with some cleanish rags we found in the downstairs bathroom. We pull our clothes back on, and I try not to watch the slight limp in his movements. Part of me wants to ask him what I can do, the other part wants to believe he will get better with time. All of me hesitates to let him go on the run today.

We both fall onto the couch as the front door bursts open, and

Juliet bounds into the living room followed by Senior, who looks winded.

"You okay?" I ask, glancing behind him for danger.

He closes the door, shaking his head as he takes deep breaths and sets down his mostly empty duffle. "I could have sworn I heard you scream."

"You did, but like I said before you left, we would be perfectly safe," Sterling says, swiping at the sweat on his forehead.

Senior looks at each of us and then over at Juliet, who is sniffing around in the hallway. "Okay, I will not ask. I am going to recommend we drive down to park closer to raid. This little neighborhood is just so spread apart from the others. We will need to go through another neighborhood if we go back down, but if we head up the hill a little further, there looks to be a few shops. We can start there, park on the street or next to a building and make quick work of places."

"I can see the pros and cons in this situation, and while I would like to be discreet, I also understand the need for the van to be nearby so we can flee if need be or so we can. Also it might be easier on us physically in some ways, but the closer we get to the places crowded together, we need to leave the van and scavenge without worrying about leading people back to it while we are busy."

"I agree with both of you," Sterling says, giving me a strange look that I ignore.

Senior moves to grab our bags, and Sterling looks at me again, this time with concern.

"Are you hurting?" he asks, reaching for me.

"No, but you are not 100 percent still, and I am worried you'll get worn out. Or that you'll overdo it," I admit, pulling away.

His brow drops as he frowns at me, and I can tell I hurt his feelings or that he is not happy with what I said. "Are you trying to put me in a protection zone?" Sterling asks.

"Are you questioning my intelligence by pretending you're not hurting as bad as you are?"

His beard twitches, the muscles in his neck rippling.

"No response because you don't want to lie to me."

"So I found all the bags, are you both ready?" Senior asks, walking into the room laden down with empty bags hanging from his arms and held in his hands.

Sterling stares at me, but instead of engaging in his stare-off, I take a few bags and move toward the door.

"Juliet, stay." I led the way out of the house through the garage, climbing into the driver's seat of the van.

The garage door slides open and Senior steps aside while Sterling gets in next to me.

"I am glad it's not so bad you couldn't focus on pleasure, but you expect honesty from me, and yet here you are keeping quiet and not telling me about your discomfort."

Sterling leans over and turns my face to force me to look at him. "It's a mobility thing, not a pain thing, you'll stretch me out effectively. But you're right, I need to be open about it." He kisses me hard on the mouth then sits back in his seat buckling in.

"Okay, Juliet's mad but inside, and we have only necessary supplies and the empty five-gallon gas jugs," Senior explains once I pul lout of the garage, and he closes the door behind us. "Oh, and I left the door to the back upstairs slider unlocked so we can get back in."

"Sounds like a plan," I agree, looking ahead, the van moving up the incline toward the few businesses easily. Nothing moves around us until we reach the top, and a random chicken scurries across a patch of grass, making my stomach yearn for some more fresh chicken. My focus moves back to the shops; one looks like a gift and card store, the next a cash checking spot, and lastly, a laundromat.

"Let's stick together and start with the laundromat and work our way out," I direct, looking at each storefront.

"What supplies could we possibly find there that would help us?" Senior asks.

I stare at him for a moment as I exit the van. "Clothes..."

Sterling chuckles, stepping up next to my right side. "Heads up, my mobility to my left isn't up to my usual par, so I will need to stay to the right side of formation today."

"We have some painkillers if you need some," Senior offers, glancing back at the van.

"I definitely do not hurt, it's just weirdly stiff."

"Maybe because of how long it took to get it popped into place?" Senior ponders, running his fingers through his beard thoughtfully.

We move to the front door of the laundromat, Sterling watching our backs as we try the door to find it unlocked.

"Grab the bell," I warn as we move to enter. Senior reaches up, and we move together to enter, scanning the large room full of washers and dryers from right to left. Moving quickly to a door to the left, we find the main room empty, but when we tug open the door marked employee, only an abomination falls from a small office space, its feet caught up in a sleeping bag on the floor.

Senior takes it out, and we check the back exit and restrooms before I set the timer on my watch and we begin methodically moving through each space, quickly discarding clothes that won't fit any of us and bagging items we can use. I reach the office first and push aside a bucket of quarters and cash, moving a grocery bag full of socks before pausing and looking back at the items. I snag two mismatched long socks and fill them halfway with coins, shoving them into the lower cargo pockets of my pants. Then I pull free any food I can find that doesn't look contaminated, moving to the exit and waiting for Senior and Sterling as the last minute ticks past and my watch vibrates an alarm.

We open the back carefully, checking for movement before going to the back of the check cashing place next door, finding the door wide open, cash spilling across the ground. We look at each other, shake our heads and bypass to the next shop. The risks of the check cashing store are not worth the few batteries we might find. As we pass, a loud sound crashes behind us, and we press against the wall. I signal for them to move around the building, which we do just as six men come stumbling and laughing from the open door. They walk through the back parking lot over to an old pickup truck where they deposit the computer and cash register they are hauling.

"Senior, go protect the van, Sterling, let's check this last building," I whisper, watching Senior dart back around to the van. Sterling and I move toward the front of the store, finding it locked, but after a quick rap on the window, abominations amble into view.

"Should we skip?" he asks, looking around us.

"No, they have too many things we need: batteries, candles, soap, and who knows what else."

"Okay, want me to smash the front window?"

"No, pretend you're an abomination and attack me, the trucks coming around this way, I can hear it."

"What if they shoot?"

"I need to know what kind of people we are dealing with. If I see a gun, we will get cover that way," I urge, pointing toward the beams holding the path above the walkway. My scream causes Sterling to jump before I throw myself to the ground.

Sterling follows me as the truck rounds the corner and slows. The men chatter for a moment, and Sterling's teeth graze my stomach, and I have to contain the moan from slipping into my scream. The truck drives away when I reach out to it. I stop screaming and watch them disappear down the road.

"You know, I am surprised by your willingness to role-play in public," Sterling chuckles, getting to his feet and offering his hand to help me up.

I stare after the truck, unamused at their decision to do nothing at all. How are people surviving if they refuse to aid each other? I take his hand and rise.

Senior walks closer with a frown. "We need the radios cause that was terrifying, I thought they hurt you."

"I think they're in the glove box. After we get in here, we should get new batteries for them. Was that scream as startling as I ask curiously.

earlier was more earth-shattering."

"I guess next time I just have to impale you and cause your brain to rattle," Sterling suggests, smacking my butt.

I smack his arm gently, snorting with laughter and turning to the windows. "Let's take out the window on the right behind the shelves. We can pull them out and make it more manageable."

We break the window, causing the whole pane to spiderweb, then crash down. The shelf follows suit, falling out with abominations on top of it. We move forward, each killing one, then dragging the carcasses away from the store window.

I grab a small statue of an elephant and throw it toward the back of the store hoping to startle anything else that could be inside, but nothing moves, so we step through the broken window, setting another timer. We pull in a haul of about twenty Our Lady of Guadalupe candles and many types of snacks, along with assorted handmade soups and warm drinks. We load all the supplies into the van and then drive down the road closer to the city. Our goal is to mark a few areas to plunder for tomorrow. We have to go deeper than expected, and we finally find a spot to park that is with lots of other vehicles to help us blend in.

The absence of abominations is honestly quite eerie. It helps that we see traces of them, the bloodstains and debris, even a few corpses. We decide to drain the cars in the lot of gas before venturing much further. So while Senior and Sterling puncture gas tanks and use their rubber pans to collect and store fuel, I move from car to car looking for anything that can make our lives a little better.

After finding very little, the guys lock up the van and turn to me, Sterling with the M16 slung on his back, sweat clinging his shirt to his delicious muscles. I avert my eyes before I can jump him, the heat must be working on my subconscious. We walk deeper into the city, marking locations on a small map of the city we have foun, and taking out the few abominations we come across. Most of the stores look pre-searched, but anytime we spot something from outside that we can't pass up like food, tampons, or bottled waters, we collect them.

As we walk, we run into more abominations, and part of me

wonders if we are further than I have calculated. The signs of blockades in the next two alleyways tell me something is different about this area. The blockades are a hodgepodge of furniture and appliances that the guys can't look over. The one closest is about 10 feet high.

"Get back 150 feet, fire from there!" a familiar voice bellows in English from the other side of the barricade. "Fall back and regroup!"

"That sounds bad," Senior says.

My eyes meet Sterling's. "No," he denies.

"I know that voice. You need to go around and take them from the left," I order. Not waiting for his response, I sprint at the barricade, jumping up onto the back of a car before pouncing against the wall of a brick structure and finally grasping the top of the dresser at the top. It shakes at my weight. Scrambling up, I lurch over it and then drop into the back of a pickup truck with a loud thud.

Screams of fear break my focus, and I am moving forward, both my knives out, one in each fist as my feet send me propelling over the top of the truck and down hard to the ground, slamming my blades into the skulls of two of the closest abominations. From down here, I can't hear the orders of the voice that had called out to my memory. My ears are now only filled with the sounds of the dead rattling abominations. I let my training take over, my body aching in protest. I run toward the people huddled on top of a car drawing the abominations toward them with their screams for help. Kicking the knees out from beneath one, my knife borrows into its skull, and I pull another back from the horde, my blade piercing through its forehead this time.

An abomination stumbles from the flock, leading five others. My forward momentum halts, and I take a step back, judging their size and my remaining strength. Then I move to the right of the advancing abominations, letting my blade swing at their outreached hands. Black blood and fingers pirouette through the air. Taking a step back, my boot lands on something hard and cylinder. As this registers, my balance pitches me back, my arms coming up to shield my head instinctively. One of my knives skirts away from where my body lands hard on the unforgiving blacktop. I push myself into a sitting position, scrambling backward, my eyes locking on the bloody baseball bat which has taken me down. I lunge for its handle before rolling and springing to my feet, slight pain tugging at my ankle. Shoving my Gerber in its sheath, my hands grasping the bat, knuckles blanching white, before I choke up on the bat, smashing it into the snapping jaw of an abomination. Teeth fly from its rotten face, its body crumbling backward. With a pivot, my next swing cracks the skull of another abomination. I kick one back that has gotten too close for comfort, my arms burning with pain. Caving its skull in with my bat, I surge left, avoiding teeth near my face. The face's relentless mouth stops mid-gnash, and it drops like a sack of coal to the ground, an arrow shaft protruding from its forehead.

Fear lances through me as I shuffle back, and a renewed strength pulses through me.

CHAPTER THIRTY FOUR
STERLING
"ENEMIES" THE SCORE

TEN PEOPLE with bows and arrows line the top of the buildings above the square where we just slaughtered a ridiculous amount of abominations. Aurora stands frozen, her back to me, body ridged. I thrust the M16 into Senior's hands and move toward her as fast as I can over the countless dead bodies. My hands raise in the air to show the armed group that I mean them no harm. Did they not see us trying and succeeding in saving their people?

"Freeze!" someone above bellows, but my focus is on Aurora, her unmoving form ahead of me.

"Are you bit?" I ask when I stumble to her side, reaching for her to check her for injury.

"Sterling, get behind me," she insists, but I ignore her demands, pulling her trembling body into my arms.

"I said freeze, congelar!" the same voice yells, this time switching to Spanish for a moment.

"Sterling, listen to him," she insists with a hissing breath.

"We just helped your people, why are you demanding anything from us?" I yell back.

A familiar-looking man moves forward on the roof, loading an arrow.

"Jaime! It's Rory. Sheriff Davin Heartclave's sister!" Aurora announces. After a long beat, she sighs. "The Cyborg 2.0!"

"Weapons down!" Jaime orders, stepping forward and looking down at us.

I look at Aurora for some sort of explanation. I do not know who Jaime is at the moment, but if he knows Davin, then obviously he isn't from her work but back from Enigma Valley.

A rush of movement happens around us as the people jump down from atop the car and rooftop centuries fill the square, causing me to pull Aurora behind me.

"Sterling, I am okay. Jaime is from Enigma, he was on my tryout team for mountain patrol. You hired him and scored his test, he was supposed to start after his trip to South America," she reminds me, hugging me.

A vague memory of the man surfaces in my mind just as he nears us.

"Holy crap, how are you guys even alive?" Jaime asks, throwing his arms up with jubilation.

"Intelligence."

"Faith."

Aurora looks at me with a smirk, and I shake my head.

"How did you guys get down here? Where is Heartclave?" he asks, turning in a circle, his eyes searching.

"Davin is with the rest of my family in a secure location at Grandfather Mountain."

"I meant Dean, I could use his brawn about now," Jaime chuckles, smacking a hand on Aurora's shoulder.

Aurora's eyes lose the brief excitement of finding her friend and are now downcast.

"No freaking way!" Jaime gasps. "How?"

"He was bitten after the wedding, on the first day while he was trying to save Quin from the first abomination we ran into," I respond, putting my arm around Aurora's waist.

"So he died that first day, well damn, I am sorry, Rory. He was a great guy. Karter, did you guys put him down after he turned?"

"Yes, we did, and you can call me Sterling, this is my father, Sterling Karter Sr. We just call him Senior," I say, gesturing over to Senior.

"What are you doing in Mexico, Jaime? Your flight should have landed in South America by the time this whole thing blew up in our faces." Aurora asks.

"We were on a layover in Mexico City, and it took us this long just to make it this far." Jaime sighs.

"We need to go, boss," a man interrupts in broken English.

Jaime looks at his watch. "We need to get off the street before the next round of detentions, we are only out here collecting supplies and gas, mostly gas."

"We have some gas you can have," Aurora offers.

Jaime raises an eyebrow and the man next to him looks at her with disbelief. "What would you like in return?"

"Nothing, I just want good people to survive this as long as possible," she says. "Also, your team needs to go inside the car versus on top of it next time, they can survive longer and be away from bites."

"How did you guys make it this far south, Rory?" Jaime asks, looking at us with disbelief.

"Walking, Driving..."

"Tornado," I add for good measure.

"We parked our van about ten blocks northwest, it is up to you guys if you would like some fuel. If you have a silicone pan, I am sure that Sterling can show you his method of gas collecting."

I follow Aurora as she leads the group of fourteen out the way Dad and I had entered. She glances back at me, looking at me and Senior a few times.

"You good, Senior?" she asks, tilting her head to catch his gaze.

He nods in response, looking around at the group uneasily.

"Jaime, this is my father-in-law. He takes some time to warm up to people," she explains, waving a hand in Dad's direction.

Senior beams at me, and I know her honest words are clinging to his heart.

"Father-in-law? He sure didn't waste any time making you his wife," Jaime laughs, nudging me with his arm.

"I asked before the world decided to die on us."

"Well, common misconception, it's the people who died on us, not the world. If anything, she's an even more fertile beast now," Jaime announces with a huge grin.

Aurora laughs, and I smile, looking around at the people agreeing with him with nods of heads and grunts of agreement. I take in their appearances in honest as we walk. They are a lot cleaner than many refugees, including us. They are all fitted with bows and arrows, as well as various knives, most look like kitchenware. What catches my attention further is the lack of malnourishment in their faces; they look relatively healthy and well-fed.

"Jaime, the bows and arrows are formidable. Where did you acquire them, and can I go trade for some possibly?" Aurora asks, eyeing the weapons we haven't seen since before the tornado.

My attention turns away from the rest of the group, focusing back on the discussion ahead of me.

"We make them, we also make our own clothes, and plan to make our own food," Jaime explains, pulling on the sleeve of his shirt.

"Wow! Sounds like you're all a bunch of brainiacs like Aurora," Senior chuckles.

"Well, you might even consider me the upgrade," Jaime laughs, puffing out his chest with pride.

Aurora throws her knife at an abomination that rattles around the next corner, then smirks at Jaime before retrieving it and glancing down the alley, the way it had come out.

"We need to pick up the pace, there are more heading this way," she warns, shaking her arms out and moving away from the group and in the direction of the van. A few people speak to her in Spanish as we walk, but I try to stick near Jaime who is seamlessly slipping from English to Spanish.

"Sterling, can I ask you a question? I need complete honesty," Jaime asks, lowering his voice.

"How bad is Enigma, did anyone survive?"

"It's pretty nasty in town, but a lot of people were brought into the safety of Grandfather Mountain," I explain with a reassuring smile.

"They are hiding in the old mines?" Jaime asks, frowning.

"The government has an underground facility in the mountain, so they are in there. The place is massive."

He frowns but nods, moving ahead to some of his men, and I walk in silence for a while until we reach the van. I remove my silicon tray from my bag, along with my screwdriver and a stubby ball hammer. "What will you want your gasoline in?" I ask a man near me.

The man stares at me, then looks around at the others.

Aurora repeats my question in Spanish as she unlocks the van.

The man smiles and holds up a milk jug that is attached to his pack, which I take and set up next to a nearby vehicle.

When the gas streams from the punctured tank into my pan, a commotion of chatter behind me causes me to look around. The group has broken apart, half watching me and the others watching Senior.

After filling the jugs and topping off our supply, I turn to Aurora.

"So Jaime has offered us to join their community. Their plan is to move south toward South America by water to establish farms at a location near the research area they were headed to originally. Any skills we possess would be utilized to help grow and protect the community," she explains, leaning against the van and watching me intently.

"Can we trust them?" Senior asks, looking over at the group.

"We can trust Jaime, we would have to grow our trusted people from there." She shrugs.

"So no Costa Rica?" I ask.

"No, you wanted to find a safe place, settle down, and I think this is as close to that as we are going to get."

My imagination takes the reins as hope fills me. An image of Aurora, pregnant and healthy, surrounded by farmlands overflowing with crops blossoms in my mind.

"Sterling, is that a yes or no?" Aurora asks, raising one eyebrow.

I shake my head slightly, focusing on the present. "Yeah, I'm in."

"Jaime, we need to go to our base to grab the rest of our supplies, and then we are at your disposal," Aurora announces, standing straight at her full height, radiating confidence.

Jaime beams, walking over and clapping a hand on my shoulder. "Let's all go. The detonations start any moment."

The ones who can fit climb into the van, and after I hot-wire a car we haven't drained of gas, the others to load up to follow us.

When we pull up to the house, we find a white pickup truck crashed into the garage door. Aurora bolts from the vehicle, knife in hand. I swear, opening my door to the piercing sounds of Juliet's ferocious barks assaulting my ears.

"Aurora?" I call, not catching sight of where she's gone.

"What is going on?" Jaime asks, moving to my side.

"This is where we have our supplies and our dog, Juliet," I inform him, looking around for Aurora.

"Maybe we can get in through the back, any expert climbers?" Senior asks, looking at Jaime to translate.

"Rory went through the gap there in the broken door," Jaime says, pointing to a small opening in the twisted metal.

Glass shatters above us, and I yank Jaime back as a man's body lands with a sickening splat on the pavement next to us.

"Juliet, stay back!" Aurora demands.

I look up to find her standing inside the broken window, then back down at the man who has a computer mouse laying next to his head with its cord wrapped around his neck. Explosions in the distance catch my attention before we are all rushing into the house, where I sink my blade into the skull of a man with his throat ripped out. Not dwelling on the deaths, we pack and clean up ruined supplies.

Soon, we are back in the vehicles, the cargo clips secured on the roof of the van, and we are heading across town, following Jaime's directions to the pier.

"For some reason, the zombies seem to congregate at piers, and along the shore," Jaime says.

"It's probably the sound of the waves on the pier that draw them to it. I don't think abominations can differentiate between human-made sounds and other sounds," Aurora replies.

"So you cause explosions to draw them away from the areas you're using?" Senior asks, looking impressed.

"Yes, this way we have less chance of being bitten., We have done everything, but the person always turns," Jaime says, looking down.

I glance at Aurora, who shakes her head ever so slightly, and then follows the group toward a fleet of boats in all shapes and sizes, some large yachts and other speed boats with cabins.

"So the leaders travel in the biggest boats with most of our community, and the smaller boats usually have our scouts. We have fitted all the boats we use with functional CBs so we can communicate. The fishing boats take off at the rear when we pull off to protect and collect," Jaime explains, pointing out to the swaying ships.

"Your idea?" Aurora asks.

Jaime nods proudly.

"When we get docked at our last stop, would it be possible to collect sailboats? That way, we won't have to rely on gasoline for fishing," she asks, watching men lug the gasoline down a dock.

"One hundred percent. See, you guys are going to make such a great addition to our group. Let's go meet with the other leaders and find out if we have space or if we should grab another boat before taking off."

"How many people are in your community?" I ask.

"63; men, women, and children. So now we are at 66," Jaime says.

"66 and a half," I remind him, pointing at Juliet, her fur pink with the blood we hadn't cleaned off of her.

"That will have to be a negotiation," Jaime admits, eyeing Juliet.

"I think taking on three able-bodied workers/soldiers/scavengers can constitute a compromise," Aurora challenges, putting her hands on her hips.

Jaime chuckles and leads us to a few curious older men standing in a group near a large yacht at the end of the pier.

CHAPTER THIRTY FIVE
RORY
"HEADSTRONG" BY TRAPT

AFTER BEING at sea for two weeks, we have learned many things, including that boats suck for privacy, and planning ahead is near impossible when many of the stops along the coast are smash and grabs. I have no skills to really offer to our hosts yet except my quick and efficient retrieval of whatever they task us to grab. Most of the women spend their days minding the children, cooking food, doing laundry, or cleaning fish.

I use a fish knife to slit open what must be my 200th fish of the day. Most of the women have stopped working with me because I am capable of doing all the work on my own. Instead, I choose to listen to what is happening around me. Eventually gathering enough information that I know all the women by name and which children belong to whom, as well as most of their husbands or the lack thereof.

The woman beside me chatters about my good-looking husband with the woman nursing a baby in front of her, causing me to roll my eyes. The crack of a gun causes my head to snap up, the knife in my hand sliding to a defensive grip in my hand. A wave causes the boat to sway dangerously, and for a moment ,I consider that the noise could have been something else. When, suddenly, a man bursts into the kitchen, brandishing a machete and screaming at the woman to get down.

The moment his words end is the moment my fist connects with his arm, breaking it. The machete falls neatly into my gasp, and his dead body collapses with a solid slice to his carotid.

"Get back, stay low," I hiss to the others in Spanish. I glance at the stairs that lead down to the rooms where other women and children spend most of the scorching afternoons. "Warn the others."

Action meets my words, and I decide I like these women. Grasping the dead man's arms, I pull him into the kitchen, another woman named Isabella, immediately assists me. I place my hand over hers, then signal silence by pressing my finger to my lips. An arm supporting a semi-automatic rifle swings into the room, the man's head looking back over his shoulder as he talks to someone behind him.

I grasp the machete with both hands. Standing and using my momentum, I sever his arm from his body, then with a quick swing with my left, stab his face and catch the falling weapon which I use as a baton on the man behind him as I adjust my stance to this new weapon. The shocked man behind the dead one turns with a handgun and the trigger twitches beneath my finger, the bullet shattering his forehead.

Dropping, I pull the gun from his limp hands and pass it to Isabella.

"If anyone other than our people comes through this door, aim for center mass," I instruct in Spanish, showing her on my body where to aim.

"No," she whimpers, shaking her head.

"Yes, we need to protect women and children. The boats for today's run won't be back for about 45 more minutes."

A tear streams down her cheek, but she nods, moving out of view from the door but aiming at it. I slide the Machete toward a woman cowering in a corner.

"Just in case," I explain to her.

I move to the door, checking my surroundings and staying low as I check the pockets of the dead before moving onto the deck. I draw my attention to our sister boat, where men are dragging women out by their hair. Dropping to my stomach, I take aim, the efficiency of my head shots is only slowed when the sound of boots on deck send me rolling with a quick burst of fire, taking out two more men.

"Evacuar!" a man screams, and that's when I catch sight of their boat in the distance, a large yacht pitching on a wave before settling back into the choppy sea, charcoal clouds darkening the horizon. Dozens of men swarm the other boat, and I know I can't let them just flee. They would be back, and next time, they won't come in while it's just two boats.

Moving to my feet, I race toward the back of our boat, taking out three more men until the dry fire of my gun causes me to drop it and speed up. I fling myself over the rail, landing in the smaller speed boat, sending two men into the water while punching another in the face before sending a kick to his sternum that causes him to fall to his knees. In my next move, my knife slices through the fingers of the men trying to re-board the boat before returning to the man groveling at my boots.

"Please, he said this would be easy!" the man screams in Spanish before the kick to his chin sends him onto his back out cold. I grab his weapon from the ground and shoot the men in the water before moving to the controls. In a blink, I memorize Jaime's movements and get the boat started, and speeding toward the yacht.

I aim right at it, using the dead man's foot to wedge the wheel before diving off and swimming toward our sister boat to check on the woman there. The yacht explodes and screams fill the darkening sky as I climb up onto the boat, women pulling at my arms to help me. Crying and talking surrounds me, but all I can focus on is the guard of the boat cradled in the arms of his wife, who is sobbing uncontrollably as he gurgles blood and then dies.

The sound of boats nearing moves me from my stupor to my feet, pushing the woman nearby behind me. My eyes lock on Sterling's before flitting to the fleet of our boats returning. I sigh with relief, scanning the water for survivors of the explosion.

"What happened?" Jaime demands, staring at the blood covering my clothes.

"You left us with two guards, and they both were killed instantly. All they seemed to want is the women. I have neutralized them for now. They did not take anyone with them."

The sound of the water slapping the boats and the crying behind me engulfs me again. I look back at the boat I am supposed to be on where no one moves. The decks are empty until a twitch near the kitchen entrance catches my eye.

"Abomination!" I scream, pointing toward the ship.

Two guns fire and the body drops. I look over my shoulder to see Sterling and Senior both lowering side arms.

"We need to get to shore. This storm coming is huge, and we can not protect all these boats with our firepower," I tell Jaime, who has moved onto this boat to dispatch the dead guard before he can turn.

Jaime sighs. "You're right, let me check out the damage before we head back, where is your weapon?"

I hold up my hands, then point at my head. "Gave a handgun to Isabella, a Machete to another woman, the semi-auto I acquired is bulletless on deck in the other boat, my knife is at my hip, and the speed boat I used to explode the yacht is that way," I explain, dryly sweeping my hand toward the ocean behind me.

Jaime studies me and then moves to check out the boat. I reach over for Sterling, and he pulls me onto his boat and into his embrace.

"Are you okay?" he asks.

"Yeah, I thought the explosion phase was behind me."

"That was a signal to us that something was wrong, we came as soon as we saw. I thought it was one of these boats," he says, kissing my forehead, his embrace tight and comforting.

"Back to shore, now all boats back to shore!" Jaime demands. The order spreads like this plague, and I see some of our people board the other boat and comfort the women aboard, before we are heading for shore, Sterling still holding me. Shielding me from the guilt, from harm, and from the new realization that everyone here now knows I have to be way more capable than I have let on.

CHAPTER THIRTY SIX
RORY
"TAKE IT TO THE EDGE" BY GODSMACK

"LEFT, LEFT, RIGHT, RIGHT, LEFT," I whisper, trying not to let his glistening, half-naked body distract me from his training. His fists connect one after another, sweat beading down his bare chest, sliding over his muscles and down his abs until it reaches the invisible region of his once-injured hip. I divert my full attention back to his training. It has been a week since we left the boats and headed inland. We now reside in La Fortuna, Costa Rica for a few days to restock and send the scouts ahead.

"Nice form," a fellow survivor named Aaron compliments, walking toward us.

I ignore Jaime's new friend who I have only seen doing the grunt work for the move south to the planned settlement area. He watches Sterling shift into his next stance, and I catch the slight smirk Sterling gives me before he switches it up and attempts to catch me off guard. I block his shot and send him a quick jab, which he deflects.

"Want a real sparring partner, someone to match you hit for hit?" Aaron offers.

My focus splits, catching sight of him watching Sterling for a reply. I look back at Sterling, rolling my eyes, then dodge his fist with a smirk.

"Rory, when you have a minute, I need your help," Jaime says from behind me.

My brow furrows. Help? Jaime never asks for help; this must be big.

"Don't hurt him too badly, Sterling," I dismiss, enjoying the slow smile that spreads across his face as he watches me back away and pull on a shirt. My stride takes me to Jaime's side, and I expect some quip about the sweat or smell, or useless physical activity, but his face is sullen, eyes clouded with worry. "What's wrong?"

"Not here, come with me."

I glance back to Sterling, who connects with the side of Aaron's abdomen. Pride ripples through me before moving to follow Jaime, down the old cracked stairs and under a bright awning that feels alien in a sea of gray and beige buildings surrounded with foliage from the vast wilderness beyond. Ducking under a few vines cascading from the rooftops, we enter what looks to be like an old church, the vaulted ceilings and stained glass windows signs of better days. Jaime stops at a folding table, looking down at a huge hand-drawn map.

"Is this your war table? What have I missed?" I ask, glancing at the men who are supposed to be agriculturalists and scientists who sit in folding chairs looking exhausted.

"Rory, the route we were going to take is going to make us move really close to Orotina, Costa Rica, and the cartel's territory. This route takes us through the overrun city of San Jose. But if we take this pass, we could easily get lost, or mauled to death by jaguars," Jaime explains, cleaning his glasses on his shirt.

I shrug. "What is it you need help with?"

"You have experience with dangerous situations, and I split us at a 50/50 vote on what direction to go. We need to make it to our new homestead before it gets too hot and before the ideal planting days are past us," he explains, tracing the map from our location to where they are planning to settle in South America.

"Well, without the dangers, the route east past the cartel is nearly a quarter of the time, based on what I know of the geographical terrain of this area. Also, why are you worried about the cartel? Humans by far are so much easier to anticipate than wild animals. It sounds like the west route holds way more unknown and more dangers than just a jaguar. The city is obviously not an option."

"The cartel is ruthless. From the scouts, we have learned that a new boss has taken over, and he and his new whore are sitting pretty in an elite hotel deep in the city surrounded by iron fences and the arsenal of the cartel."

My eyebrow arch at his crass words, knowing how he feels about swearing.

His mouth quarks, and he sighs. "I was just telling you what they said."

"Well, how close does this path get you to the cartel's territory?"

Jaime looks toward a slim man who looks like he might turn at any second. The man groans as he gets up and moves toward us, standing across the table.

"The road weaves this direction with roads that branch off toward the city in these directions. They have roving patrols at the end of each road. I am also sure that the sound of the vehicles will attract all sorts of attention and part of it can be clearly seen from the hotel if they are watching it with binoculars," the man explains in Spanish.

Jaime opens his mouth to translate, then pauses. "You know what he said?"

"Yes, I still think that the risk in the eastern route is better than the western unless a scout can give me a better idea of what to expect."

"I never told them you speak Spanish. Also none of the scouts have made it back from that direction," Jaime says.

"Why would you all consider a route that no one has come back from? I can get you through the pass with minimal issues. Shouldn't the cartel be more focused on the dead?" I ask the room to make sure it matches their Spanish dialect.

CHAPTER THIRTY SIX

Eyes shift around, looking uneasy and not very certain of my questions or offer.

"We will discuss it, who were you before the dead rose? We appreciate your actions on the boats, but you must understand our hesitance," an old man asks, his tan face weathered by years of hard work and his graying hair gleaming with sweat. His eyes are hard while his words which are asked in English are kind yet probing.

"US Marine, black ops forces. My name is Aurora Karter, I go by Rory." They meet my introduction with interest from some and ignorance from others. I nod my head respectfully at the man who had asked before leaving the building and stepping out into the breeze. The car barricades start at the end of this street, and I turn left to head back toward where we have set up camp in a few abandoned buildings and cooking areas beyond that we would use as a heat source as the sun goes down.

Stopping next to the bunks, I glance at my watch, its silence still eerie.

"Does that thing even work anymore?" Senior asks, sidling up next to me.

With a quick glance up at him, I nod then pause, looking up at his clean-shaved face, so similar to Sterling's that for a moment I am shaken.

"It is pretty cool to look so much like my son, who would have thought."

"It is quite uncanny, what did his mother look like?"

He grins, pulling out his wallet, which I look at in shock that it's still on his person and in decent condition. He pulls out two wallet-sized photos, one of a woman with glossy brown curls and a gorgeous smile, and another of a small brown-haired toddler holding a baseball mitt.

"His smile is so much like his mother's."

"That it is, I bet your son will look the same as him someday." My look makes him laugh, his hands coming up in surrender. "I am just saying."

"I have a patrol tonight so I am going to get some sleep. Introduce Sterling to whoever freed your face from the apocalypse bush, please."

Senior's laugh surrounds me before I take off to where we have claimed our sleeping spots and curl up in Sterling's scent, setting my watch to vibrate in four hours.

When I wake, the sun is nearly vacant from the sky and the hues of color across the dusk sky are breathtaking. I make my way to my post, knowing if I seek out Sterling, I will be late. From my rooftop location, I settle on a lawn chair looking over people cooking their suppers and spending time with their families. The smell of chili wafts up from below, and I smile at how comfortable this community is getting. Bats swoop overhead, and the few children in our group are being corralled into a building to get some sleep. The darkness seeps into my surroundings so completely that if it wasn't for the dancing light of fire light it would feel like being enclosed in a vast room with only the crackling sound of fire and light chatter to keep you company.

Sterling and Senior take a seat at a large fire with their backs to me and both men's silhouettes are clean-shaven, tall, and built with muscles. Aaron joins them, supporting a fat lip, a shiner, and a huge smile as he sits across from them. I watch them chat, my attention roving around the area periodically, looking for abominations or outsiders. We have had several nights here with no issues, but after a ruckus last night that sent every able man on patrol into a flurry of movement, the tension is high.

My ears pick up the sounds of the jungle to our south, the nocturnal animals calling out to one another, peace and tranquility breathing with the wind through the leaves of nearby trees. I stand from my chair, my back aching from sitting too long, and pace the rooftop, my boots silent on the gravel roof.

My watch vibrates, and I look down at it: PROXIMITY ALERT! Just like up on Grandfather Mountain, minus the siren because of my settings. I move quickly to look upon the group, my eyes trying to piece the darkness, my muscles tense. I stop at the ledge of the roof. The wind whips at tendrils of my hair that have escaped my high ponytail. The sound of movement below to my right causes me to crouch, staring down as a figure moves in the shadows. I squint, the glint of a gun in the firelight sends my heart racing. The gun shifts between Sterling and Senior.

I feel air rushing toward me before my body collides with the man aiming his weapon at my husband and father-in-law. My momentum sends us toppling into the firelight, my Gerber out in one hand, the man's gun skidding to Sterling's feet. Screams fill the air and panic blossoms around us as people flee. Launching forward at the man as he struggles to his feet, I tackle him again, this time immediately dislodged and flung away. Rolling across the ground and then up onto a knee, my eyes meet a pair of blue eyes encompassed behind a black ski mask. A snarl rips from my throat as I charge to my feet, knife ready and other fist clenched.

Panic fills those blue eyes before focusing on the knife in my hand. The gleam of the knife an inch from his neck sends my blood boiling as he dodges back, his fist catching my side. My foot hooks his ankle and he crashes to his back, his cowardly hands flying for the mask, tearing it from his face, his short dark hair sticking up in all directions.

"Moore! Stop, it's me!" Flyboy yells.

"I would know you're incompetent blank eyes anywhere, Flyboy," my voice responds with acid as I move slowly forward.

"No, that's not my name, please remember me, Patrick Heathly from TESA."

Lurching forward at the treacherous small dick prick standing before me, my mind blasts with memories of wasted time with a man who had been paid to spend time with me, all to bring me into the depths of an organization that had tried to steal my soul. My knife flings forward, embedding in his thigh before I crash into him, unloading my fists. He silences his scream with grunts as he attempts to fight back. I wrench the knife from his leg, taking it in both hands and trying to sink it into his chest. He kicks me back then turns to run, blood splattering on the ground.

My knife clatters to the ground, and I race forward, propelling myself off a low concrete planter surrounding a magnificent tree. My hand grasps his hair, one leg wrapping around his neck as the other locks me in place as I throw myself forward, flipping him. We land hard, his hands trying to tear my leg from his neck in vain, and within moments his struggling ceases, and I release my hold and roll to my feet.

"Holy shit," Aaron's voice gasps nearby.

"Are you okay, Aurora?" Sterling asks, his hand gently stroking my arm in greeting.

I let out a sigh, my eyes darting around us for others but only spotting Senior with a gun pointing down at Flyboy.

"Who is that?" Sterling asks, dusting me off.

"My ex."

I feel the stares and ignore them, glancing at Jaime as he jogs up, looking down at the heap.

"I brought some rope unless he is dead, then we need to send a blade through his brain."

"He isn't dead, we need to find out why he's here first." Dropping, I search his pockets, finding three full mags, which I pass to Sterling, his badge, a smashed granola bar, and a rectangular device with a small beaming screen.

Jaime moves close, looking down at the device before taking it from me. The lights on the screen swing to my right, and I glance at Sterling, then back at Jaime, whose jaw has dropped.

"Sterling, can you grab me one of those blankets?" I ask.

Sterling moves toward the abandoned blanket, the beam of light following him as he crosses the hundred feet there before he turns and comes back.

"Tie him up and wake him up. I want answers," I growl.

Aaron and Senior drag him over to a tree, securing ropes around him before staking torches into the soft earth around him.

CHAPTER THIRTY SIX

"Flyboy? Is this the pilot you were with when landing in Dubai?" Sterling asks, his hands moving over me searching for injuries.

I nod, my anger still simmering within me as I watch them try to rouse him.

"What is TESA?" Sterling asks, his lips brushing my ears.

"My company's name. He broke all kinds of rules speaking it aloud."

"Was he the man from the file we found in the box truck?" he asks, his hands leaving my body and his shoulders squaring up as anger takes the place of concern.

I nod again, and Sterling bristles with rage. His hand tucks my hair back before his lips press against my temple. His other hand roves over my body, searching for injuries.

A groan sends Senior back to the tree, his hands grasping Flyboys' shirt, yanking him against his restraints. "What do you want with my daughter?" he roars in Flyboy's face.

"He was here for Sterling, not me."

Sterling looks at me as Senior looks around in surprise.

"Isn't that right, Patrick?" I ask, stalking forward.

He tries to kill Senior with his eyes before turning them on me. Fear floods them before a confused look crosses his face as he looks at Sterling.

"So what is it that has you here trying to come after my husband?"

"Husband?" Patrick chokes out.

"That's right. You came after my family and divulged the company's name, which means by section 484-B I have the right to do anything to make you pay for your indiscretions. So what will it be? Tied and quartered, or flambeed?"

"Please, I will give you anything you want to make it quick."

"I want information now!"

"Okay, okay..." He gulps, looking around us before his eyes lock on my Gerber as I pull it free. "I am here to take out a Sterling Karter by orders of Corporal Allen. He knows you will return to make it even, and they can have you back in the fold. I hesitated when I had the shot because I wasn't sure which one Sterling was and didn't want to take an innocent life."

"They are both innocent, Allen just has a hard-on for my blood. But you know you're no match for me, so why even try?"

"He sent an all-call. Anyone that can deliver proof of death will be welcome into his safe zone and will again receive an award when you show up and are detained. It went out on all open agent frequencies."

"Did you ever consider just finding me and asking for my help in faking it so that you could get in without murdering someone?"

"Well... No, I figured it just needed to be handled and that I could stop running for a while."

"Because you're a selfish bastard that thinks killing is always the answer."

"Look, Moore, just cause you won't kill doesn't mean we all have that weakness. You seem to forget that we dated, I know you."

"You're mistaken. We had mediocre sex enough times for me to figure out that your vanilla ass couldn't be trained to please a woman. Also, not to be cruel, but my kill count makes yours look smaller than your dick size."

Coughs or hands cover snorts of laughter, clapping over mouths while Patrick brow lowers, his jaw set in defiance.

"Next time you accept money to entice a woman into a job or to kill someone that she cares for, you should really consider if she can kick your ass first. Also, maybe brush up on your fieldwork, Flyboy. You could have made so many choices where me dicing you into horse food wasn't an option."

"You're not feeding our horses this idiot's carcass. We can save the chunks for the biters," Jaime argues, signaling for me to follow him.

"Keep an eye on him, Senior, Sterling, come with me."

We walk silently to where Jaime stays as he passes the guard at the door, who looks uneasy. I spot our M16 on a table as he lights two lanterns and asks us to have a seat to decompress.

"So this guy works with you?" Jaime asks, peeking out of a curtain.

"Sort of, he is mostly a pilot last I heard."

"Could that have been the sounds that were heard yesterday, a small plan maybe?" he asks.

"No runways nearby, but it could easily have been a helicopter. I guess since we never see any, we didn't consider that being an option. I think we are losing our touch."

He scoffs, handing me a bottle of water, which I drink deeply from and pass to Sterling.

"Why do they want you back so bad?" Jaime asks, moving closer so he can see me better.

"I survived this virus, and I'm not an abomination. So, they want to create a cure or get rid of me. It could go either way."

Jaime stares at me in shock, the lamplight making his horrified eyes look like dark, twinkling abysses.

"He is loose, someone stop him!" Senior yells from outside.

My hand closes on the M16 as my feet carry me from the room and past the guards who have guns raised toward the West. I bolt toward the sound of running, catapulting myself over the blockade and around Senior. Slowing as I meet the dark, dense jungle. A snap and groan of pain to my left sends me charging in, ordering my watch to optimum brightness.

Barking reaches my ears, and I realize someone has released Juliet, and she's following me. I hesitate, worried she will get injured, however, my fear for Sterling outweighs my worry of his giant fur baby. My hesitation gives the others time to gain on me as I navigate my way deeper into the jungle, tracking my prey until we reach a clearing. The sound of a helicopter coming to life causes me to drop, flinching at the sound now so volatile to my ears.

Gunfire rains above me, and I dart for cover. "Fall back!" I bellow to the others as they near my position.

The bullets hesitate, so I shoulder the M16 and swing around the tree. The helio lifts into the sky, moving rather erratically as a tactic to avoid direct hit by low-impact rounds. Taking aim, I hold my breath, aiming for the windshield, clicking to full automatic, and pulling the trigger. I see the shock in his widened eyes moments before blood explodes on the windshield. The bird tilts and the propellers tear into the ground, sending rocks and earth whizzing past me before I can take cover behind a tree again.

I slide down the tree, my body fighting off the adrenaline dump, the M16 clutched in my arms as I wait. With a blast of heat, part of the helicopter explodes. My brain goes from defense to repair, fire being a genuine threat to the lives of the people in the group we have aligned with.

"Fire!" I warn, not knowing how far the others are. Rounding the tree, I take in the blaze that I am happy to see is not as bad as it could be. I pause while gauging the fire.

"We will grab all the fire extinguishers!" Jaime yells.

"Stay back, the tank hasn't caught fire yet," I warn, backing away as a warm pair of hands pull me against a strong, muscular chest. "Is everyone okay?"

"We need to check on Dad and Aaron, I don't think anyone else was engaged with him," Sterling responds, pulling me back away from the wreckage.

I set the butt of my M16 in the dirt, leaning it against my leg, my hands reaching up for the arms cradling me close, fingers running through the hair on his arms. My nose presses into his arm taking in his scent, basking in his security. Juliet rubs against my leg, whining up at me before taking a seat.

CHAPTER THIRTY SEVEN
STERLING
"A SCAR IS BORN" THREE DAYS GRACE

THE WHIRLWIND of movement in the last four days is mind-boggling. If it wasn't for our constant disagreement about how to fix this new situation, I don't think I would see much of Aurora. But she's now glued to me, and we are watching as our group begins the process of sneaking past the cartel patrols after disarming and securing the guards at the bridges. The rest of the plan is based around the time the patrol spends circulating the area.

I watch the men pushing a vehicle down the road toward the next position, taking a moment to marvel at the intricacies of Aurora's plan before looking over at her. Her beautiful face concentrates on timing the patrol, waiting to signal to me if she sees someone and for our group to hold.

"Dad is still mad at you," I whisper, pasting myself right next to her.

"He will get over it, I will make it up to him somehow after we meet back up with them. This will work, Sterling. We are stealthier together. I can get us in and out, make a deal with Sprocket to pretend to kill you, and then we are home free."

"Maybe the other assassins won't come, maybe you sent them a message killing Patrick."

She scoffs. "If they knew about his death, they would only take it as a challenge and be teaming up. I am telling you this is our best option, she is team Rory. Send a flash, I see one coming."

I flash my light toward my father, who is angrily watching us from a distance, and he signals our group to halt. When the patrol passes, I flash the light and our group moves again.

"I know you're worried about the safety of me and others, but we are risking a lot hoping she won't turn on you."

"Look like I have told you, Sprocket is all about rules. There has to be a way to make a deal. All else fails, we go down together." She shrugs.

"That's not funny."

"It's what your dad said, and you seem to be worried about him."

"Aurora, I can just take the ring off. We can put it on an abomination and be done with them," I offer, trying to tug it off my finger.

"No, I need to always find you. Also, they won't give up that easily. Eventually, they will figure out how to break Trevor's block on me, and they will come for me. It could be days or months, but they will come, and we can't risk the lives of others. We can't consider starting that family you're dreaming about until this is handled."

"I feel you're using my want to have a child with you to drive this conversation into going your way," I sigh, crossing my arms.

"It's working, isn't it? I will not bring a child into this mess when we have the crosshairs on us."

Quick bursts of light signal to us that we have made it past the turn. We move from our location, soundlessly moving to an old building that we make our way into to find Jaime sitting there waiting.

"Your father was planning on coming, but he would not let you leave, so he's detained with the group as you requested, Rory."

"You had them detain my dad?" I ask, looking over to the nearly invisible brigade of people in the shadows.

"He was going to blow the whole operation. We need to get in, make the deal, and get out," she repeats the same thing she said to me earlier. Her insistence is starting to sound like a mantra that she's trying to force herself to believe.

"I scrounged up some ammo for two handguns. Do not argue, it's the least we can do. Make sure in four days you're back here for our rendezvous. I will bring Senior with me, and we can all go toward the homestead together. Don't forget, if they will barter a deal for food for protection, try for that," Jaime requests.

"I don't think giving the cartel our location is a good idea, I can't control them," Aurora denies.

"Hence why this is a bad idea," I murmur, pulling gently on her arm.

"Thanks, Jaime, we will see you in four days," she says, accepting the weapons and handing me one.

Jaime's expression is grim, but he leaves to catch up with our people, and as planned, we wait for about an hour until we take to the outdoors. We wait for a patrol and then, when they pass, we continue on.

"Whoever is in charge here is very anal about time, but not very bright when it comes to battle strategy," Aurora whispers, checking her watch to follow the beacon that leads to Sprocket.

"That's a good thing, isn't it?" I ask.

"Jaime said that the leader is new, so it's possible the people who know what they are doing are not the ones on patrol. We can only hope that Sprocket is somewhere away from them, so we won't have to kill anyone. Our goal is to not get involved with the cartel, just with Sprocket."

I follow her as she dashes forward. We tuck around a building, edging around as voices beyond raise in anger.

"If she wants a 24-hour patrol, then she can make him do it. Why are we listening to that American bitch, anyway?" an enraged man barks at four others.

"Are you trying to get us all in trouble? You know you have options, you've chosen to be here, so shut up already," one man growls back.

"No. I am out. Tell whoever you want that this shit is useless. We should be raiding that group hunkered down in La Fortuna not trying to keep this lost city in our possession of people when more of us die every day to those dead bastards."

A scuffle around the wall silences voices, then the men all leave in the same direction. Aurora swears before leading me behind several more homes before she picks one for us to tuck into for the day.

"Do you think they are talking about Sprocket?" I ask.

"Yes, unfortunately, I do. We might just be sneaking our way right into the lion's den, and she could be his new girl they were whispering about."

"She would hook up with a cartel leader? But isn't her job to stop the bad things?"

"No, her job is to kill, and she loves it."

"We need to abort the mission. We are not prepared to take on an army of cartel men," I urge her, touching her face gently.

"No."

I sigh and settle next to her to sleep. We are choosing not to keep guard as we are in the back room of a small house on a mattress on the floor with no windows and only one door. If someone comes, we have set us a line of pots and empty cans to warn us. The dawn light doesn't penetrate our area, giving us the much-needed darkness to sleep.

When we wake, the sun is going down, and we eat silently before making our way out of the house and into the growing darkness, skirting a group getting their rotation areas as we do and then crawling through a large drain pipe to bypass the gates around a huge resort.

"This place is enormous, how are we going to find her?"

"Carefully," she whispers back, tiptoeing forward.

I hesitate then follow her toward the building. We creep door to door until we find one unsecured and unguarded. With a quick glance back at an outdoor restaurant that's seen better days and the view of the ocean sparkling in the moonlight, we are suddenly in the dark building.

"Shouldn't the beachfront be crawling with abominations?" I whisper, looking out at no movement besides the crashing waves.

"It's probably fenced off in the densely forested areas on the outskirts."

We continue deeper into the building. The hall leads up past a spa, a bellman-marked door, a stairwell, and to a large open lobby. We backtrack to the stairwell. The site makes me nervous.

"My watch says we passed her, so she must be up on another floor," Aurora whispers, leading me up to the next floor where we peek out and then creep into the hall, not finding her and the signal not getting better as we move to the open doors of the hotel rooms one by one. The dark red blood drag marks on the carpet tell us the story of why they are open, but we push on, eventually finding ourselves on the top floor of the hotel tower, sweating, but a female voice beyond a door beacons us through the dark. We find ourselves in a large room with chairs all around and lanterns shining on various tables.

The voice grows louder, and Aurora grasps my wrist, pushing me into a chair and taking a seat in my lap.

"How many do they think are in the herd next to the southern pier?" a tall blonde woman asks as she strolls into the room, holding the hand of a slim but fit Hispanic man.

"Sprocket, you're fashionably late as usual," Aurora greets, her body tense.

Sprocket's hand moves for her holster, the man next to her slower on the draw.

"I checked your security checkpoints for you, and it looks like you might need more men or a smaller hotel to guard."

"Moore?"

"At your service."

"Holy shit, how the hell did you get in here?"

"Took the stairs, mostly." Aurora smiles, caressing my arm with her thumb.

"Who the hell is this? Should I summon the guards?" the man next to her asks, grabbing Sprocket's arm none too nicely.

"No, Moore wouldn't do anything as reckless as threaten me or mine. Isn't that right, Moore?" Sprocket asks, a creepy smile etching up her face.

"I would never, as long as we are aware, it works both ways." She responds by gesturing at me.

Sprocket squints and I look around Aurora's shoulder.

"Good evening," I greet them, fear like a stone in my gut.

"My husband, Sterling Karter," Aurora introduces, not moving.

Sprocket's jaw snaps shut. "This is my boyfriend."

"My name is Lucas," he adds, stepping up next to her.

Aurora shivers slightly, and I am aware she must have made some unknown connection.

"Where is the rest of your family?" Sprocket asks, her eyes darting around the room.

"It would have been a pretty cool trick if I snuck all of them in here, wouldn't it? No, they are back home with our bosses."

Sprocket's eyebrow rises.

"They put a hit on my husband to control me, so I can't really bring the whole fam to meet you," Aurora says.

"Those bastards have your family and are still trying to bring you back? Well, I am sure they will have fun trying to catch you. Are you here for asylum?"

"No, passing through and figured I would ask you for one last favor."

Sprocket laughs and takes a seat across from us. Lucas follows, his gun still in his hand.

"Your bosses? You're an assassin?" Lucas asks.

"Lower your weapon a bit, I wouldn't want to ruin my partnership with Sprocket when you break our truce by shooting me or my husband," Aurora warns, her muscles tightening on her back.

Sprocket reaches up and pushes the weapon down, giving Lucas a look. "Lucas, Moore doesn't kill, she is not a threat to us."

"An assassin who doesn't kill? You're joking, right?" he asks, taking a seat and looking over at us.

"Have your laugh if you want. Sprocket, I am hoping you can help me by staging Sterling's death. They are sure to send you the bounty, and we can just disappear."

"You don't pull punches, I have always admired that about you, Moore, honest and straightforward. I think I can help you with this problem with just a quick picture and some well-placed blood."

"And in return?" Aurora asks, her hand clutching mine.

"Well, I mean, I get the bounty and to stick it to those old bastards, so I think that's fair," Sprocket laughs.

"Supplies," Lucas adds, jolting forward.

"Am I bartering with both of you? I can run for supplies for you or I can draw out the weak spots in your patrol if you like," Aurora counters, twirling her hair with one finger, her other still clutching mine.

"No, you're dealing with me, this is between us. However, the mock-up would be a great cherry on top. Matter of fact, we can take the picture as soon as we get some blood up here. Then you can do the drawing in the morning when we have light," Sprocket agrees, glaring at her boyfriend.

Aurora nods.

"Of course, I will send the picture only as you're leaving, you know how it is," Sprocket says with a shrug.

Aurora smiles. "Sounds good, glad to see you haven't lost your mind at the end of the world. We can go ahead and use my blood, none other is going to touch him." She pulls her knife and drags it across her palm.

"Shit, seriously?" I gasp, pushing at her to get her up off my lap, but she doesn't budge, her ankles locked around mine.

"Perfect," Sprocket purrs, getting to her feet.

Aurora releases me from her leg hold, turning to me, her face blank from expression as she gently grabs me around the neck. I study her eyes, noticing the shell cracking as a tear threatens to spill from her eye.

"Some warning would be nice. Would you like me to lay down near a blood stain?" I ask, looking at the gore-stained floor.

"That works," Sprocket agrees.

I move, laying on the ground.

"Open up those eyes so it looks legit," Sprocket instructs, twisting her watch like taking pictures with it is alien to her.

I oblige because I know this means we are halfway to being away from this craziness. Instead, I imagine Aurora holding our child.

"All set! Lucas, thanks for the towel," Sprocket says, tossing it at me.

Instead, I get to my feet and lunge at Aurora, pressing it to her hand and adding pressure.

"Why don't we find them a room and in the morning, we will find some paper to draw on and you two can take off," Sprocket offers, looking over at Lucas.

"Sure, can we get somewhere we won't bother anyone with our make-up sex?" Aurora asks, leaning into me.

"You're hilarious, I might just have to add in food if we can hear you from across the resort," Sprocket laughs, ignoring the anger her boyfriend is showing.

"Challenge accepted," I agree, pulling Aurora to me.

After a moment, they lead us down a few floors and over to a clean room on the opposite side of the hotel.

"Just one request, please don't wander tonight. We all need rest and don't want to break any deals by accident," Sprocket threatens looking at both of us to make it clear.

"No worries there, I'll keep him entertained," Aurora replies, then bolts the door locks and checks the room for any other ways in. Eventually, she opens the slider and steps out onto the balcony. After about ten minutes, I go out to look for her and find her sitting with her knees drawn up against her, sobbing silently in the darkness.

"Breathe," I soothe, kneeling next to her.

"I am so sorry, we should have talked about the plan when we met her, but I didn't know what to do. I keep picturing you laying there still with my blood all over you," she gasps, trembling in my embrace.

"Let me fill you with better thoughts, we accomplished our goal. Now I can work on turning us into parents without the looming shadow of your employers."

She snorts with laughter, her tears still uncontrollable. "Make it all go away, take me to the moon, Wolfie."

I don't need to be asked more than once. My lips find hers, and our hands work in a fevered attempt to free one another from the restraints of clothes, and suddenly, I'm base deep, staring down at her pale breasts glowing in the moonlight as they heave with every thrust, her screams sending flames licking through me.

CHAPTER THIRTY EIGHT
RORY
"LIFETIME" THREE DAYS GRACE

AFTER WHAT I wish was an eternal night of passionate lovemaking in every room, and on every surface possible, the sun eventually wakes us from our passion-induced coma of sleep. The breeze causes the curtains to move, and I wake up, looking around the room for any other signs of movement.

I use the bathroom and open Sterling's backpack to retrieve my rations and water. A wrapped item greets me, and I pull it out gently, then uncover a machete. I set it on the table and walk naked over to a stirring Sterling.

"Good Morning to the rest of our lives together, let's close this deal."

"We should take this mattress with us, it gave significant support and allowed me so many wonderful angles." Sterling smiles, a finger tracing my breasts and across my feather tattoo.

We dress before we can get distracted, finish our rations, and Sterling attaches the machete to his belt, leaving his gun in the back of his pants. I roll my eyes, and he gives me a breathtaking smile.

"I have the safety on."

I lead us into the hall, surprised to see an empty chair where someone must have been posted. We make our way back in the direction we had come last night to find Sprocket. A gun barrel nearly burrows into my eye as I round a corner.

"Where is she?" Lucas demands, his finger hugging the trigger.

"I made Sprocket a promise not to hurt you, but if you don't lower your weapon, I will easily break that promise."

"Don't threaten me with a good time. I know how your type is, I just don't know how you got the drop on her."

The gun doesn't shift from my face. I kick out, jolting to the left as I smash his hand into the wall. The gun blasts a charge before clattering to the ground.

I grab him by his shirt collar and drag him over the rail, his hands clutching my wrists in a desperate attempt for me not to drop him. He is heavy, and his flailing legs challenge my balance. "Sprocket, come get your man meat before I splatter him!"

"You don't have her?"

I growl, dragging him over the rail and dropping him onto the unforgiving marble tiles. "What the hell are you talking about?"

"I thought you took her. I can't find her, and she would never bail on meeting up with me."

I keep my opinions about Sprocket's ability to be loyal to a man to myself. "Where did you last see her?"

"She went down to medical to make sure he was releasing the infected since he won't kill the dead."

"Let's start there."

"What?"

"I can find anyone, even Sprocket. Let's go." I let him pick himself up off the ground, only glancing back at Sterling's rage-filled face for a moment as he lowers his gun. This time, we descend a grand staircase of three floors, my eyes darting around the lobby as we pass, looking for her blonde mop of hair and arrogant grin.

I pass a few of Lucas's followers, ignoring their looks mixed with anger and trepidation. We burst into a corridor that is stark white compared to the extravagance of the sparkly hotel. Past a large door that says no entry and a few doors labeled for ballrooms and finally to a clinic that strangely enough looks as if it was here before the virus. Why would a resort need an entire clinic set up?

"What now, did Sprocket not get a good enough ribbing on me already?" a man in a lab coat reads Dr. Gutiérrez, sighs.

"Where is she?" Lucas slams the self-proclaimed doctor against the wall, his anger rolling off his quivering arm muscles as the doctor gasps for air.

I pull him back, starting to understand Sprocket's infatuation might steam for this hot-headed, smash-first ideology. "What Lucas means is we need to talk to her, is she still around?"

"No, she left an hour or so ago with what was left of my pride. I don't see what you people think I can accomplish with no aid or supplies."

"That must really stink, I am sure more appreciation is in order as well."

Lucas's glare burns into me, but I ignore him, watching the doctor's face flash with gratitude before catching sight of his leader.

"Where was she headed?"

"Maria wanted a word with her about the decision to kick Carlos out."

I glance at Lucas, who looks livid now. "Who is Carlos?"

"A member of my family who didn't want to follow my rules."

I roll my eyes, looking back at the doctor and reading his tense body language. "Lucas, why don't you go check the dining room? Maybe they ducked in there to talk." To my surprise, he moves to look, and I am reminded that he doesn't know Sprocket as well as he should by now. There is only one way in and out of the dining room now, and she would never use that as a place to discuss sensitive information.

"This can go two ways, I can help you gain the noticeability you want, or I can tell Lucas you are withholding information."

"I..."

"Make that choice wisely, I can be a great asset or a detrimental advisor."

"They left out that door." He gestures to the exterior emergency door, and I frown. "She wasn't steady on her feet like usual. I thought she was drunk or sick at first. I tried not to let Maria know I saw her inject a needle into Sprocket's neck while I was cleaning up the supplies she scattered everywhere."

"Where is the syringe?"

"In the sharps bin."

"Get it for me." I watch him move and then focus my attention on Lucas and Sterling as they walk back in. His eyes dart around the room like she's going to materialize out of nowhere.

"What is Maria's job here?"

Lucas rubs his stubbled cheeks, his eyes angling to the ceiling, and I try to be patient. "Originally she was housekeeping, that's how Carlos got in after the lockdown. But I spared her leaving because she is a midwife in training, and with Crista pregnant, we couldn't risk not having someone here to help when the baby arrives."

"So she looks after Crista?"

"Yeah."

"Let's go up and find out if she's had contact with Maria or Sprocket today."

"She was asleep when I went by before. Sprocket wasn't there."

I ignore him, taking the syringe from the doctor as I breeze out of the room. Minding the needle, I pull the plunger out, sniffing at the remaining residue in the syringe. Then I hold it out to Lucas. "Do you know what this is?"

Instead of taking a whiff, he dabs it gently on his tongue, his face scrunching in disgust.

"She left her cup in here as well," the doctor says, handing it to Sterling but still standing at the doorway to the clinic.

"She drank that this morning before she went downstairs when Gage saw her," Lucas reveals, eyeing the glass.

I sniff the glass and frown. "It smells like the plunger."

"What!" Lucas asks, snatching the glass from my hand. "Whoever did this better know the digestible levels of ketamine. If she overdoses, it won't just be their necks suffering for whatever they have done with her."

"Wait, someone took Sprocket?" Sterling asks, confused.

"Maria led her out that door there," I respond, pointing to the door.

"Not a chance, that is the way toward the abomination field and not within her access area."

"While you stand here and argue, I have a feeling we need to go find Sprocket. Where are your useless guards?" I ask, pushing out the door with no hesitation.

The abominations in the area are all dead, and so is the guard outside the door. Lucas races ahead to a back gate, stopping short of another guard's body, this one with a note attached to its chest.

Tell Lucas his woman will be at Mira Maravilla pier for a trade of leadership at 1 pm

-Carlos and Maria

"Son of a bitch!" Lucas yells, tearing the paper to shreds.

I look at Sterling, who shakes his head. I know he doesn't want to get involved, but all the words about our future from last night whisper through my mind. I want all of it, and if that means helping rescue Sprocket, then so be it. "Lucas, we need to go get her."

He looks at me in shock, then nods, his jaw tightening. "She has your photos."

"Well, yes, but she also made a pact with me, and it's not over. I can't let someone kill her."

"Admirable, but my men and I can handle it. You'll only make it worse with your gun-toting American presence," he denies, shaking his head.

"That's fine. You stay here behind your gates and your title of a drug lord. I can go get her myself."

He spins, backhanding me, which causes me to smirk because it's a punk move. But Sterling grabs him by the throat.

"How dare you put your hands on my wife? You're lucky to be alive and obviously don't hold stock in the rules our women live by," he snarls, releasing the man and stepping back to my side.

"Fine, come along, just stay out of the way so I can get the exchange done with no more bloodshed and Sprocket in one piece," Lucas growls back, stalking back toward the resort.

Waiting for this imbecile to gather up a few people, a few of which we had seen on patrol, is a joke.

"Why are we waiting instead of just going?" I ask.

"The note said 1 pm."

"So let's be polite and let them set up a trap?"

"They will honor their word," he argues, lifting his chin definitely.

"Like that prick right there complaining about you and your whore the other night while we snuck into your precious hotel?" I question him, frowning.

Lucas glares at his men. "What help will arriving early give us? The pier is simple enough with the ocean at our backs so we don't have to worry about being flanked."

"No, but the abominations are obsessed with the shore so you have to worry about the hordes. And you trust this Carlos's word, but he took Sprocket, the most dangerous woman I know, with no problem," I press, leaning forward, my hands placed on a table, annoyance of the delays clear in my tone.

"He is my cousin, he is just being a child about everything, that's all," Lucas says, rolling his eyes.

I still feel like there is something more to all of this, and as we walk to the pier, my unease grows worse. Sterling is on the left, which makes me uncomfortable as he is always on my right for mobility, but with my wrapped, bandaged hand, he wants to be an aide to me.

A large fence that doesn't look too sturdy and many selling stands that could easily hide people blocks the pier. The people materialize from the shadows laden with blades and bats. I raise my gun in response and next to me, so does Sterling, leaving his machete attached to his pants.

Staring at Lucas as he faces off with his cousin, a realization hits me. I have landed us in the middle of a turf war over a cartel by helping him to retrieve Sprocket.

Sprocket is in a wobbly chair, hands bound, she looks bad. Her face is swollen, bloody slashes run down her arms like tiger stripes. How did this happen to her, of all people? It looks as if she has sustained several lacerations on her legs and abdomen. Shallow but painful. I'm not so sure she will survive her own rescue.

"Weapons down," Lucas orders, holding up a hand.

Weapons lower around the pier, and I am the only one who doesn't listen. I do not know Lucas or trust what I am now dealing with. I will not holster my three remaining bullets in vain.

"Moore," Sprocket warns, her voice broken.

I holster my weapon, remembering our promises to each other. Sprocket's oath is one that she will not break. She may not have a soul, but she has honor in her word.

"Look, Carlos, I understand you have been unhappy with the regime since the rise of the dead," Lucas begins, stepping forward.

"Unhappy?" Carlos shouts, clutching a machete in one hand and a revolver in the other.

"I am here to rectify all the wrongs, to invite every member into the sanctuary, and eliminate all traitors," Lucas insists, looking around the crowd.

"All traitors, by your definition, or ones we both deem to be a threat?" Carlos counters, pointing the machete at Lucas.

"We will eliminate all threats," Lucas agrees with a nod.

"Deal," Carlos agrees, a wicked smile flashing on his face.

There is a scuffle to my left. Sterling grabs a man's wrist, yanking a knife away from me and thrusting him away.

I pull my weapon free.

"NO!" Lucas yells, moving toward us.

CHAPTER THIRTY EIGHT

Sterling makes a grunting sound, and his back collides with me. I shoot the man closest to him in the face, grabbing Sterling under his arm as he collapses. The man drops, my eyes catching sight of the blood drenching his hands. I look down at Sterling as chaos shatters the surrounding stillness. His mouth is moving as he gasps.

"Sterling!" I scream, then my eyes lock on the Karambit handle protruding from his chest. "No, no, no, no," I chant, yanking my shirt off. As gently as I can, I wrench the Karambit blade from him, applying pressure as blood streams from the wound. Blood pools at my knees. I look at another wound on his right side. "I've got you," I tell him. My hands shake as I stare down at his face, both my hands trying to slow the bleeding from the gushing wounds.

"Aurora," he chokes, blood spraying from his mouth.

"Don't talk, I will get you help," I promise, looking up and around wildly.

Lucas drags Sprocket away from the fight. Our eyes connect for a moment, then I look back at Sterling.

"I love you," he gasps, blood seeping from his lips.

"Don't say it like you'll never say it again," I beg, trying to stop the bleeding. Too much blood covers my hands, and my brain screams. Pain flares, like a fiery blade on my shoulder, but I ignore it. "I need you." I plead, trying to stop the flow of blood.

"I..." he attempts.

A boot connects with my side, and I draw my weapon, shooting the man and another advancing. Sterling's hand loosens on my arm, all that strength and power in his grip gone. I watch as the light leaves his eyes, and my breath comes in ragged gasps.

"The dead!" someone screams, and the world explodes in chaos around me.

I feel a hand on my arm, pulling me back, but jerk free, clinging to Sterling's lifeless body. I grab Sterling's machete, swinging at the person pulling at me. Part of me recognizes him as one of Lucas's men. Carlos pushes an abomination toward me. I swing, cutting its head clear off, then diving at Carlos. I feel pain in my throat, realizing I am screaming. Rage spills out of me. Carlos's eyes bulge as Sterling's machete pierces into him. I yank it down, twisting. His followers nearest us freeze, staring at me. I pull free, rushing them. They scatter, trying to escape my rage.

Abominations amble between me and my targets, and I take them down, my arms burn, pain ripples through me, and my screaming does not stop.

An abomination closes in on Sterling's body. I dodge a blow of a bat that would have surely sent me into Sterling's arms in the beyond, spinning and chopping into the man's arm with the machete. I throw myself at the abomination before it can bite into his sun-kissed skin. With a look down at Sterling, I will him to blink, for his chest to rise and fall. I've failed. My brain weeps. I get to my feet, turning to the hoard pressing in on the pier. My vision blurs with tears. "He is MINE!" I bellow. *Kill me*, I beg inside as I fight their relentless teeth off to preserve Sterling's body.

Thunder crashes overhead, sprinkles of rain patter on my face, and darkness presses in. My senses overwhelm me as my consciousness connects to my brain. Sterling's scent swims around me, tainted by the sharp scent of blood. I lay on his chest, rain falling lightly on and around us, Sterling's lifeless hand clutched in mine. Bodies surround us, and shouts and gunfire in the far distance carry over the sound of the rain.

"I am so sorry." Our song trembles from my lips in a choked whisper when I finish. I release his icy hand, kissing his fingers, the tears burning back into my eyes.

I stagger to my feet, backing away from him, tripping over the slain bodies, my eyes glued to him. The rain pelts down now, lightning streaking across the sky.

"Daddy!" My eyes rip away from Sterling, my focus on the ocean. Stumbling down the stairs to the beach gasping for air. "I need to be with him!" The force of my words causes me to collapse to my knees at the edge of the water, the wet sand caking my trembling legs. "He is mine," I whimper, punching the soggy sand, trying to reign in the terror and pain rippling through my veins.

"Our God took you. Why does he need him? Sterling!" Tears battle with the spray of saltwater from crashing waves.

Movement behind me on the stairs reaches my ears faintly. I look back at Sterling's body, jerking as it moves. Arms slumped, head tilted to the side. Memories blast into my mind, our first meeting, our first kiss, his smile, his touch. He draws closer, and I shut out the rattling, the raspy sound escaping his mouth. Reaching out, stopping him, my hands caressing him as gently as I can as I restrain him.

"I loved you, dammit!" Not looking into his handsome face, I fall against him, hugging him one last time. My entire world feels as if it is crashing around me now. His lips reach my neck, and I allow myself to remember his tender kiss.

The End

AFTERWORD

In Memoriam of Sterling Karter Jr. May He Rest in Peace

Those better be tears of victory I see there, cause Sprocket's ready to tell you how it truly went down. Join her in paradise and you decide if is she the villain of the story, or is she a misunderstood heroine.
Book Four The Contracted Things Coming Soon!

ABOUT THE AUTHOR

B.E. Fidler is the mother of four, currently residing in the midwest. She began to write after the death of her late stepfather in 1999. Fidler has 35 books in process and enjoys what she calls chaotic writing. Music cranked up, singing at the top of her voice, and typing for hours on end. She enjoys writing retreats with her author friends and researching her books, and practicing the skills her characters utilize on their adventures.

ALSO BY B.E. FIDLER

AGENT MOORE SERIES

The Little Things
The Abominable Things

PRISCILLA'S STORY

Catastrophe

Made in the USA
Monee, IL
02 August 2024